# "CRAIG! CRAIG MATLOCK!"

The woman stood in the shadow of a doorway, beckoning him. "Craig! Over here! Hurry!"

He knew only one woman who had such a soft, conspiratorial voice. Her fingers gripped his and wound around them. "I know somewhere where we won't be disturbed," she said. "Come with me."

With rapid steps she went ahead of him and turned into a side corridor. She opened a door, and, after Craig had entered, she turned the key and pulled it out of the keyhole. She smiled at him from under her broad-brimmed straw hat. "No one will disturb us here."

And no one did . . . until the deep voice of her husband sounded in the hall.

# Sandra Paretti

# TENANTS OF THE EARTH

Translated by
**RUTH HEIN**

A KANGAROO BOOK
PUBLISHED BY POCKET BOOKS NEW YORK

TENANTS OF THE EARTH

POCKET BOOK edition published December, 1977

ISBN: 0-671-80941-5.
Library of Congress Catalog Card Number: 75-44424.
This POCKET BOOK edition is published by arrangement
with M. Evans and Company. Copyright, ©, 1973, by
Verlagsgruppe Bertelsmann GmbH. Translation copyright, ©,
1976, by M. Evans and Company, Inc. All rights reserved
under International and Pan-American Copyright Conven-
tions. This book, or portions thereof, may not be reproduced
by any means without the permission of the publisher:
M. Evans and Company, Inc., 216 East 49th Street, New
York, N.Y. 10017.

Printed in the U.S.A.

# Cast of Characters

JOHN TYLER MATLOCK—*patriarch of the Matlock family, President of the Empire State Railroad*

ROSE MATLOCK—*John Tyler's wife*

ALICE, MAY, and VINNIE—*the Matlock daughters*

CRAIG MATLOCK—*the youngest Matlock son, just returned from the Civil War, married to Margaret Poynder Matlock*

LANGDON MATLOCK—*the oldest Matlock son, director of Empire State Railroad's New York headquarters*

IRENE MATLOCK—*Langdon's wife, Craig's lover before the War*

LOFTUS POYNDER—*John Tyler Matlock's adversary, owner of the New York Railroad*

MARGARET POYNDER MATLOCK—*daughter of Loftus Poynder, Craig Matlock's wife*

JOSHUA and SINCLAIR—*twin sons of Craig and Margaret Matlock*

EDNA CHILD—*Margaret's aunt*

JUSTIN KRAMER—*Loftus Poynder's lawyer and right-hand man*

WENDELL SYDENHAM—*John Tyler Matlock's accountant, keeper of the Matlock empire's secrets*

KITTY SCHOFFIELD—*Craig Matlock's mistress*

MY INTEREST IN AMERICAN HISTORY
LED ME TO FABRICATE THIS FICTION.
ANY SIMILARITY BETWEEN THE CHARACTERS IN THE
NOVEL AND HISTORICAL FIGURES IS UNINTENTIONAL
AND PURELY COINCIDENTAL.

# BOOK ONE

# WILLOWBEACH, CONNECTICUT

July 1865

# 1

THE HIGH BEACH grass completely concealed the four-year-old boys running along, hunched over, their arms pressed against their sides, close on each other's heels. It was the hour for their afternoon nap, but they had waited until the house was silent. Moving quietly, they had left their beds and pulled their blue denim overalls over their nightshirts. They were still holding their shoes, begrudging the time it would take to put them on; but their feet had become so toughened that they never felt the sharp blades of grass and grainy coastal sand.

The day was hot. Not a bird, not a cricket stirred. The only sounds were the rustle of the boys' footsteps and the sharp inhalations of their breath. The forest of pale-green reeds moved no more at their passing than it would in a gentle breeze.

They had already covered half the distance to the place where they could get a glimpse of the train, when there was a shout from the house: "Joshua! Joshua!" The woman's high-pitched voice lingered so long over each syllable that she had to stop to catch her breath each time. "Jo—shu—a."

The boy in front looked back at his twin. Sinclair had come to a stop, suddenly uncertain.

"Hurry, or we'll miss it," Joshua said in a loud, tense whisper. "The train will be here any minute. Hurry."

But Sinclair still hesitated. He looked back along the path they had taken the past few days, a narrow rut through the high grass that continued to sprout despite all the gardener's efforts. "Are you sure the train will come?" he asked.

Joshua pointed to the house near their own, its white walls shimmering behind the dense stand of old trees. Both houses—the sinister, fortresslike Poynder mansion, from which the boys had come, and the white, rather modest summer cottage of the Matlocks—sat on a hilly spit of land that reached out into Long Island Sound. "If the shutters are open, they're coming." Joshua's voice was assured. "And look, the swings are up."

Once again the shout of "Joshua" rang through the garden, more gently than before, almost an echo of the first. The twins looked at each other, this time in agreement: Aunt Edna wasn't going to come after them. She hated the Matlocks; she would not set foot on their property.

Joshua took Sinclair's hand and together they ran the rest of the way to a spot where they could see the tracks. The railroad ran along a small willow-fringed stream, ending in a wide circle behind the Matlock house. In the noonday sun the rails cut a shining, silver streak through the green. Only two days before, thickly overgrown, they could not be seen. Then a group of mowers arrived. Greville, the gardener, had told Joshua and Sinclair, and they had taken off at a run to see for themselves. They had been waiting for the train ever since.

Sinclair climbed up on the tree stump Joshua, the lookout, had discovered and leased to him for two cents. The boys often made deals, and invariably Joshua came out ahead. Joshua sat down in the grass and put on his shoes, never taking his eyes off the spot where the train might appear at any moment.

They were not so alike in looks that it would have been difficult to tell them apart. About all they had in common was their coppery-red hair, an inheritance from the Poynder side of the family. The Matlock side was less evident. It showed only in Joshua's dark eyes and the typically square Matlock jaw.

"I wish Papa was on the train, too," Sinclair said.

Joshua got to his feet, shaking his head. "I don't think he will be. That's Grandpapa's train. It runs just for him. It belongs to him—the engine, the cars, the tracks." He squinted up at the sun. The willows were brighter at the top, where the breeze curled the silvery leaves upward.

"Can you see it?" Sinclair called. "Tell me! Is it the train?"

Joshua did not reply. Then it appeared—gliding between the trees, enveloping them in the white smoke, the black engine and two yellow cars gleaming in the sunlight. The boys stood motionless, awed at the sight, al-

most afraid to believe what had been only a figment of
their dreams.

"I saw it first!" Sinclair looked at his brother, but the
expected denial did not come. Joshua glanced once more
at the train, then turned and ran back toward the house.

Edna Child stood waiting on the porch of the Poynder
mansion. She was extremely nearsighted, and before she
could grasp what had whisked past her, the twins had
disappeared into the house. On the stairs of dark-stained
oak that led from the entrance hall to the upper floors,
Sinclair skidded, giving Joshua the advantage he needed
to be first to tell his mother. Sinclair yelled at him, but
he did not stop. He ran along the hallway to his mother's
bedroom, with its large balcony facing the sea. Nor did
he hesitate when he reached the high balustrade of the
balcony; he knew he had to climb it. Now he stood on
the top—right up in the sky, it seemed to him. Long
Island Sound stretched out below. For a moment he was
dizzy, but the feeling was marvelous, as if he were flying.
Slowly his eyes returned to the shore. The color of the
sand depended on the time of day. In the morning it
was red as coral, while at dusk it turned to the soft purple of the little fat fish that wriggled in the fishermen's
nets. Now, though, it glowed with the same burnished
hue of his mother's hands and arms.

His eyes searched the beach for her. In the shadow of
the dock, softly rocked by the surf, seagulls were swimming. The boat lay at its mooring, sails furled. The soli-
tary green beach umbrella seemed translucent in the sunlight, as did the figure in the white dress resting beneath
it on the wicker lounge.

Joshua put his hands to his mouth and took a deep
breath. "Mama!" His voice cut cleanly through the stillness. "It's here! The train is here!"

The residents of Southport and Willowbeach saw the
train twice a year—early in July, just after Independence
Day, when it brought the Matlocks to their summer
home; and at the end of September, after John Tyler
Matlock's birthday, when it came to take them back to
Albany. When the Matlocks arrived, everyone knew that
summer had come; and when they left, everyone knew
that the Atlantic would soon be pushing autumn gales
into the Sound.

The Matlocks' white house, with its many porches and chimneys, had been the first building on this deserted stretch of coastline, where only fishermen came to cut willow branches for their creels. For a long time it stood alone on the isolated spit of land. The first Matlock, who had emigrated from England, built it after he became rich on his mail-coach empire, the boundaries of which extended far beyond Connecticut.

His progeny had remained loyal to the old house. Even after the family acquired extensive property in the Hudson Valley and moved to Albany, the Matlocks did not abandon Willowbeach; year after year they came for the summer. It was a long time before others discovered this part of the Sound. Their houses were usually larger (the sinister granite castle of Loftus Poynder, the Matlocks' closest neighbor, was an out-and-out threat, sheathed in stone), their gardens and parks more extensive, and their boathouses more costly. But the oaks, locusts, maples, and larches around the Matlock house were older; the gravestones in the little fishermen's cemetery more numerous; and most important, the Matlocks had their own railroad. A private line eight miles long had been laid from Southport Station to the house for the sole purpose of bringing the family to Willowbeach in the summer and taking them away in the fall.

For decades the Matlocks, like everyone else, had come by coach over roads that grew more impassable as they neared the shore. Five years ago, however, Irish workmen had arrived and laid the tracks, and three months later the black engine with the two yellow cars had first steamed through the willows along the river. Each successive year the engine had grown larger and the cars more luxurious. Only the colors remained unchanged. The cars were yellow, the curtains were blue, and on the front of the engine, below the lantern, a resplendent seal with a large gold *M* led the way.

It was a long journey from Albany to the Connecticut shore. The road ran through Greenbush, Chatham, Springfield, and New Haven, and the train had to use the tracks of four different railroad companies. With all the stops, the trip took seven hours, and the children of the Matlock daughters, who had the second car to themselves, would squirm with impatience at the last. There were nine children who could not keep still, fighting for window seats from which they could get the first glimpse of the house. They paid no attention to admonitions and slaps from travel-weary mothers. For all of them it was the second day on the road. The day before, Alice had brought her four children from Troy to Albany, Vinnie and her two had come from Utica, and May had traveled with her three from Rochester. Today they had set out for the Connecticut shore at six o'clock in the morning.

In the general excitement only one person remained calm—Rose Matlock, John Tyler Matlock's wife and the children's grandmother. Rose was in her element. She could never understand women who complained that their children "drained" them; her children and grandchildren were what had kept her young. At sixty-six she had the figure and bearing of a woman of thirty. She was much quicker than her daughters to try out new fashions; right now she cared not a whit that the breeze from the open windows was mussing her upswept white hair, for like the children, she was concentrating on the moment when the house would come into view. The way she looked gave no clue to the fact that she had been on her feet since four that morning. Her gray eyes were glowing, her cheeks rosy, as if tinted by the sun. With a smile she was passing out what was left of the chocolate she carried in her reticule. When Alice saw that Lance, her youngest boy, was being given seconds by his grandmother, she lost her temper. She slapped his hand hard and took the chocolate away from him. "That's right," she said, turning to her mother, "go ahead—reward them for misbehaving."

Rose Matlock held out the chocolates to her daughter. "You should have some. It's good for the nerves. It's high time you had a vacation. I don't like the way you're acting. You're irritable. I've been noticing it all day." In spite of Alice's disapproving frown, she handed some chocolates to Lance. "A train trip is no time to worry about good behavior."

"You make it easy on yourself," Alice said. "You never let us get away with anything. But your grandchildren can do as they wish."

"When you've raised as many children as I have, you have a right to stop." Rose Matlock took Lance in her lap and opened the window a crack more. "Over there behind the trees," she told him, "you'll see the house any minute now. You remember from last year?"

The expression of chronic irritability on Alice's face, which made her look older than she was—at thirty-three she was the youngest of the three Matlock daughters—intensified. "You seem to want us all to get sore throats on top of everything else. Last year, for the first few weeks, the house practically turned into a hospital."

Amused, Rose Matlock nodded. "Stomach aches, sore throats, sunburn, scraped knees, runny eyes, buzzing ears—it's always that way at the beginning. Look at your children. They're pale and soft. Whatever do you do with them? Don't you ever let them go outside? I'm sure the sun shines in Troy, just like anywhere else. I daresay Joshua and Sinclair are tanned and the soles of their feet are so calloused that not even a wasp can sting them. When I think what would become of my grandchildren if it were not for Willowbeach—"

"You may call it toughening them up," Alice said, "but I say it's Spartan torture."

Rose Matlock gave her daughter a searching look. "Why don't you tell me what's really on your mind? When you got to Albany, you were already sporting that gloomy face. I thought it would change, but if anything, it's gotten worse. No one is forcing you to come to Willowbeach. I would gladly have taken the children for you."

Alice hesitated. There had been more favorable moments to have a talk with her mother, but she had let them go by. If she could not summon up the courage now, she would go on being silent; that much she knew. "I don't like to leave Everett, at least not for so long."

"Why doesn't he join us later, like George and David?" When Alice did not answer, Rose continued. "Your Everett simply does not like the beach. He doesn't swim, he doesn't sail. He doesn't even like sitting in the sun. He's a bookworm. But you knew that when you married him. A man never changes in things like that. Did you think he would? If I were you, I'd enjoy every minute of the next three months."

"There's another reason," Alice said. "To put it bluntly, it's Father."

"Father?"

"Are you surprised? You don't mean it. After all, you've known him longer than the rest of us, and you'll have to admit it's not entirely pleasant to spend the summer under his thumb. And the way Father treats Everett —if I were him, I wouldn't want to come to Willowbeach either. If Father would only understand that he cannot treat his sons-in-law that way. He was impossible throughout that whole business of the patent for the new luxury cars. Everett did all the work. The ideas are his, every one of them, and now he's expected to hand over all the profits. Now don't tell me Father doesn't mean it and that he treats George and David the same way. He goes too far. Just the other day he told Vinnie's husband that he'll give him the construction contract for the new railroad terminal in Albany only if George agrees to hand in invoices with faked expenses."

The clamor that suddenly broke out in the compartment saved Rose Matlock from having to answer. The children had spotted the white house in the distance, flashing among the trees. "There it is! Our house! It's ours!" Their shouts mingled as they pushed their way to the windows.

Rose Matlock gave a contented smile. All the Matlocks, old and young, really cared about only one thing— whether something belonged to them. Though the children had other surnames, when it came to property, they were all Matlocks. Even in appearance the Matlock heritage shone through, especially in the boys. All of them looked like Rose Matlock's sons had looked at the same age: dark hair, dark eyes, a thin face that would have appeared overbred without the sturdy chin, and the stocky frame which they would keep until they were seventeen or eighteen, when they would shoot up within a year. The Matlock boys had always been handsomer than the girls, as if the men represented the family's real capital. Without exception the girls were plain, at least while they were young. Only later did they take on color and fragrance, like a Northern Spy apple, which doesn't mature until the leaves have turned. The comparison had originated with Rose Matlock; she remembered what it was like when, in her mid-thirties, she had suddenly realized that men's heads turned when she passed. Her husband had discovered her anew. It was a wonderful time, perhaps the best in her whole marriage, and that was why she loved her youngest son, Craig Lyman, the most. She had not deliberately conceived the other six, but this one she had wanted: the spit and image of his father. Like all her other children, he had been born at Willowbeach, in the southwest bedroom on the ground floor, in the wide double bed placed near the window.

Rose Matlock passed Lance to Alice and took her hat from the rack. "I'll speak to your father. I know he values Everett's work, and on days like this, he's most easily approached."

"I didn't mean it that way," Alice mumbled. "I don't want you to get in any trouble. By the way, have you heard from Craig? Is he at Willowbeach already?"

"I haven't heard anything, but it can't be much longer. So many of the men have already come home from the war. Your father offered—through me—to take steps to speed up his discharge, but Craig wouldn't hear of it. You know how it is between the two of them. Craig is his own son, but he's even tougher on him than he is on his sons-in-law." Rose Matlock buttoned the jacket of her pale-green traveling costume. "Do I look all right?"

Alice scrutinized her mother as only a woman can examine another. Nothing sharpens the eye more than rivalry, and the Matlock daughters saw their mother as their chief model as well as their most dangerous rival. "If I dared wear that shade of green, I'd look like a ghost."

Rose Matlock laughed softly. "Wait until you're my age and your hair is white; then green will suit you, too."

John Tyler Matlock's private car was coupled to the engine. It was brand new, having been delivered only a few days before from the factory in Troy. It was built so that John Tyler did not have to forego the conveniences of home when he was traveling. The car had a kitchen, parlor, sleeping compartment, and office. The walls were paneled in black walnut and red cedar. The floor was deep in turkey-red carpeting and red-velvet drapes framed the windows. No papers, no writing utensils, no newspapers littered the desk top in the office, which Rose now entered.

The sound of splashing water came through the open door to the adjoining sleeping quarters. Rose Matlock stepped closer, but he did not hear her. His chest bare, he was bent over the cobalt-blue china wash basin. He had the body of a seventy-nine-year-old man (they would be celebrating his eightieth birthday on September 20 at Willowbeach), but the mottled skin, which had grown almost transparent, was stretched tautly over firm muscles, and his spine was as straight as a young man's.

Rose Matlock picked up the clean shirt lying on the bureau. She undid the buttons and set aside the stock. John Tyler Matlock came in from the wash closet. He was drying himself with a turkish towel. "You're just in time," he said.

She smiled. "That is the secret of my success. How do you suppose our marriage would have worked out if I had not always had a sixth sense to tell me when you need me? Patience is not one of your virtues."

"Don't say that. I can wait when I have to. To get certain things, one must wait." He threw the towel across the chair and pulled the shirt over his head. Like his body, his face had preserved its youthful tone. Age had only etched the features more deeply: the arch of the high forehead, the square lower jaw with the jutting chin, the hint of scorn around the mouth. Age had not even drawn a veil over the large, dark eyes which had retained their sparkle and fire. "I don't know about you," he continued, "but this year the trip hasn't left me nearly as tired. These cars are a giant step forward. The windows really close, the ventilation is much more effective, and the suspension is first rate. No comparison with the old cars. This new model puts us way ahead of the competition. We can easily double the fare for luxury class. This isn't railroad travel as we knew it in the past. Now it's luxury, pure and simple. People will pay for that. We're not running any risk by going into production with it."

He held an arm out to his wife so she could button the cuff. "This model is a good example of a transaction that required a good deal of patience. I looked Everett over carefully, knowing that if I gave him time, he would make something of himself. You'll have to admit, I have a flair for picking sons-in-law. Everett is a first-rate railroad-car designer."

Rose Matlock made it a rule never to interfere in her husband's business affairs; that was his domain. She had carved out her own—the family. Maybe that was another reason why her marriage to this despot had run so smoothly. But now she said, "I think it might do Everett a great deal of good to hear that from you, for once."

"Has he been complaining to you? Has Alice? My father never once had a good word for me. That's why I became what I am. He kept telling me I was no good, until he finally had me where I would have moved heaven and earth just to prove him wrong."

Once Rose Matlock had decided to take up a cause, she was persistent, though she always remained gentle. "You've said yourself that as an inventor Everett is a genius. People like that seldom have very good heads for business; they're dreamers. Perhaps you have to be like that, a little wolly-headed, to think up new things. Don't you really believe you're treating him unfairly?"

John Tyler Matlock waited until she had tied the dark cravat. "Unfairly! Who was Everett Lunden when he married Alice Matlock? A bum with big ideas. They're a dime a dozen. Ideas never made anyone rich, much less kept him rich. Without me, he'd still be hawking his sketches. I gave him a Matlock in marriage. I let him have the factory. I'm the customer for his cars. Today he's somebody. And one day Lunden Cars will be a byword all over the United States—maybe all over the world."

Rose Matlock's gentle nod did not mean that she was giving up. "Perhaps I didn't express myself properly," she said. "The cars and the factory bear his name, but you are the boss. Everett has to run to you for every little thing."

"He who pays the piper calls the tune. I'm the owner, and Alice has her share of the stock. Don't forget that."

"That's it exactly. Everett is in his wife's employ, in a manner of speaking. Try to put yourself in his shoes. It's not a good feeling to be dependent on your wife."

"Everett was lucky to marry a Matlock, and so were George and David. I'd be a fool if I so much as lifted a finger to help them. Trust me. I've seen families lose everything to their sons-in-law in a single generation."

"And what about the patent? I hear it was taken out in your name."

"A precaution. I don't want him running to Loftus Poynder with it—or one of the other railroads."

"Hasn't he earned some part in it? Even a small one?"

"Do you want me to turn hired hands into partners? What about my sons? Langdon is almost fifty. He's one of my directors—amply compensated, sure, but that's all he is. He's my heir. One of these days he'll own everything, the whole kit and caboodle, but *he* never asked for a partnership. I settled with Craig for three hundred and fifty thousand dollars, and he legally renounced all future claims. I'm not about to grant a stranger rights that I refuse my own sons. Next time tell Alice to come to me. Is she forgetting the three hundred and fifty thousand dollars' worth of stock I settled on her on her wedding day? Alice is one of those people who worry about starving in the midst of plenty. All my daughters have short memories." He went over to the red-leather settee and picked up his coat. "By the way, Loftus Poynder is joining us for dinner tonight."

The news surprised Rose. She searched her husband's face for a clue as to whether the invitation should be taken as a good or a bad omen. Loftus Poynder was Craig's father-in-law, but the marriage of Craig Matlock to Margaret Poynder had not improved relations between the two fathers, archrivals in the railroad world. "Was this a personal invitation or a business one?"

"Business. But I thought it best to lend a family air to the matter. I gave it some thought. It hasn't yet occurred to him to ask us to his house."

"I'm glad you took the first step. Especially because of Craig and Margaret. I could never understand why you disapproved of the marriage."

"You can always find something good in everyone. If I'd lived by that rule, I would never have become what I am today. In this world—"

It was not Rose Matlock's way to interrupt her husband, but when he started in on his philosophy of life, she took the liberty. "Craig knew what he was doing. Margaret has some sterling qualities that he never found in any other girl, not even in the heiresses you treated him to every weekend in Saratoga Springs."

"If by sterling qualities you mean that she's Poynder's only daughter—so one of these days she'll inherit the lot —don't forget that Loftus Poynder is fifteen years younger than I am and every bit as tough."

"My father would have said that Margaret is the kind of person who'll always find a four-leaf clover. Not many women would have borne up so well while Craig was away in the war."

"He didn't have to go. He could have sent a substitute. Four years! Other men made their fortune in that time. And he hasn't come home yet."

"All the same, she was left alone with the children. And Joshua and Sinclair—"

"How you dote on those twins. Red-headed Matlocks —that's a new one. I have to admit it though—I do like that Joshua. I have a feeling he's a true Matlock. He's the first one of all my grandchildren who understands the meaning of money. And he's only four. That's one good thing about the marriage contract Poynder negotiated for his daughter: Craig won't have any financial obligations if it doesn't work out. Proud to the point of stupidity. Self-made men are all the same."

Rose Matlock had stepped over to a window. The train was slowing down. The house was near now, and as she gazed at it, she asked herself once again how she could have lived with this man for fifty years without growing to hate him. There had been times when she had come close, as well as times when she felt her strength was gone. At such crucial times she had had help—from her children and later her grandchildren, and always from Willowbeach, the house and the sea which had robbed her of two sons and yet had given her so much strength and inner peace. She turned from the window. "I hope your meeting with Loftus Poynder won't make more trouble for Craig and Margaret."

"I have no intention of being unfriendly, but I see no reason for being especially amiable, either. I am not in the habit of encumbering my business dealings with sentiment. Poynder is a sensitive plant, and stubborn, to boot." John Tyler calmly went on dressing. "Before the children use the swings, I want Brewster to check the ropes and hooks. I don't want an accident in the first ten minutes."

"Don't worry. The Reverend Yarring looked after everything. He wrote me that all the details have been seen to. The window frames have been painted, the trees are pruned, and the dock has been repaired."

"Yarring! There's another one you waste your charity on. We pay a hundred dollars for the pews, and the bill for cemetery care is sky high. It sounds suspiciously like he needs another new furnace for his church. It's the damnedest thing: every two years—whenever they devise a new kind of church stove in England—Yarring's heating plant mysteriously breaks down."

Rose Matlock lowered her head and looked at her hands, a signal that she was not prepared to discuss the matter. After a pause she changed the subject. "Is it all right with you if we have fish for dinner tonight?"

He nodded. "I believe this year Joshua and Sinclair can join us at table."

"I was about to suggest it myself."

"They'll never grow into anything worthwhile on the slops they're served at home. Watery vegetables. I don't think they know there's any other kind of food. Fish—very good. But please have it served whole. The children must learn to handle the bones. By the way, last year's fish bill was pure extortion. We would have had to be eating fish day in and day out." He pointed out the window. "It was an impertinence of Poynder to plant that gray box right in front of our noses."

"You could have bought the property. But you thought the price too high."

"Anyway, if Margaret intends to fill *that* house with children, she'd better hurry. When you were thirty-one, you already had six."

Thirty-one, Rose Matlock thought. It seemed like yesterday and yet as distant as a previous life. "If I had it to do all over again, I think I'd wait a few years to get married."

He looked at her, the hint of scorn fleeing from his features. "That's a very belated admission." He put his arm around her. "I don't think there's a man alive who could have tamed you once you reached twenty-five. It was difficult enough when you were seventeen." His hand traced the curve of her forehead. This had been one of the first caresses he had dared to make when he was courting her. It had never disappeared, neither the gesture nor its meaning—a deep feeling of oneness, one couple, one tree with two trunks.

The train jerked to a stop. They clung to each other. "McCallum isn't as young as he used to be," John Tyler Matlock said. "I'm going to have to let him go." He was smiling.

# 2

Joshua's shout reached Margaret down at the beach, at her favorite spot. Though she knew better, the call roused a flicker of hope that, along with the rest of the Matlock family Craig would be returning to Willowbeach.

"Mama, the train! The train is here!" She saw the boy, standing up high, and from the distance made a warning gesture, as if she could prevent Joshua from committing some folly. She took the straw hat from the back rest of the wicker lounge and began the walk back to the house.

Margaret knew the train would come today; the letter in which Rose Matlock had informed her of their arrival was in the pocket of her white linen dress. But *letter* was not the proper word. The small envelope with the embossed initials R.M. (like a royal coat of arms, Edna had said, and had lectured Margaret on vanity and transient things) usually contained hastily scribbled notes: the recipe for a medication, a swatch of cloth with a query as to whether Margaret would like a dress of that fabric, a newspaper clipping mentioning Craig's regiment. She sent news and not an unnecessary word; sometimes even the signature was missing. Rose Matlock's love encompassed everyone who had a part in her life, no matter where that person might be. She always found ways to let them know they were in her thoughts.

Surely Rose would have written if she had had news of Craig. And if Rose asked about Craig, what could Margaret have told her that Rose did not already know? She did not even have answers to the questions she asked herself over and over. Her thoughts were constantly on Craig and therefore on the Matlocks, and time and again her feelings were in conflict. There were many Matlock traits that Margaret could not tolerate—their way of look-

15

ing at someone disparagingly, as if the only people who
counted in this world were those who were born Matlocks; their exaggerated self-assurance; their scornful
smiles at those who were weaker, who handled a sailboat
less deftly, who swam shorter distances out into the ocean
(like herself); their evident contempt for anyone who
wasn't like them. It was an open, almost joyous contempt, which they never tried to conceal. Even their way
of walking enraged Margaret at times, as if the earth had
been created for the sole purpose of supporting them.

Margaret had grown accustomed to these thoughts and
feelings long before she became the wife of a Matlock.
Craig and Margaret. They had a long history, though the
first chapter belonged to her alone. It covered the years of
her childhood, when she had watched the inhabitants of
the white house from a distance, from the attic window,
from the beach tent used by her mother, who was already
ill and who did not allow young Margaret to leave her
side. Whole afternoons she had spent watching the strange
children, who came with the summer, at their wild games.
That was when she learned that it was not absolutely
necessary to throw a ball so that it could be caught
effortlessly, that these children appeared to enjoy tricking
each other. The cleverest was the boy they called Craig.

Until her mother's death the Matlock garden was a
forbidden Eden. On the day of the funeral, in the cemetery of the fishermen's chapel, the ban was lifted. Surprisingly, Rose Matlock had appeared at the cemetery,
and after offering her sympathy to Loftus Poynder at the
graveside, had asked him and his daughter to visit the
following day. Margaret remembered everything as if it
had happened yesterday: the church with the empty front
pews which belonged to the Matlocks, where every seat
held an embroidered cushion; her mother's coffin, raised
on the bier; the words of the Reverend Yarring. Nor had
she forgotten the warm pressure of Rose Matlock's hand,
her voice, her invitation. When she actually entered the
Matlock house, Margaret had clutched her father's hand
like a child, though she was fourteen years old.

On that day Margaret had first experienced the warmth
of a house inhabited by a large family. For the first time
in her life she sat at a table where there was not a
moment's silence. And Craig Matlock, a year her junior,
had become the center of her life. And had remained it.

That had been seventeen years ago. She was no longer Margaret Poynder, but the wife of a Matlock, a Matlock herself. She bore the name that stood for everything she wanted out of life.

The path from the beach to the house zigzagged through a rock garden. Its loosely and romantically piled rocks, its shrubbery of juniper and broom, owed their existence as much to the imagination of Margaret's mother as to the architect's ambition. It had been sinfully expensive, almost impossible to maintain in this climate, and it blocked direct access to the Sound.

Edna Child made a valiant effort to keep the twins from running to meet their mother on the steep coastal path, but when Margaret reached the garden, there was no holding them. "I saw it first! This time I was first!" Sinclair, the more affectionate of the twins, rushed up to his mother, pressing close to her, while Joshua, not bothering with preliminaries, asked the question uppermost in his mind. "Can we go over there? Naptime is over."

Before Margaret could answer, Edna Child intervened. "That rough Matlock crowd! In an hour these two will come back bruised and battered, and we can consider ourselves lucky if they're still in one piece."

"But Edna, you're always the one who advocates toughening the body. When I think of my childhood, how you persecuted me with cold compresses and massages, and I survived . . ." She turned to the boys. "All right, go on."

"At least you could caution them against letting that woman fill them full of sweets."

Not an hour passed that Edna did not point out the dangers to health lurking everywhere. Sweets, alcohol, tobacco, meat, and bleached flour were, to her, the prime causes of disease, with which her imagination was ceaselessly engaged. Years ago she and her brother had edited a journal, advocating hydraulic cures, and for a long time it had been her dream to establish a home for all those misguided persons who had ruined their health by errors in living and eating. After she had discarded this dream —together with her other lifelong dream, to become the second wife of Loftus Poynder—she concentrated on those nearest and dearest to her. At heart she abhorred healthy people, whereas the idea of keeping vigil in a darkened room at a sickbed quickened her imagination.

She noted at once Margaret's bare, tanned feet. The soles, bleached by salt water and carrying traces of reddish sand, looked so provocatively healthy that they struck her like a personal insult. "I assume you'll be running over there yourself," she said sharply. "I also assume that there is no need for me to fix supper here tonight."

"Why don't you come with us?" There was not a hint of mockery in Margaret's voice.

"Me? Visit people who refused to receive your mother while she was alive?"

"That was many years ago."

"Not long enough for me to forget. Don't trouble yourself. They haven't deluded me with all their riches. One day your eyes will be opened . . ."

"Please, Aunt Edna, let's not go into that. If you need me, I'll be over there."

Edna turned silently and went into the house to take care of what she considered a more pressing need. She went to the first-aid chest, selected surgical gauze, court plasters, and ointments, and carried them into the kitchen. The thought that from now until the Matlock's departure in the fall she would be needing these items every single day filled her with bitter gratification.

Unlike the private train, the Matlocks' house offered few clues to the owners' wealth. It had often happened that tradesmen delivering their first order from the Matlocks automatically drove up to the imposing gray fortress of their neighbor, Loftus Poynder.

Joshua and Sinclair had disappeared into the garden, which was as unassuming as the Matlocks' house. It was a paradise for children. Instead of formal beds and borders there were trees, lawns, swings, sandboxes, and unobstructed access to the beach. From afar Margaret heard her sons' voices, Matlock voices already—clear, penetrating, strong enough to communicate from boat to boat, but without any edge, sounds bubbling over with the joy of living. As she listened to them, everything fell into place: she was a part of this world. She was a Matlock; her sons were Matlocks. The smoldering quarrel between her father and old John Tyler Matlock was no concern of hers. Her life was built around Craig—Craig and the children, including those she would have in the future, until her house was just as full of life as this one. Nothing else mattered.

Margaret had turned into the path to the open porch outside the housekeeping rooms at the back of the house. As she turned the corner, she saw, not Rose as she had hoped, but her father-in-law, supervising the transfer of the wine from the train to the cellars. Two men were carrying the clumsy crates.

"Slow down," he admonished. "Careful. Watch the steps. Carry it gently. Are you purposely trying to spoil it?" His voice was muffled, distressed.

Margaret knew this tone only too well, it was used to indicate where each family member stood in the old man's estimation. Measured on this scale, his welcome to her was warm. Spontaneously he reached for her hand, a gesture he did not use freely. "You're looking well," he said.

The eyes he turned on her seemed to consist entirely of dark irises. As always, at this first moment of reunion in the summer, Margaret felt herself being examined closely. John Tyler's look searched out the state of her health, her appearance, and whether she would be able to bear more children.

"I've put aside another thousand dollars each for Joshua and Sinclair. In treasury notes," he said.

Margaret should have been inured to his ways by now. "Treasury notes?" she said stiffly. She could not bring herself to utter a single word of thanks.

"They're as safe as houses and bring six percent. The trust will continue after my death. A thousand dollars a year. When Joshua and Sinclair turn twenty-one, they will have a considerable sum of money. I wonder if it wouldn't be wise for your father to invest an equal annual amount for them—or perhaps you should."

Margaret was glad that Rose Matlock came around the corner and John Tyler turned away to follow the workmen into the house.

"What's the matter?" Rose asked. "Did something go wrong with the wine and he took it out on you?"

"No, no," Margaret said as the two women embraced. She felt better immediately. "I'm so silly. I'll never learn to take him as he is. He has subscribed for treasury notes of a thousand dollars each for Joshua and Sinclair—'safe as houses, at six percent'; that's his welcome to me after a year. I know I'm being foolish, but it's like a slap in the face. I didn't even thank him. Perhaps I should have called Joshua and Sinclair to come from the garden so that they can say thank you properly. But they wouldn't understand what they were thanking him for."

"I'm not so sure about that," Rose mused. "With a Matlock, you can never tell when his love of money is born." She walked ahead of Margaret into the house. "Have you heard from Craig?"

"Since he wrote from Savannah three weeks ago, not a word. Every morning when I wake up I think, this is the day he'll be home. In his letter from Savannah he said it wouldn't last much longer. The war has been over for three months. So many men are already home."

"And the children?"

"They haven't been able to sleep properly for days, they've been so excited waiting for the train."

Rose Matlock stood at the table in the center of the kitchen and picked up her list, a kind of overall campaign plan, which she used every year to organize the move into Willowbeach in half an afternoon. She checked off an item before looking up at Margaret. "I suspect you were the one he wanted to please with the treasury bonds. That's his way of loving—the Matlock way of loving. A child may not have much use for that sort of thing, but the accounts he keeps for his grandchildren—for him that's not just money, it has to do with imagination, it is an attempt to thwart the future. His wines are the same thing. There are more than five hundred bottles in the cellars here, and each year he brings a few more cases. He'll drink thirty bottles this summer, and I suspect he won't even like them very much. The wines are too heavy, the vintages too old. But what inspires him is that he has acquired the last bottles of a particular year or a particular vineyard. It's an investment. That fires his imagination, and his palate has to go along." Rose Matlock's eyes met Margaret's. "When Craig first went off to the war, I couldn't understand it myself. But I think that too can be explained. He must have expected to gain by it in ways we cannot fathom. God knows, it can't have been material gain. Of course money is important to the Matlocks, but it is only the springboard for their dreams. When you can understand that, you can begin to understand them."

"It's already July," Margaret said, "and the war ended in April. Almost everyone I know in Southport has come home. In his last letter, Craig wrote that they wouldn't be mustered out just yet because there was work for the Construction Corps even after the surrender. I've learned to live with his volunteering, but surely with your connections in the War Department, his discharge could have been speeded up."

"He'll be here soon. It can't take much longer."

Margaret knew that these words put an end to the topic. Her mother-in-law would now turn back to her checklist. For years Margaret's life had been made up entirely of household duties, of daily tasks. In this respect, she was starved for someone to talk to. Aunt Edna did not count, nor did Joshua and Sinclair; they only preyed on her strength. She needed Craig; it was the longing for him that had hollowed her out, and the only thing she wanted from Rose was a chance to talk about him.

But comforting someone was not something Rose Matlock did well. Nor was she any good at typical women's conversations that circled a topic for hours. This kind of intimacy had never been of help to her any more than had words of sympathy. For her there were only two sources from which she could draw strength—the family and keeping busy. "You don't mind, do you?" she said. "I've got to get back to work."

"Let me help you," Margaret answered quickly, afraid that Rose might send her away.

"Do you have time? My daughters have travel migraines, whatever that may be. It seems to be the fashion. I've never had a headache in my life. I told all three of them to lie down until dinnertime. They'd only get in my way anyhow." Rose Matlock smiled. "But you and I, we make a good team. Let's start upstairs, in the nurseries."

Making beds, laying out towels, unpacking countless valises and stowing their contents in wardrobes—every motion seemed senseless to Margaret. Two ants carrying grains of sand from one place to another. The pillows they plumped up, the flowers they arranged in vases, the biscuits they placed on all the night tables—none of their actions would endure. Running to the beach and swimming out until all thought, all feeling disappeared, leaving only the roar of the sea in a shell, only something driven along on the tide—day after day that had been her medicine, her drug against waiting. But now she would not have left even if Rose had ordered her to go.

When, two hours later, the two women came back to

the kitchen and Rose made check marks against all but a few items on her list, Margaret watched her as intently as if the moment could reveal to her the full nature of the woman. Rose was sixty-six. Early that morning she had boarded the train, but within hours she had turned a house that had stood empty for nine months back into a home. Now each lamp had a lucifer lying beside it. Each washbowl was equipped with its own soap—seven different kinds for the fifteen Matlocks who had arrived this day. She did not begrudge a single motion. She knew exactly which of her grandchildren liked two pillows and who would need an extra blanket. And now, in the kitchen, where the serving girl was busily mixing great pitchers of lemonade for the children, Rose watched to see that there were plenty of thin lemon slices.

From the sideboard she took the bell used to summon the children to their meals and opened the window. It was not long before a pack of children came through the trees, charging toward the house. A moment later they stood breathlessly in the kitchen, their hair rumpled, streaks of dirt on their faces. Lance sported a broad scratch on his forehead. With a contented smile, Rose Matlock handed out glasses of lemonade. There would be more bumps and bruises before dinner and at clean up time some bandages would have to be applied.

"He's a liar," Joshua suddenly screamed and began to hit his cousin Lance. "He's a mean, dirty liar."

In one bound Margaret reached Joshua and separated them. "What a way to talk."

"He *is* a liar, a common liar. He says Grandfather Matlock built the first railroad, and that's a lie. All he did was *buy* it. Grandfather Poynder—my grandfather, not his—built the first one."

"Let them be," Rose Matlock whispered to Margaret. "They'll work it out by themselves." She maneuvered the children to the other side of the large kitchen, where she refilled their glasses, blew noses, and tied shoelaces. Gradually the kitchen emptied. When the children had all drifted off, she waved Margaret to her side and stepped out with her to the stairs leading to the garden. "Did you know that we are expecting your father?"

"My father? He's coming to Willowbeach? Has there been another quarrel?"

"No, no, just the opposite. John Tyler invited him to dinner."

The children's voices rang through the garden. All of them were now gathered around the locomotive, an old discarded model John Tyler Matlock had set up in the garden. Joshua's and Sinclair's red mops of hair stood out among the dark heads of the others. Joshua was the loudest of the lot, their spokesman.

"It's strange how these traits are inherited," Rose said. "None of my children spoke as early as Craig, and none was so wild and enjoyed scuffling so much. Sinclair is the quiet one, isn't he?"

Margaret nodded. She was still thinking about John Tyler's invitation to her father, wondering what was behind it.

"I still remember the first time I saw you," Rose Matlock continued. "You were the same age your boys are now. It was a sunny day, like today, but you were wearing a coat and wool stockings. I thought there was something wrong with your legs. I don't know why, but someone was always leading you around by the hand."

"Aunt Edna saved my baby shoes," Margaret said. "I must show them to you sometime. They had steel inserts, to prevent fallen arches, splayfoot, and hammer toes. It's a miracle that I learned to walk at all. The doctor came from Southport once a week to examine me. Everything was dangerous—the sun, the wind, walking fast, cold drinks, playing in the sand. And if anyone dared to pull me on his lap and kiss me, my mother was convinced that I had contracted a terrible disease. She hardly ever kissed me herself, for the same reason. . . . I think she must have been a very unhappy woman."

"That's how she wanted it." Rose Matlock's voice was cold. It could sound cruel to someone who did not know her well. "She made it her life's work to suffer," she continued. "I don't have any sympathy with that sort of person. It's undignified. Happiness? A mirage, nothing more. The day isn't long enough for me to ask myself whether I'm happy or unhappy. Your boys have come a long way since last summer. It's time they had a little brother or sister, or they'll start thinking too well of themselves. You're not planning to stop having children, are you?"

"No."

"It doesn't have to be another set of twins. I've checked the family tree. They're the first. There have never been twins in the Matlock family." She laughed. "To enter the the world as a pair, to share such an important event with another person—surely that's not to the Matlock taste."

For a while they listened to the children. Rose Matlock's hands were on the porch rail. The wood was warm from the sun. "I used to think that once my daughters were grown up, I'd be able to leave everything in their hands," she said.

"Why don't you give it a try?"

"Sometimes we want things that we wouldn't know what to do with if we had them. Things are just fine as they are." She paused. "It's occurred to me that Alice, Vinnie, and May are just pretending to have the migraine. Perhaps they know me better than I know myself. Perhaps I'd be unhappy if all at once no one needed me."

"Do you know why my father is coming to dinner tonight? Are you sure there hasn't been a quarrel?"

"There is something they have to discuss. Business. I am never told about such arrangements until the last minute. I hope your father arrives from New York in time."

"What exactly is the trouble between them? The way they avoid each other—surely that's not natural. Sometimes I think they hate each other. At least that's the way my father responds to the name John Tyler Matlock."

"It's probably an old story, and they themselves don't remember how it started. I keep out of such matters. Trying to force your way in to mediate usually only makes things worse. I hope this is the beginning at drawing a line through the past. I must see to dinner now. We're having fish. I hope your father likes fish."

"You can put whatever you like in front of him. He won't notice what it is. The only thing he doesn't like about meals is the time he has to spend on them. He has always preferred to live like a bachelor. It suits him."

"John Tyler would like all the grandchildren at the table tonight, including Joshua and Sinclair."

"Seven-thirty, as usual?"

"As usual." Rose clasped Margaret's hand in one of the silent gestures which she could imbue with so much warmth. Another summer at Willowbeach had begun.

# = 3 =

As THE YEARS passed Loftus Poynder found it increasingly difficult to leave his New York house. The narrow four-story brick building—fronting on Warren Street and backing on the New York Railroad terminal, with its sidings, train sheds, and ticket counters—had been home to Loftus Poynder since he first settled in New York. Neither his marriage nor the newer house in Willowbeach had altered that fact. Willowbeach was an illusion. It had been planned as the home of a large family, but it had remained empty, a refuge for a sick wife. Loftus Poynder visited it only to see his only child Margaret. Even after his wife's death he had never been comfortable there, and since Margaret's marriage to Craig Matlock he felt no more than a tolerated guest at Willowbeach.

It would have been simpler and more convenient to take the steamboat to Bridgeport and continue from there to Willowbeach by coach. But he preferred the more troublesome rail route, though it required changing trains before he was even out of the city in order to get to Woodlawn Station where the train for Southport began. He knew every mile of the route. He had been there when the embankment was laid, and he had been there when the tunnel was dynamited out of the hard schist of Murray Hill. The line leading from Woodlawn out to Greenbush, the terminal at the eastern shore of the Hudson near Albany, was one of the two New York lines he owned and to this day he personally hired the locomotive drivers, stokers, conductors, and stewards. Usually he got on in front with the engineer, but today he picked a seat in the least crowded carriage. Even the few words he was forced to exchange with the conductor cost him an effort. Every mile along the way reminded him of the slowness and hardships of his road to riches and of the man who had cudgeled him along the way: John Tyler Matlock.

Not that Loftus Poynder was feeling gloomy; rather, he had no wish to be cheerful. To be wide awake, on the alert, that was his resolve. He was not an impetuous man easily swayed by his emotions. He had to sort out his feelings, place them like a set of rails. It was hard work; it took time. He had chosen this means of transportation because he needed plenty of time to get himself in a fighting mood for the coming encounter with John Tyler Matlock.

Loftus Poynder had been surprised by the invitation. He had discussed it at length with Justin Kramer, his right-hand man. Poynder had been sorely tempted to refuse but had finally been persuaded that it would be better to find out what was on Matlock's mind, especially to get it from the source. It was hardly a gesture of family solidarity. If it had been, Rose Matlock would have extended the invitation. Poynder thought about her. If she were not John Tyler's wife, he would surely have found her enormously likable. As it was, she was merely one of the heads of that hydra-headed snake called Matlock. No, a Poynder had no reason to expect anything good from the Matlocks. Whenever their territories impinged on each other, he, Loftus Poynder, lost.

He was about to undergo a trial of strength. He could feel it. But if Matlock thought he would be encountering his old antagonist, he was mistaken. During the last few years Loftus Poynder had learned much. He had come to understand that it was not enough to be in the right when you were up against a man like John Tyler Matlock.

Few travelers got off the train at Southport. Most of those who did had families who spent the summer at the shore. It was the ambition of practically every New Yorker to own a house at the shore. To spend the summer in New York, as Loftus Poynder did, was scorned, considered an admission of poverty. There were even some who pretended to be away though they remained in the city.

In front of the station—actually an extended wooden shed, stemming from the time when Southport was a flag stop—light one-horse shays were drawn up, waiting. Loftus

Poynder had also ordered one, but first he went to the telegraph office.

The room was small and dark. Among the telegraph machine, desk, and worn, leather-covered bench there was just room for the clerk's swivel chair. Something about the man in it was familiar to Poynder. He remained standing in the doorway until the ticking of the machine stopped.

"I'm expecting a telegram," Poynder said. When the man raised his head, he recognized him. "Daniel Place! What are you doing here, working a telegraph?"

The man took off his headset and turned in his chair. His face was blank as he looked up. He reached for a cane leaning against the desk and whacked it against his right leg. "Ash wood," he said. "Ash and steel. Movable knee joint. The latest English patent." He put the cane back. "Don't take it personally, but all railroad owners ought to be hauled into court. Every couple of months they give the cars a new coat of paint, but somehow they never seem to have the money for any safety precautions."

"How did it happen?"

"I've been telling them for years, those couplings are no damn good. You'd have to be a monkey to get out alive." With a jerk Place pulled up his trouser leg and extended the wooden leg. "Disability caused by work-man's negligence—that's what the lawyer for the insurance company said. They claim I wasn't quick enough. They turned me down flat when I asked for an indemnity." He brushed the cloth back over the leg and leaned back in his chair. "But you know their methods. You got accidents on your railroads, too, don't you?"

"Where did it happen?" Loftus Poynder asked. "On the Housatonic?"

"Yup. Six months ago. In the depot at Chatham. I've seen worse legs, and nobody thought to amputate 'em. But the hospital they've got there—it's nothing but a wooden-leg store. An Englishman, of course. He's not a doctor, he's a butcher. It's a miracle he didn't take it off all the way to the hip. Three weeks ago they transferred me here, and I've got to be glad to have the job."

Poynder shook his head. "You Irishmen. You were always damned careless. Have you ever met an Irishman who worked on the railroad and still had all his fingers?"

Daniel Place chuckled and raised his left hand with its missing middle and ring fingers. "Eight fingers is good enough. Less to freeze in the winter." He chuckled again.

"They'd have to stand over you with guns to make you pay attention to the safety rules," Poynder said. "Remember that time we had to get through the blue limestone? We blasted for weeks. Day and night. At first you were careful of the signals, but then you got reckless. You didn't even bother to get down on the ground. At most you held your shovels over your heads—and you laughed when the rocks crashed down on you."

Place nodded to himself. "God knows, we were a wild bunch. Great times, especially in the winter, when the crews were resting and we had money in our pockets. I never ate better turkey or drank greater whiskey than those years. We were all kings. A railroad engineer earned more than the governor of New York. When you come to think of it, all of us should have amounted to something." He looked sharply at Poynder. "It worked for you." He gave his chair a swing and made a quarter-turn. "Here's a telegram for you. From Albany." He looked at the time stamp. "It came in an hour ago."

Loftus Poynder examined both sides of the envelope and put it in his pocket. He used to tip the telegraph clerk, but was uncertain what to do now that Place was the operator.

Place reached for his cane, rose, and followed Poynder outside. All the carriages but two had driven off.

"You don't spend much time at your house," Place said. "I was surprised when you built it. The biggest house in these parts, that's for sure. From the boat it looks like a castle. That's not your style." Falling back on their old intimacy, he gave Poynder a poke in the ribs. "At least you don't think you're too fancy to come by the regular train. Boy, you missed a sight this morning. The Matlocks' private train." Air hissed through his teeth. "A palace on wheels. Brand-new McQueen locomotive that can pull ten cars without even straining. The surprising thing is, our tracks here held up to it. Right now old Matlock is giving you a run for your money, right?"

"As far as I'm concerned, he can put whole houses on wheels. In New York I'm the boss. He can't stick so much as a sack of flour in there. I've got to be going. See you again. Would you like a job with me?"

"Thanks, but it's cheaper living here than in New York. My wife inherited her parents' little house. Her brothers are fishermen, and my son delivers the telegrams. We manage."

This place doesn't suit him, Place thought as he watched Poynder walking toward the carriage. He tried to remember how long he had known Poynder. Must be nearly thirty years. Once upon a time, Loftus Poynder had started at the bottom. When they met, he had already worked his way up to supervisor. He was a man who believed in railroads at a time when most people were still laughing at them. And today he owned the New York Railroad. He had not changed much since then. Even in the old days he had had deep lines around his eyes and across his forehead. It didn't matter that his hair had turned white. The red flames around his head had become white ones, that was all. Poynder had never been what you would call a young man, but he would never be an old one either. A block of granite knows no age. Watching him walk, you got the feeling that the earth clung to his feet, that he was taking root.

As Daniel Place returned to his office, he realized that Loftus Poynder was the only rich man he respected.

Loftus Poynder was disappointed by the telegram. He did not read it until he was settled in the carriage. Of necessity its wording was vague and obscure. Many eyes would have seen it before it reached him. Justin Kramer had gone to Albany in hopes that in Matlock's home town he could more easily learn Matlock's plans. Though he had reliable informants among the politicians, lawyers, and brokers in Albany, the trip had not, it seemed, borne fruit. Whatever hand John Tyler Matlock held, he was playing it close to the vest.

Loftus Poynder did not look out the windows as the shay drove along. He was blind to the scenery, to the sky and the setting sun. Since he had not let anyone know he was coming the front gate was locked. But even if it had stood wide open, he would have dismissed the carriage there and walked the rest of the way. He never allowed himself to be driven to the front door, perhaps because what Daniel Place had said was true: the house was not his style, and therefore he behaved like a stranger in it. As he paid the coachman, he ordered him to return the next morning. "Get here in time to make the first train to New York."

As he opened the side gate, a feeling of pain mingled with his sense of estrangement. The narrow door moved awkwardly on its hinges. The difficulty was intentional; no child should be able to open it. When he built the house, he was proud of this conceit. The house was full of such details. The window sills were so high that a child could not climb them; the table lamps in the nurseries were screwed down, as on a ship. He had not wanted to build the house; but when he did give in to his wife's urging, he had invested everything in it—his hopes, his energy, and untold amounts of money. All in vain. His wife had not regained her health; she had never borne him the sons he wanted so much.

Slowly, with heavy steps, he approached the house. No one came to meet him. None of the many windows was illuminated, while across the garden, at the Matlocks', light fell on the lawns from the ground-floor windows. Silence and abandonment greeted him as he entered the great hall, carrying his bag. He could not hear the children. Behind the closed library doors someone was playing the piano. Edna Child. Whenever she played, all the pieces sounded alike.

He went to the door and opened it quietly. The lamp on the grand piano lit up the high walls of massed books. More than a thousand books. Susan Poynder had acquired them and presumably had read all of them. He had never taken one from its shelf. Except for technical materials about railroad building and *The American Railroad Journal*, he read nothing.

Though Edna had broken off her playing, she remained sitting at the keyboard, her hands on the keys, in exemplary pianistic fashion. Nor did she stop the metronome, as if she intended to resume at once. "So you came after all. I didn't think you would. Nothing is ready. You could have sent us a telegram—or are we not worth even that much? You must have known you were coming."

Loftus Poynder set down his valise. "Where is Margaret? And the boys?" He went over to the fireplace, where a fire was going in spite of the time of year.

"Where do you suppose? The Matlocks are back. You'll have to hurry if you plan to dine with them. Is that really what you want? I'm told you and old Matlock are going to have a cozy chat. So you're going to knuckle under. You too! If Susan knew!"

She got up and stopped the ticking metronome before walking toward her brother-in-law. But when she found herself face to face with him, she resisted the impulse that had almost made her embrace him. It was not the first time she had felt that way. Their relationship was cramped, inhibited. Poynder, who gave it little thought, ascribed it to the atmosphere of the house. He did not have the slightest suspicion that Edna had still not gotten over the fact that thirty-six years ago he had married, not her, but her sister Susan. Nor did he suspect that after her sister's death Edna's hopes had flickered anew. She still hoped, seventeen years later, that she would become his wife. Though he had never given the remotest sign that he shared her vision of the future, Edna felt entitled to her hopes, if only because of the number of years she had already lived in the house in Willowbeach. "You could have sent us a telegram," she repeated.

"It would have come too late."

"It would have been in time. Since Daniel Place's son has been delivering them, we receive all telegrams from Southport within the hour." She gave her brother-in-law a searching look. "You don't look well."

"I feel fine. I've never felt better."

But Edna went on probing. "Do you still take your meals at that French place? Those spices, so much fat. You're ruining your health. One of these days you'll have to pay for it. I hope you haven't started smoking again."

Poynder's reserves of equanimity were more quickly exhausted than might have been expected in a man who was outwardly so calm. Because he was already on edge, he answered with sudden vehemence. "Spare me the lecture. In my whole life I have never needed a doctor—and I will never let one near me, I can promise you that."

Edna's shoulders straightened. "Of all people, you shouldn't talk like that. But of course you haven't learned a thing. Susan would be alive today if she had been under a good doctor's care in time."

"She had a dozen doctors. That was the mistake. My mistake, because I let it happen."

"By that time it was much too late. Earlier, when it could have done some good, even a stay at the seashore was much too expensive for you. I remember the endless arguments over every bill. You always begrudged her this house."

He seemed to be listening to his wife, to accusations from a distant past. "Why do you think this house has eighteen rooms?" he asked. "There's room here for a dozen children. A house like this doesn't make sense unless a large family lives in it."

But Edna was not listening. "You know perfectly well that Susan hated the house on Warren Street. But you forced her to move in with you. She wanted a carriage, but you told her, 'It's only a short walk for me to the stock exchange.' You even begrudged her a pew in St. Paul's." Her voice was rising.

"It's not necessary to have a chair that costs two thousand dollars a year to pray properly."

"She hated you. I know, I was there. All week long she felt fine. But the closer the time for your arrival, the worse she felt. She knew you wanted only one thing from her. All you men want that. A child a year—yes, that's what you wanted."

Their voices stopped. Outside, dark was falling, washing the walls with blue. In the grate the fire sputtered and hissed.

"I didn't come to fight with you," Poynder said.

"I'll get your room ready." Edna sounded weary.

"Don't go to any trouble. I'm only staying one night." He was already homesick for New York, for his desk and for the toots and screeches from the railroad station below.

"If you want to change before you go over there, you'll have to hurry," Edna said. "Dinner is served promptly at seven-thirty."

Loftus Poynder stood with his head lowered. "Send Greville. I want him to take a message. Tell Matlock, if he wants to see me, he can come here." No sooner had he said this than he regretted it. In his refusal to go to Matlock's house he had merely betrayed the fact that he was in a black mood, and that was a sign of weakness, something he could not afford now. But here, in front of Edna, he could not afford to take it back, either.

"Greville will be happy to deliver the message," she answered.

Loftus Poynder reached for his valise. "I want all the

lamps in the house lighted. All of them. I want a bright house." He motioned toward the grand piano. "And clear out of the library. This is where I'll see him if he comes."

= 4 =

SEVENTEEN PEOPLE SAT down to the first dinner in Willowbeach, eleven children and six adults, John Tyler at the head of the table, surrounded by his grandchildren. Family custom assigned the seats immediately next to him to the male grandchildren who were allowed to join the family for the first time, and this year Joshua and Sinclair occupied these chairs.

Though the women and girls were assigned no particular seats, Rose Matlock always occupied the place at the opposite end of the table. From this vantage point she could best direct the serving girls. More important, she was far enough away from her husband to control the inevitable incidents. In August, when Langdon and Irene joined them on weekends, bringing their children or friends, sometimes as many as thirty people sat down to dinner. But the more of them there were, the better Rose Matlock liked it.

Years before, the table had been built according to her instructions, so that it could be enlarged at will. For her the year began, not on the first day of January, but when she arrived at Willowbeach and saw her children and grandchildren gathered around her at the special table. Anything she might have overlooked at other times, she noticed here. Here she had discovered the first fuzz on Langdon's lips, as well as Alice's buffed fingernails. The growing up of the children, and later the grandchildren, had made her more aware of the stages of her own life and even more of those of her husband. Fifty years, fifty summers at Willowbeach. For the first few years there had been only four of them at meals. Now three generations met around the table, and when, as now, she gazed at the group, it seemed that she had been granted more good fortune than a single life could hold.

Today the meal had been served half an hour later because they had waited for Poynder. Once at table, his name was not mentioned. The entrees had been eaten. The maid who was clearing the table for dessert remained standing next to Rose Matlock's chair. Though Greville had told her to give the message to her master in person, in this house all avenues to John Tyler Matlock led through his wife.

"Greville was here just now," the maid whispered. "You know—the gardener from next door. Mr. Poynder has asked Mr. Matlock to come to his house. After dinner, of course." She was used to speaking softly so that no one else at the table could hear and to take the sting out of messages of this nature. In her experience, bad news invariably rebounded on the messenger.

"Thank you, Celia," Rose said. "I'll take care of it." She looked down the table at her husband, but he seemed unaware of any interruption. Margaret, on the other hand, only two chairs away, had seemed uneasy throughout the meal; now she perked up, dashing a questioning look at her mother-in-law. Rose did not respond. She had an infallible intuition for the proper time to impart unpleasant news to her husband. She decided to wait until after dinner when the children had gone to bed and he would be alone in the smoking room, drinking his coffee.

When John Tyler indicated that dinner was over, she motioned for Margaret to remain. In front of her husband she could control her displeasure, but she was open with the younger woman. "Your father arrived from New York, but he did not accept the invitation to dinner. He sent Greville to say that if John Tyler wants to see him, he can come to his house. Was that necessary? Must he always be so stubborn?" Rose had remained seated. Now she put her face in her hands, as always when she was momentarily ashamed of being tired and old.

Margaret felt that she should say something in defense of her father, but she could think of nothing; deep down she agreed with Rose.

"I'll have to tell John Tyler." Rose Matlock got to her feet. "God knows I don't want to. He'll explode."

"I'm sorry."

"Never mind. Come with me."

"Me? Go with you?"

"Yes, why not? He likes you, and he likes your boys."

Margaret had to agree when she thought of her father-in-law's patience in showing Joshua and Sinclair how to remove the fish meat from its backbone. "I'll apologize for my father," she offered.

"No. No apologies. Leave it to me."

It was unusual for Rose Matlock to follow her husband into the smoking parlor immediately after dinner. He was therefore somewhat prepared for bad news.

"So he came after all?" John Tyler asked. He was sitting by the fireplace. On the table by his side was a stack of business reports.

"He sent a message," Rose began. "The train was late. He asked that you come to see him." Her tone of voice did not betray the reluctance with which she delivered the message.

He turned his head. As always when he was angry, his jawbone became even more prominent. "He sent a message? He wants me to go over there?"

Over many years Rose had learned to deflect his rages by making his anger her own. "I'll send word that you can't go. It's an extremely rude answer to your invitation. If I were in your place, I'd refuse to go. There's no doubt in my mind. I'll send Celia."

"Wait." John Tyler looked at Margaret. "Your boys pleased me tonight. Joshua can talk very sensibly. He asks clever questions. He will be at home in this world, and one day he will take whatever he needs. I know. Sinclair will have a harder time of it. He is a dreamer. His questions are of quite another sort. When Joshua asks me, 'Where does money come from and where does it go?' what he means is, what do you have to do to keep it? If Sinclair asks the same question, he means, why does there have to be such a thing as money? Pour my coffee for me, Margaret. A little milk, no sugar. You haven't forgotten?"

Margaret obeyed, saying nothing. She knew that this attempt at warmth was no more than a form of tyranny, the most dangerous kind. Yet she could not help but admire his style. Everything he did, even his malice, had the glow of newly minted gold.

"What do you want me to do?" Rose asked. "Shall I send Celia?"

"Do you remember what I told you on the train today? He's a delicate plant." John Tyler's look once again wandered toward Margaret. "I liked that in your father from the outset. He never made a secret of his feelings about all Matlocks. But I'm afraid his world is full of Matlocks. He's worked like a madman all his life. But sometimes he doesn't know how to reap the rewards of his work." He sipped his coffee. "What is it like outside?" he asked without transition. "Must be a glorious evening."

The two women exchanged looks. John Tyler rose, picked up the papers, and locked them in the concealed wall safe. "I had planned to take a walk anyway," he said.

John Tyler Matlock went straight to the Poynder mansion, without detours and without delay. Only now, confronted with the wall of brightly lit windows, he stopped. Loftus Poynder's provocation had bothered him even less than he had let the women see.

In sight of the house, which he had considered ostentatious from the first, he asked himself whether he had ever taken Poynder seriously. The wealth of the Matlocks was old, secure; a Matlock was born to lead a rich life and to die a rich man. Poynder's wealth was new, barely thirty years old. He had seen a lot of upstarts. New York teemed with men who had grown rich overnight and were impoverished again just as quickly. He had thought Poynder another flash in the pan, but he was mistaken. Loftus Poynder had staying power. He had secured his wealth, his power had grown, and now he was even muddying Matlock's waters, putting obstacles in Matlock's way. That was a new and unexpected situation for a man like Matlock who, as he grew older, was less and less willing to take the long way around to get what he wanted.

Twice before, there had been crucial struggles between Poynder and himself. Twice he had forced his will on Poynder, but this time he sensed that it would not be so easy. It had been for this reason that Poynder's behavior of this evening came as a relief to him. It showed him that his antagonist had allowed his feelings to overcome his better judgment. And where the emotions ruled, John Tyler Matlock immediately scented weakness.

They had last seen each other at the twins' baptism—literally seen, for immediately after the ceremony in the little fishermen's chapel in Southport, Loftus Poynder had disappeared. Now as they faced each other in the brightly lit library, they looked each other over with the curiosity of men who have made it a habit to measure their own vitality by others' decline.

"You are seldom here," John Tyler Matlock said in greeting. "Though the climate is particularly healthy. I live all year for the months I spend here."

"I find that New York agrees with me much better."

As if in the habit of meeting every evening, both men settled in armchairs near the fireplace.

"You don't spend much time in New York anymore," Poynder noted. "Aren't you homesick for your ships? I can remember when New York harbor was full of Matlock ships. Now it's all railroads. You haven't always considered them a profitable capital investment."

"Times change," John Tyler Matlock said, "and we must change with them. Perhaps I'll come back to New York one day. Perhaps soon."

"Matlocks have always known how to follow the times." Poynder was determined not to let himself be provoked and therefore tried to sound friendly. "A glass of wine? I don't know if it's any good. I don't pay much attention to such things here."

Matlock made a gesture of refusal. "You have a couple of splendid grandsons—we both do. I've set aside a thousand dollars in treasury notes every year for Joshua and Sinclair. I wonder if you shouldn't do the same, or something like it."

"Why not?" Poynder rose, and Matlock followed suit. The two men, so dissimilar in many ways, were alike in their need for movement when they wanted to speak and think. "Is that what you wanted to talk to me about?"

"In a way. All of us work too hard. At our age we ought to keep something in reserve. We should put in order whatever there is to be put in order. Otherwise too many loose ends remain. One always starts on something new. One thinks and acts as if we were granted life eternal. But one day we realize that the time has come to reap the harvest. To stabilize, to establish order, to take care that there is no way for one's heirs to make mistakes —yes, that's what I wanted to speak to you about."

"You don't seem to have a great deal of faith in your sons."

Matlock paced slowly around the room. "Sometimes I actually do think that we are made of different, tougher stuff. In any case, I want my sons to have an easier time of it."

"You really mean your older son, Langdon. Craig has already been paid off."

"I mean all my children. Money melts away, especially in a large family. My work will have meaning only when I succeed in securing my fortune in such a way that even the children of my grandchildren can live on the income."

"That doesn't sound much like a Matlock," Poynder said.

John Tyler passed his hand over his eyes. When he dropped it, his features had been smoothed out by a smile. "And yet that is what I think about night and day. I am looking for a solution. And a solution for the problems Craig's marriage caused. What I am aiming for is in both our interest. At least, I hope so. We both have a good scent for—what did you call it—sign of the times. Both of us have invested in railroads. The times are working for us. Every immigrant, every new-born child, every factory, every new house—all raised the value of the railroads. The West becomes more and more interesting. Across the Great Lakes the population is exploding, and our roads are part of the principal routes. They can't do without us. If they want blood, it must flow through our veins. In America, distance doesn't mean a thing anymore—if it ever did."

Loftus Poynder stood still at the center of the room, his head lowered. Listening to Matlock, he had felt a wave of hot emotion washing over him. "It took you a long time to discover your passion for the railroad," he said. "I remember that you rejected my proposals as pipe dreams. It was in your office on Broome Street. At the time I was looking for partners. I offered a high rate of interest, but you called me a fool. And that's not all. You saw to it that in all of New York not a single bank would back me with so much as a penny."

John Tyler Matlock laughed without embarrassment. "So? Wasn't I right at the time? The interest payments would have choked you—if you could have paid them at all. To this day I'm proud of the fact that you didn't succeed in borrowing money. Admit it. What you called a railroad in those days! Wooden tracks! All of them had to throw good money after bad. Not a single road was profitable. From a business point of view, it was sheer madness in those days. I'm not a railroad pioneer; I'm a man of business. As long as an enterprise devours money and earns nothing, it doesn't interest me. Get in, get out, both at the right time. That's the secret. It was that way when I bought my land and when I got rid of it at the right time. It was that way with shipping. I pushed my competitors to the wall when the freight rates were high. And I was the first to sell when this war became a real possibility, though it should have been clear to everyone that no ship would remain safe from the Southerners."

"Is it smart to remind me?" Poynder stood before the fireplace, staring at the flames.

"My dear Poynder! I know you are proud of your early railroads, even if they did cost you an arm and a leg. There is no one who has greater respect for men of your stamp than I do. Without men like you, mankind would still be huddling in caves. But to open the doors of the future, one has to be something like a sleepwalker. One must walk with closed eyes along a parapet. Canals, ships, railroads—they're all the same. They wanted to prove to all the world that the impossible is different. I'm not like that. I've never changed from being a small merchant. My bible is the ledger, where the numbers are recorded."

Loftus Poynder had promised himself to let Matlock talk, to be purely a listener, to offer the other no points of attack. But his patience was growing thin under Matlock's steady stream of words. "What are we talking about? Many years ago we had a conversation which you introduced with similar prolixity. In the end it turned to blackmail. At that time I had to back down. Forty thousand dollars to keep you from competing with me on the Hudson. A pretty penny. But I paid, and I learned. What is it you want this time?"

When Matlock had prepared himself for this meeting, he had imagined Loftus Poynder as he had been years ago, a man whose bizarre character betrayed itself in both stony silences and sudden outbursts. But the Poynder he now saw before him was a different man. "People like ourselves have to be rivals," Matlock said. "There's no way around it. I believe we've reached the point where it would be unnatural, not to say unprofitable, to insist on continuing the rivalry. This time both of us will have to pay a pretty penny. Look at the situation upstate five years ago, when I began to get into railroads. A dozen small lines, obsolete, feuding among themselves. The most you could say for some of them was that they were keeping out of bankruptcy. In spite of very generous concessions and land grants. Everyone built for himself. Each chose his own gauge. Most of the lines failed. Some idiot could always be found to buy up the rubbish, but then he didn't do any better. He didn't even have enough money to repaint the cars or undertake the most essential improvements. After all, he bought the line to make money, not to spend it. In no time the cars rotted, as did the tracks and locomotives. I've seen the books. They paid dearly for their lesson—all of them—simply because they couldn't get along with each other."

Loftus Poynder had only a minimal sense of irony. In addition, he lacked an understanding of the strange transformation to which past events may be subjected in the mind of an imaginative person. "Of course the way you tell it, it sounds a lot better," he said. "But you're forgetting the bribes you paid so the directors of the lines would deliberately let the tracks and yards rot. When the stock fell sufficiently, when the company stopped paying dividends, when the newspapers had blown the whole thing up into a scandal—then who emerged as the savior? None other than John Tyler Matlock."

"Pity," Matlock said without explaining what he meant. Loftus Poynder was not the man to spar with. He was too direct. He behaved toward other people as if he were blasting a tunnel through a mountain. "Whatever you want to call it—late love or bribery—the result is the Empire State Railroad, which I control. No other state in the country is crisscrossed by a more extensive rail network. From Albany to Buffalo there's nothing left that doesn't belong to the Empire State. Three thousand miles of tracks, and more than half of it two-way. I tell you, Poynder, the time of small companies is over. The Empire State Railroad is just a beginning. The potential is enormous. That's what we need—big companies, combines, mergers."

Whether Matlock was twisting the facts or presenting them fairly, Poynder was caught either way. He sat down, perching precariously on the outermost edge of the leather armchair. He leaned forward, ready to strike. "I assume you haven't finished."

Matlock nodded. "You're right, I'm not through yet, any more than the Empire State Railroad is. A rail line that dominates the state of New York is a monstrosity as long as it has no access to the state's principal city—New York."

The expression on Poynder's face was one of deep, expectant stillness. "I thought that was what you were getting at."

"It seems to me the lines are clearly drawn. With your roads, Poynder, you control the city, access to the city, the connection with Albany. My hands, the hands of the Empire State, hold the state, the whole hinterland. That's what we must talk about."

"Talk?" Loftus Poynder felt that he had been listening to John Tyler Matlock for a long time, that this alone put him at a disadvantage. "You didn't build your network with pretty speeches. As far as my railroad is concerned, I don't need a savior. Everything is running smoothly. Last year the New York Railroad carried thirty million passengers, and it paid a dividend of ten percent, while your Empire State Railroad paid no dividends at all— and hasn't for the past four years."

"Granted," Matlock said soothingly. "I don't under-estimate what you have to offer. I am laying out the facts. Up to now we've been rivals, simply in the nature of things. But we didn't get in each other's way. Now we have reached the point where any further expansion—no matter whether it originates with you or with me—would intrude on the territory of the other. Why let it come to that? The world can change, and we can too. The competition we've been engaged in up to now was a natural stage of development. But now we're on the threshold of a new era. I believe there's a solution which would not only make it possible for both of us to avoid unnecessary and expensive competition, but would profit each of us as well. Think of the railroad bridge over the Hudson near Albany. We agreed to build it jointly, and we both came out ahead."

Poynder was seized with a wave of discouragement. Sometimes at night, bent over his drafting table, the same feeling came over him. But not when he was working on a new project. As long as he was coping with problems, his courage remained high and his faith unshaken. But afterward, when the project had been completed, when he had cleared away the drawings and computations, then the moments of emptiness came on him. It was at those times that he was devoured by the feeling of having robbed himself, of having given away something he would never be able to retrieve. He rubbed his hand over his face as if to brush away the weariness. "You're right about the Hudson bridge," he said. "But what about the years of negotiation about a rate agreement? Kramer has explained the situation to your son Langdon a hundred times. In the winter, when the Hudson is frozen over, we carry all the freight of the Empire State Railroad. But in the summer you don't pay because you can transport the goods more cheaply by water. That's pure extortion. For about ninety days in the winter, when the Hudson is closed to traffic, eighty of my locomotives and more than a thousand freight cars are put at the disposal of the Empire State. But I have to bear the costs of maintenance, material, and storage all year long. So far you've refused to pay any part of these costs, and you don't come across with decent freight charges. What would happen if I refused to carry your loads during the winter? I don't see any readiness to come to an agreement. I see only the age-old methods for getting rid of a competitor."

With all the righteousness of a man who sees himself unjustly accused, John Tyler Matlock spread out his arms. "My proposal solves all that automatically. *You* have converted me. You have opened my eyes to what the railroads mean to the future. Now must I remind you? The fruit is ripe, ripe for plucking. The harvest is ready. Since the war, even the general public knows as much. Now it's clear to everyone that the Union won only because of its railroads. How else could we have transported our soldiers to the front, sometimes thousands of miles away? There would have been no victory at Vicksburg without the railroads. And what would General Sherman have done with his ten thousand men and twenty-three thousand horses in Atlanta if the railroads hadn't supplied them daily over a distance of more than three hundred and sixty miles? That's what convinced the people. Before the war, many people were opposed to this new means of transportation, but the war made the railroads popular.

Life without locomotives is no longer conceivable. What was impossible for twenty years—agreement on a uniform gauge—has come about almost by itself. Traffic will grow by leaps and bounds. There will always be new lines. Speeds will increase; soon a mile a minute won't be a dream. Fifty years ago, Buffalo was a little border village with a few trappers, whiskey-sellers, and smugglers. Then came the Erie Canal and then the railroad. In the eighteen thirties Chicago was nothing but a village. When I was there, there was a single hotel. It was called Hotel, a hut near the water. Last year ninety-five million pounds of meat were dispatched from the Chicago yards alone. And Cincinnati, St. Louis, Detroit, Indianapolis. I don't have to tell you what's been happening in the last thirty years in New York City.

"And the immigrants! Three million through New York alone in the last thirty years. They'll be spreading throughout the country. After all, how else could your New York Railroad have grown? Every Irishman, every German has helped pay your dividends. And that's only the beginning. Everyone is looking to the cities. Everyone wants the same thing to happen to them. The farmers, the manufacturers—all of them are rail crazy. Rochester raised a million dollars for a switch line to the coal mines —not the city of Rochester, mind you, but the citizenry. They signed for a million in bonds. There's no way we can stop it; we must invest. Or would you rather wait until the directors of the Pennsylvania or the Baltimore and Ohio put a knife to our throats? Do you want to leave Detroit, Cincinnati, St. Louis, Indianapolis, and Chicago to others? We must reach an agreement."

Loftus Poynder let the other man speak. It was absurd to hear the thoughts that plagued him day and night from the lips of a man who had never felt on his shoulders the weight of a sleeper, whose hand had never touched the switch that disengaged the gears of a locomotive. Investments, dividends, interest—that was the world of John Tyler Matlock. Poynder wondered where a Matlock would place man in the scale of values. Were people also nothing but property? Was the cult he made of his family simply another way of exercising power? But then, why were they so fond of him? He was a tyrant, but he was loved just the same. Poynder had often seen Joshua and Sinclair rush up to old Matlock in the garden, at the beach, wherever he showed up. And his own daughter, Margaret, also seemed fond of her father-in-law.

"If we don't draw the proper conclusions, others will," Matlock continued. "The hour has come for great railroad systems. It may be that there will be a time when other measures are necessary. But the present situation——"

"What conclusions? You've taken a lot of time to explain things I know all about. You make it sound very plausible. Certainly these are subjects that should be discussed. But just what conclusions do you have in mind?"

"There used to be two telegraph companies operating between New York and Buffalo by way of Albany. For years the two owners feuded. They were so busy with their price war that both of them were losing money. When the Civil War began, they suddenly had twice as much business as before. Then they saw the light and made a deal. Today they have a monopoly and dictate prices. Both are now millionaires several times over."

"Your example does not apply," Poynder said stiffly. "I have no competition in New York City. My railroad is flourishing. The profits grow larger."

"Well then," Matlock said, "I would like you to sell out to me. The sum I'm offering——" But when he saw the abrupt change in Poynder's expression, it seemed wiser to break off. With the cordial condescension that was the stinger in Matlock arrogance, he changed his tack. "No, I didn't expect you to agree, though that would be the simplest solution. How would you feel about leasing the New York Railroad to the Empire State? For a period of no less than twelve and no more than ninety-nine years. For the term of the lease I will guarantee an interest return of seven percent a year on your stock. On top of that, I will pay a fixed sum—immediately and in cash—for the take-over of all movable and immovable installations. What you do with the money and the dividends is your affair. All you would have to do is give me a guarantee not to invest it in other railroads."

"Is there a third possibility?" Poynder spoke with difficulty.

"You are a stubborn old man." Matlock's reply did not stem from mockery but from the respect he felt for his opponent, who had proved himself an equal. "Forget the two offers. Let us jointly found a new company. You bring in your stock; I'll bring mine."

"And the division of the partnership?"

"We won't quarrel about that. If we were to go by the size and track network of the Empire State, it would have a ten-to-one advantage over your line. But I appreciate the importance of access to New York. So let's say the partnership will be fifty-fifty."

During the ensuing silence Poynder's eyes traveled over the pattern of the black-and-red carpet. He had not expected Matlock to go so far. Almost against his will he said, "It sounds like a fair offer."

"It *is* a fair offer."

Loftus Poynder got up again and paced back and forth before the fireplace. His habit was to make such decisions alone, and yet he wished Kramer were there. Most of all, he wished he were in his office on Warren Street. This house hemmed him in. It made him unsure of himself. "Do you want an immediate answer?"

"There is only *yes* or *no*. I make an offer such as this only once. You can accept here and now, or you can turn it down."

"I see the advantages," Poynder said, but his tone of voice betrayed mistrust.

"I can see nothing but advantages. Don't do anything foolish just because the offer comes from me. Remember, too, the decrease in administrative costs. We can combine stations and ticket sales; we can save a lot of personnel; we can take out joint advertisements, buy coal together, and so on. Furthermore, we can come to grips with that outrage, the free rides. Last year the Empire State handed out three thousand free passes to politicians, newspaper people, and their families." His voice grew more insistent. "In time to come we will need to undertake enormous capital expenditures. You know that as well as I do. The public grows more demanding. In future they will choose the railroad that offers them the most comfort and luxury. I intend to order thirty luxury cars, my own patent. Each car costs nineteen thousand dollars. And people are asking for more safety. The way they used to feel about alcohol, they feel about the railroads today. The reformers and the journalists jump on every accident and blow it up into a catastrophe. Nobody mentions the fact that more murders are committed every day in Boston or that more people die of heat exhaustion in Connecticut. But when a drunk decides to sleep it off on the tracks and promptly gets run over, that's a banner headline. I have a pretty good idea that new laws will saddle us with elaborate safety regulations, to the point of giving locomotive engineers tests for color blindness. All that's going to cost money, Poynder, and more money. Automatic signals, overpasses. . . . Do you intend to pit yourself against the lawmakers? And think of the freight rates. You remember what happened to the shipping rates on the Hudson. Should we wait for the same thing to happen again? When you were just starting out, you could get seven dollars for transport from New York to Albany. Today it's two dollars. Right now, because of the war, freight rates are higher than they've ever been. But who knows how long that situation will last. There are senators who feel we're earning too much as it is. I'm telling you in confidence, in Albany they're drafting a law intended to freeze the rates at four cents a mile—top limit—for companies that pay six percent in dividends. When they reach eight percent, the companies are supposed to lower the rate to three cents. At a dividend of ten percent, we're supposed to be content with two cents a mile! The same with wages. A machinist already gets two and a quarter a day. And nobody works more than a ten-hour day. And that's now, after the war, when there's a surplus of workers. But if we pull together, we can bring wages back down to a dollar seventy-five in spite of everything. Really, Poynder, I can see nothing but advantages. I want you to say yes."

While Matlock was speaking, Poynder had been asking himself one question: what—and where—was the catch? He stopped pacing, his face expressionless. "What about the board of directors?"

"You're beginning to get used to the idea, are you? What I propose is a board of twelve. You choose six, and I choose six."

Poynder's gaze returned to the carpet. Black pattern on a red background; squares, lozenges, stars; the shadow of Matlock's shape, coalescing at his feet. His eyes traveled over Matlock's brown shoes as if identifying rock samples. Shoes from the workshop of Ginery Miller on Canal Street. Margaret had persuaded Poynder to order his shoes from the same firm, and on that occasion he had seen a whole shelf filled with lasts for the Matlock family. Since then, he had never placed another order with the bootmaker. His glance wandered upward. Fortunately he had never seen the tailor's dummy where Matlock's suits were fitted, but he could imagine it. Narrow hips, stomach still flat even in old age, straight shoulders. Yet a man who had never done hard, manual work. And then that face. Poynder did not notice the details; he knew only that he was looking at a man who paid more attention to his whims than to his conscience.

He resumed the discussion. "Each of us with equal rights. Each of us with the same number of votes. Each of us with the same amount of stock. That leaves the positions of treasurer, manager, and president of the company. How are they to be assigned?"

John Tyler Matlock smiled. "Nowadays the manager is more important than the president. He must be a specialist, an expert. And that's you. I would be satisfied with the position of president. A figurehead. It suits my age much better."

"With one vote?"

"One vote."

"That leaves the treasurer. Do you want to split him down the middle?"

"You know Sydenham. There isn't a better man for the job. I believe you can put your full trust—"

Loftus Poynder made an abrupt gesture of dismissal. "There's no point in continuing," he said. "Sydenham may be the best, but he's your man. He would give you the deciding vote. Your offer sounded fair, Matlock. Fair except for that one vote. A Matlock vote. That's too great a risk. One vote the first year. How about the second? I am refusing your offer. I suspect I would have refused it even if there had been an equal number of votes. I do not trust you, Matlock."

The smile on Matlock's face froze. For a moment it seemed that he would leave without another word. Then he said, "I could do with a glass of wine now. I don't care about the quality." He waited until Poynder had poured it. He added water and sipped until the glass was empty. "I am assuming that you have considered the consequences. Your *no* has consequences, as your *yes* would have. You will lose much of the Empire State's revenues. One word from me and tomorrow all freight goes to New York on the Hudson."

Poynder was relieved. He felt serene now, surer of himself. "Feel free to say the word. Use the Hudson by all means. I see no problem in that. I will lose timber and rock, but not the freight that pays—meat, butter, cheese, wool, skins, hides. My customers have grown accustomed to prompt deliveries. I doubt that they will go along with your proposal. And even if you manage to talk them into it, it's summer now; the river is clear. But winter will come; then you will need me again."

Matlock set down his glass. The fine gray lines on his face looked like cracks in an old painting that are visible only when the light falls at a certain angle. He said, "I hear you are having a hard time finding land for a new freight station in New York. There's a movement in the Common Council to stop the traffic of trains down to Warren Street entirely, and the station and depot on Twenty-sixth Street are said to be bursting at the seams. They say you have your eye on St. John's Park. You couldn't have chosen a better location, except that some of the houses are privately owned—by Matlocks, as it happens. The Hudson isn't my only battlefield, Poynder."

"It's beginning to sound better," Poynder said. "That's the language that suits you."

Matlock was displeased with the turn the conversation had taken. It was coming dangerously close to an exchange of roles. Poynder should have been the one to flare up, to threaten. He was not meant to be the calm, relaxed, invulnerable combatant. If only somehow the roots through which this man drew nourishment were visible. But he was like an erratic rock, a solid block of stone, gray and alien in this landscape of bright earth. Years ago it had been easy for Matlock to lure the man trapped in the stone —Poynder was insecure, abrupt, proud, as vulnerable as an exotic bloom—and seduce him into bad decisions. But he was not ready to give up yet. "How about the railroad bridge across the Harlem River? It's your most important route out of the city. Do you know what is hanging over you—a city ordinance to bring the bridge up to the prescribed height. It's an attempt to make the river navigable to warships, and it requires raising the bridge. A senate committee is studying the matter. I'm sure it can be given a little nudge. I have even been told that the cost of the new bridge and the raising of the roadbed on either side of the river will be over a million dollars." His voice rose.

"You'll have to pay every cent of it out of your own pocket. And there are still other plans. New York will no longer tolerate your stinking trains puffing through the city and dirtying the air. You will be forced underground. The costs will swallow you up, even though you could have it all for nothing. If you and I were working together no amount of legislation could bring us to our knees. We would get the bridge and the raised roadbeds, overpasses and a network of tunnels, and it would cost us only a pittance, what with city and state subsidies. Is that what you want? Or do you want war?"

"The war has already begun," Poynder said.

"It will ruin you."

"Or you."

"You will regret this evening. Your fate will be that of the others. In the end, all you'll have left is a bitter memory of defeat." Matlock's voice sank almost to a whisper. "I'll draw blood. I'll bleed you until there isn't a drop left in your veins."

With these words he left. His steps were short and firm, as if Poynder's house were his own and every square foot of ground familiar.

# ═ 5 ═

DURING THE HOUR between dinner and bedtime, while Rose Matlock sat with her grandchildren leafing through bright picture books or reading fairy tales and stories to them, quiet returned to the house. All day long the children had been noisy and wild. Even at dinner, when they were freshly washed and groomed—the boys in starched shirts with narrow collars and cuffs, the girls wearing taffeta bows in their hair—their pugnacity remained, though it was transferred to another field of action. They enjoyed vying with each other as to which one could be most like the grown-ups. They sat the same way and communicated their choices to the serving girls with the same sureness. Finally, they did not kick their neighbors but settled differences of opinion like grown-ups, by discussion. Meals at Willowbeach were lessons in self-discipline, and not for the children alone. As soon as they had gathered in their grandmother's sitting room, there was no further need for admonitions. They grew quiet, forgot the mistakes of the day, and sat peacefully around Rose's armchair.

Sinclair lay stretched out on his back, his arms under his head. Even Joshua had broken off his whispered bartering with Lance. On the grate a fire of applewood crackled. The children absorbed in listening to Rose Matlock: the scene made Margaret jealous. When she read to her boys, they were never silent; she asked herself what it was that her mother-in-law did differently. Though she was distracted and restless, she was the first to notice that the door to the parlor was opening. Margaret could not recall anyone ever daring to interrupt the reading hour, not even John Tyler. But now there he stood on the threshold, framed by bands of bright light. His face was hidden in the shadows, but his rigid posture told Margaret enough.

Rose Matlock lowered the book. The children, too, were now alert, looking at their grandfather. "Tomorrow night we will read on." Rose closed the book and put it on the table beside her. "We've had a long journey and a long day. Tomorrow I'll read you two stories, to make up for it. Now go to bed without any fuss." She motioned to her daughters, but to Margaret said, "Stay."

John Tyler Matlock stepped to one side to let the children pass. Then he closed the door behind them and came toward the two women. "I'm sorry to interrupt you," he said. "But I must speak with you." He was looking at his wife.

"What happened? Did you quarrel?" Rose became aware of the look he was giving Margaret. "I think she has a right to know."

"What I have to say is not pleasant."

Under his gaze Margaret lowered her eyes. "I'll leave," she said.

"No, wait. All right, what happened?" Rose Matlock was insistent. "If you have quarreled, it affects us all—the whole family."

"It is more than a quarrel," John Tyler Matlock said

slowly. "I made him a fair offer, but he suspects traps everywhere." He continued to look at Margaret. She's a Poynder, he thought, his only daughter, his only heir. Until now this last fact had legitimized her marriage to Craig. But now he scented danger exactly in this fact. Such things often, in the end, spelled victory or defeat. Something one left out of his calculations, something that arose unexpectedly, something beyond his influence. In the coming struggle, Margaret and his son, Craig, were an unknown factor. "Your father will be telling you his version," he said. "I don't want to anticipate him. He is your father, and I'll understand your siding with him."

"What does that mean?" Rose's voice was sharp. "How can that concern us women? Don't let him confuse you, Margaret." To her husband she said, "She is a Matlock. Don't forget that."

"Is she? Are you a Matlock, Margaret? Perhaps you were until now. But when something like this happens between two families, the name often loses its meaning. Only blood counts. It really would be better if you left us alone."

He turned away and in turning bumped into the table. The book from which Rose Matlock had been reading fell to the floor. Margaret bent over for it. As she picked it up and put it back, she felt as if she were saying good-bye to something undefined yet of great importance.

Rose Matlock took Margaret by the arm. At the door she said, "Don't take it so hard. The world of men—that's one side; ours is the other. Tomorrow is another day . . ." She completed the sentence with an affectionate squeeze.

It was only three days after the new moon. The night was clear and cloudless, and the slight breeze from the east was a sign that the next day would be similar to today. Margaret clung to this thought as she walked home with Joshua and Sinclair. Tomorrow at the beach, the voices of the children playing would fill the air. That, and only that, was real.

The rooms on the ground floor in the Poynder mansion were still brightly lit. The children noticed it at once. "Who's here?" Joshua asked.

"Grandfather. But you must go to bed at once. I let you get away with it this afternoon. You may say hello to him, but that's all."

The children ran ahead. Margaret followed slowly, anxious to postpone meeting her father. The door to the library was ajar. She could hear Joshua's voice, loud and boastful. "I beat him up. He's older, but I'm stronger. He was lying, wasn't he? You built the first railroad! Tell me about how you built it."

Margaret entered the library, speaking irritably. "What did I tell you? Come with me at once."

"Good evening, Margaret." Loftus Poynder went toward his daughter, arms open to embrace her. She slipped past him.

"Just let me put them to bed. They've been on their feet all day. It's very late for them."

Poynder stood there awkwardly. "Do as your mother tells you." He put out a hand to stroke Sinclair's hair as the boy stood near him, but Margaret pulled the child away. "You come along at once; you, too, Joshua—yes, I mean you." She walked the children to the door.

"Did you bring me the cars?" Joshua asked as he let himself reluctantly be pulled along. "You promised." Before Loftus Poynder could answer, the door closed behind them.

Margaret took her time with the children. Even after they were asleep she stayed in their room, listening to their even breathing. She went to the windows which Edna, as usual, had opened wide and closed them. The garden below was abnormally bright. Light was coming from the windows of the library. Across the lawn, in the Matlock house, there were more lights burning than usual. Margaret unlooped the curtains and pulled them until they overlapped tightly, thinking that her father would be gone by the time Joshua and Sinclair woke up.

She found Loftus Poynder standing where she had left him. She did not recognize this as helplessness; she felt it as secret terror. That had always been his method. He was not openly tyrannical, like John Tyler Matlock. His tyranny manifested itself in other ways, in his absences, his silences, and his terseness.

"Where is Edna?" she asked. "Did she fix you something to eat? Would you like something more?" Loftus Poynder made a gesture that could mean either yes or no. "Did you quarrel with her again? It takes me days to get her calmed down again when you do. Is that your only

reason for coming here—to sow dissension? How long are
you staying?"

"Just until morning."

"Why didn't you join us for dinner? You had accepted
the invitation . . ."

"I want to talk to you about that," he said, looking
around the library. "But not here. Let's go to your room."
He meant the room, at one time his wife's music parlor,
which Margaret had furnished for herself after her
mother's death. The grand piano had been put in the
library; the potted palms and other Mediterranean plants
from the conservatory bay had been moved to the garden, where they had long since perished. Now the bay
held Margaret's writing desk which was, as always, littered
with lists, like Rose Matlock's. Next to it stood a sewing
table where Margaret took care of small tasks immediately. Nearby was the settee where she occasionally
rested. The bay gave a wide view of the Long Island
Sound. In the evenings she often stood at the windows
and followed the lights of ships making their way along
the Sound. This bay, which was larger than many
chambers, was where Loftus Poynder had gone while
Margaret put out the downstairs lamps. While his back
was still turned to her, he said, "I wish you would come
to New York with me."

"To New York? To live in New York? With the children in the house on Warren Street? Are you serious?
You want Joshua and Sinclair to live there in that gloomy
neighborhood?" Her voice was sharper than she had intended. "It's because of John Tyler Matlock, isn't it? Because you can't get along with him. That's why we're
supposed to leave here. But you're forgetting one thing:
their name is mine. I'm the wife of a Matlock, my
children are the sons of a Matlock. I'm the wife of Craig
Matlock. He will be coming home, and whatever he decides, I'm on *his* side. If you make enemies of the Matlocks, you are making an enemy of me."

Margaret's outburst had a soothing effect on Poynder.
The paralyzing feeling of being a stranger in his own
home, which had not left him since he had arrived, began
to loosen. He recognized this young woman as his
daughter. He recognized himself in her as he had been in
his younger days, impetuous, hot-headed, unable to think
clearly when he saw his rights threatened.

Margaret had fallen silent, stunned by the vehemence of her own words but still more by the animosity she had allowed herself to show. He is my father, she told herself; he isn't my enemy.

"It cannot be explained in one sentence," Poynder began.

"Then don't try. I won't understand anyway. Why did you accept an invitation and then turn around and send Greville to tell John Tyler to come to you? What does that mean? You seem to have lost any idea of how to get along with people. Even when you have the best of intentions, you hurt them. Why must you always quarrel with Edna? Why do you make promises to the children about things you'll bring them and then forget all about it? You haven't been here for three months. I heard nothing from you, not even a note to ask about the children, about my well-being."

He had lowered his head, but Margaret responded to the vulnerable gesture as if he had tried to defend himself. "Love is different. You don't have to bring them expensive presents. That toy train—how little trouble it would have cost you. And when I have a request, you tell me, 'Make a note of what you want,' and in New York you send a secretary out shopping, and then it arrives without a word from you. So much for your presents. When I heard today that you would be having dinner with the Matlocks, I thought that you would finally be reconciled. All these years there has been tension between you two." She spoke more calmly and deliberately. The aggressive tone faded from her voice. She could fight only as long as she was angry, but with her anger gone, what remained was merely bitterness.

"I could not agree to Matlock's proposal."

"And did you think of me for even one moment when you acted as you did?"

"John Tyler Matlock is my enemy. He wants to see me ruined."

Margaret laughed bitterly. "What big words. I can't listen to such talk. Isn't there enough room for both of you? Don't you already have everything? What more do you want? Must you destroy everything before you're satisfied?"

"It's a long story. If you knew it, you would understand a lot—why I'm so attached to the house on Warren Street, for one thing. Your mother hated it, and apparently you can't stand it either. Yes, it's an ugly brick house in a gloomy neighborhood. But to me it's something more. To me it matters that Castle Garden and the Battery are close by. They remind me every day of the long road the Poynders have had to travel to make something of themselves in America. That is where my father first stepped ashore. He was twenty-four and my mother eighteen, and at the end of the trip they had a hundred and fifty dollars left with which to buy land. I know that my father hated New York; it took twelve years of his life. They did him out of his hundred and fifty dollars in the first couple of weeks he was in the city—for storing the trunks, for rent security, for who knows what all. Robbing the new immigrants, the greenhorns—some people made a science of it, and they're still at it. The city kept my father in its clutches for twelve years. That's how long it took him to save enough for a farm of his own. He took any work he could get, hard work that paid miserable wages. For years he worked as a stonecutter on the East River, where the granite from Portland was unloaded and piled. In later years he often said, 'I don't believe there's a sidewalk in New York without stones I split.' In the winter, when huge blocks of ice were delivered in New York from Maine and Boston, he chopped ice and drove it to the breweries. It took him twelve years to escape from New York. He was thirty-seven when he left New York by boat and went up the Hudson to buy three hundred acres of land near Lebanon Springs. Lebanon Springs was wilderness in those days. And when he talked about it, he would say, 'In those days the sailors knew the way to China better than they did to Albany.' "

He was almost immobile on the settee, his hands around his knees, his eyes staring straight ahead. When a man as uncommunicative as Poynder suddenly opened up, the effect was usually disturbing, but Margaret wished he would continue. Yet she said, "What does all that mean? What has it got to do with John Tyler Matlock?" In this, too, she was like her father. She allowed only one thought, one feeling at a time to possess her, warding off all others.

But Loftus Poynder, impassive, continued. "If I say he bought land, you must not take me literally. It was a wilderness. Fir, pine, larch, the kind the Indians called hackmatack—the toughest wood there is. Trunks so big two men couldn't get their arms around them. Hardly any sun reached the ground because the trees grew so thickly. When I was growing up, root stocks were still all around. They had been used to enclose the house and the land. The world began on the other side, but we were in paradise."

He was silent, lost in thought. "We were poor. We had no money. Whenever we acquired something, we bartered for it. But the rivers and streams were full of fish. Sometimes we caught them with our bare hands. The woods were full of game. The summers were hot and the winters so cold that the pond froze almost solid. Some winters the cold even burst the trunks of the trees; it was like firing a cannon. When I brought the cows home in the evening, their hides were stiff with hoarfrost; clumps of ice hung from their nostrils. There was only one problem in this paradise—contact with the outside world. It was difficult, sometimes even impossible. There were no roads for us to transport the products Father might have sold. What we called roads were paths through the forest. Mail reached us only by outriders. In the spring, when the snow melted, even these paths disappeared beneath the mud. We tried to secure them with tree trunks and make a kind of dam. But the wood rotted, and the following spring we were marooned again. It was better in the winter, as soon as the snow was high enough for sleds to travel across the fields to the Hudson. I often went along on these trips, sitting in back with the sacks and kegs. We carried dried fruit, butter, chesse, lard, honey, nuts, flour, whiskey, potash, and sometimes even a barrel or two of frozen pork. My father exchanged his goods for silver. Yes, if there had been roads, my family might have become rich. But there were no roads. A trip to Europe was easier than a journey from New York to Albany." He rose and unbuttoned his coat. "I think I would enjoy a glass of wine now."

Margaret had loosened her hair while she listened. It was something she did every evening. She put the hairpins in a tin bowl and, raising both hands, smoothed the long auburn cascade down along her back. "Something to eat as well?" she asked.

"If it's no trouble."

She came back with a large tray of wine, butter, bread,

cheese, cold meat, and fresh radishes and set two places on the table before the fireplace.

"If I'd known that you'd be eating with me, I'd have said something sooner," Poynder said.

"It wasn't until I was in the kitchen that I realized I was hungry." Eating with the Matlocks was something Margaret had to get used to all over again each year. During the first week she always got up from the table hungry because she could not talk, keep an eye on the children, and eat all at the same time.

They had taken seats at the fragile little table. Loftus Poynder poured the wine. "I've never seen you drink wine before," he said.

"That's because we don't spend much time together."

Poynder could feel the distance between them growing again. "Perhaps you think that I'm rambling with these anecdotes that have nothing to do with the Matlocks. But they aren't beside the point. The Matlocks play an important part. I told you that what the farmers of Lebanon Springs needed were roads, and because the state did not provide them, the farmers decided to build their own. A year-round connection with Rensselaer on the Hudson was what we needed most. My father took the initiative, and the other farmers joined him. It took them two years to build the road, two years for twenty-four miles, because they had to start from scratch. They had to bridge rivers and fill in marshes and ditches. During those two years they neglected the farm work; they sank every bit of cash they could lay their hands on into the road. I often went with my father. He loved working on the road. He even toyed with the idea of giving up farming to take up road-building as a trade. 'What this country needs,' he would say, 'is roads, freedom of movement.' I never forgot that.

"Well, after two grueling years, the road to Rensselaer was finished. It's still there, as straight as can be, because that made it cheaper. Throughout its twenty-four miles it deviates very little from the straight. A considerable accomplishment, given the primitive surveying instruments they had in those days. So now they had their road. They could get to Rensselaer in all kinds of weather. The road attracted new settlers; the population grew. Everyone prospered. Lebanon Springs grew. We acquired a church and a school. They soon forgot the sacrifices they had made."

Poynder pushed back his chair, but he still felt

hemmed in. He got to his feet. "Then the Matlocks came.
It was the middle of the summer. I was fourteen then,
and I was allowed to go along with my father. I was one
of those who listened to what no one was prepared to believe at first: a man had sent his agents from Albany to
tell the farmers that their land no longer belonged to them."

Loftus Poynder looked at his daughter, possibly wondering whether she was beginning to understand. "The
farmers were thunderstruck. They couldn't believe their
ears. But it did them no good. Before the Revolution the
land my father and the others had bought had belonged
to a large landowner, a British nobleman. Because of the
Revolution, his property had come into the possession of
the United States, and the state of New York had, in
turn, subdivided the property and sold it to immigrants.
A certain Lyman Matlock, John Tyler's father, now conceived the idea of buying the seemingly worthless deeds
from the heirs of the Englishman. Matlock sued the
United States, claiming that the expropriation had been
illegal. His lawyers took the case all the way to the Su-
preme Court. They won, and overnight Lyman Matlock
became the owner of the lands that had become valuable
primarily because of the road the farmers had built. And
now the farmers were his serfs, in a manner of speaking.
Matlock sent his agents to make them what he considered
a generous and fair offer—as fair an offer as the one John
Tyler made me today. According to the letter of the law,
he could have expelled the farmers or forced them to pay
for the land all over again. But he behaved generously
and fairly. He let them keep the farms. But in return, he
demanded fifteen percent of the yield. They could choose:
either they stayed and paid, or they left the farms they
had carved out of the wilderness."

He had not been mistaken. Margaret was beginning to
understand. But even as she sensed the truth of what her
father was saying, she was still on her guard. She was
thinking of what lay behind his story. He wanted to get
her on his side, entice her away from the Matlocks. She
was afraid of the time when she would have to decide.

Poynder went on. "Some of the farmers submitted. But
many refused to accept Matlock's terms. My father belonged to this group. They chose him as their spokesman.
He came right out and told Matlock's man that the farmers would sooner set fire to their lands than pay. His ef-

forts were interpreted as a signal for revolt. He was arrested and jailed. The rest of the farmers went to the Rensselaer jail, threatening to storm it if my father wasn't freed immediately. The sheriff let my father go, but it was a short-lived victory. Lyman Matlock got the state militia to move in on the farmers. They barricaded themselves on their farms, but they were powerless against the militia. It finally came to a little war, and one of its first victims was my father."

Poynder lowered his voice. "That was the Poynders' first encounter with the Matlocks. With my father's death the resistance of the other farmers was broken. They gave in and paid the rent to Lyman Matlock and later to his son, John Tyler Matlock. It was said that he made three hundred thousand dollars a year out of all his holdings in the Hudson River Valley. There were many petitions to take the land away from him again, and in eighteen forty-six, more than thirty years later, the court ruling was actually overturned. But by then John Tyler Matlock had secretly sold the lands. When the buyers learned about the court's decision, they knew they'd been cheated. For some it meant ruin, but by then Matlock had invested heavily in shipping."

"Does John Tyler know anything about your father?"

"John Tyler was thirty at the time."

"You mean you're not sure that he does know the story?"

"Why do I have to be sure? I know that his father called in the militia, and I know that the militia killed my father. It's not likely that John Tyler remembers the name of a dead Dutch farmer. But I have remembered the name Matlock; it is indelibly engraved on my brain. After all, I was fourteen when my father was killed. My mother was buried six months later. My older brother fell the same year, in the war against England, just before it was over. I stayed in Lebanon Springs three more years. A friend of my father's, the blacksmith, took me in. He had a son my age. He and I left together. They were just starting to build the Erie Canal. Thousands were working in the marshy country between Utica and Salem, ruining their health for a pittance. We worked fourteen hours a day for fifty cents. But all I could think about was what my father had said and what I had learned in Lebanon Springs, that a country begins to come alive only when there are roads. Roads, rivers, canals. I had been expelled from Eden, but I found something new I could believe in."

"And that's what you have against him? After all these years you still hold what happened in Lebanon Springs against John Tyler Matlock?"

"That was not the end of the Matlocks in my life. He followed me—John Tyler Matlock, a man who never built anything with his own hands. He sees something. He sees that it is profitable. He calculates whether it is profitable enough. And when he has determined that it is, he grabs it. That's how it was in Lebanon Springs. That's how it was when shipping flourished. That's how it is with the railroads. Until five years ago he mocked everyone who had anything to do with them. Until he found out that they had become good business. Money—that's the only thing in the world he knows about. What I have built up was created in a different way." He raised his hands. "That is how I made it, with these hands."

"And you didn't want to be rich?"

"Oh yes. I wanted to be rich. I wanted riches and wealth, to protect myself from men like Matlock. I have grown old in the process. But I achieved what I set out to achieve. The New York Railroad—that is the sum of my life. At the place where my father first set foot on this land—that is where I have put down my roots. And Matlock wants me to sell out to him and give it all up. Do you understand now? It is important to me that you understand. I'm not being arbitrary; nor am I being obstinate. To give it up means the end of my life."

Margaret understood, but that was no comfort. Earth, water, railroads, inanimate things—for these her father had lived and fought, and it was them that he was now defending. He was proud of his ability to estimate with the naked eye how many cubic feet of earth were contained in a hill he wanted to level. But to see into a human being, to put himself in another person's place—that was beyond him. Her mother had suffered because of this, and now Margaret suffered. "What are the consequences of your decision?" she asked coolly. "I mean, actually, what effect will it have on my life?"

"I don't know," he said avoiding her eyes. "That will depend on Craig. Where he stands in the matter."

"Do you really expect him to take your side?"

"I'm not sure. I'm not convinced that he will automatically side with his father."

"You're going back to New York in the morning?"

Loftus Poynder nodded. He had said everything he could think of to justify himself. But in matters of the emotions, he was helpless. Like all people who find it easier to endure loneliness than to act against their pride, it was impossible for him to press her. He felt that he had done it all wrong. What could his past mean to Margaret? People she had never known; places she had never seen. He noticed her hands nervously playing with the dripping candle wax. She wore no rings except for the narrow gold wedding band. She had not grown stouter after the birth of the twins but more slender—like Poynder's mother between children. The softness of youth had disappeared, and now beauty was beginning to take its place, a serious, austere beauty which seemed to increase distance rather than closeness. "Try to remember that you are my daughter," he said. "Try."

Margaret looked at her father, but she could not think of anything conciliatory. "You seem to be recalling that fact very late," she said. She sensed that he was about to put his hand on her arm, and she dreaded the emotions the gesture would release. She got up quickly and hurried from the room.

She did not see her father the next morning, though she was awake when the carriage came for him. She heard his steps in the hall but stayed in her room. When she came downstairs later, she found a brown cardboard box in the entrance hall. It contained the toy train Loftus Poynder had brought from New York for his two grandsons.

# BOOK TWO

---

# NEW YORK CITY

---

## July 1865

# ≡ 6 ≡

CRAIG MATLOCK STOOD on the small platform of the last
car, shaded by the protruding tin roof. The smoke from
the locomotive blew past his head out into the gray morning sky. If it had been burning coal, the Conness, a new
locomotive manufactured in Massachusetts, could have
covered the distance from Baltimore to New York in six
hours. But only a load of wet poplar had been available
for the Hundred and Twenty-sixth Regiment in Baltimore.
They had been traveling all night.

The door behind Craig opened, and two men stepped
out on the platform to get some air after a night in the
sticky compartment. Seeing their superior officer, they began automatically to button their tunics. The twelve shiny
brass buttons were the only thing that lent a military air
to the uniform of the Construction Corps. Perhaps it was
because of their appearance that these soldiers were given
such scant attention at railroad stations. They were not
one of the famous regiments whose deeds had filled the
newspaper columns. They had not taken part in any of
the great battles. Their task had been to repair demolished railroads, rebuild bridges, stretch new telegraph
lines, mend locomotives.

"You needn't bother," Craig Matlock said. "In an hour
I won't be wearing these insignia any longer anyway."
Nothing was left of the elation Craig had felt two weeks
before, when he had begun the journey home from Savannah. It had turned into the past, something that no longer
belonged to the present, like the uniform. A sudden gust
of wind whirled the smoke upward. The morning sky was
tinged with a delicate green, and the color of the meadows
through which they were traveling was beginning to change.
In the grass close to the tracks Craig recognized sorrel
blossoms. "I believe we've almost made it," he said.

"We'll see the Hudson any minute now." He knew of no other river where sorrel grew so red.

A switch beat under the wheels. Three, four more sets of tracks appeared. The train slowed down. Trained by years spent more on rolling wheels than on firm ground, the men on the platform absorbed the shocks. Then the train came to a stop.

Fuller, the smith, was the first to swing himself to the running board. "Jersey City. We're really here. In beloved, filthy Jersey City. I've never seen a more run-down station. I just hope we won't have to wait hours for the ferry."

For a few seconds there was no other noise than the ear-splitting whistle of the locomotive. On the next track a cattle transport was being loaded. Steers obediently trotted up the planks into the freight cars.

Baggage came flying through the windows of the military train onto the platform, while men shoved their way off the high running boards. Craig Matlock grabbed his canvas satchel and jumped off.

"Not a single porter," Fuller said, his head pushed forward, assuming a stance as if he were facing, not the New Jersey train station, but some enemy terrain. "That's not how I imagined our rousing reception."

"What did you expect?" another man said. "Bands? Reporters?"

The train emptied rapidly. The platform came alive with soldiers looking for their luggage.

"We'd better hurry if we want to get a seat on the ferry," Craig Matlock said.

Dried-out birch branches put up to honor the first returning veterans were still clinging to the black pillars of cast iron that supported the station canopy. Fuller began to laugh. "Maybe I'm not in all that much of a hurry to get to New York," he said.

"For four years I've been listening to you telling me how you're going to turn New York upside down when you get back," Craig said. "What's become of all that? What about lunch at the Astor House? Or oysters on Canal Street? What about all the girls?"

Fuller looked down at the shabby sleeves of his uniform, at his large, red hands. "As long as I thought each day might be my last, New York was paradise. And now? When I think the same old routine is going to start all over again. . . ." He picked up his sack and threw it over his shoulder. Silently they set out for the ferry across the North River.

The men queued up in front of the ferry slip. The clock on the tower showed a few minutes after seven. The air still held the chill of night. The broad, bluish-green river was as flat as a mirror. On the other side of the water the city loomed. It floated in a cloud of light, weightless, almost transparent in the white rays of the rising sun.

Craig had often thought about the sea at Willowbeach —the salt air, the foaming of the water at the prow of the boat, the wet cables slipping through his hands, the sails trembling under the impact of the wind. But New York? There was a forest of ships the length of the piers and docks: the bright masts of the clippers, the black smokestacks of the steamers, some of them with steam already up. Behind this rampart rose the rooftops of New York.

Why New York? Why hadn't he boarded a ship in Savannah and gone straight to Willowbeach? Once more his glance took in the city's skyline, that fortress which even at this hour had something sinister about it. Why? Maybe because this was where he had left to go to war, and because he wanted to see whether he could resume his life in the same place. One of the rooftops in the distance belonged to the house on St. John's Park. Did he really wish Margaret were there? A hand came down on his shoulder, and he looked up. Blinded by the light, into which he had been staring, he saw Fuller in silhouette.

"I really do wonder why I'm in such a damn hurry." A deep furrow wrinkled Fuller's brow. "What are you going to do? Same thing as before? I always thought I loved the railroad above everything. I grew up believing that. My father, my brothers—all of them—work on the railroad. Right next to the block where we live, on Tenth Avenue, there's a railroad depot. Nothing but soot and dirt. My mother lugged the laundry to the attic to dry, but the soot got to it there, too, right through the cracks between the tiles. And if she forgot to cover the milk, soot got on the top cream. And to work over ten hours a day for that—ten hours for two dollars! I used to think that life was like that. Never occurred to me it could be any other way. That damned war. All of a sudden there was plenty of time to think."

The bond between Craig and the men around him was not based merely on his being their superior officer. That was unquestioned from the first day and had become more secure during the war, for there was no situation in which Craig Matlock did not know what to do. They had also become friends. Without becoming too familiar Craig possessed the gift of making people feel that he understood them. On the other hand, he himself remained somewhat mysterious. No one thought anything about the name Matlock, since from the outset he had not mentioned his middle name, Lyman. Any other questions his name might have caused had been answered on the first day he joined the regiment. At the sight of Craig's hands, rough from sailing in the Sound, Fuller wondered what a fisherman knew about railroads, and Craig had merely laughed. After all, he had enlisted precisely in order to lose himself in the anonymity of a uniform, to cease being the second son to the mighty John Tyler Matlock, to leave all that behind, to start out in search of himself.

"What are your plans now?" Fuller persisted.

"Plans? I don't know." The unshaved stubble made Craig seem older than his thirty years. He seemed distant, aloof.

Fuller had never seen him like this. "How about you and me going into business together? Before you go back to your fishing village and me to my railroad yards, we ought to be able to find something better than fishing and railroading. What do you think of church ovens? 'Dealer in Clerical Stoves' sounds pretty good to me. Or how about the Union Pacific? Conquer the West! You seen the posters on all the railroad stations? They're starting to lay tracks at Omaha, and they're looking for people. Four years with the Construction Corps ought to be worth something. In a couple of years we'll be rich." He grew serious again. "You don't believe it any more than I do, right?"

They were caught up in the pushing, shoving mass of men and said no more. Everyone was eager to get on the first ferry. It was not easy for Craig to allow himself to be pushed and shoved. On the other hand, he was glad the crowd was separating him from his men. Nothing would come of the great binge they had talked about so often. They would have a couple of beers in one of the bars on Cortlandt Street at the foot of Pier Seventeen. They would promise each other to have a reunion every year.

Then they would go their separate ways as if those four searing years that had bound them together had never happened. Craig thought the others sensed this just as he did.

Craig and Fuller found a place at the prow of the ferry. Craig put his canvas satchel between his feet and leaned against the railing. The planks vibrated as the paddle-wheels began to turn. Wings of spray unfolded to the left and right of the ferry and swiftly bore it away from the slip into the green Hudson River, toward the city.

A house that stood unchanged for nearly forty years was a rarity in this part of the city. If, as was the case with 19 Laight Street— one of the streets around St. John's Park— it was a lavish Greek Revival structure, it almost deserved the rank of a curiosity. Craig used to pay no special attention either to the panel with the classical relief over the doorway nor to the statuary on either side of it, for many houses on Laight Street were similarly adorned. But now, in the midst of the gray, monotonous tenements that had taken the place of the old buildings, the house was a remnant of the distant past. It had been built in 1827, five years after the great yellow fever epidemic that had prompted the migration of the rich from lower Manhattan. Battery Park, Bowling Green, and the area around City Hall Park, which until then had been the residential area of the well-to-do, were abandoned. Instead, the neighborhood of St. John's Park became fashionable. John Tyler Matlock had acquired the house at 19 Laight Street, together with some other property, in the 1830s, while he was involved in shipping and was spending more time in New York than in Albany.

The pavement in front of the house was ripped up, and wagons and carriages jammed the road. The trees across the street had been cut down. The ice-cream vendor, whose cart used to stand under the trees in summer, was gone. As Craig crossed the street to the house he noticed that one of the statues had been broken in two.

The door to the porter's apartment opened and a huge man with spidery arms and legs emerged. "Hold it, mister; you can't just sashay in here. Who you going to see?"

Craig stared at Joe Cristadoro. "You're still here, then. And just as polite as ever. Have I changed so much, Joe?"

"Mister Matlock!" The porter inspected the uniform and the soiled canvas satchel.

"Go ahead and say it, Joe. What did you take me for?"

"You must excuse me. I didn't recognize you at first. You got to be careful nowadays. The neighborhood's not what it used to be; St. John's Park is going downhill. The Mowinkels moved away. Did you see it? They turned the building into a Turkish bath! We're just about the last respectable house. Nothing but trash moves into those tenements. Not like when you were a boy. In those days you could call everybody by name. What's coming now is no good. If it goes on like this, we'll have the Irish here in six months." Joe Cristadoro smiled maliciously. "But you're back. Now that's *good* news."

"Why are they tearing up the street?"

"They do it all the time. This time to lay a new gas main. There's always trouble with the gas."

"And the ice-cream man?"

"Maretzek? He's dead, run over on Greenwich Street in broad daylight, him and his cart. The kids fought over the spilled ice cream."

"And how is Mrs. Cristadoro?"

"Bless you, she's still the same. Still jealous of this stuff." He pulled a flask out of a bulging jacket pocket. "May I offer you a welcome-home drink? No? You don't mind if I do?" He took a long swig. "She's been looking after your apartment all these years. She aired it out once a week, and in the winter she made sure there was a fire. So you're still in one piece? Why didn't you let us know you were coming? I'll send my wife upstairs right away."

"There's no hurry."

"You'll be wanting ice for the icebox. Like before. The most important thing was always that there be ice and newspapers. My wife will take care of it, and anything else you want. Even though prices are running away since the war, and the Clinton Market's not what it used to be either. Do you remember when Mrs. Matlock used to buy eggs there and asked if they were fresh, and Willy Bagiola took a couple of eggs and broke them right in front of your mother to show her that they really were fresh. Then he threw them away. All I can say is, I hope that now you're back, they won't tear down the house. Every time Mr. Sydenham came by, I said to myself, watch out, this is it; now it's our turn. Now they'll tear us down and build one of those tenements that bring in more money."

"May I have my keys?"

"Of course, the keys." Cristadoro hurried into his apartment and came back with the keys. "Well, then, welcome home. Are you sure you won't have a drink? Wait, I'll carry up your bag. When will Miss Margaret be arriving? That was something, that last night, when we had to send for the doctor. I'll be glad to take it upstairs."

"It's not necessary," Craig picked up the satchel.

At the foot of the stairs the porter detained him. "I almost forgot. Somebody's been asking for you."

"For me? Who?"

"Yes. I thought it was pretty queer, too. For four years nothing, not even a letter for you, and then for a whole week a guy comes by every single day."

"What did he want?"

"He wouldn't say. I told him to go see Mr. Langdon, but I guess he'd been there already. A very queer bird. Always came by late in the day, about dark. Not exactly pushy, though. Just one of those men who's seen better days."

"What was his name?"

"He didn't want to give it to me. But I told him, I said, 'I won't even listen to you if you won't tell me who you are.' If he's telling the truth, his name is Thomas Wilmurt. A very strange guy, very nervous, like somebody who hasn't been sleeping any too well. I'm sure he'll be back." Cristadoro grinned. "And don't worry. The ice will be up. The missus, she'll drop everything when she hears you're back."

The apartment was on the fourth floor. Craig had not been there for four years. He had spent his leaves at Willowbeach, staying at the St. Denis Hotel during the few days he spent in New York. After four years of living in freight cars on sidings and in barracks and tents, he found the apartment gloriously spacious. But the air was stale. The red silk wall covering in the parlor reminded him that Margaret had suggested doing the apartment over. On the mantel he discovered the gold cigar case she had given him as a wedding present. He thought it had been lost, yet he felt no special joy now that he had found it.

He snapped open the lid. It was filled with the thin, dark cigarillos he preferred. They were dry as straw.

Four years. It had been July, as it was now. Here they had spent their last few days together. He had not smoked because Margaret, who was in the last weeks of her pregnancy, could not tolerate the smell. In the bathroom he found the brown bottle of medicine Margaret had taken by the tablespoonful after each meal. That week had not been easy for her, but she had insisted on going with him when he joined his regiment at City Hall Park. Four days later Joshua and Sinclair had been born.

He went from room to room, opening windows to let in the morning air. Many of the locust trees in the park had been cut down. The artificial hillocks had been leveled and the artificial watercourses filled up. A train, pulled by a team of horses, was moving down the street. Its five cars were carmine red. St. John's Park really was running down, but Craig felt no regret.

# ▭ 7 ▭

JOHN TYLER MATLOCK'S possessions were labyrinthine, layered in a deliberately opaque arrangement. Aside from Matlock himself, there was only one initiate—Wendell Sydenham. When he was in a good mood, John Tyler Matlock was even ready to admit that Sydenham was more knowledgeable than he was himself.

For more than forty years Wendell Sydenham had been working for Matlock, and for more than thirty of these his office had been located in the five-story building at the corner of Broome and Crosby streets, which had been bought at the same time as the house on Laight Street. There he kept the Matlock books. Every dollar invested in loans and in bonds, every dollar earned in interest, every bribe paid out to this or that person—frequently by Sydenham himself—were recorded. He kept track of every square foot of ground owned by the Matlocks or previously in their possession; all sales contracts; the balance sheets for the mines in Orange County and the salt works near Syracuse; the losses of the tanneries in Glens Falls; the cubic footage of lumber cut in Ticonderoga; the daily output of the textile mills in Oneida; the investments in the Lunden Carriage Works in Troy. Sydenham put together the annual reports of the Empire State Railroad—the private ones for John Tyler Matlock's eyes only, as well as the official figures for the stockholders and the tax assessors. In his books the investigators from the tax commission found everything that pandered to their pedantic needs; the only missing facts were those that might have been of interest to them, for the principal books of the Matlock fortune were kept in Sydenham's head. An empire concealed in ciphers—that was Sydenham's world. He lived in it so exclusively that it had been a long time since he had had a life of his own.

Sydenham was now sixty-three. He was of middle height, with a slender frame and stooped posture. His health had been undermined by chronic asthma, and his eyesight worsened from year to year. He bore his ailments without complaint. According to his philosophy, which divided life, like a ledger, into debits and credits, he was willing to accept the negative signs for as long as his brain continued to function properly. As other men are proud of their physical strength, so Sydenham was proud of his memory; a set of numbers he had memorized could not be erased again.

He had discovered this talent as a boy. His father, a chemist, ran a small dye factory and on the side concocted medicines—cough elixirs, hemorrhoid salves, sarsaparilla, a remedy for syphilis. His greatest financial success came when the temperance movement was at its height and the imbibing of alcohol was frowned on. He marketed a stomachic. But trouble ensued when a woman died of it, with all the symptoms of poisoning. The indictment dwelt on the lack of prescription books in Sydenham's business. It was true, there were none. The judges did not believe the chemist's explanation that both he and his son had infallible memories, which made such books unnecessary. The sentence ruined Sydenham's father. His property was confiscated and he was sentenced to Fort

Lafayette for ten years, where he died after serving three of them.

At the time of the trial Wendell was twenty. He had nothing but his gift for carrying in his head the most complex chemical equations, formulas, and combinations of numbers. John Tyler Matlock, who had followed the trial with interest, approached him, having recognized the young man's gift. Thus Wendell Sydenham, over a period of time, grew into a living repository of all Matlock's secrets. He earned himself a secure place in the Matlock organization. Since the day he had moved into the house on Broome Street, nothing had changed in his office; only the strongboxes grew ever larger. Though he had been able to postpone the installation of gaslight for several years by pointing out the cost of repairs, he had finally been outvoted by Langdon Matlock.

But there was another technical innovation that he could not warm up to—the shredder John Tyler Matlock had had installed in Sydenham's office. Sydenham continued to carry anything not meant for strange eyes in his black briefcase to his house, where he burned it. Each day ended with this interplay of fire and paper, the flames darting upward as numbers were turned into ashes.

Hunched over a long column of figures, he was so absorbed that he did not hear the horse-drawn train. The stop, directly below his window, was a constant source of irritation, but right now, submerged in the ocean of figures, he was as deaf to it as he was to the knock at the door.

Sydenham's first reaction was to glance at the safe, to make sure its steel door was firmly closed and locked. The unannounced visitor had not stopped in the doorway, as Sydenham had expected, but boldly walked toward the desk. Sydenham nervously groped for his glasses under the papers scattered over the desk top.

"Your eyes haven't gotten any better." Craig Matlock had picked up the spectacles, holding the thick lenses up to the light.

"Craig! I beg your pardon—Mr. Matlock!"

"I know you still think of me as a little boy." He handed the glasses to Sydenham. "Do you dare to venture out in the streets with these?"

Sydenham looped the elastic sidepieces over his ears.

"Craig Matlock! Is it really you? But where is your uniform? The newspapers said you had been promoted to captain."

"My uniform is in a rubbish bin on Laight Street. I never suspected that you harbored so much patriotic fervor."

"My mother is the patriot. She read every report from the front, all because of you. She never forgot the flowers you sent her that time she was in the hospital. She knows the name of every hamlet where a locomotive was blown up. When the Confederates——"

"I can see," Craig interrupted, "I won't be allowed to forget the war quite so easily. How is your mother?"

"Well on the whole, in spite of being ninety. I can't imagine life without her or an evening when I will have to come home to an empty flat. She saved all the newspaper clippings. She kept the whole office supplied with them."

"And how does my father feel about the staff reading newspaper clippings during office hours?" Craig sat down on the window sill and stretched out his long legs.

"I thought the war, the experience of war, taught people to be more charitable," Sydenham said.

"You hoped I would return as a dutiful son? A wolf without teeth. Good for nothing but wagging his tail before the great king, his father."

Sydenham folded his hands. "Whatever your father did, you would reject him. Even though there are few men of his caliber. It is a great deal for a man to accumulate a fortune in a lifetime, but he has accumulated four fortunes. Not because he was luckier than others or more ruthless, but simply because he was more farsighted, because he could see trends coming that no one else saw." Sydenham took off his glasses and polished the lenses. "When did you get to town?"

"A few hours ago. They've built a Turkish bath on Laight Street. They say it cleanses a man inside and out. I've come here straight from there, cleansed through and through."

"Other troops came back weeks ago."

Craig laughed. "They kept us in Georgia as a clean-up squad. During the last days of the war we managed to destroy three hundred miles of railroad from Atlanta to

Savannah, then we rebuilt it again. A very meaningful way of life."

"Have you telegraphed to Willowbeach?"

"My dear Sydenham, I arrived by train in Jersey City at seven o'clock this morning. I crossed on the ferry. I had a farewell drink with my men. Then I startled Joe Cristadoro, went to the Turkish bath—and here I am."

"Would you like me to put through a telegram to your mother? Your family has been at Willowbeach for two weeks."

"I don't know yet when I'll be able to join them. By the way, what about the house on Laight Street? What are my father's plans? Joe Cristadoro is afraid you'll tear it down and put up a tenement."

"That would be best, if we're talking about making a profit. When your father bought it, things were different. The neighborhood was in fashion then, and an elegant apartment house with one large apartment for each floor brought in good money. Nothing changes so fast in this town as 'good' neighborhoods. A few years ago Bleecker Street was the border. Now 'everybody' has moved farther north. You can hardly find tenants for the St. John's Park neighborhood. You must have seen what's going on. The park is ruined. The noise, the dirt, the tenements. I don't suppose you'll want to go on living there."

"I don't know yet."

"We would probably have torn the house down a long time ago, but we waited for your decision."

"I assume in the meantime you've been withdrawing the rent from my account. I'm afraid my father is quite right when he thinks me a fool. Who else would pay rent for an apartment without any value. Only a few memories."

"In any case, I'm glad to see you," Sydenham said. "Do you need money?"

"Did I say that?"

For the first time Sydenham smiled. "You always needed money when you came to see me."

"Fine," Craig Matlock answered. "That hasn't changed either."

"How much?"

"A thousand."

"A thousand dollars?" Sydenham, who had already turned toward the safe, swung back. "That much? Your credit is good all over town. I'd rather that you have all bills sent here."

Craig felt as if he were back in college, when he had to haggle with Sydenham over every book he needed. "You're right," he said. "A thousand won't get me far. You'd better give me five thousand."

As always when he had to screw up his courage, Sydenham brushed his thinning gray hair back with both hands. "That is more than there is in your account at the moment."

"What do you mean?" Craig had jumped up from the window seat. "Not in my account? What expenses can you have had except the rent and the two hundred dollars a month that I contribute to the joint household? The interest alone on my inheritance comes to twenty-four thousand five hundred dollars a year. So I must have ninety-eight thousand dollars in my account, without compounding."

Sydenham had returned to his desk, but he was too troubled to sit down. He took an itemized list from a drawer. He felt confused, not by the calculations Craig had performed, but by the fact that he had performed them at all. Craig—who never bothered about money, whose only interest in money in the past had been in spending it—was now spouting figures with the best of them. A mute who suddenly opens his mouth and speaks could not have disconcerted Sydenham more.

"Your shares did not bring in any interest," he finally said, hoping somehow that his words would restore the familiar situation.

"What do you mean, no interest? You'll have to be more specific. I was promised seven percent. I know what I signed. I allowed myself to be bought off with a pittance and now I'm told, *no interest.*"

"Your inheritance consists of stock in the Empire State Railroad. The line has never paid dividends."

"So that's how it is. Surely you made plenty during the war. And still no dividends?" Craig did not raise his voice. His words only came more swiftly, more cuttingly than before, like whistling arrows. "Was the Empire State unable to pay—or simply unwilling?"

The conversation struck Sydenham as increasingly unreal. He had known Craig from birth; he had seen him grow up. He had been waiting for John Tyler Matlock's true son to emerge. He had hoped for it, but now it frightened him. "The Empire State was not willing to pay dividends," he said finally.

"And because it did not pay dividends, the market value has dropped?"

Sydenham nodded. "The shares have fallen below the rate of issue."

"How much?"

"The fifty-dollar face value is down to forty and three-quarters."

Craig, who had been pacing, suddenly stopped and laughed. "You mean my three hundred and fifty thousand dollars has dropped twenty percent in value, aside from the fact that it has accumulated no interest?"

"If you were to sell the shares now. But they will go up again, as soon as we start paying dividends. After we merged the various companies into the Empire State, we controlled barely twenty percent of the voting stock. Should we have bought up shares at the price they were fetching? We had no choice but to hold back the dividends and thus lower the market price. That way we were able to buy at a more favorable rate. Now we hold forty-five percent of the shares, counting yours and your sisters' portions."

"Then you played the same trick on Alice, Vinnie, and May? Splendid. That's really a splendid piece of news. I come back and my own family has cheated me out of a hundred and sixty-eight thousand dollars." Craig took the list from Sydenham, studied it, and placed it face down on the desk. "Sell my stock. That way the family can annex a few more shares at a favorable rate."

"You want to sell?"

Craig was growing impatient. "The shares are my property. It's true, they're kept in your safe, but I can do as I like with them. After these last four years I've had enough of railroads, believe me. When I was a boy, my father was a shipowner. I can still hear him—'I have sixty sailing vessels and three thousand sailors.' And when I heard him talk about Calcutta, Canton, or Sumatra, about holds full of coffee, tea, cinnamon, and spices, I was proud to be the son of a shipowner. Weren't you proud of each new clipper? Didn't you always go to the shipyards? Weren't you there each time a new ship was christened? Do you remember the *Silver Cloud?* It made the trip from New York to San Francisco by way of Cape Horn in record time—ninety days. Where do you take your walks now? To the railroad depot? And what became of the crews, the captains? Your friend, Jan Beelt—what's he doing now? Is he the engineer on a big shiny locomotive?"

Craig had touched a sensitive nerve. Sydenham harbored a deep dislike of anything having to do with locomotives and railroads. His asthma became chronic only after the tracks of the New York Railroad had been laid through Broome Street and smoke and fumes began to penetrate his office. Fortunately those times were over, since locomotives were now banned below Twenty-third Street; the trains had to be pulled by horses. But the horse-drawn trains also bothered him, if only because their vibrations, running through the building each time a train went by, threatened to jiggle the clerk's desks, imperiling their neat columns of figures.

"I see Jan Beelt now and again," Sydenham replied. "We have dinner together occasionally, and sometimes we meet at The Merchant's on Portland Street; the oysters are good, and it's close to the harbor. You're right—the clippers were the most beautiful and fastest ships of all. I liked those days. I remember when your parents went to Willowbeach in a horse and buggy, never faster than five miles an hour. There was time then, time to stop on the way to get a bite or look at the scenery. Now it's all hurry, hurry—faster all the time. But that's how it is. Nothing lasts forever. But if your father hadn't gotten rid of his ships in time, he would have lost a fortune. Behind a desk is the place for me. I'm one of those who love yesterday more than tomorrow." His glance wandered over the gas lamp on his desk and across the unused shredder. "It wouldn't be good if everyone were like me. There have to be people like your father."

"And how is Jan Beelt doing in these new times?" Craig had spent a year sailing on Jan Beelt's *Silver Cloud*. "Did he save enough to live on?"

"He is captain of a passenger boat on the New York–Albany line."

"Does that satisfy him?"

"The new boats are very luxurious."

"Yes, except that the cook is more important than the captain. My God, a man like Jan Beelt, captain of a passenger ship on the Hudson." Craig was standing by Sydenham's desk. "Give me the money now."

"I believe it would be best if you spoke to your brother about it."

"Langdon? Is Langdon here in the office? Did he give up his farm on Staten Island?"

Sydenham nodded. "You can talk to him about the stocks at the same time."

"My brother comes here every day? Where is his office?"

"He is using your father's."

"I *have* been away a long time." At the door Craig turned once more. "By the way, do you know someone named Thomas Wilmurt?"

Sydenham clutched his chest, as he always did when he felt shortness of breath coming on.

"Thomas Wilmurt," Craig repeated slowly and distinctly.

Sydenham coughed. "I do not know any Thomas Wilmurt, and it would be better if you did not know him either."

## = 8 =

IN SPITE OF the closed shutters the room was filled with sunlight. The windows stood open, and the light fell in broad slashes through the louvered blinds, bathing even the corners in golden warmth.

Craig Matlock stopped in the doorway when he saw that his brother was not alone. The visitor had already risen to leave. At first glance Langdon Matlock, seated behind the massive desk, might have been part of the painting set into the dark wood paneling which covered the entire wall behind him. He held out his hand to the visitor. "I believe that's all, Scrutin. I want to thank you for myself and in my father's name for bringing the matter to my attention so promptly. I always knew I could count on you and your paper." Langdon did not rise to accompany the man to the door, nor did he trouble himself to go to meet his brother.

"Just let me finish this," he said to Craig, "then I'm all yours." He seemed neither surprised nor glad to see his brother. He took up a sheet of paper, thought briefly, wrote a few lines, and reached for the bell. One of the two secretaries Craig had seen in the anteroom came in, and Langdon handed him the paper. "Have this sent to Willowbeach immediately. Take care of it personally. Hand it in at the main telegraph office on Broadway, not at a branch."

"Hold on," Craig Matlock said. "Not so fast. Perhaps I'm not so eager to have my return broadcast to the winds."

Langdon nodded to the secretary. "Do as I said." He waited until the man had left the room, then turned to his brother. "You can rest easy. I sent Father a message about a pressing matter. I will continue to honor our old agreement. Neither of us interferes in the other's business. You don't tell me what I'm doing wrong, and I don't try to set you straight." He came out from behind the desk. "Let me look at you. We haven't heard from you in a long time. But you're looking well. Welcome home."

The embrace was stiff. It was more than a difference in age and temperament that separated them. Langdon, the first-born, was nineteen when Craig was born, an event that distressed him in a number of ways. The very existence of this latecomer seemed monstrous to him. It destroyed his image of his parents. The discovery of adultery on the part of his father or mother would not have troubled him as much as did the idea that these two people, who seemed to belong to a higher order of beings, were just another married couple. Further, the appearance of a brother threatened Langdon's hereditary right as his father's sole heir.

Langdon had learned to live with the facts; he assumed a kind of avuncular tone with Craig. In confrontations between the younger son and their father, he had taken his brother's side, even when Craig married Margaret Poynder. The tactic, which suited his intelligence and his phlegmatic temperament, was also intended to make Craig feel dependent on him, at the same time, putting the greatest possible distance between Craig and their father.

Craig looked around the room. The amber-yellow curtains of ribbed fabric had faded. The floor was still covered by the same carpet, in many spots worn down to the backing. The only new acquisition was the large painting Craig had noticed on entering. Now he walked around the desk to examine it more closely. "At first I thought you had bought up Rembrandt's 'Night Watch.' How many square feet of canvas would you say you have here?"

"Six by three yards."

"That's some work of art, all right. Somehow or other, several of these gentlemen, who are so self-conscious that they can barely stand up straight, look familiar. This one over here bears a remarkable resemblance to you—and I assume this one is meant to be Father?"

"It was painted by Bower." Langdon spoke as if the name of the painter would make the entire enterprise legitimate. "I must admit, I find it impressive. Bower is unique in his control of such a colossal format."

"And what does it depict?"

"It's the Empire State Railroad. The founders, directors, agents, builders—all the men who had a part in bringing the Empire State into being. Bower worked on it six months; it was finished by the February deadline. A gift to celebrate Father's reelection to the presidency."

Craig was thoughtful. "The Empire State. Mr. Bowers' fee ate up the dividends. Is that correct?"

"You've seen Sydenham?"

Craig turned toward his brother. Langdon was one of the few people he had to force himself to look full in the face. But right now Langdon seemed to have the same difficulty, for he lowered his eyes.

"I was quite surprised," Craig said. "You know that I renounced all inheritance claims, and I promised never to contest the settlement. I did not get one cent more than Alice, Vinnie, or May."

"You admit that you entered into the agreement of your own free will."

"Sydenham told me that the stock stands at forty and three quarters. That means my shares are down twenty percent. That adds up to seventy thousand dollars. Besides, by not investing my portfolio, as we had agreed, you caused me to lose another ninety-eight-thousand-dollars. Did you really think I'd be pleased?"

"Sydenham can't think of anything but figures," Langdon said. "Of course we could have paid dividends. But it was a matter of scaring off investors by presenting them with seemingly negative balance sheets."

"You can save your breath. I heard all that from Sydenham. I want my money."

Langdon pulled on his small mustache. Craig noticed that his fingernails were longer than he used to wear them. "Nothing to worry about. The shares will go up. They can climb to a hundred in the blink of an eye. Then you'll be twice as rich as before."

Craig had turned back to the painting. "A good thing it didn't cross your mind to immortalize me in this thing with the rest of your stockholders. If Father had had himself painted in the company of his sea captains, I would have understood. He must have changed a great deal to let himself be put in one pot with these gents here. The great pirate who stays in the background, whom no one ever sees, but whose black flag rules the seven seas." Craig threw a final glance at the canvas. "Besides, it's crude. No light, no depth." He turned away and dropped into the leather chair at one side of the desk.

"Would you like a drink?" Langdon asked.

"No, thanks."

"Just wait until you see Father. He's still the old pirate. His black flag flies over trains now, that's all. Railroads are the wave of the future."

"You're telling me."

"Forgive me." Langdon cast a sidelong look at Craig. "You've been promoted to captain."

"I didn't know you cared about such things. A captain's salary isn't impressive. Sydenham was quite disappointed that I did not appear in full-dress uniform." Craig chased a fly that was about to come to rest on his hand. "Do you come into the office often these days?"

"Sydenham isn't getting any younger. And, you know, his asthma."

"He seemed chipper to me. How is the farm on Staten Island? You used to say that an office wasn't for you. Is that why you gained weight? But it suits you."

Langdon made a wry face. "The family is at Willowbeach, as usual. Otherwise there's not much news. My oldest girl got engaged, but I'm sure Mother wrote you about that."

"Is she marrying the musician from Saratoga Springs?"

Langdon shook his head. "A Rothenstein from Boston. A banker. The musician was killed the first year of the war."

"I hope he knew the fate he was spared. To be the husband of a Matlock daughter. My God, look at Everett, George, David. I'll have that drink, after all."

Langdon set two glasses on the desk. "Sherry or something stronger?"

"Whatever you're having."

"I stick to whiskey." He did not touch glasses with his brother but drank rapidly. Afterward he seemed more relaxed. "To think that I will soon be a father-in-law and then a grandfather. I can tell from the children that I'm getting old."

"Never say anything like that around Father. It's his belief that he remains young through his children and grandchildren. He is the trunk and we are only the leaves. We live only one summer, while he has countless ones."

"One thing you've inherited from him anyway—his malice."

"That's not the only fault of his I've got. I learned that much during the war, and I was happy whenever I discovered another one. That was the only good thing about the war." Craig spoke slowly and thoughtfully, as if he were only just realizing what he was saying. "A hawk has sharp eyes, a beak, and claws. People aren't so lucky. Our only advantages are selfishness and a passionate attachment to this life. The very fact that I'm sitting here now I owe, not to luck, but to the unbridled employment of all my 'faults.' "

Langdon was twisting the whiskey glass between his fingers. "Are you going out to Willowbeach? Margaret has been waiting for you."

"I'll go as soon as I've taken care of a couple of errands. I have to do something about my shares, for one." He thought a moment before continuing. "I would like you to instruct Sydenham to hand them over to me."

"What do you mean, *hand over?*"

"That I want them."

Langdon gave a pained smile, like someone who does

not get the punch line of a joke but is unwilling to admit it.

"I hope I have expressed myself clearly enough," Craig continued. "I want my stock certificates."

Langdon still refused to understand his brother. "You can be absolutely certain that they will go up in value. Probably even more than I indicated. And of course we will make restitution of the interest for the past four years. The accounting was simply overlooked. Father always honors such agreements."

"Langdon, listen to me, please. If I put my stocks in a bank's safe-deposit box, I can get at them whenever I want. You're my bank, as it were, and I want you to hand over my shares. Do you understand? I simply want to have them. I want to take them away from here—in a cardboard box—I don't care how. It is my inheritance. I am entitled to it. I do not want it lying here with all the other family papers. I want my portion. It's only paper, but I want to be able to touch it, rummage around in it, maybe burn it. I want it; I want to do with it as I please."

Langdon wondered if his brother were bluffing. Craig had once staged a similar scene to get a ten-thousand-dollar boat out of his father, simply by insisting that he was about to join a polar expedition. That had always been his method: out of a clear blue sky a tantrum, a crazy notion, a tactic for the sole purpose of getting his own way in another matter. "What is it you really want, Craig?"

"The stock certificates."

Langdon had never heard the words spoken in this way. Suddenly they contained flights of poetry. This, too, was something Craig had in common with his father, this gift of intoxicating others with words while himself remaining quite cool, quite unmoved. Both Craig and John Tyler could start fires in other men's hearts without feeling anything themselves. They could turn people into life-long friends without giving off a single spark of warmth.

"Surely you don't want to sell them," Langdon said, probing. "You can't be serious?"

"Are you refusing to hand them over?"

"No, but . . ." Langdon made sure the door to the anteroom was shut, and for a moment he seemed to be about to close the windows as well. "If you insist on selling them, I will make you an offer."

Seconds passed. "I'm listening." Craig's voice was expressionless.

"All right. I will give you fifty, though they stand at forty and three-quarters. That way you won't lose a cent."

"Nor gain anything either. You just told me that they would go up to a hundred."

"I'll give you sixty. But Father must not find out that I am buying for myself."

"I don't want to get you in trouble. I won't sell."

"But you just said—"

"I've changed my mind."

"Your shares must not come on the market, not at this time," Langdon explained. "I mean it. You'll understand when you hear my reasons. I ought to leave it to Father to bring you up to date, but perhaps it will be better if you learn it from me. War has broken out between Loftus Poynder and Father."

"Has it really come to that?"

"Yes. Dominance in New York, the state and the city, is at stake. Father made Loftus Poynder an offer. Are you listening?"

Craig, who seemed absorbed in contemplating his hands, briefly raised his eyes. "And Poynder refused?"

"We'll get what we want without him. You can be sure of that. But it will be a hard struggle."

"You're hoping that sooner or later he'll knuckle under, as he did before?"

"He'll have to if he's got a spark of reason left. I hope you know which side you belong on. That's why your shares are so important. You can't sell them over the counter. Poynder would buy them up at once."

"I understand." Craig brushed his fingers over the rim of the nearly full glass on the desk in front of him. "I can promise you and Father one thing. I will not offer the shares to Poynder. But that's another matter. First of all I want to have them. It would be best if you told Sydenham."

"He'll need a little time. And I don't know how Father—"

"Don't give me that! I can't bear it. I never want to hear it again. 'Father says. Father wants. Father does not like. Father must not find out.'" Craig stared at his brother. "I don't have your thick skin. To spend a life-time waiting, waiting, waiting. No moneybag can be big enough to make me spend my life as the puppet of a tyrannical old man."

Craig did not take his eyes off his brother. "What is it like, Langdon? How do you manage to keep him from seeing how eager you are for him to die? Do you let your-self think of it only when he's not around? You don't have to defend yourself. Don't abuse me of the notion that deep inside you, hidden under your hypocritical good na-ture, there lives a man who cannot share—a Matlock. Do you think I don't know that it was crazy of me to let my-self be fobbed off with such a ridiculous inheritance? But I was sick to death of waiting. If I ever catch myself thinking of Father's dying—wishing, hoping—I'll begin to hate him. You *must* hate him. You won't admit it, but it's true. Your love, your submission, that's just another form of hate. I'm better off. I can go to Willowbeach and enjoy the ocean. There will be at least one person at my father's table who is glad to see him healthy and well."

"You'll see that, all right." Langdon's laugh was tenta-tive. "This winter we were all sick, every one of us—ex-cept him."

"I'd appreciate it if you'd call Sydenham now."

"Fine, I'll take care of it. Don't worry. Can you come back for them tomorrow morning?"

"Good enough."

"Anything else?"

"Yes. Restitution of my interest payments for the past four years. See to it that Sydenham takes care of it in a few days. I'll take an advance now."

"I'll write out a draft. How much?"

"Five thousand."

Langdon, who had seated himself at the desk and opened the green writing case, looked up. "Five thousand? In God's name, what do you want with five thousand dollars?"

"Don't start in on me again," Craig replied. "What do I want with it? I don't know what I want with it. I just want to have it." He patted his pockets. "I want to feel the money here, just the weight of it. I want to feel that all I have to do is reach for it. Maybe I won't spend any of it. Maybe I'm already as corrupt as you. But I want to have it with me, on my person, so that my pockets burst with it." He spoke without an edge, in that soft voice that was a warning to anyone who knew him.

"Done." Langdon reached for his pen and wrote out the check. "It's on my account," he explained. "We can straighten out the details later. Next time please come to me right away. Don't bother Sydenham." He handed the colored slip of paper to Craig. "I wish I could ask you to spend the evening with us, but I have an appointment out of town. I'm sorry. We'll get together in a day or two if you stay in New York that long. Irene will be delighted to see you again."

Craig folded the draft. "When will you speak with Sydenham?"

"Immediately. Send him in here after he has cashed your check. Tomorrow morning you'll have your stock certificates. If you'd like me to recommend a bank where you can deposit them. . . ."

"I'll sleep on it," Craig said. "At least for one night."

"You're the same crazy fellow you used to be." They were at the door. Langdon put his arms on Craig's shoulders. "I'll be back day after tomorrow. Let's meet."

Craig turned back at the door to put the same question to his brother that he had earlier asked Sydenham. "Who is Thomas Wilmurt?"

The name had a similar effect on Langdon. He closed the door. "Where did you hear that name?"

"This Wilmurt character seems to be something of a time bomb. My curiosity is aroused. Sydenham reacted the same way you did."

"You spoke to him about Wilmurt?"

"I asked him, as I asked you, whether he knew the man but he wouldn't give me a straight answer."

"You said you only got to town today."

"Yes."

"Who told you about Wilmurt?"

"Don't keep me in suspense. Who is he?"

"It's an unpleasant business. Not dangerous, just unpleasant. A man like Father always has enemies; that can't be helped. His kind of deals involve serious contests, and of course there are losers."

"You're already talking like Father. I can almost hear him."

"Wilmurt . . ." Langdon hesitated, pulling at his mustache. "Actually, Thomas Wilmurt performed some little service for Father, expecting it to be more profitable than it was. What he did for Father perhaps wasn't quite legal, and it gave Wilmurt the idea that he had Father in the palm of his hand. First he tried it on Father—you know, blackmail—but Father threw him out. I was his second port of call. When he didn't get anywhere with me either, he ran around New York with his documents, making the rounds of the newspapers. The visitor in my office when you arrived was Allan Scrutin. Wilmurt offered his material to Scrutin for publication."

"And Scrutin came straight to you?"

"Something like that. He's too clever to get mixed up in any shady business."

"He came for no other reason, simply out of high-mindedness?"

Langdon shrugged. "More or less. We are very good advertisers."

"Is that why you sent Father the telegram?"

"Yes. But tell me what you know about Wilmurt."

"He's been asking for me at Laight Street. All last week, every day. What kind of 'service' did he perform for Father?"

"Why trouble yourself with that? One way or the other it will soon be settled. If he should call on you again, don't agree to anything. But I'm sure he won't bother you again."

Finding Langdon at his father's desk, official viceroy of the New York office where John Tyler had ruled so long and high-handedly—Craig had not counted on that. Not that he envied Langdon. He felt envy only when he saw a buzzard in the sky with wings widespread, still, seemingly unmoving, as if sleeping on the wind, keeping its prey in sight for minutes on end—a battle that consisted of endless waiting and an almost immeasurably tiny instant of thrust. Craig had never envied other men, least of all someone like Langdon, who awaited his master's orders and rewards like a lap dog. Langdon was probably already regretting that he had used his authority to such an extent and was thinking of having to justify his actions to his father. His older brother had never been a model to Craig; on the contrary, early on he had made an effort to be different, going so far as to reject out of hand foods

Langdon liked. In time Langdon had come to represent everything Craig abhorred.

"Craig! Craig Matlock!"

He was so lost in thought that he had not heard the first soft call. The woman stood in the shadow of a doorway, and he saw only the hand in the fawn-colored glove, beckoning him. "Craig! Over here! Hurry!"

He knew only one woman who had such a soft, conspiratorial voice. "Irene."

Her fingers gripped his and wound around them—her old, practiced ritual of understanding, discreetly secret even in the presence of others.

"Take care," she whispered. Irene had a clear view of every situation; she smelled out opportunities as quickly as dangers, so that in the nine years of her affair with Craig she had seen to it that there was never a whisper of suspicion. Her eyes traveled the length of the corridor to the door leading to the anteroom of her husband's office. "I know somewhere we won't be disturbed," she said. "Here, hold this and come with me." She handed Craig some magazines and a few small packages. With rapid steps she went ahead of him and turned into the side corridor. She opened a door and, after Craig had entered, turned the key and pulled it out of the keyhole.

She smiled at him under her broad-brimmed straw hat. "No one will disturb us here. Since Father Matlock left, there hasn't been a director's meeting here. You can tell from the dust. Craig! Fate made us meet like this." She took her packages and magazines from him and put them on the conference table.

Craig watched her. Her motions, even when performing the most ordinary tasks, had always delighted him. She raised her arms and pulled two hatpins from the hat. Her way of lifting the hat off her head to let it fall on the table while its ribbons fluttered, of running her hands through her hair to smooth it—was almost enough to explain why he had fallen in love with her as a young man and had never broken off the affair.

As she turned toward him now, he remembered what a friend had once said about her: "That kind of fruit grows only in a clergyman's orchard."

"What are you thinking?"

"Something very nice." He pulled her close. "I'm thinking that, all at once, New York is a wonderful town."

She had to stand on tiptoe and staggered a little when he let her go. "Craig! I've got you back! I still can't believe it. It had to be thought transference. I don't often come to the office. Only at the end of the month, when I go over the bills with Sydenham, or when I pick up Langdon and we go out to dinner at Kane's. Craig Matlock! I knew I'd have a pleasant surprise today. When I woke up this morning, my left foot was itching."

She began to take off her gloves. No other woman Craig knew of could divest herself of her clothes with so much charm. The fabric seemed to dissolve, flutter away. The conference room, with its bare white walls and two uncurtained windows, was very bright. A map of New York State and one showing all the rail lines in the country hung on the wall.

Irene followed Craig's glance. "We can close the blinds," she said.

"Well, I don't know."

She busied herself with the narrow belt of her dress. He would not have been surprised if she had taken it off. But it was only a playful gesture, one of those wordless signals she delighted in. "You've just been to see Langdon. How was your reunion?"

Craig shrugged. "You know I make him nervous. That hasn't changed."

"He likes you, though—at least in his way. Probably more than you like him."

"He wasn't exactly overcome with joy."

She laughed deep in her throat and took a step toward him. Her hands burrowed their way under his coat, wandered softly up his back. "You feel the same—all muscle. I believe your heart is just another muscle. It reacts only when you want it to. Langdon, now, he has a heart as soft as a down pillow." She moved a couple of steps away. "Is it me or you who has changed?"

"We'll find out."

"How did you like the Southern belles?"

"We were at war."

"Yes, and you were the victors. All women have a weakness for conquerers, just as I have a weakness for Matlocks. Really, every time I thought of you, I hoped you were enjoying some nice girls. How is Margaret? She ought to be getting to the right age. I think she's one of those women who have a child before they get a taste for it." She looked at Craig with the smile of an accomplice. "Did you bring her to New York with you?"

"I haven't been to Willowbeach yet." Once, such questions amused him. The first time he had refused to answer Irene was when she had tried to elicit the details of his wedding night.

"You haven't been to Willowbeach?"

"I only just got to New York."

"And run into me first thing! It's magic. We have to celebrate such a wonderful coincidence. And then you'll tell me all about Southern women. Are they really as clever as people say? I always looked forward to the day when we would trade roles and you would be the teacher. You're staying in town? No, I won't let you go to Willowbeach now. My claims are older than Margaret's, especially since I don't have as much time." She became serious. "You still like me a little, don't you? Look into my eyes. Tell me you still like me, that I haven't changed."

"You haven't changed."

"Be honest. For a woman my age, every year counts as two. I'll be forty next year."

"How many men turned to look at you on the street today?"

She laughed. "It's the hat and the scent. Lily-of-the-valley. I know it's too youthful for me. You wouldn't believe all the things women do." She put her arms around his neck. "You still like me a little?" Her lips were at his ear. "A little bit? Do you want to show me? Today is Thursday, isn't it?"

"Yes, why?"

Her arms loosened, her eyes were downcast, and her voice grew soft. "Langdon goes to Albany on Thursdays. On the night boat, so as not to lose a working day. He won't be back until late tomorrow night. Our good angel is still watching over us."

"What is Langdon up to in Albany? Don't tell me he works there."

"The directors meet on Friday. That awful railroad. What do you think they're up to? They talk about cows run over on the tracks, about fires in locomotive sheds, about freight tariffs. Things like that. His boat leaves at eight."

"And all I ever saw in Langdon was a farmer, a horse-breeder."

Silent, Irene slowly put on her hat. When she spoke again, her voice was low. "Staten Island—those were terrible years for me. I grew up in the city. I need the city. I really only did it for Langdon. Langdon Matlock, the country gentleman—that was your father's plan for his oldest son. What could I do but put a good face on it? And it was healthy for the children, of course. Now they're old enough to be away at school, thank goodness. Only Celia is at home. She spends her days embroidering monograms on her trousseau linens. She insists on doing it herself. I wonder how long she'll keep it up."

Craig, too, had become thoughtful. He could not get his brother out of his mind. "I never understood Langdon," he said. "All his life he's played the part of the dutiful son who lives in fear of his lord and master."

"I understand him better than any of you. You underestimate him. Langdon is the heir. One day it will all belong to him. That's worth waiting for."

"Such a long wait? If he's unlucky, he'll wait another twenty years. Father is mean enough to live to be a hundred."

"To listen to you, one would think there's room for only one man on this earth. Langdon is a different breed. He has adapted. John Tyler is a tyrant, but Langdon knows how to handle him. Your image of Langdon's life —it was never like that. He doesn't shout it from the rooftops, but for years he has had deals of his own."

"Is that how it is? He wanted to buy my shares."

"You see. He knows how to take the old man. Every chance he gets, he talks about the farm, acts as if it were a sacrifice that he can't be there instead of living in New York. Now you will finally get to see our new house. The best neighborhood, Murray Hill, Fifth Avenue at Thirty-eighth Street. The land was part of my father's estate, and the house is in my name."

"And what do they say about all that in Albany?"

"Your father hasn't seen it yet. We didn't even ask him for permission."

"Don't go getting any big ideas. Father knows all about it, just the same. He could tell you the price of everything, down to the last penny. He's just waiting quietly for the right time to play his trump card against Langdon."

Irene carefully and deliberately pierced the white straw with the pins and then reached for her gloves. There she stood, quite still. Suddenly, without knowing why, she had no more strength, no courage. She felt old and ridiculous. When Craig asked, "When can we meet?" she listened to him suspiciously, trying to tell whether he was sincere.

A loud voice in the hall saved her from having to answer. It was Langdon. "What is it? Still no answer from Willowbeach?" Footsteps and voices going back and forth, then again, loudly and drowning out the rest, Langdon's voice. "I don't want it lying around for half an hour, like last time. I want to see the telegram as soon as it comes in." The footsteps faded, doors closed, the silence resumed.

"When?" Craig repeated.

"At nine, at the St. Denis."

"I'll reserve the room."

"Perhaps you can get Five-oh-six again."

"I'll try. At nine, then. I'll come to the side entrance on Eleventh Street, as usual."

Irene nodded. The wide brim of the hat hid her face.

"Is something wrong?" Craig asked.

But Irene had herself under control again. She took his hand, held on to it, and said, "Let me leave first. Wait until I'm in Langdon's office." She picked up her things from the table and, without looking back, left the room.

THE FIVE POINTS was notorious for its slums, misery, and dirt and for its many crimes. Craig Matlock had allowed friends to drag him to this part of Manhattan only once, during his student days. At that time there was a bookmaker on Mulburry Bend who took bets on the races at

Saratoga Springs. But Craig's dormant passion for gambling, which his friends had meant to arouse, had not surfaced. Nor did they succeed in opening his eyes to the dark beauty of the slums. Craig had seen nothing but the dirt, misery, and decay. His revulsion at anything connected with poverty was so profound that he had no wish to learn about it even in books. He had never understood his sisters' passion for Dickens' sinister *American Notes*.

Why hadn't he gotten a hack to take him to Chatham Street? But now he was too close to his goal to hail one. Chatham Street was a canyon of gray buildings, their walls covered even in summer with dark, damp spots. Sometimes an open door allowed a glimpse of a sunless back yard. The windows of the bars, which were open only in the evening, were covered, the doors locked. Craig felt uncomfortable when he thought of the five thousand dollars in his pocket.

He quickened his step. Every other house sported a sign indicating the junk dealers' trade. They had placed their wares on the sidewalk—old stoves, chairs, bird cages, racks of clothing. Craig could not imagine how anyone could wear such rags. He cursed the fact that he had to fulfill this particular promise; but it would be the last chore to remind him of the war.

At this time of day the shift ended for the girls who worked in the clothing and shirt factories and sewing rooms on Chatham Street. But their bright clothes did little to make the street more cheerful. Craig examined the house numbers until he saw a sign stretched across a narrow façade: B. POCOCK, FINE GLOVES. EXCELLENT WORKMANSHIP, EXCELLENT PRICES. The windows were grimy. A tin hand at the corner pointed to the entrance, which was reached by way of an iron staircase leading alongside the house to a rusty iron door. The door opened onto a large room cluttered with shelves. Next to the entrance, in a kind of niche formed by the racks, a man in a gray smock was sitting behind a desk. Above him a gas lamp with a green shade shed a narrow band of light.

Craig approached the desk. "Mr. Pocock?"

The man picked up a white tablet, popped it in his mouth, chewed it, and then spoke hoarsely. "Can't you read? Commercial travelers welcome only in the mornings. I'm not buying. I'm oversupplied now." He reached for the lamp swaying above his head and turned it on his visitor. Craig's expensive, elegantly cut suit changed his attitude at once. "You must forgive me," he said. "But if you knew everything they tried to sell me today—lightning conductors, life insurance, railway stocks." He spoke with a foreign accent.

"It's all right. I'm looking for a Mrs. Kate Schoffield. Does she work here?"

Pocock let go of the lamp, which began to bob over his head. "What do you want with her?" he said, his face sullen.

"I have something to give her."

"I can do that for you."

Craig pulled a small box from his pocket. He had been carrying it around for a long time and was glad to be rid of it at last. For a moment he was about to let Pocock have it. Whoever she was, Mrs. Schoffield would only ask him questions to which he had no answers. But he said. "I'd rather give it to her personally. It's from her husband. He died in Savannah."

"She insisted on marrying him. That's all they think about—marriage. Did he leave her something at least? If it's money, you better give me thirty dollars of it. She owes me."

"Where can I find her?"

"You don't believe me?" Pocock rummaged around in a carton. "The other day the whole house almost went up in flames because of her. Three bolts of shammy were charred. Nobody else but Ben Pocock would have been so generous as to charge her only the wholesale price and let her work off the debt."

"Will you tell me where I can find Mrs. Schoffield?"

"Here it is, her IOU. These girls spend money faster than they earn it. And then they say we don't pay them enough. They blame us for everything. The price of sewing thread has doubled since the war began. Thirty clams is what she owes me. Anyone else would have put her in jail for less."

"This way at least you get your money back," Craig Matlock said coolly.

Pocock lowered his head. The light fell on his gray hair which showed the marks of a broad-toothed comb. "She's upstairs in the cutting room." He pointed to a stairway. "Up there. You can't miss her. She's alone."

Upstairs, too, the light barely penetrated through the

grimy windows. Shelves full of boxes blocked Craig's view. The area smelled of leather and leaking gas. A circle of light fell through the gray dusk from a lamp over a cutting table. The tinfoil cover on the shade increased the brightness. Kate Schoffield stood in the garish light. A strand of her pale hair was hanging down into her face. She was bent over a piece of black kidskin stretched over the table and held down by pins. Absorbed in chalking along the stencil placed over it, she had not heard Craig enter. Even now, when he was on the other side of the table, she did not look up. She undid the pins, reached for the scissors, and began to cut along the chalk lines.

"Mrs. Schoffield? Are you Kitty Schoffield?"

She jumped, and the scissors slid through one of the chalk lines. "You startled me. Who are you? How did you get in here?" She blew the strand of hair from her face.

Craig looked at her but did not speak. Her face, which was a mixture of earnestness and childlike purity, took his breath away. "Did Mr. Pocock see you? And he let you come up?" She became aware of the ruined piece of leather. "Do you know what that's going to cost me?" she said. But her eyes sparkled, as if she had deliberately played a prank on Pocock.

"I have something for you from your husband." On his way up the stairs Craig had once again pocketed the little box.

She looked at him, her eyes containing both openness and suspicion. "You were a friend of my husband's?"

He felt vaguely irritated by the room. "How much longer will you be?"

"Three hundred hours." Again there was a sparkle. "He pays ten cents for every hour of overtime, and I have to put in three hundred of them to work off my debt —three a day." She pointed to the ruined piece of leather. "And now this, too."

Her manner was infectious. "Before you do all that, could we go somewhere and talk?"

"Is that an invitation?"

"That was how it was meant."

Without hesitation she began to clear off the table. She hung the stencils on a hook behind her, leaving the ruined kidskin on the table. Craig noticed that she was not wearing a wedding ring. He wondered if she had pawned it.

Kate turned off the lamp. "I want you to be prepared

for Ben Pocock's explosion," she said. "Besides the fact that he pays badly, he's uncommonly jealous of any man who calls for one of his girls."

"Do you often get called for?"

"More often than I like, because they're always the wrong ones."

Pocock was waiting for them at the foot of the stairs. "One moment, Mrs. Schoffield," he said. His voice sounded even hoarser than before. "No overtime today?"

She looked at Craig, amused. "What did I tell you!"

"No overtime—and in debt," Pocock said. "If you leave now, Mrs. Schoffield, you don't need to come back. I'll get the thirty dollars from you somehow. Probably a lot quicker."

Craig reached into the outer pocket of his coat. He counted off the ten-dollar bills. As Pocock reached for them, he said, "First the IOU."

"I'll tear it up."

"You'd better give it to me." Craig took it and tore it into small pieces. "You're losing a good cutter," he said.

Laughing, Kate went down the iron steps, but by the time they reached the street, she had become solemn. Craig was already getting used to these sudden changes of mood.

"That was very generous of you," she said. "I should thank you. But in the first place, now I'm in *your* debt, and in the second, I'm out of a job."

"How much did he pay you?"

"Six dollars a week."

"Six days. Ten hours a day?"

"Eleven."

"Then you should be grateful to me. To work for such wages!"

She brightened again, as with secret amusement. "What kind of world do you come from anyway? Where can a girl get more than six dollars a week doing work that's clean and easy?" She gestured as if to embrace the entire street. "I know a lot of girls who would give their eyeteeth to work for Ben Pocock. He pays regularly, and he lets you alone. Not all of them do."

"I could go back and ask him to give you another chance."

She stopped, her eyebrows raised. The strand of hair was down over her forehead again. She seemed childlike now, taken by surprise. But another need was written on her face: hunger, There was no other word for it—a hunger for life. "No," she said. "Anything but that."

They walked along. "How old are you?" Craig asked.

"Young enough so I don't have to lie about it."

"Seventeen?"

"Is that meant as a compliment? I'm twenty."

"You grew up in New York?"

"Worse." But she did not follow up this ambiguous answer with an explanation.

"What can be worse?"

She looked straight ahead with an alert expression. "Worse than New York? The Convent of the Sacred Heart. They have a wonderful house up north. Usually they educate only the daughters of the rich, but sometimes they make an exception for orphans. Can you believe that I had already completed my postulate and was about to become a novice?"

An alarm rang in Craig's head. He had gone to Chatham Street to carry out a pledge made to a comrade not to hear a confession—and not, as had almost happened, to forget that he was to meet Irene in a few hours at the St. Denis. Nevertheless he said, "Where are we going?"

"You decide."

"Would you like to have dinner with me?"

"Remember—I've already set you back thirty dollars."

"Where would you like to go?" He recalled too late that this was a rash question. He did not care to take her to one of the fashionable restaurants where he might be recognized.

"You mean, without thinking about money?" She glanced at the houses along the street. "The Fifth Avenue has a better kitchen, but the St. Cloud is fancier."

She continued to surprise him. He did not know whether she meant it or whether she was making fun of him. "Is that your world?" he asked.

"I'm sure John told you about it. We were both crazy that way. Whenever we had money, we went straight to the St. Cloud."

"I have a better idea. We'll take a Hudson River boat, go to Claremont, and come back on the return boat. If we get hungry, we can eat on board, the trip is long enough. I'm told they cook very well on the boats." He paused. "You're not saying anything."

"I love the river. If I were rich, I'd buy a boat and have them run me up and down it all summer long."

"Let's hurry, then."

"I live near here. And I won't take long. That's the advantage of having only one nice dress."

They quickened their pace. They were on Vandewater Street. Kate went toward a tall tenement building, where she stopped by a dark passageway. "Here," she said. "I'll be right back." She stepped into the entrance, but then turned back. "You really will wait, won't you?"

They did not eat until the return trip from Claremont. The dining saloon on the upper deck of the *Elysion* was elegant, with thick carpets, gold-framed mirrors, crystal chandeliers, and marble tables. But Kate Schoffield moved among the opulence as if she had spent all of her life here. Craig had suggested the boat ride to avoid being seen with her, and her question whether he would wait had anticipated this reluctance of his. As he paced up and down in front of the tenement building, wondering how it looked on the inside, there had actually been a moment when he did want to leave. But that feeling was long forgotten. She had enthralled him totally.

During the evening he noticed that she aroused attention, from the coachman who drove them to the pier to the stewards and waiters in the dining saloon. Something emanated from her that worked directly on men. Even the piano player had sent over to their table to ask if she had a request.

Craig disliked women who pleased too easily, but he had to admit that Kate did nothing to provoke these attentions. Even her dress surprised him. It was a frock of yellow linen, simply cut, bordered in black at the collar and cuffs. She wore no jewelry.

It was dark when they left the dining saloon. The promenade deck was brightly lit. They looked for a spot away from the lights, far enough from the other people on deck. They found two seats on the quarter deck. Only then did Craig remember that he was still carrying the package that had been the occasion for seeking her out. "In ten minutes we will be docking," he said. "The trip downriver goes faster."

Kate had lowered the back rest of the lounge chair. Her arms crossed under her head, she lay still. "You're probably in a hurry," she said. "For me, the trip can't be too slow."

After they disembarked—he thought, he would have only a few minutes in which to get to the St. Denis, but it was merely a passing worry. He said, "I was almost born on one of those boats. My mother was on her way from Albany to New York."

"I was born at sea," Kate said. "Maybe that's why I'm drawn to the water."

"Where was that?"

As always when he asked her a personal question, she hesitated. "Before I came to this country."

There was only the noise of the paddle wheels, the rush of water, and the soft thumping from the ship's machinery. Craig reached into the pocket of his coat for the package. "How long were you married?" he asked her.

She sat bolt upright. The shawl draped over the back of the deck chair slid to the ground. She bent to pick it up and folded it carefully. She seemed absorbed in the task. "I know everything ends," she said finally. "And always when I start to forget it, I'm reminded all over again. But have no fear. These hours mean a great deal. I expect nothing beyond them. The Hudson, the dinner, to know for one evening that it's summer. . . ." She got out of the chair and went to the railing. After a while she turned and faced him. "I married John two years ago last May. We spent eleven days and seventeen hours together. We got married only when it was settled that he had to go to the war. I never saw him again. Didn't he tell you?"

"He did not have much time to talk. He was dying."

"He didn't tell you about our wedding trip? It was on one of these boats. We went as far as the Catskills and from there to a hotel in the mountains, two thousand feet up. From the window in our room we could see the Hudson though it was ten miles away. Then we took the train to Niagara Falls. I got dizzy on the suspension bridge over the river. John had saved up four hundred dollars. When we got back, we had just enough left for a big dinner the night before he had to report." She looked at Craig. "Go ahead, say it."

"Say what?"

"That I'm crazy. That I could have lived very well on the four hundred dollars."

"Couldn't you?"

She laughed, as she had laughed on the street when he asked her if he should go back to Ben Pocock.

"John's parents harp on that four hundred dollars to this day. I was a great disappointment to them. They have a bakery near City Hall. When John first introduced me to them, they liked me. An orphan; that was as good as a gilt-edged guarantee that I would be grateful, unassuming, and frugal. And then such extravagance. After the honeymoon they wanted nothing more to do with me. I never saw them again, except the time when we got the news of John's death. In their eyes, I'm to blame for everything—including that." She was silent. "He didn't tell you about our trip? Every time he wrote, he mentioned it." A forlorn smile played around her mouth as she waited for him to answer.

Craig was tempted to make something up. "What were you told about his death?"

"Not much. The usual things." She put the shawl around her shoulders. "But I read the newspapers. A burning ship, men trapped below deck. The newspapers said it was a boiler fire. There were four hundred men on board, all on their way home."

He had seen many terrible things during the war, but the burning of the *Marvellous* was the worst. The ship was at anchor in Savannah, and the wind carried the thick clouds of smoke across the city. It was a sweltering, hot day. All the windows in the hospital were open. But for the men on the stretchers there was no relief. They lay there just as they had been fished out of the water, some of them looking more like charred pieces of wood than human beings. What was the sense of talking about it?

Kate was staring at him. "You said your name was Craig Matlock?"

"Yes, why?"

"One of the newspapers said the *Marvellous* used to be owned by John Tyler Matlock, who sold it to the government when the war started. And in his last letter John said he'd never seen such a dilapidated old tub. The crew was just waiting for it to fall apart. He meant it as a joke. John wasn't afraid of anything—except the day when he would have to take over his father's bakery.

I never, never would have believed that something could happen to him." She raised her hand as if to ward off some danger. "No, don't tell me what you saw." She stood by the rail, isolated and vulnerable.

"He was looking for someone from New York," Craig said. "A nurse came through the wards, searching for someone. I happened to be there."

"Then you spoke with him?"

"He told me your name; that's all. And he gave me this."

Kitty did not put out her hand immediately, but instead said, "Please, you open it. You do it. I'm afraid I know what's in it."

"Are you sure you don't want to . . . ?"

"No, you do it. Please."

He tore the flimsy paper wrapping. A piece of white cotton cushioned an amulet.

Kate turned white. She took the charm from him. For a moment he thought she would throw it in the river. "I gave it to him," she said. "On our last day together. It was supposed to bring him luck. My mother believed in such things. She wore it on the trip over. But they never arrived. They only got as far as the Quarantine Station on Staten Island. The city was right there in front of them. It was almost close enough to touch. A good-luck charm. . . ." For a moment she was lost in thought. "During the journey smallpox broke out on the ship. By the time they brought me to Manhattan, my parents were dead—both of them. They told me about it later, when I was older. Do you believe it?"

"Believe what?"

"That there are people who succeed at everything, who have a long lease on good luck, while others. . . ." Again her voice trailed off. When she spoke again, it was in a different tone. "We're almost there."

The boat was slowing down. Dark smoke curled from the smokestack as the *Elysion* turned in the current and headed for the pier. They stood together at the railing. She laid her hand on his. "Thank you."

"It's all right, there's no need to thank me."

"It never really got dark. Or is that just the city?"

Craig glanced at the illuminated clock on the ferry house. It was a few minutes to nine. "You had better take a cab." He pointed to the turnouts at the shore.

Kate was looking at him with bright eyes. "Are you glad?"

"What do you mean?"

"To be rid of me."

"I really am sorry, but I do have an appointment. I had no way of knowing. . . ."

"What was it exactly that you had no way of knowing? Can't you just forget about your appointment?"

"It's not that easy."

"Why don't you come home with me?" She sounded offhand, as if she were asking an ordinary question. "Is it Vandewater Street? You don't approve of the neighborhood. I noticed that." She laughed. "If you'll close your eyes, I'll lead you by the hand. You won't see the house or the stairs, and upstairs, in my room. . . . Did I frighten you?" Her face was close to his; she was staring at him again. "You could make it easier for me. It's supposed to be the man who makes these suggestions."

"The first time?"

She stepped back as if to avoid a slap. Her voice was suddenly hard. "You've more than paid for it. Thirty dollars to Ben Pocock, the tickets to Claremont and back, the dinner. Probably you'd pay for my cab as well, to be rid of me all the sooner. That's a lot of money, a great deal more than girls get around here."

"You're hurting yourself," he said.

"Better I than you. But you're already finished with the whole thing."

The ship's bells were answered by the shouts of men standing on the shore, ready to make fast the hawsers.

"Forget what I said," Kitty said. "Maybe some evening you'll have a free hour. You know where to find me. Come along. It's time to get off."

They left the steamer. It was exactly nine o'clock, and it would certainly take another quarter of an hour to get to the St. Denis Hotel. Craig had reserved the room that morning, Room 506. Irene would be waiting for him at the side entrance. In his mind's eye he saw the closed carriage, her hand at the curtain while she kept watch. He had never kept her waiting, and it was difficult to imagine how she would react if he did not come at all.

She lay beside him, still and silent. The room was dark. Her hair was the only bright spot in it—that and her arms neatly arranged on top of the coverlet. She slept deeply, taking long breaths, as if in sleep she required more air than awake. Her nude body touched his. It was smooth and hot. Though she wore no perfume, an aroma emanated from her—from her skin, her breath, and her hair —which attracted him more than anything else.

He wanted to light a lamp so he could see her face, but he was tired, a good tiredness with heavy limbs. Only his heart beat restlessly, pounding harshly within his chest, almost painfully. It was a new sensation.

His eyes fell closed, but he forced himself to stay awake until a clock struck. He counted laboriously and afterward could not remember whether he had heard three or four bongs, but he recognized the bells of St. John's Chapel on Varick Street, reminding him that in the middle of the night he had brought Kitty here to the house on Laight Street. Already half asleep again, he turned toward her. He pulled her closer, and in her sleep she wound her arms around him.

He was awakened by a noise in the apartment. It took him several seconds to come awake and realize that someone was knocking at the door. Though it was daylight, the blue-velvet curtains allowed little light to get through. The yellow dress with the narrow black border on the collar and cuffs lay crumpled on the floor next to the bed. He released himself from Kitty's embrace. Her eyes were closed, but this time he could not tell whether she was really asleep or whether she would be watching him when his back was turned. The knock at the door was repeated. Craig pulled on his dressing gown and went into the hallway.

Joe Cristadoro stood at the door with a telegram in his hand. "This just came for you. I thought it might be important. Good morning."

Craig took the envelope. There was no indication of its point of origin, but he had his suspicions. "Tell me, how late is it?"

"Ten o'clock. You had left yesterday by the time the missus came back from shopping. She took care of everything. Did you find what you needed?"

It was an ordinary remark. The porter's face betrayed nothing, but Craig was certain that Cristadoro knew perfectly well that he had not come home alone. Even if he had not actually seen Craig during the night, a man like Cristadoro had a sixth sense about such things.

"I have a visitor," Craig said with his accustomed assurance. "It may be she will stay for a while. If she asks for anything, please take care of it for me."

"Of course." Cristadoro affected indifference. "What if anyone should ask for you?"

"I'm not expecting anyone." Craig was curt.

The curtains were partly open when he returned to the bedroom. Kitty was sitting up in bed, still nude, her hands folded around her drawn-up knees. Craig laid the telegram on the mantel without opening it. He picked up the dress and sat down next to her. "You're not cold?"

"I'm hot. What time is it?"

"Ten."

"Why are you looking at me like that?"

"I'm wondering what it is about you."

"What about me?"

"That's what I keep asking myself. In the night, too, when I woke up."

"Why didn't you wake me? You can always wake me. I can fall back asleep at once."

"I don't mean that. I lay next to you, and my heart was beating hard. Now it's like that again—now that I'm looking at you." He took her hand. "Here."

She looked at him. It was the old look, the first thing about her that had struck him, uninhibited and on guard all at the same time. She lowered her head. "I know how it is," she said.

"How?"

She answered without hesitation, "Like dangling from the hook."

The answer surprised him, and the image she had used disturbed him; it damaged his self-esteem. But she had clearly expressed what he felt. He nodded. "Yes, that's how it is."

"Is it bad?"

"I'm not used to it," he said shortly.

"You're the first who's been willing to admit it. Usually it happened only to me. I dangle from the hook every time. It hurts, and the more I try to tear myself loose, the more deeply the barb sticks into me." Without transition she burst out laughing. She jumped up, threw herself across the bed, and laughed until the room echoed.

Then she reached for him and pulled him down. Still laughing, she said, "I caught you, Craig Matlock. I've got you on my hook, really and truly. I've got you on my hook. I have Craig Matlock on the hook."

# ═ 10 ═

THE YEAR HE had spent on the *Silver Cloud* with Captain Jan Beelt, Craig lived through a storm that terrified even the most experienced seamen. Three days of eternal night, of unremitting rain and wind drenching the ship with huge waves. Never before or since had he been so intensely aware of the value of life. He could not imagine that the storm would ever end. He had learned that sometimes submission was the only way to survive.

In the days following Kitty's moving into his apartment on Laight Street, Craig was often reminded of that experience. They closed themselves off from the world. All the clocks had stopped. There was no Willowbeach and no Margaret. Craig opened none of the telegrams that followed the first one. Whenever Joe Cristadoro appeared in the doorway with another envelope, Craig put it, unopened, on the bedroom mantel. There was, however, a clear break between the days and nights with Kitty. Often during the day irritating confrontations arose. Kitty would start a quarrel from one moment to the next over nothing at all: Craig hadn't heard a question of hers, or he hadn't touched the glass of wine she poured out for him, or he smiled at the lengthy orders she gave Cristadoro. During the days he often wondered why he endured it. But the nights removed all doubts; they allowed only submission.

On the fifth day an event made it impossible for Craig to shut himself off from the world any longer. Shortly after dark that day he went around the corner to the ice-cream parlor to get one of the huge servings of vanilla

ice cream Kitty could never get enough of. When he returned and unlocked the apartment door he was surprised to hear Cristadoro's voice in the kitchen. The
porter and Kitty had gotten along from the first. He no
longer left all the errands to his wife. Early every morning the two of them sat down in the kitchen and compiled
the shopping lists while they had a drink together.

He opened the kitchen door. Kitty and Cristadoro
were seated at the table.

"Hello, Craig," she said without ceremony. "Come have
a drink with us. Joe has a fantastic voice, and he knows
lots of wonderful, funny Italian songs."

But Cristadoro was not at ease. "I only come to bring
you something," he said to Craig. He picked up a large
yellow envelope from the top of the ice chest and held
it out to Craig. "This came for you. It was delivered
while you were out. Thomas Wilmurt. I told you about
him the first day you were back."

Craig picked up the flat, square packet. It was
wrapped in heavy yellow waxed paper, tied with string,
and sealed. "It's from Wilmurt personally?" he asked.

"Yes," the porter answered. "At first he didn't want to
leave it with me. He claimed to know you were back in
town. Wanted to speak to you in person. But I told him
it was not possible, at least before tomorrow, and certainly not until I'd spoken to you. 'Tomorrow,' Wilmurt
said, 'tomorrow is too late. See to it that Mr. Matlock
gets the papers.' He was in even worse shape than before." Joe opened the kitchen door. "I wanted to deliver
the package at once. Good night."

Craig followed Cristadoro into the hall and locked the
apartment door behind him. Then he brought the package
into the parlor. He sat down, the package in his lap, and
he began to undo the sealing wax and string. Kitty appeared in the doorway, holding a full glass. "I was having
such a nice time with Joe. He sings, you know. Funny
Italian songs. You drove him away. At least have a drink
with me now."

"I don't feel like it."

"You don't feel like it! It's boring to drink alone all
the time." She perched on the edge of the table and dangled her legs. She wore only a flimsy, loose gown against
the heat, and her feet were bare. "I want us to do every-

thing together. Why do you have to look at that package now?"

"Why not?"

"You didn't open the telegrams."

The string was off, but he hesitated before taking off the wrapping paper. "Give me your glass," he said.

Kitty was transformed. "Oh, darling you're going to have a drink with me. Wait, I have something special for a special occasion." She ran back to the kitchen and returned with a dark, bulbous bottle. "Champagne! The best kind. Joe got it at Bang's on Broadway. Bang is the only one who carries it."

Craig could not help smiling. It had become Kitty's habit to shop only in specialty stores. China, hats, lingerie, shoes, tea—for every item there was one shop that was superior to all others. Even the ice cream he had just returned with was not quite right. She knew that the best ice cream came only from Weller and Hudson's. It was as if, while cutting gloves in Pocock's workshop, she had let her imagination range over a different, more luxurious life.

She carefully filled a glass for Craig and one for herself. As they drank to each other, she did not take her eyes off him. "I'll leave you alone now," she said, "because you've been so nice."

"You can stay if you want to." But even as he spoke, he hoped she would go. She poured herself another glass of wine and left the room.

Craig meticulously unfolded the stiff yellow paper. It concealed pieces of paper, documents, obviously copies of legal forms. Many carried the stamp of the War Department, and all were in the same neat copperplate hand.

While Craig scanned the documents, he remembered the hints Langdon had dropped. Wilmurt had tried to blackmail his father. Craig quickly realized that he was holding the proof of that extortion. It was an ample bundle; even at a glance he began to understand what was at stake. A straightforward deception, a cunning swindle by which John Tyler Matlock had made millions. He had sold to the government of the United States old ships, some of them ready for the scrap heap, at horrendously inflated prices. And in these deals Thomas Wilmurt was the front man. It was all there. The list of ships' names was as complete as the record of payments.

Craig laid the papers aside and shook his head. He could not help but admire his father. What made him uneasy, however, was that somewhere in New York there was a man with the evidence of what his father had been up to, who knew the whole story. Had his father actually seen these documents and still sent Wilmurt packing? Admittedly, the go-between was in it up to his neck. But how could Langdon dismiss the entire matter, how could he call it trivial? Whoever possessed the papers could set in motion a scandal that would, at the very least, ruin old Matlock's reputation. Even a John Tyler Matlock could not bribe as many judges as it would take to win this trial.

Craig had not heard Kitty coming back. As he got up, he saw her sitting on the floor, her legs crossed, glass in one hand. In her other hand were the unopened telegrams. Her presence reminded him that the *Marvellous* was also on the list.

"What about this fellow, this Wilmurt?" Kitty asked. "Will he make trouble for you?"

Craig gathered up the papers strewn on the table, wrapped the waxed paper around them again, and tied up the packet.

Kitty held out the envelopes. "As long as you're at it, why not open these too?"

Craig took them from her. "I have to leave you alone tomorrow," he said. "I have to see my family."

"Your family?"

He had said *family,* but he meant only his father. Without mentioning Margaret, he had told Kitty about Willowbeach. He did not deliberately avoid the subject; it had simply ceased to exist.

"Your family?" Kitty repeated. "You mean your wife and children?"

There was a silence.

"Is that what you talk to Joe Cristadoro about?"

Kitty put her glass on the table and went over to the desk. When she came back, she was holding a daguerreotype. "These are your children, aren't they?"

The picture of Joshua and Sinclair had been taken in front of the house last year. His mother had sent it to him, enclosed in one of her letters. On the back someone, probably also his mother, had carefully noted the names, dates, place, and height and weight of each child. Rose Matlock preserved everything as if it were meaningful for eternity, or at least for several generations.

"Just so you know, I didn't go looking for it," Kitty said. "I came across it when I was trying to find some writing paper. The picture was right on top."

"When did you find it?"

"The first day—or yesterday. Does it matter? I knew one day you would tell me everything. And someday you'll tell your wife everything too, won't you?"

Craig put the photograph in his pocket. As he felt the stiff cardboard, he was reminded that throughout the war he had never carried any pictures. He had only rediscovered this one when he unpacked his satchel.

Kitty really had found the children's picture by chance. Afterwards, though, she had systematically searched the apartment for traces of the other woman. She had found only a morning gown in the dressing room—white satin trimmed with ermine. She had tried it on, but it was too long and full for her figure.

"You're going to see your wife, aren't you? I knew from the beginning," she said. "It couldn't have been any other way." She refilled her glass but held onto the bottle while sipping at the delicate goblet.

"Stop drinking." He reached over and took the glass and bottle from her.

"Why didn't you go to see her right away? She was alone a long time. You wouldn't treat me that way. Do you really have to go? When will you be back?"

He did not look at her. "Soon," he said.

"How soon? One day, two, a week, a month?

"How can I tell? I really have to go. It's important. I told you." His voice was calm, but Kitty understood that she could expect nothing more.

"We'll talk about everything in due course. But please, let me pick the time."

"Is she pretty? Her parents are rich, I'll bet. I'm sure you can talk to her about more things than you can me. Look at me. Are you going to sleep with her?"

Craig wished he could believe that she was drunk. The full glass still stood somewhere near her. It was as much a part of Kitty as were her abrupt mood changes. "Can't you think about anything else?" he said coldly.

"She's your wife. She's waiting for you. She hasn't had you for a long time. It's the most natural thing in the world."

"Not every woman is like you."

"Will you and I have children someday, Craig Matlock?" She often addressed him like this, using his full name. "Or does Craig Matlock have children only with women who are his social equals? Are you already sorry? Do you begin to see me as I really am? Don't worry. Just tell me when you want me to leave. You won't even have to put up with a scene." Her voice broke on an odd sound. It might have been the beginning of a laugh or an attack of hysterical weeping.

Abruptly she ran from the room.

The apartment door closed with a thud, and a few moments later he heard her footsteps on the roof terrace. He shrugged his shoulders and picked up the telegrams. He opened them all before reading them in sequence. One was from Irene, two were from Langdon, and one was from his mother at Willowbeach. Irene's had been sent first. It was typical of her. Just a question. It sounded hurt but at the same time affectionate and forgiving. Langdon informed him that the stock certificates were ready for him to pick up and in a second telegram that restitution of the interest had been approved by their father. His mother's telegram reminded him that he was very much missed at Willowbeach and that he should not do anything rash.

He had hoped that the telegrams would distract him from the footsteps overhead, but the reverse was true. The sound never let up. It grew fainter, then louder, then fainter again. The roof terrace came with the apartment. Kitty had spent many hours up there. The iron railing around it was only eighteen inches high. Margaret had felt dizzy the first time Craig took her up there. It was a stormy day, and she clutched at his arm for support as she looked down at the streets below.

Kitty's pacing had stopped. The silence frightened him. He thought of her state of mind. She had been drinking; she was angry with him. And it was dark up there. He would not be able to hear her cry out if she were to fall. The more he tried to banish such thoughts, the more they haunted him. The more he refused to admit that he was afraid, the greater the power she seemed to have gained over him.

He listened. No more steps, no sounds of any kind. He tore the telegrams into tiny scraps. He could endure the silence no longer. He quickly left the room, hurrying out of the apartment and up the stairs.

In the dark the roof seemed very high above the city which lay somewhere below in the dusk. "Kitty!" He thought he saw her behind the topiary boxwood. "Kitty, come here." No answer. He began to search. Not a trace of her.

He rushed back to the apartment, looking in every room. When he thrust open the door to the bedroom, she was sitting on the bed, laughing.

Fear still burrowed in his guts. "Stop," he shouted at her. "Stop laughing."

But her laugh grew louder and more abandoned. He grabbed her by the shoulders, but he could not stop her laughter. When he let her go, she stopped at once.

"You were afraid, weren't you? You thought I'd jump off the roof. I almost wanted that to happen. At least once to see you afraid, Craig Matlock."

"Kitty," he said. "Kitty." Only now did he notice that she no longer wore her dress but had changed into a green gauzy shift. "Yes, I was afraid."

"Then how can you leave me?" she asked. "Imagine what will go on here when you're gone! Maybe I *will* jump off the roof the very moment you get into the carriage downstairs. Maybe not. Maybe I'll invite Joe in, and we'll get hopelessly drunk and turn the place into a shambles. I have a lot of friends. Maybe I'll ask them all in, and we'll have such parties that all the other tenants will complain. You don't think I have any friends? I'll fill the apartment with them. How can you leave me alone if you have to keep thinking of all the terrible things I might be doing here?"

"Please, Kitty," he said. "Please don't talk that way. Please."

"Say it one more time. Just once more."

"Say what?"

"That you're worried about me."

He nodded.

She smiled. From one moment to the next, her beaming

face returned. She reached for his hand and, with her other, turned down the light. She pressed against him. "Will you miss me?" she whispered, and later, "Will you miss *that?*"

# ═ 11 ═

SINCE THE TIME when the first sailors from the Old World had dropped anchor in the North River, lower Greenwich Street, together with its many narrow side streets, all of which led to the water, had made its residents rich. The shipfitters who had their workshops there provided whole fleets with hawsers, sailcloth, and anchors. In the houses of the auctioneers, more cotton and wheat were knocked down than in any other port in the world. And at night countless beerhalls saw the flow of money saved up by seamen during long months at sea.

But the golden age of sail was over, and on this July morning Warren Street was abandoned. There was nothing to recall the days of wealth. Many doors and windows had signs that read "Closed" or "For Sale." New York was quick to forget. Because it changed character rapidly, one of the wealthiest neighborhoods had turned into one of the ugliest. Now there were narrow old houses under whose soot-darkened roofs hundreds of people were crammed together. Streets sank into mud every time it rained, and lanterns shattered by the last storm remained broken for weeks.

This was where Poynder had settled when he came to New York in the late 1820s. Here his life had changed and his luck had turned, and here he still lived, at 68 Warren Street. The house was left over from the time when the street was still a canal fed by the North River when it flooded. The house was of red brick. The windows were leaded in black and there was a high, projecting ground floor and cement steps leading to the front door. The Dutch had built solidly to last. The house was still intact. It had even survived the Great Fire of 1835.

Loftus Poynder had bought the house cheaply, for a down payment of four hundred dollars on the total price of twelve hundred. By now the property was easily worth twenty times as much; and with the growth of the New York Railroad terminal, which lay immediately behind the house, its value would continue to rise. Still, living in the house, in that neighborhood, required a certain amount of obstinacy. Poynder had remained loyal to the house in spite of his wife's wishes, and he remained loyal to it now in spite of Justin Kramer, who for years had been pointing out that the owner of the New York Railroad could not possibly live on Warren Street, aside from the fact that the office space had long ago become inadequate. There were many reasons why Warren Street should be abandoned, but equally good ones for staying.

One of the latter was the French restaurant across the street from Poynder's house. The restaurant was called La Tricolore, after the two blue-white-and-red flags in the dining room which flanked a large painting of the battle on the Paris barricades. But to most of its customers it was known simply as the Frenchman's Café because of its owner, Captain Catull.

Year in and year out, summer and winter, at seven o'clock every morning Loftus Poynder had breakfast there. In the summer he sat outside at the table to the left of the entrance; in the winter he occupied one of the small round marble tables in the back room where seamen played billiards and dominoes all night long. In the mornings he was usually the only customer, and so it was today. Because of him, Captain and Madame Catull had to get out of bed. Madame complained daily about this strange friend of her husband's who was to blame for her not being allowed to get her beauty sleep and who was in no way prevented by this friendship from checking over his monthly bill with meticulous care. But say what she would, her husband was deaf to her complaints.

The two men had been friends since 1825, when they had met in Buffalo. Catull was one of the first captains on the newly opened Erie Canal. His appearance then was startling. He wore his blond hair long, and his hands were adorned with rings. An act of heroism had given him a certain reputation. There had been a fire on his passenger boat. While the flames ravaged the wheelhouse around him, he remained at the tiller and brought the boat to shore, saving all the passengers. His hands and arms still showed the scars.

Poynder and Catull joined forces soon after they met. They bought a boat and six mules to pull it. Soon they added more boats and mules. The Frenchman took care of the ships and animals while the Dutchman sought passengers and freight. It was a lucrative business but a difficult one. There were many competitors, men who loved nothing better than to force their way through the canal locks and who were not finicky about enticing passengers away from other boatowners. Then there were the winters, which often used up all the profits of the summer months. The canal usually closed down in October, when the water was drained. Then the boatmen sat in their hotel rooms in Buffalo with nothing to do.

Buffalo in the winter. In the days before the railroad, it was like a straggling army in winter quarters. Roads buried in the snow, the only transportation by sleds that were never on schedule, a port where ships were caught fast in a six-foot layer of ice. Endless winters. Sometimes it was May before the canal could be opened. After the third winter, which was so cold that the Hudson was frozen from Albany to Newburgh, a distance of more than eighty-five miles, Poynder and Catull had had enough and set out for New York.

They had to start all over again. They bought a second-hand boat. The division of labor was the same as before: Catull ran the boat on the Hudson, between New York and Albany, and Poynder looked for business. After four years they owned ten ships and after seven years, twenty. Calling it the Dutch-French Line, they dominated the Hudson, Long Island Sound, and New York Bay and were thinking about going into transatlantic trade. For many years it had been Captain Catull's dream to carry overseas passengers. But when the time came, he found he was tired of a hustler's life. He sold out to his partner and established La Tricolore on Warren Street, for, as he said, a man who has run a ship can do anything.

For Loftus Poynder, Catull's decision came at an opportune time, just when he discovered railroads. The years on the Erie Canal had reinforced his faith in good transportation routes. Cities had blossomed along the entire length of the canal. The fare from Buffalo to Albany had shrunk to a tenth of its former price. Farmers who used to have to feed their excess wheat to the pigs could now sell it. While merchants in New York still had their sights on the transatlantic trade and swore by shipping, Loftus Poynder was turning to railroads, learning how to build and maintain them from the ground up. For several years he held onto his ships, putting an agent in charge of the operation. Eventually, however, he sold all of them to John Tyler Matlock.

There was no breeze to rustle the tassels on the striped awnings over the windows of La Tricolore. The air was still. It had not cooled off during the night. Loftus Poynder, tapping the wall barometer, guessed that there would be no change in the weather for a least twenty-four hours.

Few of the Frenchman's patrons failed to tap the large barometer. Poynder had given it to his friend when he opened the restaurant. Catull lavished on it the same care he had once given his nautical instruments. When one of his customers claimed that a barometer just like it could be found in Hudnut's Drugstore on Broadway, he went there at once and satisfied himself that not only was his barometer larger and more splendid, but also that the other lacked the engraved signature of the famous Brussels instrument-maker.

Behind the door that led to the kitchen Poynder heard noises and for a moment was tempted to go in. A crackling kitchen stove—on his parents' farm the big one in the kitchen had been the heart of the household. On Warren Street the kitchen was a small, soot-blackened chamber, unused for years, and at Willowbeach the kitchen was too far away from the living quarters.

"Good morning." It was the clear voice of the Frenchman. "She'll be bringing your breakfast in a minute. Shall we sit outside?" Catull held his habitual glass of chilled claret.

"It's going to be hotter than yesterday," Poynder said.

Catull stopped to tap the barometer. "Weather forecaster—that would have been a good job for my old age. You would have invented the instruments, and I would have surrounded them with the mumbo jumbo without which people don't believe anything. It's going to be hot, eh? Well, it can't be too hot for me. I don't think I've got enough blood left in my veins."

As long as Captain Catull kept silent, he seemed old, older than Poynder. But as soon as he spoke, his rugged features became smooth and fresh. And when he smiled, he was once more the vibrant young man who got a second look even from women not in the habit of looking men over.

After he had sat down in the chair across from Poynder, he repeated, smiling, "I really don't think I've got enough blood left in my veins."

"I wouldn't be surprised. How can anybody start the day with chilled claret? Your blood can't help but turn to ice."

"I'll be going to the market later. Would you like anything special?"

Annie Catull, a short brunette, came in carrying a breakfast tray and set it in front of Poynder. Each morning she waited for a friendly word from him, and each time he said only, "Thank you, Madame Catull." She habitually wore dark dresses that hugged her neat little figure. After giving one last look at the tray to make sure nothing was missing, she said to her husband, "I thought you were in such a hurry to get to market."

Catull leaned back and looked up at her. Long ago he had stopped arguing. "Do me a favor and bring me the basket," he said. "I left it in the kitchen." He lifted the lid of the coffee pot and sniffed. "She knows how to roast coffee, that's for sure." He poured himself a cup. "All right, then, what do you feel like eating? Roast veal, roast pork; surely you're tired of those. I feel like something special today."

Poynder made an impatient gesture. "In this weather I don't eat much anyway."

"No one is asking you to eat *much*. Hors d'oeuvres, entremets, fish, roast, and the rear guard brought up by God knows what; I loathe big dinners. You can't accuse me of ever having put you through that kind of torture. A single tasty dish. If it were a foggy autumn day, I wouldn't be asking you. I'd make a pot-au-feu. We'd have a feast tonight you wouldn't soon forget. Do you know what a stomach binge is? For days after, you feel like a big sleepy snake." He shook his head. "The way you live— that's no way to live. Last night your lamps were lit until long after midnight. You need fresh air, exercise, activity. Sometimes you used to come for a game of billiards of an evening, at least. Really, I've never been sorry that I said good-bye to shipping. Always the same routine, that's what makes you a fossil." He nodded to himself. "I can understand Annie's perpetual churchgoing. It's the same thing. She can't stay in her kitchen all the time. A change of scenery—instead of garlic, the odor of lilies and incense. Instead of sailors, a pale, lisping priest. Change is what's missing in your life. I've been noticing it for some time. I don't like the way you look. Are you in trouble?"

"Why trouble?"

"I just thought. . . . After all, I keep track of the stock market, too. Your stocks have fallen considerably these last few weeks. I still own enough of them to care where they stand."

"Speak to Kramer. If you're worried, sell. Let him pay you what they were worth three weeks ago. I don't want you losing money."

"Don't be so touchy. That's just what I mean. What good does all your money do if you jump out of your skin at every little thing? Look at me. My first thought every morning is that I own enough never again to have to lift a finger. I don't have to get up and open up the place; I do it because I enjoy it. And whenever I pour myself a glass of claret, I think that to the end of my days I can drink as much of it as I want. And if I go to market now, that's not work but pleasure. When I see them bargaining and begrudging each other every penny, I'm glad all that's behind me. You can accumulate as much as you like, but one day it flies out the window anyway."

He looked over his shoulder into the restaurant to make sure his wife was out of earshot. "The day I pack it in, everything I've acquired goes up in smoke. It will start with the masses Annie orders for my soul. She'll throw everything into the priest's maw. The rest will go to a home for invalid seamen. And why not? If I outlive Annie, I won't do much better. I'll run through my money. It'll be gone so fast, it might as well have wings." He spread out both arms. "Believe me, wings."

Poynder laughed. "I'm trying to think how you'd have turned out if I'd never run into you. My penny-pinching forced you to become a rich man."

Catull sat up straight. "I've learned a lot from you, I admit it. But now it's my turn to teach you something."

Poynder pulled out his fat chrome-plated watch. "He should be along about now," he said. And indeed, the boy who sold newspapers in the neighborhood was just coming around the corner. He approached at a trot, the heavy bag around his neck banging with every step. Annie Catull who, like Loftus Poynder, waited for the newsboy every morning, took the pile of papers from him. She picked out the French newspaper for herself and put the others on the table between the two men. Each picked up one, and for a while there was no sound but the rustle of turning pages.

"You don't have to look any further," Poynder said after a while. "They fell another half-point."

Catull nodded absently. "Did you see this? They fished a man called Wilmurt out of the water. It's on the last page."

Loftus Poynder looked up sharply. "Thomas Wilmurt?"

"Yes, if it's the same one. They found him in the harbor near Pier Fourteen, dead as a doornail. According to the statement of a cabman, Wilmurt asked to be driven there. They don't know whether it was an accident or suicide. No next of kin. Motive unknown. That man who kept asking for you here, wasn't his name Wilmurt? Thomas Wilmurt?"

Loftus Poynder rose and folded his paper. Catull rose as well and picked up the basket his wife had put next to his chair. "What did he want with you anyway?" he said. "A very strange fellow. Now that I think about it, I must say that even then he looked like a candidate for suicide."

Poynder gave his friend a piercing look. "You never saw Wilmurt here. You do not know the man or his name, nor can you recall that he was ever here and asked for me. Do that for me."

Catull nodded. The two men crossed the street. In front of number 68 they came to a stop. The sun was already hot.

"Did you think of anything you'd like for dinner?" Catull asked. "No? Then I'll see if I can get some fresh shrimp. Shrimp salad on ice, that's the proper dish for this weather, and cheap this time of year too. All the fancy New Yorkers have left town." He looked at Poynder. "Is it something to do with Margaret? Are you worried about her?"

"Just worry about your shrimp." Poynder looked down the street toward the North River. "And as far as Thomas Wilmurt goes, I ask you again—forget him."

He knew that at this time of day he would not find Kramer in the office. His managing clerk's day began at the stock exchange. Poynder himself did not act as a broker. He had found it best to remain in the background. This sort of business did not suit him; it was too abstract, too rarefied. Kramer therefore took care of that function. He seldom appeared at the office on Warren Street before eleven o'clock, after the first call, and when he did arrive, he usually did not stop to take off his hat and coat but reported at once to Poynder's office on the third floor. Nevertheless, Poynder asked his secretary to send Kramer in as soon as he arrived. To send a messenger to the exchange did not seem advisable; it would be noticed, especially now, when rumors were already circulating about his confrontation with John Tyler Matlock. He had no choice but to be patient.

He walked slowly to the elevator at the end of the hall. At the sound of his ponderous tread, his employees bent more attentively over their desks. Loftus Poynder was a generous employer when it came to wages but a martinet about wasted working time.

The tiles in the corridor were as old as the house itself. Some were damaged, while others were loose. Many of the oak stair treads were also in need of replacement. The whole place needed renovating, especially Poynder's private rooms on the fourth floor. But Poynder refused to make any changes.

It was a different matter when it came to technical innovations. Over the years he had spent enough money on them to pay for a new building. The first improvement was a central-heating system. A network of air shafts and louvers had been inserted in the old brickwork, and the huge furnace in the cellar had been adapted to provide the whole house with hot air. A few years later Poynder had the heating plant converted to gas, and now he was thinking of attaching a hot-water storage tank to the furnace. He loved gadgets. His most expensive toy was his steam elevator. The first model, in the Latting Observatory, had been one of the marvels of the New York World's Fair of 1853. Poynder did not hesitate for a moment. He had the equipment installed in his house, though it necessitated new retaining walls. In all of New York there were only two other such elevators, one in E. V. Haughwout's new store on Broadway and the other in the Fifth Avenue Hotel, uptown. Poynder's elevator, which went from the parlor floor to the third floor, was usually out of commission, and the confidence of Poynder's staff did not increase with the hours of repairs. Finally, only Poynder used it. Strange, it always worked for him.

In his office Poynder, still standing, bent over the newspapers spread out on his desk and read the report of Wilmurt's death again. Then, as he always did when he was trying to sort out his thoughts, he paced.

His office consisted of two rooms. He had removed the folding doors dividing them. In the smaller room were his desk, bookcase, and safe. The second room was twice the size of the first. His drafting table near the window was strewn with plans, sketches, and drawing instruments. One wall was covered with the charts and timetables of the New York Railroad. The rest of the space was given over to the open shelves where Poynder piled what was dearest to his heart: miniature models of steam boilers, locomotives, cars, railway stations, freight sheds, steamboats, bridges; sample cards of screws, nuts, bolts, clamps which he had had developed especially for his lines; carpet samples for the floors of his parlor cars; models for folding and sliding doors; safety devices for windows, doors, and car couplings.

Poynder held all of these items in equal regard. They were part of his life. When he contemplated them, he got a warm feeling in his heart, a feeling that people could seldom awaken in him.

A locomotive whistle blew. He glanced at his watch. All the clocks on all the stations of his lines were set by his watch. Every day at noon, all the way up to Greenbush, the time was transmitted by telegraph. No other time was accepted on the New York Railroad.

Poynder went to the window that looked out on the back, from which he could see the end station of the River Line. The other line, the Harlem, had its terminal and depot at Fourth Avenue and Twenty-sixty Street. He opened the window. At this time of day there was always a great deal of activity. The sheds stood open. Men were working all over the tracks. A freight train was slowly being pulled down the street into the station. A signalman rode ahead of the locomotive, his horse picking its way between the tracks. It was the outrider's job to wave two red warning flags at every crossing.

As he watched the train, a frown crossed Poynder's face. How much longer would the city allow trains to pass through residential streets? The railroads were his life, his passion. The obsession had begun early, shortly after he moved to New York. He remembered it as if it were yesterday. An Englishman from Liverpool had docked at Pier 6. Catull had been given the job of taking on part of the freight, but there were problems because of its weight—a machine weighing more than six tons. The "machine" was a locomotive, one of the first to be imported. To Loftus Poynder it seemed like a miracle. He had personally supervised the loading onto the barge, and he did not leave its side during the trip up the Hudson. When, a few weeks later, the locomotive made its maiden trip along a short stretch of track, he went to see for himself. The trial run had been disappointing. The pinewood tracks could not handle the six-ton locomotive and its speed of eleven miles an hour. It jumped the tracks, overturned, and crashed.

Poynder still remembered what he charged for transporting the locomotive up the Hudson: ninety-three dollars and thirty-three cents. He had not kept any of his wife's letters, but he still had the bill of lading for the locomotive. It was a treasured relic, which he kept in his safe.

He could still hear the laughter of the spectators who witnessed that unsuccessful maiden run. He could still see the mocking newspaper headlines. All had agreed that those "machines" would never replace the horse. New Yorkers continued to believe in the waterways, and they continued to put their money on the clipper ships which were setting new speed records on each voyage abroad. But Poynder was one of the "fools" who believed in the machines. A vehicle that moved under its own power—the power of fire caught, tamed, and translated into motion. Movement that would pulse throughout the country. Tracks that would carry people everywhere. An earth no longer at the mercy of the elements but of man who would put a yoke on the elements and make them serve him.

His father had come to America to find a piece of land that would bear fruit. He had put seeds in the ground and produced wheat, barley, and oats. Basically Loftus Poynder had repeated this ritual when he laid his railroad tracks over the soil, except that his harvest took more than a spring and summer to ripen. And there was another difference: Loftus had no son to pass all this on to.

It took many years and many failures. Poynder had begun as a building contractor for railroads. There were winters when the frost tore the new tracks out of their sleepers and broke them. He had taken on building contracts on the basis of firm cost estimates, and he had lost a great deal of money when he underestimated the problems posed by roadbeds, subsoil, and bedrock. When he built his first line, the first five miles, the germ of the New York Railroad, it took him a year to complete the stretch from Twenty-sixth Street to Harlem because of the tunnel work through Murray Hill. And when he appealed for a subscription of shares, hardly anyone would entrust his money to such an uncertain enterprise. For many years the railroad's income was so modest that there was no thought of dividends. On the contrary, dunning notices from the bank piled up.

But Poynder had survived. He had attained his goal. His way had not always been straight; there were stains on the image of himself he liked to project. But he was thinking of John Tyler Matlock now, and of the fact that he, Poynder, had more at stake than his opponent, and that he must therefore be the stronger man.

Its brakes screaming, the train came to a halt. Poynder slammed the window shut. *John Tyler Matlock.* He thought again of the conversation at Willowbeach. No, he had not built his railroad just to lose it to that man. Poynder had never fought for people, but he would fight for his railroad.

# = 12 =

EVEN WHEN HE spoke, Justin Kramer formulated his sentences with the precision acquired when he was in the judiciary, drafting the legal documents. Loftus Poynder could not rid himself of the suspicion that Kramer's meticulous speech was intended primarily to keep his German accent from surfacing. Whatever it was, the precision indicated important traits in Kramer's character: his striving for perfection, his desire not to be conspicuous, and his ability to preserve the proper forms at all times.

This morning he arrived at Poynder's office earlier than usual. Although he had rushed up two flights of stairs, his entrance was calm and measured, and although he was the bearer of bad tidings, he gave no indication of it. He carried with him a stack of morning papers. When he saw the newspaper lying on Poynder's desk, its back page uppermost, he said, "So you've seen it."

"Captain Catull called it to my attention. I probably wouldn't have gotten beyond the business section. It's only a brief notice. Do the other papers give it much play?"

Kramer put the newspapers on the desk. "All of them are brief. Without exception they play the story down. Not a single paper refers to Wilmurt's earlier role in the shipping business. There are a dozen suicides every day, and his is simply one of them. It looks like collusion."

"That's not our worry." Poynder was sitting behind his desk. He always kept the writing surface bare except for his watch. Now he took the newspapers and stuffed them into the rack on the wall.

"Do you believe it was an accident?" Kramer asked.

"Does it matter? We didn't know Thomas Wilmurt. He was never here. He never looked us up. He never existed for us. And now he does not exist at all."

"And his records? I wonder what became of the documents."

"I don't believe they would have done us any good."

"This outcome comes very conveniently for John Tyler Matlock." Kramer sat down in the chair facing the desk. "Matlock is lucky—or he makes certain that he is lucky."

"John Tyler Matlock told me what would happen when we talked at Willowbeach. When he says war, he means war. He has always begun his wars without formalities, without diplomatic declarations, without preliminary skirmishes. I was prepared. How is the market today?"

"Unchanged," Kramer replied.

"Still bad, then."

"The afternoon call will be even worse. We'll go down by more than half a point."

"What's happened?"

"An accident outside the Woodlawn station. Jones came to my apartment to report it." Philo Jones was in charge of the technical aspects of the New York Railroad.

"The early train?"

"It was involved in the accident. It had just pulled out of Woodlawn when a train came from the siding and rammed it. The cause was probably a switch thrown the wrong way."

"Were both trains carrying passengers?"

"No, thank goodness. The one from the siding was empty except for a few cleaners on the cars. The Woodlawn train tried to stop. The bad break was that in the collision one of the stoves in the empty train tipped over and the car caught fire. There were no fatalities, only a few wounded. One man sustained burns in putting out the fire."

"We must speak with the firm. There has to be a way to fasten the stoves more securely. We should install some kind of device to prevent—" Poynder stopped. "A lit stove in an empty train? At this time of year?"

Kramer nodded. "And the reporters were on the scene at once. Jones is at the site of the accident now. He's questioning people, but I can tell you now that he won't learn a thing. I would take an oath that Matlock is behind it. But until we have proof. . . . There have been too many accidents lately."

They had begun soon after Poynder returned from Willowbeach. A damaged telegraph line which interrupted the connection between two stations; a fire in a freight shed. They were ordinary, unavoidable accidents, but they did not usually occur at this rate. Never before had the pins of the tracks loosened within the length of a single mile, derailing a number of trains; never before had the dishes served in the dining cars left passengers nauseated. Equally odd was the prompt appearance of newspaper reporters at the scene of every accident. Each time the headlines grew larger, and editorials concerning the "scandalous conditions" on the New York Railroad had begun to appear.

"We'll feel the effects in the market today," Kramer said. Poynder played with his watch.

"Three weeks ago, before your conversation with Matlock, our stock was listed at ninety-one and three-quarters," Kramer pointed out. "Yesterday we were down to seventy-eight and a half. A loss of almost fifteen points in less than a month. And I see no end to it. Just wait until late today."

"This is his war. He told me."

On impulse Kramer got up and went to the window. He opened it a bit and then closed it again. As he came back to the desk, he pulled out a white handkerchief and wiped his hands. In his youth, in his parents' house, it had been printer's ink that bothered him; but here in Poynder's office, it was the soot. In spite of the fact that locomotives were no longer allowed this far downtown, there was still soot. Maybe it had lain there for twenty years, he thought. *News from the Old World* was the translation of the newspaper his father, a German immigrant, published in the cellar of their house on Second Avenue. He had brought the fonts with him, and he clung to them as strongly as he did to his native tongue. Justin Kramer had never understood why his father emigrated in the first place. He refused to speak English. He was interested only in the people in his own neighborhood, which was known as "Little Germany"—people like himself, who wanted to read in German what was happening back home and who used handsome, well-formulated German sentences in their newspaper announcements of baptisms and funerals. Justin had never seen his father with clean hands. No matter how carefully he washed them, the skin, and especially the cuticles, retained the patina of printer's ink. He had his mother to thank for not having to attend the German school. She sent him to the best private school in New York. There he had become an American with such a vengeance that now he could not pronounce his name correctly in German. He was determined one day to replace the K with a C. To be an American, a New Yorker, was the motive behind all his actions. It was why he lived on elegant Washington Square. Little Germany was only a few blocks away, less than a thousand yards; yet it had ceased to exist for him. His world was the New York of Washington Square.

Loftus Poynder had not missed Kramer's use of his handkerchief. He knew Kramer was not at ease in the house on Warren Street, and he was also aware of his ambition. When Justin Kramer first set foot in the Warren Street house, he was an employee of the tax office. He had come with instructions to check Poynder's books. The two men had fallen into conversation. Kramer let Poynder know that certain laws could be circumvented and had hinted at effective ways to go about it. Poynder promptly hired him. Kramer was paid a handsome salary, twice as much as he could have earned in his own law office. During the years he had worked for Poynder, Kramer had saved enough so that his name was included in the 1864 edition of Moses Beach's *Biography of Wealth,* which listed only those with an estate valued at more than a hundred thousand dollars. Moreover, Kramer was still young; he had not yet attained his goal. It was not enough for him to be Poynder's right-hand man. He had wanted to become his son-in-law, as well. After Margaret married Craig, Poynder knew he could not hold the clerk forever. Kramer had political ambitions and was flirting with the idea of a senate seat. Poynder knew of these plans, but at the moment he needed Kramer more than ever.

Poynder resumed the conversation. "I'd like to hear Jones's report for myself. Leave word at his office."

Kramer nodded. "He'll come on his own. You know him. He's one of those who are always blaming themselves. You should have seen him. He was as upset as if it were really his fault—though ever since the first accident he has had every available man in the field."

"Then we have to assign more men to him. We must stop these plots. Have him post a man every mile along the road."

"To do that, we need three hundred more men, who must be given special pay—at least a dollar and a half a day."

Poynder traced invisible lines on the surface of his desk. "We'll pay them. Let's start with two hundred men."

"Even that comes to eighteen hundred dollars a week. And our income is decreasing. We lost a major part of the Empire State freight to Hudson shipping, just as Matlock promised you. But more crucially, we are losing passengers because of the accidents. By the end of the month, I calculate, we will be down twenty points. Admittedly, July is always a bad month, but this one is going to be the worst in years. Not only are our shares dropping, so is our income."

"We won't allow ourselves to panic," Poynder said, still tracing invisible lines. "The market losses won't hurt us as long as Matlock doesn't buy. He isn't buying, is he?"

"Not so far."

"I'm sure he hopes to get in more cheaply still," Poynder noted drily. He had risen and was pacing the length of both rooms.

"I'm sorry to say it, but there's still more bad news," Kramer went on.

Poynder was smiling. "Go ahead. Today is a good day for me. I can't tell you why, but I've felt it ever since I woke up."

"I don't know if you'll feel the same when I get through. What Matlock has done so far is only the beginning. His next move will hit us hard. He's now attempting to gain entry to New York with his own lines."

"His old tactic. An empty threat. He doesn't dream of actually building a line. It would take too long."

"I know for a fact that he's applying for a concession."

"And how does he plan to get into the city?"

"By way of Broadway, to Twenty-sixth Street."

Poynder shook his head. "Broadway is sacred to New Yorkers. Besides, if a concession were to be granted, the Common Council is on our side. Where did you hear that?"

"From Vibard personally. He informed me officially, as it were, that an application from John Tyler Matlock is under consideration at City Hall. Matlock is offering a yearly royalty of a hundred thousand, or one million in cash, in return for a concession for fifteen years."

For a moment Poynder's immovability had the effect of the calm before the storm, but then he merely said, "Matlock seems to have an agent on the Common Council who is every bit as reliable as Vibard. We made the same offer, didn't we?"

"Except that John Tyler's official offer is secured by considerable sums in bribery. That element was missing from our offer."

"If that's all that's worrying Vibard, of course we'll pay that, too. I have no intention of being more moral than the world I live in."

"Would you go as high as two hundred thousand?"

"Two hundred thousand. Matlock is really determined. What does Vibard think?"

"Sums like that don't arise every day, even in the Common Council. The gentlemen can already feel the money in their pockets."

"That means they will stick with us if we make it worth their while."

"The matter was initiated very cleverly. Langdon Matlock invited all the council members to his house. He made the offer in his father's name, not surreptitiously but out in the open, in the presence of the entire council, so none of them had a chance to get more for himself. For once, even the little fish have a chance to profit."

Poynder had returned to his desk. "I told you about my conversation with Matlock," he said. "Afterward, I thought for a long time whether my reaction might not have been too subjective after all. I even thought that it would have been better to let you conduct the negotiations. But now I can only say that I'm glad the time has come." He warded off Kramer's question. "Let me think."

Matlock's tactics had to be taken seriously, not so much because the concession might be awarded to him, but because it had revealed a vulnerable spot. The New York Railroad was not as free of problems as Poynder had represented it to Matlock. There were already too many railroads in the city. Everyone knew it and, until now, everyone had closed his eyes to it. Other industrialists had followed Poynder's example. Over the years rail lines had been laid along Fourth, Sixth, Seventh, and Eighth avenues. They were purely intracity lines, some of them licensed only as horse cars, but even so, the trains blocked all other traffic and represented an increasing danger to pedestrians at every crossing.

Poynder was not blind to these events. He had not forgotten that last winter an aroused crowd had ripped up the tracks of the railroad along the Bowery. He knew of the citizens' committee that had been formed to banish freight and passenger traffic from the center of the city. The day was near when only one solution would remain: put the railroads underground or on elevated tracks. Poynder saw this clearly; he was prepared. In his safe were plans for a line beneath Broadway, to Thirty-fourth Street and north from there, under Sixth Avenue to Central Park. He had also secured the patent for an elevated line. This development was unavoidable. The demand for it would grow. To be forearmed, he had to hold on to his capital and increase it. But how could he do so if, thanks to Matlock, his stock dropped, his revenues fell, and he was forced to sink two hundred thousand dollars into the Common Council? He had never discussed this fear with anyone, not even Kramer. He must not show weakness. Any mistake in this struggle counted double, and weakness was the most serious mistake. He would be defeated if Matlock so much as suspected his soft spot.

The striking mechanism of his watch began to whirr. As if it had activated his own machinery, Poynder rose and went to one of the rear windows. "The eleven o'clock is late," he said. He stepped back and consulted the timetable. "Thompson again."

Kramer was silent. At times like these he did not understand Poynder. "What are we going to do?"

"Most important, we need time," Poynder said. "We must drag out this business as long as we possibly can."

"Vibard wants me to tell him what position we're going to take."

"I knew this was going to be a good day," Poynder said. "Tell Vibard we want City Hall to take Matlock's money."

"You want them to take the money?" Kramer did not know what to make of Poynder's words and his high good humor. "Does that mean you're giving in?"

"It means that I'm going to take John Tyler Matlock for a ride." Poynder was beaming. "He set his own trap. And I'll see to it that it shuts on him. He's going to have a bloody paw!"

"I don't understand."

"Matlock has always boasted that he can get along without lawyers. In this case a legal adviser could have given him valuable counsel." He had gone to the shelves behind the desk, pulled out a white pamphlet, riffling the pages until he found what he was looking for. "Here it is. The bill was passed three years ago. Listen. 'The assignment of concessions by the City of New York requires the consent of the state legislature. Concessions assigned without such state consent are null and void.' " He handed the pamphlet to Kramer. "See for yourself. It's watertight."

"I'm familiar with the statute. I should have thought of it myself. I should have remembered it immediately. And Vibard didn't think of it either. . . ."

"Who knows? Perhaps he didn't want to remember. For us it's a good thing all around. I very much hope City Hall will go through with it. Let them take Matlock's money. Let John Tyler pay. Let him rejoice in his concession. I don't begrudge him his triumph for a few days or weeks. I've been hoping he would make a mistake, but I didn't expect him to make it so soon."

"Then you want me to tell Vibard that the council should accept Matlock's offer?"

"You seem to have some misgivings."

"Not misgivings exactly. I'm still not over the fact that it did not occur to me. I'll personally go to Albany to make sure the gentlemen there don't forget what laws they've passed."

"The important thing is, Matlock made a mistake." Poynder ran both hands through his hair, a gesture that was habitual with him. "How you tell Vibard is your business. It should not be hard, given the expectation of pocketing two hundred thousand dollars for doing nothing. And Matlock will take care not to ask for the money back. Vibard must insist only on getting payment *in advance* from Matlock. Wait." Poynder was smiling. "Hint to Vibard that the concession is probably worth much more to Matlock and that it might be possible to get a quarter-million out of him. He's so eager for the concession that he will probably come across with the money."

Poynder stuck a piece of paper between the pages of the pamphlet to mark the place and put it back on the shelf. The two men were silent. Then Poynder said, "What is important is for us to gain time and to make sure that our real plans do not become public knowledge. Vibard and the others must not suspect our intentions. Let him believe that, for the present, we don't have the strength. Our advantage in this case depends on everyone else's ignorance.

Understand me, Kramer—we mustn't alert them. They must stay in the dark a little while longer. The longer we can drag this business out, the better. City Hall must play hard to get as long as possible. Let them leave Matlock dangling; that's all right. Let them have misgivings. As long as Matlock is counting on the concession, he might leave us alone elsewhere."

"How to string people along—that's one thing they do well at City Hall. They have had a good deal of practice."

"We must prepare ourselves for one event, though," Poynder said. "For the moment when Albany revokes the concession. Until then the shares of the Empire State will climb as it becomes known that Matlock has been given the concession. But as soon as the concession is revoked and that becomes public knowledge, his stock will drop so fast that our market losses will be nothing compared to his. And when that time comes, *we* will buy. Get ready for it. Engage reliable middlemen. I give you a free hand in the matter of commissions, too."

"Matlock has a solid majority. I have informed myself because you wanted to know. He himself holds about eighty thousand shares; his three daughters and his son Craig together have twenty-eight thousand. Given the total sum of two hundred and fifty thousand shares issued by the Empire State, he's not far short of forty-five percent."

"We'll buy just the same. Who knows, some good might come of it. I've learned a great deal from Matlock. And I'm about to learn some more, Kramer. He *has* to be able to bring his Empire State into the city, and I, Kramer, I *must* break out of my isolation within the city. I have to grant him that much. He saw it clearly. The future lies out there in the West, in the major cross-country lines. Whether I want to or not, I must press him hard. I have to attack him on his home ground. There's no other way. Until now I have been afraid of him; but we must see to it that he grows afraid of us."

Kramer stood with his head lowered.

"You are skeptical?" Poynder asked.

"I have only one reservation. It would be the first time Matlock has lost."

"And you think he will win this time as well?"

"I have to tell you. The proposition he made you at Willowbeach wasn't bad, in my opinion. The merger of the Empire State and the New York railroads would have brought nothing but advantages to both partners."

"John Tyler is no one's partner."

"After all, the only point at issue was the position of treasurer. Perhaps an arrangement could have been found even in that. The position could have been shared by two people, Sydenham and myself."

"It occurred to me. But John Tyler Matlock doesn't know how to share. And I—I can't do it either."

"It may be a long struggle."

"The longer, the better; I'm fifteen years younger than he is."

"He has sons."

Poynder tried to hide his pain. It was a sore subject, and the older he grew, the more it hurt. Often, when he heard Kramer's footsteps, when Kramer appeared in the doorway, he was reminded that he could have sons Kramer's age. Just as Kramer denied his father, they too might deny him—not his money but his origins. Perhaps they would show little interest even in his railroads. But they would be his sons, all the same. "Aren't you overestimating Langdon Matlock? Or are you thinking of Craig?"

When Kramer did not reply, Poynder asked, "I take it you still have not gotten over the fact that he married my daughter?" The topic had not been broached between them before, but it had to arise sooner or later. Perhaps it was a good thing it was happening now. "How can I put it?" Poynder said. "To appeal to Margaret, you might have been anything except this: a man who works for her father, who shares his interests, who devotes himself to these. That alone made her reject you completely. With Craig Matlock, she knew from the outset that I would be against it. I believe that was reason enough for her to marry him."

"As far as I'm concerned, the matter is finished," Kramer said. "But since you brought it up, why did you not forbid her at the time, if you were so opposed?"

"I know Margaret, and John Tyler Matlock apparently knows his son Craig. Otherwise, we would both have said no."

"Forgive me, but I always saw that marriage as a kind of peace treaty."

A melancholy smile flitted across Poynder's face. "You're not the only one who saw a political ploy in the alliance. But wait until you have daughters of marriage-able age. Once they make up their minds, the father's wishes don't count, not nowadays. Girls are no longer raised to be obedient. I don't consider that progress. How can they become good wives if they haven't learned to obey?"

"How do you think Craig will act now? It might be important."

"I don't know my son-in-law well enough to speculate." Poynder wanted to change the subject. "Let us wait and see. I have no high hopes in that quarter."

Kramer rose. "If you need me, I will be in the office for a few more hours. This afternoon I will be going back to the exchange."

"Would you like to have lunch with me? I don't know the menu exactly, but Captain Catull felt it was time for something special."

"Many thanks, but I have a lot of work piled up."

Poynder briefly rested his hand on Kramer's shoulder. "Don't work too hard," he said. "I need you. Afterward, when it's all over, we will talk about your plans. You'll see, we will win this fight." He walked Kramer to the door. "You won't forget to send Jones in to see me."

Kramer was glad Poynder's last statement had saved him from having to reply to the previous one. "I'll meet with Vibard tonight," he said.

Poynder nodded. "It will be a rude awakening for Matlock. It'll have cost him a quarter of a million dollars, and then he will know he finally has the war he wanted."

# ═ 13 ═

A MAN WHO had spent the greater part of his life outdoors at manual labor, Loftus Poynder could not stand being cooped up for long. The beauties of nature meant nothing to him. The only notice he took of the changing seasons

was through the changes in the timetables. Good or bad
weather was about the same to him as market indicators
for rising or falling numbers of passengers. He was drawn
outside because that was where his railroads were. It was a
compulsion. When it overcame him, he had difficulty holding back.

If he did not have sufficient time for an extended inspection of the lines, he at least made the rounds of the
Warren Street station. He could always find a pretext. He
looked over the new bookkeeping system for the freight
lists; he spot-checked the registers at the ticket windows;
he asked the workmen at the baggage dispatch how the
new labels were working out. Simply marking the travelers' valises with chalk, as was customary on all the lines,
had led to too many complaints. While the other lines denied responsibility, taking the attitude that lost or mis-
placed luggage was an inevitable risk a traveler had to
take, Poynder had ordered some special labels, in duplicate, which could be affixed to a piece of luggage, while the
duplicate label was given to the traveler along with his
ticket.

There was nothing on his railroad that did not interest
him. Men who worked at his other depots felt sorry for the
poor guys who were forced to work at Warren Street under Poynder's nose.

For the ambitious, however, Warren Street was the
ideal springboard for advancement with the New York
Railroad. The best example was Philo Jones, who had
started as a simple section hand and today was general inspector of the whole railroad. There was also Decker, the
wagon inspector. For the first three months of his employment at Warren Street, the newly immigrated Austrian
was put to cleaning the train toilets. When Poynder spoke
to him on one of his inspection tours, Decker suggested an
improvement in the flushing mechanism—the first of many
improvements Decker was to devise. Now, three years
later, he was inspector of all the wagons. No new parlor
car or cattle car was either ordered or put in service without his approval. It had been Decker who had urged the
acquisition of the four new cars delivered that morning
from West Point. He had been waiting for Poynder to appear in the yards.

In speaking with Kramer, Poynder had actually forgotten the delivery of the new cars. But when he recalled

it, he was delighted to have a good reason for leaving his office. His hands crossed behind his back, as a sign of his good mood, Poynder strode toward the new cars, accompanied by Decker.

All the New York Railroad cars were a brilliant carmine red. The four newly arrived cars, however, were painted a dull brown to distinguish them from the rest.

"They're not exactly handsome," Poynder said. "The color turned out even uglier than in the sample. What do you call this shade of brown?"

"There's no name for it," Decker said proudly. "But the paint contains a dye that will repel any kind of vermin."

Poynder shook his head. "I've seen hyenas in the Bowery Menagerie that were the same color. Is that what inspired you?"

"God knows, the cars aren't beautiful, but that's why they cost only half as much. Our main concern was to get by as cheaply as possible so we can lower the fare."

They entered one of the cars. Poynder went through the compartments, checking the carrying capacity of the luggage nets and the steadiness of the coat hooks. "Everything seems in order," he said. "Except the ventilation. Can you smell it?"

"Anybody who takes this train will probably have just come from steerage on the transatlantic ships. I myself . . ."

"Could it be the paint that causes the stink?" Poynder said. "Open a few windows."

"They can't be opened. They're built in." Decker seemed as proud of this fact as he was of the ugly brown paint. "We agreed on that, to cut costs. Besides, we know our customers. Some want the windows open during the ride, others want them closed. It leads to arguments."

"I'd smash a window," Poynder said, "if I had to travel a mile in one of these cars. The passengers must have fresh air. Haven't the ventilation domes been raised?"

"I know, an effective dome would have to be at least a foot high," Decker said. "But these cars give us only eight inches of leeway on the Harlem River bridge. Back to our old problem. And it's impossible to build lower cars. The bridge crossings would have to be raised. No one thought of it at the time."

Poynder had opened a door. "Only one toilet to a car?"

"Yes. The train makes plenty of stops."

"Tomorrow morning I'll ride out to the Morris Bridge. I want to see for myself." He thought of Matlock's prediction that City Hall would demand that he raise the bridge. "Another thing, Decker. You know about the recent spate of accidents. Something else happened this morning. How are people taking it?" When Decker hesitated, he added, "Speak up, let's hear it."

"You honestly want to know what they think?"

"I wouldn't be asking you if I didn't."

"Well, they think of themselves first. There are two camps. Some are afraid of going to work. The others—well —they see a good side to it."

"A good side?"

"You asked me. They think that now you need all the hands you can get, and that means you won't cut their wages."

"Why would I cut their wages?"

"There's talk that the whole thing is a put-up job between the New York Railroad and the Empire State. The men have their own ideas, that's all. If you don't mind my saying something else. . . ."

"Go ahead."

"Be careful when you take on new men. The army was a good hiding place for all kinds of riffraff, and a lot of them are looking for a new burrow. I have no idea how to weed them out, but if I were you, I'd look the new ones over very carefully."

They had walked the length of the car and came out on the back platform. "In any case," Poynder said, "I thank you very much. I would like an official report concerning the brake mechanism this time." As he slid the car door closed, he looked again at the compartment. "Automatic ventilation. The man who invents that will be on Easy Street. There'll always be trouble with windows. But an automatic ventilation system—something to carry off the old air and let in new—someone should invent that."

They went down the steps. Poynder's hand rested on the rail, which was made of heavy iron rods, as was the fence enclosing the platform. "It looks like a cage for wild animals," he said.

"Until people stop jumping on and off moving trains, those railings are necessary."

"But must they be quite so sturdy? Why don't you have

a talk with the West Point factory. Maybe they can come up with something a little less ponderous."

Decker had stepped back two paces to contemplate the new cars. He was not offended by Poynder's reference to hyenas; he liked it. *Hyenas*—perhaps the cars should be called that. He was distracted by the sudden appearance of Justin Kramer, who could barely be stopped by two workmen from walking through a spewing jet of water that was being sprayed on a locomotive.

"Mister Kramer is looking for you," Decker pointed out. "I'll take care of the brake control as soon as the other cars arrive. They should be here tomorrow."

Kramer never set foot in the yards unless there was a crisis. "Is there no end to the bad news today?" Poynder asked.

Kramer had come to a halt just in time. "I don't know if it's bad," he said, pointing over his shoulder at the house. "You have a visitor."

Poynder, who had difficulty seeing at a distance, narrowed his eyes. He could not recognize the figure outlined against the bare gray wall of the building at once. The man was wearing a white suit.

"Did you know your son-in-law was in New York?" Kramer said.

"Craig? He wants to see me? Has he been waiting long?"

"I was not sure that you wanted to see him." Kaplan hesitated. "I told him I would look for you."

Poynder smiled at Kaplan. "Is there any reason why I shouldn't see him?"

"In the present situation you cannot be too careful. If you want me to be present. . . ."

Poynder did not reply. He raised his hand and gestured for Craig to join him. The back yard of the Poynder house had gradually become the repository for superfluous railroad equipment. The wheels of the heavily laden carts had left deep ruts in the ground, but Craig stepped over them as though he were familiar with every rill and hollow.

"This is a surprise," Poynder said. "You're back? When did you arrive? You know Justin Kramer?"

The men shook hands. Craig looked relaxed and self-assured, while Kramer seemed ill at ease. "The agent from

Aetna is waiting in my office," Kramer said. "He wants to discuss passenger insurance."

"Listen to what he has to say," Poynder said. "I'll agree to it only if they have come up with a reasonable suggestion. Passengers must be able to take out a policy when they buy their tickets. The procedure must be simple. Otherwise we won't sign a contract."

"Don't worry; I'll get them to come around." With a slight bow toward Craig, Kramer left.

"What's bothering him? Does he have a grudge against me?"

"There are days when he has a grudge against everyone," Poynder said. "When did you get back? Does Margaret know?"

Craig was looking at the station and yards. "Everything here has grown larger. It's bursting at the seams."

"Four years is a long time. And in my business each year is like two. I had no idea you were in New York."

Craig was watching a tender being shunted to the coal dump to take on fuel. He was not trying to avoid his father-in-law's questions; he was genuinely interested in the station. "Anthracite?"

Poynder nodded. "We use it exclusively. It comes from Pennsylvania. Costs us ten percent more the ton, but, in return, it gives us thirty percent more power than bituminous."

"Have you converted to the new metal tracks?" Craig said.

"For most of the road; but the trouble is in the roadbed. That's where we're stuck. Engineers today aren't interested in that sort of thing. They care only about the machines. Speed, that's all they care about, them and the passengers as well." He looked at Craig. "To be honest, I did not really believe that you would take my advice and join the Construction Corps. You've learned a lot."

"It wasn't very much—how much dynamite it takes to blow up the boiler of a locomotive; the quickest way of burning up storage sheds or putting telegraph lines out of commission or derailing trains. That was what we did, more or less. But is that kind of knowledge very practical?"

Loftus Poynder could not help himself. "For John Tyler Matlock, it is extremely practical. He could make good use of your training." Poynder fell silent, angry at himself for having said so much.

"I heard about your fight," Craig said. "But that's not why I'm here. I need some information. Could we go to your office?"

"If you like." Again Poynder was annoyed with himself.

Craig had not at first thought of looking up his father-in-law. But Joe Cristadoro arrived, out of breath, with the morning newspapers and showed him the article about Wilmurt. He decided to take a later train to Willowbeach and to see Langdon first. But as always on Fridays, Langdon was in Albany. Craig collected his stock certificates from Sydenham and took them, together with the envelope containing Wilmurt's material, to the bank, where he rented a safe-deposit box. Then, as he bought a ticket to Southport, it occurred to him to go to see Loftus Poynder, since Poynder had once been in the shipping business. Craig was sure that Wilmurt was not unknown to him.

But now, in the office, he hesitated to put the question. They sat across from each other, the desk between them. Craig searched in vain for his favorite cigars in the pockets of the white linen suit he had put on in anticipation of Willowbeach. His father-in-law would not have any. Since Poynder had given up smoking, he kept his house free of smoking paraphernalia. "I won't keep you long," he said. "I only stopped in for a moment. I'm on my way to Willowbeach."

Poynder indicated a white strip of paper on his desk. "The road has been cleared. There was a brief interruption of traffic because of an accident."

"When was the last time you went there?"

"Three weeks ago. You're looking for something to smoke? Would you like me to send across the street?"

"It doesn't matter. It would only annoy you."

"I don't know. I've thought about it. Maybe I'll take it up again. Catull gave me a lecture this morning. . . . I'll send for some for both of us." He went to the door, called a clerk, gave his order, and returned to the desk. "So you're going today. Not that Margaret has complained. She never speaks to me about such matters. But I get the feeling she's very anxious for your return."

Craig would have liked to avoid the subject but it gave him time to gather his thoughts. "How is she? Did she spend much time in New York? Warren Street must be heaven for the boys."

"Do you think so? Margaret is of a different opinion. She feels at home at Willowbeach. That's where she's put down roots—and Joshua and Sinclair are turning more and more into true Matlocks."

"They're growing up in the shadow of Matlocks."

"Yes. I only saw them for two minutes, but when it comes to railroads, they always side with me. There was a fistfight between Joshua and Lance Lunden about it. If you want to give them pleasure—and you have time—stop in at Gillott's on Broadway. They always have the latest English toys. That will show you how the times are changing. A few years ago boats and steamships were all the rage. Now railroads are in vogue."

"Do you ever talk about anything else?" The joking words betrayed the sympathy Craig felt for his father-in-law just then. That it was possible at any time to feel anything for Poynder surprised Craig. He had not forgotten the negotiations over his marriage. "You are, and remain, a proper railroad fool."

The clerk returned with the cigars. Craig lit Poynder's. The harmonious atmosphere that had prevailed between them in the yards began to return, but Poynder was on his guard. He must not forget that he was talking to a Matlock. And one of the Matlock's dangerous weapons was their power to win people over to their side. That was how they had won Margaret, and that was how they had won his grandsons.

"Why did you marry Margaret? Surely it was not romantic love."

Craig blew thin threads of smoke through a minute-opening between his lips and watched intently as they floated straight ahead before gradually dissipating. "If you had asked why I didn't marry Gloria Hamilton, in spite of her million-dollar dowry, the answer would have been easier. No Matlock has ever married for romantic love, I'm afraid."

"Why, then?"

"Stop, please. Be glad that I did marry her. No one else would have had the courage to become your son-in-law. Perhaps that's what attracted me. Not even your marriage contract deterred me. Shall I quote? 'That he, Craig Matlock, now and in the future, shall make no claim on the estate of his wife, and that as long as he may live, he shall contribute the sum of two hundred dollars per month to the common household.' "

"Do you hold that against me?"

"Of course not. Why should I? The contract has some advantages, too. Suppose I make a huge fortune of my own and maintain a splendid establishment. I need never contribute more than my two hundred dollars." He laughed.

Poynder had leaned back in his chair. He was enjoying the cigar. Suddenly it gave him great pleasure to think of lunch at the Frenchman's Café. "You said you had heard about the struggle between your father and myself."

"Yes."

"During the war your father made some easy money with his roads, and he doesn't want that situation to change."

"But what have you to reproach others with? Did you act any differently? Didn't you make money? Should I remind you of the railroad stocks in the South? The summer before Lincoln was elected, you held a great many of them. And you got rid of them, down to the last piece of paper. Not because your love for the railroads had suddenly cooled, but because someone gave you a tip that all southern railway shares would fall with Lincoln's election. You sold at a profit, while others were ruined."

"My compliments. Your memory is first rate."

"I assume yours is also. They say you know everyone who works for you. Do you know a man named Fuller?"

"Fuller?"

"George Fuller. His father works for you, as do two brothers. They put in a ten-hour day, and you pay them two dollars for it. Or have you already begun to pay less because now, with the end of the war, there is a surplus of workers? Not that I'm outraged. I only meant that you run your business much as my father does. I cannot get it through my head that you two still insist on quarreling. Why can't you reach an agreement? Surely it would be advantageous for both of you."

"Your father thinks me a headstrong old man."

"Aren't you?"

Again they were united in a feeling of closeness and understanding, and again the sensation triggered a defensive reaction in Poynder.

"I once trusted your father's word," he said. "It was

once too often." He put out his cigar. "What brings you here?"

Craig regretted that he had not asked about Wilmurt immediately, when they were down in the yards. Now he wondered whether he should bring up the subject at all. But he knew that his father would either refuse to tell him anything or give him only the sketchiest information, and intuition told him that it would be good to know everything there was to know about Wilmurt.

"I have a question for you." Craig had noticed the stack of newspapers on the shelf behind Poynder's desk. He reached for one and folded it to the page with the report of Wilmurt's death. "This man here. What do you know about him?"

Poynder pulled the paper closer, as if he were unfamiliar with the story. "Thomas Wilmurt," he said at length. "Many people in this part of town knew him. At one time he was a very important person. Why are you asking?"

"He was in shipping?"

Poynder nodded. "When the war came, it was important to know Wilmurt, especially if you had too many ships or ones that weren't quite seaworthy. But why do you ask?"

"It's sort of a personal matter. A friend from the war. He died on a ship Wilmurt sold."

"Wilmurt was only the go-between."

"Whose?"

"To know that, it is necessary to understand the background."

"That is precisely why I'm asking."

"The period just before the war was a bad time for ship-owners," Poynder said. "When I sold my ships to your father in the late forties—not quite of my own free will— it seemed to many people that I made a big mistake. Trade was booming, and it was influenced even more by the gold fields in California. Every ship was booked for months in advance. But overnight there was a change: no freight, no passengers. Those were thin times in New York harbor—until the war."

"And Wilmurt? What did he have to do with it?"

"The war was a godsend for the shipowners. Until then, they had been struck with a lot of useless ships. They couldn't even sell them abroad, because they had been built too poorly and hastily. Many had been nailed together anyhow. But then the war came. The War Department was looking for ships to transport troops south—lots of them, and immediately. The war was the shippers' big chance."

Craig nodded. His ability to listen was one of his better gifts. He looked steadily at Poynder, who had not yet mentioned anything that was of real interest to him. He had already understood from Wilmurt's documents how such sales of ships were handled. But he let Poynder go on.

"The War Department appointed a man to take over the purchase of ships for the Union. A government employee was out of the question, because any chance of influence or bribery was to be eliminated. They were also looking for someone from the shipping trade. The choice fell on the largest shipowner in New York, a man who had already proven his patriotism as soon as the war broke out by making the government a gift of one of his ships. That man was John Tyler Matlock. Do you want me to go on?"

Craig nodded. This, too, he had deduced from Wilmurt's papers, though most of the sales invoices merely carried the notation, "Commission passed on to J.T.M.," followed by the sum.

"Your father accepted the post. You can imagine how the other shipowners courted him. But everyone who wanted to see him was told to apply to Thomas Wilmurt."

"How did my father happen to pick Wilmurt, of all people?"

Poynder pushed back his chair. "Perhaps this is the point where I should stop. The matter is over and done with. And Thomas Wilmurt is dead."

"Perhaps I am asking *because* he is dead."

Poynder rose and took a few steps. "It had all been carefully thought out. Your father was, as it were, above the fray. All the details were in Wilmurt's hands. He negotiated with the shipowners. He inspected the ships. And he bought on condition that the owners pay a commission on the agreed sales price without its appearing on the official form. This commission varied from five to ten percent. Without exception, the shipowners paid. Each one made a profit. The owners got rid of their scrap ships for good money, while your father, that disinterested patriot, pocketed the commissions. Only Thomas Wilmurt, the poor little go-between, ended up with next to nothing. If it had become necessary, John Tyler Matlock could easily have claimed that he knew nothing of Wilmurt's intrigues."

"I don't believe that."

"Of course, you don't believe it! But then, why poke around in ancient history?"

"Who else knew about this?" Craig asked. "How is it, for example, that you know the whole story?"

"Anyone who applied to your father and carried on business through Thomas Wilmurt knew what was going on. But, why should they publicize it? They were making a very good profit, in spite of the percentage they had to give your father. I knew some of the ships that were fobbed off on the government."

"Did you by any chance know a ship named *Marvellous?*"

"The one that burned in Savannah harbor?"

"Yes."

"For fifteen years it traveled Lake Ontario under the name *Oregon*. Your father owned it. The model was built especially for inland navigation. It was unsuitable for the open sea. Nevertheless, the government bought and used it. Who would have cared to point out the facts to the government? The owners? Or Wilmurt, who was dreaming of a career with your father?"

"Can you prove it?"

"Now see here! You came to see me. I didn't bring up the subject. It was not my intention to enlighten you about your father's methods. It is true that the claim cannot be proved—by anyone. Only Wilmurt could have done that, and he's dead."

"Let me ask you one more time. How is it that you are so well informed. At the time you no longer had any ships to sell."

"I knew many of the people who were involved in those deals. They all vilified John Tyler Matlock behind his back. And then there was Wilmurt. Your father doesn't seem to have treated him very generously. He was the only one who lost out."

Craig was convinced that his father-in-law was telling the truth, but he shook his head. "My father would not have been so careless as to antagonize Wilmurt."

"You should know your father. When he dropped Wilmurt, he was being consistent. That way he kept the matter at a distance. All he left was a minor functionary of the War Department who, all on his own, skimmed the cream off government business. Who do you think people were more likely to believe, Thomas Wilmurt or John Tyler Matlock? Unless, of course, Wilmurt had proof."

"And you know all this only through gossip?"

"Thomas Wilmurt came to see me." Poynder had stopped evading the question.

"To see you? Here?"

Poynder nodded. "I don't know why I'm confiding in you. Nor do I know what you plan to do with the information. After your father showed Wilmurt the door, once and for all, Wilmurt came to see me. I don't know what went on between your father and Wilmurt. Probably Wilmurt wanted his share. At any rate, more than your father gave him. And when your father didn't agree, Wilmurt probably tried to blackmail him. I believe I was the next person he came to. Wilmurt knew his way around in the shipping trade. He knew about the old rivalry between your father and me. In any case, he offered me the evidence he had amassed against your father. He told me he had personally copied it from War Department files, and I have no reason to doubt it."

Noticing that Craig was about to interrupt, Poynder raised his hand. "For a few days, whenever Wilmurt called here, I pretended to be out. I could figure out what he wanted. But when he came back day after day, here in the office and across the street at the restaurant, I saw him—if only to put an end to his conspicuous comings and goings. They were beginning to make me nervous. There he sat, right where you're sitting. He held a yellow package on his lap and clutched it tightly with both hands. His face was gray. It looked as though he had slept in his clothes. He said, 'With these papers you can destroy John Tyler Matlock.' "

Poynder had lowered his voice. It was important to him that he keep his feelings to himself, but his very lack of expression gave him away. He could tell from the way Craig looked at him. He would have preferred ending the conversation there and then, but that would have left him more exposed than ever. Calm was not one of his stronger traits. Over the years he had affected it in order to check his natural impetuousness. But it had not been extinguished; it smoldered like a volcano thought to be extinct.

When he continued, his voice was as calm as before.

"When I did not agree to his proposals, Wilmurt left and offered his evidence to the newspapers. I could have told him that he wouldn't get a hearing, but he didn't ask me. This was about two months ago."

Craig could not take his eyes off Poynder's face. He tried to find something there that would help him understand his father-in-law. Craig firmly believed that the man who was always able to speak the truth and nothing but the truth had not been born yet. What, then, must he deduct from this narrative, which might be nothing but subjective embellishment that said something about Loftus Poynder but nothing about Wilmurt? "Why did you refuse the documents Wilmurt offered you?" Craig asked.

Poynder raised his arms and slowly lowered them to the desk again. "Yes, why did I? I keep asking myself the same question."

"Did he ask for too much money?"

Poynder stared into space. He could still visualize the scene: the restless man, his trembling hands holding on to the yellow packet. "Thomas Wilmurt was past that point," he said. "The man was at the end of his rope. Money was no longer important to him. What he wanted now was someone who would help him find justice—or revenge. Sometimes it amounts to the same thing. When he went to the newspapers, he did not ask for money either."

"Then I understand even less why you didn't take the documents. Did you doubt their authenticity?"

"No, it wasn't that." Poynder seemed reluctant to continue. "I've already told you: today I might act differently, now that I know how your father intends to wage our battle." Poynder was still, as if listening to himself. Then his features relaxed. "Why worry about it? Wilmurt is dead."

"Was Wilmurt the kind to kill himself?" Craig had risen and was now leaning against the back of his chair. He remembered Joe Cristadoro's description of Wilmurt and he felt that what Poynder had said about him confirmed the description. For one fleeting moment, the thought struck him that Wilmurt might be alive today if Craig had taken the time to see him the night before. "Was he likely to commit suicide?"

"I've told you everything I know. I don't know what he was likely to do."

"Do you have a hunch?" It was an important question

to Craig. Just how had Thomas Wilmurt died? And yet, he was glad Poynder would not answer it for him. "I think I know enough now," he said. "I'm very grateful to you."

"Now I have a question for you. It concerns your father and me. Where do you stand in this matter?"

"Is the conflict really inevitable?"

"Perhaps your father has only the best intentions. But it's too late for such reflections. It had to come to this sooner or later. We are too different; we exclude each other. I don't care to discuss it further. The time for words is past. He wants my blood—and I want his. You can tell him that. I will defend my property by every means at my disposal, as I know he will. Tell him that, too. I want him to know it."

"I will tell him."

"Perhaps we can prevent this affair from casting a shadow over you and Margaret."

"I don't know. . . . If it does, it won't be because of me."

"I myself was not fortunate in my marriage. I cannot advise you. Today I only know that for a long time I did not pay enough attention. I allowed too much to come between us. Later, when I began to notice and try to set things right, it was too late. I don't know whom Margaret takes after. I like to think that she favors me. If that is so, you have a wife you can count on. We have a great deal of staying power, especially when we are least expected to show it. We do not develop many passions in our lives, but when we do, they last."

The two men had become closer in the past hour than they had ever been before. If they had given in to their feelings, a quick embrace would have been the appropriate gesture of farewell, but both, mistrustful of emotion, merely shook hands formally.

"I really haven't made up my mind where I stand," Craig said. "When in doubt, a Matlock always thinks of himself first."

When the door had closed behind Craig, Poynder went to the window that looked out on Warren Street. He waited until he saw his son-in-law go down the street, past the Frenchman's. Once again he was struck by Craig's relaxed and self-confident manner. He understood why his daughter had chosen this man. But the choice had not automatically gained him a son. Craig was a Matlock; he would always be a Matlock. Poynder thought back over their conversation, examining each answer and reaction, to determine whether they might be interpreted as weakness.

# ⸗ 14 ⸗

STARTING AT THIRTY-fourth Street, Fifth Avenue was the domain of the rich. Only one name plate graced each front door, and no one went on foot. That the man in the white linen suit with the dark hair and tanned face was walking confounded the coachmen, and for the fourth time a cabbie slowed to offer his services.

Craig Matlock waved the carriage on. He wanted to walk, as he always did when he needed to sort out his thoughts. He had this trait in common with his mother, who could stride for hours on the sand at Willowbeach, alone with her thoughts.

After what Irene had hinted about the place, he was prepared to find a house that broke with the Matlock tradition of living in modest, inconspicuous dwellings. He was nevertheless taken aback at the pomposity of the marble façade, featuring bronze candelabra between the pillars of the portico. He felt no envy. Rather, his sense for the proper measure was offended. Langdon and this house—the two did not dovetail. Or did they? Did Langdon require a palace in order to feel strong? Was this what he had dreamed of during the years of waiting: to walk on stairs of black-and-green marble and in the evening to bathe his house in the light of candelabra? Perhaps, too, Craig's reaction was particularly strong because he had just come from a visit to the harbor police, where he had seen Wilmurt's corpse. Though his conversation with Loftus Poynder had cleared up many questions, it had left unanswered the crucial one: how had Wilmurt died? And so Craig had gone to the harbor police and asked them to show him the dead man—the gaunt body, the hollow-cheeked face slimed over with a grayish-yellow mask. . . .

He had a clear picture of Wilmurt now, running from office to office, obsessed with justice. But why had he suddenly given up? What had stopped him? The recognition that he himself was too deeply involved to be able to appear as the accuser? Or was it neither accident nor suicide? Looking at the corpse, Craig remembered his brother's words: "One way or the other, the thing will be settled soon." Now he read still another meaning into that statement. He must find out the truth.

Craig had expected the door to be opened by Charles Gilpin, the onetime ship's steward who had been Langdon's domestic factotum for many years. But the butler who unlocked the door was a stranger, a face as new as the house. The black hair, slicked back, shone with pomade; the cheeks were rigorously clean-shaven, the narrow lips barely parted to speak. "You wish, sir?"

Craig Matlock did not consider it necessary to reply. The butler tried to bar his way. "Sir!"

"Don't call me sir," Craig snapped. "And get out of my way."

He pushed the butler to one side and crossed the foyer and hall with his quick possessive footsteps. The butler came scurrying after. He was in livery, complete with white gloves. "I don't know what gives you the idea. . . ." At the last minute he swallowed his "sir."

"I am notorious for my impossible behavior," Craig said. "Better tell me where I can find my brother."

"Mister Matlock? He is out of town."

Craig had counted on this. Wilmurt had appeared at Joe Cristadoro's door the night before at half past eight. If Langdon had really taken the eight-o'clock boat to Albany, as usual, everything was in order. "Please announce me to Mrs. Matlock."

While he waited, he looked around. The gloomy splendor of the façade was continued inside the house: marble, bronze, ebony, all on a scale befitting a monument, not a home. Above the tall fireplace hung a portrait of Langdon, obviously also painted by Bower. The setting reminded him that he was looking at the designated Matlock heir, while he had let himself be fobbed off with $350,000, a pittance it now seemed to him. And to think he himself had wanted it that way.

The folding doors at the back of the hall opened again and the butler returned. Bloated with self importance, he planted himself in front of Craig. "Mrs. Matlock regrets. She does not wish to receive you."

Craig had difficulty controlling his urge to laugh. He could already hear the sound of his laughter resounding through the house. When he was a child, his laughing fits had sometimes disturbed the whole family. He stared at the butler. "Did you ever laugh?" he asked him. "This hall must have wonderful acoustics. How about it? Have you ever tried it when no one was "home?""

The butler took refuge in his "sir!" and stiffly pointed to a small table with writing materials. "If you would care to leave a message?"

Before Craig could decide what to do next, the folding doors parted again. There stood Irene Matlock in a pale pink dress, her hair gathered up simply with a ribbon. The butler took a step toward her.

"That will be all, Daniels. I'll call you when I need you."

She preceded Craig into the parlor. It was decorated in white and gold; silk rugs in pastel shades covered the floor. Three windows looked out on the garden, which was landscaped in the French style. Its special attraction was a glass birdhouse.

Irene closed the folding doors and approached Craig hesitantly, with an expression in which sternness and unease were mingled. "Must you behave so impossibly?" she said. "There *is* a limit. I did not find it very amusing. In any case, I would not like to lose my butler over you. It is not easy to find a good one, you know. All right, what is it you want, besides upsetting the servants?"

"He was so ridiculous," Craig said. " 'Mrs. Matlock does not wish to receive you.' How can you stand having such a puffed-up fellow around all the time? What became of Gilpin?"

"The house was too much for him. He was here only a few days before he asked to be allowed to go back to Staten Island." Irene addressed him with cool formality, the way she might speak to a stranger. She turned her back and went to one of the windows. "Now then, what brings you here? Have you come to apologize?" She was pleased with herself. Since the abortive rendezvous at the St. Denis, she had had sufficient time to check her anger, but she had not been sure whether, when it came to it, she would be able to avoid a scene. But when she had heard Craig's voice in the hall, she realized that, on the contrary, she must take care not to forgive him too quickly. All he had to do now was come near her and put his arms around her, and she would forget her pride and her cunning. Only one feeling would remain: the desire to use to the utmost the time she had left, that short span in which she was still desirable to him.

She turned toward him but avoided looking at him directly. "At least you remembered that today is Friday."

Craig was not the least disconcerted by this reproach. The fact that he had abandoned her a week ago Thursday—that was past history. Not even Irene's presence could bring it back. He was possessed by the thought of Thomas Wilmurt. Chance had put him onto this scent, while intuition told him that everything connected with it would be of the utmost importance to his family, but most especially to himself.

"So Langdon is in Albany? And he took the night boat yesterday?"

She threw him a quick glance, the precursor of a smile. "I didn't expect you to get down on your knees to me. But is that your apology?"

"Did Langdon leave at eight last night?"

"No." Irene's face had closed again. "No, he couldn't leave yesterday."

"No? But your butler told me Langdon was out of town."

"What are you talking about? You asked about last night."

"Yes. Where was Langdon last night?"

"We had guests. People from City Hall."

"And Langdon was home all evening? Starting when?"

She still could not believe that Craig had not come solely to see her. His questions must be a pretext, a diversion, the typically male fear of a scene. But surely he must have noticed by now that he had nothing to fear. Why not go along with his little game? They had always had to pretend. Why not, for once, carry on the charade with one another, why not act as if nothing had happened between them? "Yes, the party went on all evening," she said. "A boring affair. A formal dinner, and afterward a little game for the gentlemen. Only the host ever loses. The whole thing began at nine and lasted until after midnight." Involuntarily she had strayed back to her easy conversational tone.

"And after that? Langdon went out again?"

"Of course not. He went to bed at once. The last carriage had barely left when his head hit the pillow. Any time Langdon isn't in bed by eleven, the entire next day is shot."

"And where is he now?"

"At Willowbeach. He took the early train."

"Was there a particular reason?" Craig was thinking of the morning papers.

"Father wished to see him. After evenings like last night, John Tyler expects a personal report. Those are the sacrifices Langdon is called on to make."

Craig looked at her searchingly. "You could swear in a court of law that Langdon did not leave this house all night?"

She laughed. "Why all these questions? Won't you at least tell me what this is all about?"

For a moment Craig was tempted to tell her about Wilmurt but thought better of it. He had already made enough of a fuss, and he still was not sure whether Langdon might not after all have some part in Wilmurt's death. His alibi, at any rate, was almost too good. He had witnesses whose veracity was unimpeachable. Craig looked at Irene musingly. "Surely you remember what you once said about the consciences of Matlocks," he said.

"I never knew you had one."

"Exactly. That's what you said. You went on to say that to us something is bad only when it has bad consequences for us. This particular matter will probably have no bad consequences, and we may therefore forget all about it."

"Forgetting," Irene said. "That's another thing you Matlocks are good at. All your traits are advantageous for you and detrimental to others." She put her hand on his arm. "All right, we'll forget it. I'm almost a Matlock already in that respect. But the hour in the carriage in front of the St. Denis—I do not want to have to experience that again. I paid for all my sins that night." As she looked up at him, her eyes sparkled. "Even those I haven't committed yet."

Craig knew that she had forgiven him, more generously than he wanted.

To distract her, he asked while looking about the room, "Tell me, Irene, are you comfortable here? This house would impress people, I'm sure. But can you live in it? When I think of your house on Staten Island. . . ."

"You don't like it?" She was busying herself with her hair.

"Is the whole house like this?"

She laughed briefly and took his arm. "No. Come, I'll show you."

He thought he knew what she was thinking. There wasn't much time before his train left for Willowbeach. But he allowed her to lead him upstairs, where they went from room to room. He also thought he knew where they would end up. On the third floor, at the end of a long corridor, Irene put her hand on the door latch and said, "This is my realm."

The thick carpet into which his feet sank, the cascades of gossamer lace around the wide bed, the pale green curtains and wall covering, the furniture of cypress— the room was a faithful copy of Irene's bedroom in the farmhouse on Staten Island. The shutters outside the windows were closed, the blinds slanted. The perfect setting for an hour of love. For the second time since he had entered the house Craig felt like laughing. This time he found it even harder to resist. What a comedy! What a rotten, miserable comedy!

"Green is still my favorite color," she said. "You haven't yet said hello to me properly."

As he embraced her, he was aware that even as he held her close, she was kicking off her shoes. He used to share her impatience, her determination to make use of every second they had.

"Do you like it better here? Everything is as it used to be. Wait here for me," she whispered.

At the door to the bathroom, a transparent negligee hung from a hook. For a moment he hesitated, not because Irene still held sway over his senses, but because he still owed her something. The affair between them was ended. He had known that from the moment she led him into the room. But he was bothered by something else. He still owed her for that night at the St. Denis.

"Wait," he said quickly before she could reach for the negligee. He hurried to the door, opened it, and looked out into the corridor. This, too, was part of the comedy.

He did not fool himself into thinking that he was playing his part very well, either. He shut the door and said, "I wouldn't be surprised if the butler were spying on us. Who hired him, you or Langdon?"

Irene stared past him, her eyes large and vacant. She had seen through him at once. If there were a way to hold Craig, she had told herself over and over during the past week, it was only through unshakable serenity. She must remain for him the woman she had been from the outset: the adventure without risk, without complications. "You've learned," she said. "When I remember Staten Island and Willowbeach . . . I was always the one who had to be cautious."

"I don't want to make trouble for you."

She sat on the edge of the bed, looking at him a long time before speaking. "I have one request, Craig. One day, perhaps soon, you will find me too old. For a man of twenty, a thirty-year-old mistress is wonderful. But when he is thirty, it changes. What I want is simply this: leave it to me to decide the time. You understand what I mean. Otherwise, I'm afraid, I wouldn't be a good loser."

He sat down next to her. Taking her face in his hands, he kissed her on the forehead. She knew that this silent answer meant the beginning of the end, perhaps the end altogether, and she wondered how she would be able to bear it.

"I always admired you," he said, "and I always will."

"I'd prefer anything to that." Her voice was grave. "But don't forget. Don't forget what I said."

"Listening to you, one might think that life is as easy to administer as property."

"One can actually run one's life like that. I learned that —or was forced to learn it, if you prefer. My father was a clergyman. I don't know where he stood with heaven, but I know his relationship to this earth. His church was always full. His congregation was one of the most well-to-do in New York. He asked for and got as much as two thousand dollars a year for one of the better pews in the front rows. Unlike other clergymen, he didn't have to go running after his sheep; they flocked to him. He was their advocate, their property administrator. What he preached to his children may not sound much like the word of God, but it has always helped me. 'Good luck,' he would say, 'is nothing but an arithmetic problem, one that can be solved. Most people don't find it out until the answer comes out wrong.' I was always my father's obedient daughter. I always followed his advice. Luck *is* an equation that can be solved, and I will see to it that it remains so in my life."

"Why did you marry Langdon, Irene?"

"That's easy. Langdon Matlock was the best catch in my father's congregation. Besides, there were four of us girls. Each one wanted him, but I got him. For a girl of sixteen, that's reason enough to fall in love with a man."

"And are you happy?"

"I got him!" She made a gesture that took in the whole room, the whole house. "And all this with him." When she continued, her voice was different. "I've been thinking a lot this last week. You and I—the reason we got into this with each other wasn't that I was unhappy. I wasn't even discontent. I was happy, but I wanted to be happier still. I did not want to have to tell myself later that I had missed something. I wanted to have it all, to have my fill of it—of everything." As she spoke, she did not look at him. Even now she remained still, motionless, staring into the middle distance. "A strange sermon for a clergyman's daughter, isn't it?"

"Not to me. It's the same old Matlock litany: trust only in yourself; think only of yourself. It doesn't sound very noble. There was a time when I hated my father for such maxims. Today they only make me laugh. One day, probably, I will preach the same sermon to my sons. And so it goes, from generation to generation. At heart nothing ever changes. The race for good luck, the fear of missing something. Never being satisfied, always wanting more."

"Except that some get it and others don't. That some are satisfied and others are not. Living with you Matlocks, one gets so that one always wants more. Everything there is on this earth, you want to own. Land, houses, ships, railroads—and women. When you have everything you want, it still isn't enough. It will never be enough."

"Am I really like that?"

"Of course you are. Wait. Young men always think they're different. It probably has to be that way. But you'll find out. You're a Matlock. It's in your blood. You have to prove to yourselves, to the world, that you're stronger than the rest. That will always be your aim. You will not rest until you have achieved it." Looking up at him, she thought she caught a glimpse of something new in his face, merely a hint of something.

"You do not know yourself yet," she said. "You've been away for four years. When you do find yourself, I suspect you'll find that you've become a bird of prey."

# BOOK THREE

# WILLOWBEACH, CONNECTICUT

October 1865

# ≡ 15 ≡

Normally John Tyler Matlock spent the hour before the midday meal taking a walk on the beach or, if it was a very hot day, sitting in the garden in the shaded arbor of ivy. But today he had not left his room all morning. His breakfast stood untouched on the tray, just as Rose had brought it to him. It was his usual breakfast: oatmeal, scrambled eggs, bacon, smoked salmon, three kinds of jam, bread, and a bowl of fresh figs. He was in the habit of eating well, believing that a person with regular digestion could not fall ill.

But this time not even the sight of the figs was able to whet his appetite. On the contrary, the green damp fruit had caused him to be nauseated. He spread the napkin over the tray and threw open the door to the balcony. And there he remained. He placed his wicker chair on the sill, so that he had a view of the Sound but was himself invisible to everyone, even the children who were playing on the beach and whose voices came up to him.

It was a hot, bright day such as often occurred in October on the Sound. The weather had been like this for some time, a second summer apparently, which might end any day. A rain shower or change in wind direction, and it would turn gray, wet, and chilly, and it would suddenly be late autumn. The sun no longer had sufficient power to warm Matlock. He put a blanket over his knees, but the feeling of cold, of withering, would not leave his legs.

On the terrace below the balcony he heard footsteps. Alice was loudly calling the others to lunch. On the beach the children's cries of protest rose, rolled toward the house like a wave, lost themselves in the house. Finally there fell the silence he had been waiting for, and he closed his eyes. The sun sent red flames through his lids. Warmth coursed through him. He seemed weightless. He no longer needed anything.

Sitting around the big table, they would glance at his empty chair, but no one would say anything about it. The empty chair would not be conspicuous; it would not cause as much of a stir as there had been yesterday, when John Tyler had left all the dishes put in front of him until they were carried off again untouched. Rose acted as if she had not noticed. But if it were repeated, she would be upset. No, it was better to sit here alone in the stillness. He was a man of moods. They were all used to that. His family had no choice but to accept them. He smiled at the thought that his moodiness was now helping him conceal from those close to him the fact that there was something wrong with him.

The train had arrived punctually on September 22, two days after his birthday, to take them back to Albany. Since then it had been standing behind the house. How many days was it now? Seven? He was too indolent to figure it out. Perhaps it was more, for Rose had hinted last night that the villagers were already gossiping about the wheelwright's widow and McCallum, the locomotive engineer, who was boarding with her. Every other year, after the long summer in Willowbeach, Matlock had impatiently anticipated the return to Albany, so that the departure from Willowbeach seemed hasty. How often in earlier years had Rose begged him to prolong their stay by a few days, for the first half of October was one of the best times on the Sound—Indian summer, with the trees resplendent and oysters that never tasted better. But at no time had he allowed himself to be softened up by his wife, and now suddenly it was he who would not hear of departure.

For a minute he dwelled on the image of those astonished faces. Only the children, who had been kept penned up in the house, dressed in their traveling clothes, all the morning of the twenty-second, had begun to shout for joy when they heard that the departure had been postponed indefinitely. Of course he was accountable to no one, but this time he had thought it proper to clothe his mood —he stubbornly called his reluctance to return to Albany a mood, although he knew that it was something else— in the robe of good sense. He had explained to his family that he had finally decided to enlarge the house, saying, "I asked Harry Chubb to join me here. He will draw the

plans for the addition right here. Please get a room ready
for him. He'll be staying a few days."

If he had ever surprised anyone, it was with that announcement. Summer after summer he had been deaf
to the complaints that the Willowbeach house had long
ago become too small to hold all the grandchildren.
"You can do all that when I'm dead," had been his un-
varying reply. "Then you can make all the changes you
want. Until then, you'll just have to wait." And now suddenly he had commissioned Chubb, the architect who had
built his house in Albany, to do the job.

No one understood what he himself was unable to
explain. His wife had left without a word and not returned
until dusk. She knew him better than anyone. Perhaps she
understood him better than he did himself, and perhaps
he should have talked to her. Even now, in the lonely, silent room, he felt her presence and her concern. She suspected that the building plans were only a pretext,
something to divert their interest from him.

Why? Because he was tired, because he felt unwell, because he was disturbed? He pushed such thoughts aside.
Next summer it would be forgotten. Next summer, when
the house had grown to three times its present size. Two
single-story wings, to the right and the left, to maintain
the proportions of the old house while still gaining so much
additional space that the next two Matlock generations
could multiply unhampered—that was what Chubb and
Matlock had agreed on. Yesterday the architect had returned to Albany. Construction would begin as soon as
the Matlocks left Willowbeach. When they returned next
summer, everything would be completed. Next summer. . . .

He must have fallen asleep. The sun, which had been
shining on his knees, had disappeared. He had dreamed
about the addition to the house, about next summer.
Dreams—they had never had any effect on him other than
to arouse his mistrust. And so it now became clear to him
that the building plans obligated him to nothing. As
soon as he was back in Albany, he would make a detailed
examination of the cost estimate. He could still take it
all back. The thought comforted him.

The blanket had slipped off his knees as he dozed. He
wrapped it around his legs again. The finely carded cash-
mere was like a silky hide; he felt warmth when he ran his

hands over it. His hands were narrow, the fingers long and bony. The backs were covered with brown spots that had grown more numerous over the years, so that the original skin color hardly showed. An old man's hands. It seemed to him that a stranger's voice had spoken. He sat upright in his chair. He listened for the voice to return, but he heard only a dull thudding in his chest. It was his heart, and that frightened him more than the voice. He sank back in his chair. Gradually the beating grew calmer, more measured.

"You are an old man," he said aloud to himself. "Admit it. You are an old man." He repeated it several more times, and what he had hoped for happened: the words lost their power. What had frightened him moments before became nothing more than objective fact.

He was old, true. Ten days ago (now he remembered) he had celebrated his eightieth birthday. But what did that mean except that he had grabbed a large slice of life with both hands, the same hands lying there in his lap? And they would grab still more of it as soon as they were rested, as soon as the weariness had fled from them. No, it wasn't true that life was withdrawing from him. He himself had withdrawn from life for a few hours, had given way to the whim of absenting himself for a while and being alone with himself. The house was silent. He stood up and fetched the hand mirror from the bathroom. As he returned to his chair, he noticed the covered breakfast tray. The nausea did not return, but neither was his appetite aroused. The clock on the secretary showed a few minutes past four. Soon the biting scent of freshly brewed tea would drift through the house. But they would respect the fact that he had retired. He took care to make no noise as he resumed his seat in the wicker chair in the open balcony door.

He placed the mirror on his knee and bent over it. As he had examined his hands earlier, he now examined his face. To his surprise he saw that he was unshaven, that the stubble was several days old. He ran his hand over the whiskers. They were thick and white, whiter than his hair. They made his cheeks seem fuller, his chin broader, his eyes darker. A good thing he hadn't gone down to dinner. Rose would have been seriously worried, for no one could remember his ever having gone even a day without shaving.

Should he send for the doctor? Doctor Shyne from Southport? The idea of the doctor's being startled cheered him. He did not trust doctors, yet he valued their company. Since he took an interest in his health, he had been friendly with doctors all his life. It had been their job to entertain him with detailed case histories from their practices. He had already survived three of them. One had died only last February, and Matlock, who never missed a funeral, had paid him this last honor. During a cold wave—many of the mourners caught a chill—he had stood at the graveside with his coat open, without scarf, gloves, and the fur hat Rose had so insistently urged him to wear. On the drive home in the carriage he had warmed his wife's clammy hands between his own warm fingers. And now he sat in the sun and felt cold. What was the matter with him?

He sensed that he was no longer alone. He was not certain, might the noise have come from the terrace below? He tried to remember whether he had locked the door. He did not turn around when he heard footsteps. Then he saw Joshua's mop of bleached, sun-faded hair rising up beside the armrest of his chair.

It had taken all Joshua's courage to violate a prohibition imposed by Rose Matlock. Now he was astonished at his own boldness as he stood before his grandfather. Seconds passed before he realized that no one had stopped him on his way through the house and that the door to his grandfather's room had not been locked. Whatever the silence meant, Joshua was determined not to be sent away. "What are you doing with the mirror?" he asked as he came closer.

"I was wondering if I should shave."

"I can fetch you some hot water." As he spoke, Joshua leaned against his grandfather's knee.

Matlock felt the warmth of the child's body. It sent well-being coursing through him. "Weren't you told that I wanted to be alone?"

"Of course. But you promised me something. Sinclair and me."

"Promised?"

"The gold coins."

"Have I ever forgotten them at the end of the summer? You always get them, each of you."

"But maybe this time you'll leave so suddenly that you'll forget after all."

Matlock nodded. He saw the boy standing before him expectantly, and a picture from the past rose before his eyes. A ninety-three-year-old man in an armchair, a wolf-skin rug over his knees, on his lap a plump leather pouch. Whenever someone entered the room, the old man reached for the pouch, pulled out a gold coin, and gave it away. That had been his father. After a serious accident with the carriage, he had lived on for eighteen months, unable to speak. But day after day Lyman Matlock had himself dressed and shaved. Then he sat in his chair and distributed the gold coins to any member of the large family who came to visit, especially his grandchildren. Even as the door opened, his hands reached for the money pouch.

"You promised," Joshua said. "Really."

"I keep my promises." Matlock listened to the sound of his own voice. Compared to the boy's, it seemed puny, lacking resonance. Had Joshua even heard him? He raised his voice. "You will get your gold coin, and so will Sinclair. Even if I had forgotten—after all, I will be returning to Willowbeach. There will be many more summers." He noted the disappointment in the child's face and said, "Go to the dresser, the top drawer." He stopped, suddenly distracted by the brown envelope Joshua was clutching. "What have you got there?"

"I found it in front of your door. It was lying on the floor when I came upstairs. Somebody must have put it there while you were sleeping. They didn't want to wake you up. It's a telegram, isn't it?" He handed the envelope to his grandfather. "The top drawer?"

There was no answer, and Joshua did not dare to press further. His grandfather tore open the envelope, and Joshua stared, hypnotized, at his grandfather's lips, which moved soundlessly as he read. Suddenly they froze—not just the lips, his whole body. Only the left hand retained a sign of life. It was lying on the old man's knees, just at Joshua's eye level, squeezing the telegram so tightly that it showed through the fingers.

"Grandfather!" No answer came from the old man. For a moment Joshua was tempted to run to the door, away from the room, away from the stiff body. But, instead he stood still, as though he too had turned to stone. He could not take his eyes off the hand that still clutched the telegram.

Joshua, leaning against his knee as before, was the first thing the old man became conscious of: an island of warmth on his cold legs, the smell of a boy who had spent all day at the beach and who even at night, after his bath, still harbored pink sand under his nails and in his hair. The boy's red hair—would he see it if he opened his eyes? He wanted to rest his hand on that mop of hair, but he was afraid he was only imagining the boy's presence. He was equally afraid of frightening the child by his condition. He dared not open his eyes, not yet. He remained motionless, listening to his body. The numb sensation was in his right side, in the arm and leg. He pressed his lips together, closed his eyes tighter, and moved his tongue around in his mouth. The assurance that he would be able to speak gave him confidence.

Apoplexy—it had been foretold by the symptoms he had experienced during the last few days. His mind was working clearly. You are going to die, he told himself. Not now, not tomorrow; but it's beginning. The great game with death had begun. But it did not seem to him that his opponent had the advantage. In every game there is a first move, and his enemy had heedlessly squandered his.

John Tyler Matlock had never had much use for God. Why had He created the earth if He were not going to live on it? Death, on the other hand, was at home in this world, always a neighbor—and from now on, an enemy.

He opened his eyes and then moved his head. He saw Joshua standing before him. "What's the matter with you?" he asked the boy. "You're pale." He noted with satisfaction that his voice sounded the same as ever.

Joshua looked at his grandfather. He was still afraid, but already curiosity was beginning to replace the fear. "Shall I go for the doctor?" he said.

"No, no doctor."

"There's one in Southport. Doctor Shyne. He comes to see Aunt Edna all the time."

Matlock smiled. "Doctor Shyne has more important things to do, believe me."

"What if you die?"

"That would be worse for Doctor Shyne than for me." It did him a world of good to speak—to hear his own voice, form words, observe a thought emerge. He did not care whether the boy understood him or not. "A doctor's career depends on his keeping the right patients alive. I could ruin a doctor by calling him in to my deathbed. No matter how good a doctor he is, from that moment on he would be the one who brought John Tyler Matlock to his grave. No one would ever trust him again. What about the fire? It's cold in here. Put on more wood."

Joshua ran to the fireplace. Matlock used the interruption to make a more detailed examination of his condition. He began with the left side of his body, the one that still had sensation. As he opened his left hand, the crumpled telegram fell in his lap. He had not given it a thought all this time, but now anger flared hotly up in him.

Loftus Poynder. For two months, since late July, he had played possum. He had swallowed one setback after another—the loss of freight commissions, the accidents on his lines, the newspaper campaign, and then the major blow, the Broadway concession which had been assigned to him, to Matlock, two weeks ago. He had already begun to interpret Poynder's passivity as weakness, as an admission of defeat. But he had been mistaken. It was for this, then, that the concession had been delayed for so long. For two weeks he had gloried in his victory, and now this—revocation.

Anger brought with it a sensation of strength. The anger that had almost killed him in the first few moments now became a source of life. Where a moment ago there had been coldness and rigidity, he now felt warmth and vigor. Even his right arm and leg were no longer as heavy as stone but only half numbed, as if asleep. It took great effort, but he managed to open and close his right hand. Slowly he repeated the motion. He was tempted to help it along with his left hand, but he did not give in. That would be showing weakness.

Joshua, who had returned from the fireplace, asked, "What is the matter with your hand?"

Matlock put his hand in his lap. "What do you think? It fell asleep. Hasn't that ever happened to you?"

"No."

He sensed the boy's mistrust; it was a challenge. He supported both hands on the armrests of the wicker chair. "I am going to shave now," he said. "Will you fetch me some water?"

"The water in the kettle over the fire is hot."

"Then carry it into the bathroom for me." He knew that Joshua was determined to stay. He also knew that without the boy's presence, he would not summon the necessary strength. He pushed himself up with both arms. As his foot touched the floor, it moved against the mirror which had fallen to the floor. His right leg seemed heavy and unfeeling. He did not know what would happen when he took the first step—whether the leg would crumple under him, whether he would fall. Had Joshua not been there, he would have sunk back into the chair, but the boy's watchful eyes forced Matlock to keep on.

Slowly, step by step, he dragged himself through the room. At the bureau he stopped for a moment and reached for whatever object lay there. Thus he concealed from Joshua that he was afraid of every step.

The boy held the door for him and followed him into the bathroom. He poured the hot water into the bowl. Matlock awkwardly tested the temperature. He picked up a shaving brush with his left hand and began to stir the lather. He could no longer put off the moment when he would have to hold the razor.

Joshua stood close to the marble counter. "You didn't strop the razor," he said.

"It's sharp enough. Watch." Matlock was holding the razor in his right hand. The blade was heavy. He felt that he would never be able to raise it to his face. But his grandson's eyes drove him on. After every stroke he wiped the lather off the blade with the thumb of his left hand.

He nicked himself twice, lightly. Not until he removed the hot cloth that he spread over his face like a compress after shaving did he see the red spots on the white material. He took a piece of alum and dabbed at the spots until the blood congealed.

When he returned to his room, Matlock suddenly felt hungry. He folded back the napkin covering the tray and took a piece of bread from the basket. He looked at Joshua, who was still there by his chair. "Do you know where your father is?" he asked.

"He's out in the Sound, sailing. With Hugh Sewall's new sailboat."

"You're going to run down to Sewall's Harbour," Matlock said, "and you are going to wait until your father comes back with the yacht. Then you are going to tell him that I want to speak with him. But don't tell anyone else! How old are you?"

"I'm going on five. Next year I start school."

"How would you like to go to school in Albany?"

"The same school where my father went? You'd take me with you?"

"Why not? At least your meals would be better. Now go to the bureau."

Joshua stared at his grandfather, not understanding.

"You wanted your gold dollar. Isn't that why you came? In the top drawer, in the brown leather pouch. Get your coin. Go ahead."

"Two," Joshua said quickly. "One for Sinclair and one for me."

Joshua carefully made his selection of two coins, compared them with each other, and tied them up in a handkerchief.

Matlock was exhausted, but it did not occur to him to sit down. He must keep moving, keep walking to and fro. And he must talk to Craig.

"Thanks a lot." Joshua held his hand out to his grandfather. "I have a place where I keep my coins. Nobody can find them there."

"That is best," Matlock said to his grandson. "It is better to keep them hidden from others. Don't tell anyone about your coins. And don't tell them that you paid me a visit. Take care that no one sees you leaving. And run to Sewall's Harbour."

When Joshua had gone, Matlock stepped out on the balcony. The wind had shifted. A cold autumnal breeze was blowing, turning the sea dark and rough. He breathed deeply, and with each breath the fire of rage that burned in him grew stronger.

# ≡ 16 ≡

THE BOAT REALLY needed a three-man crew, but as long as the mild south wind was blowing, it had been easy for Craig Matlock to handle it alone. Seduced by the boat's speed, he had gone farther out in the Sound than he had intended. He noted the signs in the sky, the tattered clouds on the northeastern horizon, presaging a wind shift. An hour ago the fishermen had hauled in their nets and returned to shore. He had also been warned by Hugh Sewall, the man in whose shipyard the boat had been built and who knew the weather in the Sound better than anyone around. But he was used to that from Sewall. Sewall was too anxious when anyone took one of his boats out. Craig wondered whether somewhere on the beach, Sewall was watching him through a telescope.

In fact he wished he had Sewall with him. The boat was new, and it had never been out in such heavy seas before. Every maneuver was an experiment. If he intended to bring the boat back to Sewall's Harbour in this wind without an accident, he would need all his skill and plenty of luck.

The wind was from the northeast, a stiff, whipping gale. Ragged clouds drifted deep down in the sky. Creaking, the boat jumped over the waves even now, though he had hauled in the mainsail. Water occasionally washed over the deck.

He glanced at the shore again, to orient himself. For a moment he thought he recognized the Matlock and Poynder houses. On the hills behind the shore smoke was rising from chimneys. The first autumn fires. But it took all his concentration to handle the boat. He lashed the tiller in place and went forward to haul in more sail. Before Sewall's Harbour there were shallows. At ebb tide the water was no more than a couple of feet deep, and during

170

high seas the drift was too uncertain. He decided to avoid the area. To run aground only a couple of hundred yards offshore—he wasn't prepared to entertain Hugh Sewall with such a delicious farce.

Finally he had the sail down. He returned to the tiller. It took a long time for the shore to come closer. He let the boat run with the wind, past the shipyard, the boat shed, and Sewall's house. They flew past. He could not understand the shouts from the men on the shore, who were signaling excitedly. Below the harbor he turned the boat. He had hoped that when he reached shore, he would be out of the wind, but the final stretch to the dock was the hardest part.

Hugh Sewall and his workmen had run out on the jetty. Their hands cupped around their mouths, they were still shouting advice, but their voices did not reach Craig. The jetty and the men grew larger and smaller in rapid alternation, and for the first time since he had been surprised by the storm, he would have liked to close his eyes and let things run their course.

The boat bumped slightly against the dock, which was protected with jute sacks. Sewall was the first to reach him. The dark-blue cap with the broad visor hid his face. Without speaking, he caught the hawsers, fastened them, then jumped into the boat and helped Craig gather in the rest of the canvas.

"All right, say it." Craig spoke first.

Hugh Sewall stood before him. The cap with the broad visor left the upper part of his face in shadow. That was why he wore it, why no one ever saw him without the cap: it concealed the disfigured eye that had been plucked out by a seagull when he was a child. "You're crazy," he said. "Crazy to stay out so long. You almost lost the boat."

"The boat? What about me?"

"The hell with you. I tell you—if it had been *my* boat, I'd have wished both of you'd stay out there."

For a while they worked in silence. The workmen had withdrawn from the jetty and were talking on the beach. After they had taken care of the boat, Craig and Sewall returned to the shore. Sewall's house—not much more than a cabin on stilts—was covered with shingles. It had a narrow, roofed porch and was painted green with white trim.

The front door, unlocked as usual, led into a parlor

which served as kitchen and living room. Craig was at home here. He went to the stove where a coffeepot was bubbling. "Do you want a mug?" he said to Sewall. They sat on the window seat while Craig poured two cups. He warmed his hands on the mug while sipping from it. Craig felt exhausted but healthy; he hadn't felt this well in a long time.

He finally broke the silence. "And you have nothing to say about the way I brought her in? It's a marvelous boat. Never handled a better one. It's faster than I thought it would be. Without a doubt, the best one you've built."

Sewall bent over his cup. He was still angry. "It's not my boat. I told you. Why won't you get it through your head? The time is long past when I can afford to build boats for myself. Before I even start hammering the first planks together, it has to be sold." He looked up. "I'm sure Henry Tribe would be tickled to know that Craig Matlock ran his new boat aground." Sewall held his mug in both hands.

"What's the matter with you?" Sewall continued. "Ever since you came back from the war, right from the first day, I noticed something was wrong. Why do you take such risks?" He was looking over the rim of his mug at Craig. "You always took risks, but not like today."

Craig stretched his legs under the table. "Four years' holiday; it shows. I had forgotten what the Sound can be like in October."

"Maybe it would have been a lesson to you if you'd had to pay Tribe for the boat. Except, probably, you wouldn't have even noticed."

"That's enough. Don't spoil my good mood. I feel good here. Your coffee is good and strong." Since his return two months earlier, his favorite place had been Sewall's Harbour, on a boat in the Sound or here in the cabin, at this table, with Hugh Sewall. "What about my proposition?" he asked. "Given it any thought?"

Sewall refilled their mugs. He got a bottle from the kitchen cabinet and poured whiskey into his. Craig refused.

"I used to fall for your jokes," Sewall said.

"This is no joke. I told you, I want to stay out of the war between my father and my father-in-law. Let the two old fighting cocks settle things between them. Why won't you take me on as a partner?"

"You? My partner? Even if I never get out of Sewall's Harbour, I have more sense than that. Why should you put your money in boats?"

"We could enlarge the shipyard. Isn't there any money in shipbuilding? The prices you demand are high enough. You and me; together, we could make the business pay off."

"Maybe I don't want it to pay off. And my prices barely cover my expenses. No, Craig, there's no money to be made here—not the kind of money Matlocks have in mind. It used to be that way; but those days are gone. Men like your father now put their money in railroads and industry, not in shipping, especially not in pleasure boats. Name me one shipyard along the coast here. All of them have gone under. Think of my father and all the other small boatbuilders along the coast. There was enough work for all of them. They had their freedom. And where are they now? Only a few managed to hold on. They have trouble finding workmen because they're being lured away by the factories in Norwalk and New Haven. Only a few loonies like me keep at it."

"That could all change if you'd make up your mind to build the right kind of boats, not just these big things that only a few people can afford." He looked at Sewall as the shipbuilder took the whiskey back to the cupboard. A letter and a telegram were stuck between the green glass panes. Sewall picked them up and handed them to Craig. "These came an hour ago," he said.

Craig put the wire and letter in his pocket. That was the other reason that brought him to Sewall's Harbour day after day: the letters and telegrams from Kitty. He had told Sewall only a little about Kate, not much more than that now and then letters would be arriving from New York. He asked his friend if he would hold them for him. Sewall was the kind of man who could be trusted with such confidences.

The two men had stepped outside on the porch. Sewall's Harbour—named for generations of Sewalls who had built cutters, barges, and light schooners to transport wood and granite along the coast—lay in a natural bay. Sasco Creek, which flowed into Long Island Sound powered the saw mill in Sewall's shipyard.

The wind had not abated. It rattled the shutters of the cabin. The gulls, which had fled to the beach before the storm, now sat with folded wings on the jetty and beached boats. Hands in their pockets, walking with a slight stoop, Sewall and Craig stepped out together, into the wind and across the yard. A boat, somewhat larger than the one Craig had taken out, was up on the bench.

Craig headed toward it, but Sewall waved him on. "That's not for you. A family yacht with cabins; much too slow."

"Not everyone wants to enter races. Boats like that one attract women, the nice young ladies who understand nothing about sailing, who will never learn but think it's a wonderful topic of conversation. There's our clientele. You'd be surprised how many of them there are in New York."

"That's as may be." Sewall was pensive. "But I couldn't build that many big ones. I'd need more machinery. I don't use pumps and capstans like I used to. I need special equipment. I'd have to find someone who can manufacture the parts to my specifications."

"You seem to have given some thought to enlarging."

"And I still wouldn't have the workmen. I'd need carpenters and smiths. But they can make better money in the factories." Suddenly he said, "Come with me. I want to show you something." He headed across the yard to a long shed. The wide door was fastened with a lock, unusual in Sewall's Harbour, where there were only wooden latches that could be put on from the inside.

Sewall undid the lock, and the wind blew the door out of his hand. He pulled it carefully closed behind him. The walls of the shed did not reach the ground but instead rested on stone pilings, allowing air to get in. It was filled to the rafters with lumber, which Sewall pointed at. "There's my capital," he said.

Craig's eyes quickly became accustomed to the dark. Sewall had never brought him here before. "Lumber?"

"Yes, lumber." Sewall caressed the long straight slats of one pile. They were precisely stacked, separated by narrow wooden crosspieces. "Some of it was my father's. There's practically a whole forest from Maine here. You won't find one piece of field maple, or fir, or birch; just the best oak and the best white pine."

Sewall had walked the length of the first piles. Others came into sight behind them, all carefully stacked. "Here we've got a thousand tons of oak for ribs." He pointed to other stacks. "That's pitch pine for planks and decks, and that over there is hackmatack. Nothing better for the keel. I think I'm the only one still using it."

"There's enough here to last for years," Craig said, but Sewall did not seem to hear him. He paced along the rows as if he were alone. Craig felt like an intruder. He went outside and waited until Sewall had replaced the lock and turned it. "Well, how about it?" Craig said.

"Do you want me to be honest?" Sewall looked at him.

Craig laughed. "When have you ever been anything else?"

"All right. It sounds tempting. But two things are against it. You are and I am me."

"Start with yourself."

"I might turn out to be a more uncomfortable partner than you had bargained for. I've got no experience in working with someone else. I was always my own boss. I have my own ideas, especially where boats are concerned. The rest has to do with you. Don't take me wrong. It wouldn't be a good thing if you made such a decision simply because right now you're involved in—may I say this?—a personal matter. That doesn't seem a good time to me. I still think it's only a passing fancy with you. You'll change your mind. You'll never be satisfied with being Hugh Sewall's partner. I know it, and you know it. So think about it for a few days. Then if you still haven't thought better of it—well, it can't be worse than the Empire State, which never pays any dividends."

It was less than three miles from Sewall's Harbour to Willowbeach. The road ran straight along the coast, where many willow trees still grew, bordering the path. For the past few days they had been bare. When Craig came back to Willowbeach, the grass had almost overgrown the path, but now it was trampled down and barely distinguishable from the light sand. He walked with his eyes on the ground.

He was thinking about the conversation with Sewall. It was not a bad idea to sink his money into Sewall's shipyard and build it up. Still, the plan really was a mental pastime, a fantasy, a momentary whim, nothing more, as Sewall had recognized.

His thinking shifted to Margaret. He had not told her about Kitty, nor did he think he ever would. He was too well schooled by his long affair with Irene. But he had not broken off with Kitty, either. Kitty. Only yesterday he had seen her in New York. He had gone to town for a day and night, as so frequently in the past weeks. Although he had sent her a telegram, he had to wait for three hours in the apartment on Laight Street, which she had completely refurnished. Then she had driven up, dressed from top to toe in brand-new finery and so loaded down that Joe Cristadoro had to make four trips to get all the packages upstairs. One of them was a hamper with a complete supper from Delmonico's. The bill for it—over a hundred dollars—she had handed to Craig, saying, "It's cheaper than taking me out and being seen with me."

Sometimes he no longer knew whether it was love or hate that chained him to her. But even in the moments when it was hatred, the tie between them was not damaged; it merely grew tighter.

A flock of wild geese started up before him with a loud, frightened beating of wings. Craig turned into the bypath leading to a duck blind. In the last few weeks he had shot so many ducks that the rear wall of the blind, where he hung them to bleed, was dark with gore. He shot them with the same determination he brought to sailing, and he had stopped only when both the Matlock house and Poynder mansion, and even Sewall, had firmly refused his gifts of ducks.

He sat down on the wooden bench. On the floor lay the ashes of letters he had read and burned here. The telegram Sewall had handed him consisted of only two words: "Forgive me." What gave her such power over him? He did not know. He had been able to endure the twenty-four hours in New York only because he knew he would get on the train that would take him away from her; but he also knew that no more than a week would pass before he would be chafing at the bit to leave Willowbeach for New York. He tore open the letter. Her delicate script, delineated in green ink. He did not need to read the words to know that they too would not yield the answer to his question. He loved her, and yet he hated her, and one did not negate the other. *A personal matter.* He had been surprised by Sewall's remark. What could Sewall know about it? What had he, Craig, known about such things before he met Kitty? When had it happened? How had it happened to him? His attachment made him ill. It was against his nature. Two months had not brought him any nearer a resolution.

In a rage he tore up the telegram and letter. He burned both, scattering the ashes with his feet, and left the duck blind. The wind had let up somewhat; the sky was growing lighter. The sun was breaking through weakly. The temperature had dropped. On the shore path he heard the soft footsteps before he recognized the red hair. "Joshua," he called loudly and hurried back to catch up with the boy.

Joshua stopped. "Is that you?" Then he came running toward his father, out of breath. "Come quickly. Grandfather . . ." He had to gasp for air.

"What about Grandfather?"

At the last moment Joshua remembered his promise. "Did you go sailing?" he asked. "In this weather? Mr. Sewall said you would capsize. I wanted to see that. You didn't capsize, did you?"

"He would have liked that," Craig said. "And you too, probably. Now, about Grandfather?"

The question reminded Joshua again that he had promised to keep quiet. He pulled his knotted bandana out of his pocket. "He gave me two gold dollars." He undid the knot. "I mean, one of them is for Sinclair."

"Is that why you were running so hard?"

Joshua avoided his father's eyes. "He sent me for you. He wants to see you—in his room."

"Grandfather wants to see me? I thought he didn't want to see anyone. Speak up. What happened?"

"He just wants to talk to you."

They were on the way back. Because the path was too narrow for them to walk side by side, Joshua went ahead. They did not speak until they were near the Matlock house. "I have to go home," Joshua said. "What do you think? If I give Sinclair my rabbit for his gold coin, do you think he'll do it?"

"Probably," Craig said. "But that isn't fair. It was a gift."

"But if he wants the rabbit? He begs for it all the time. Is it still not fair then? You won't tell him that it's a bad trade?"

"I won't if you tell me what's the matter with Grandfather."

Joshua looked up at his father. "I promised him—and you have to promise me. Grandfather . . ." He hesitated. He was frightened at the memory but at the same time relieved to share it. "Grandfather was dead. I was there. For a minute he was dead."

"What do you know about dying?"

Joshua's pride was touched. He answered earnestly. "You know Greville—no, not our gardener; his brother, the one with all the dovecotes in front of his house. He builds them all himself, real little houses. They stand on posts in his garden. They have windows and doors, and he paints them white and blue, with red roofs. And he does it only to attract the pigeons. Then he kills them."

"Fred Greville, the one who whittles flutes for you?"

"Yes. Everybody thinks he likes the pigeons, because he feeds them and builds houses for them. I was in the attic with him. There's a big window right next to the chimney. The pigeons like that place especially. It's always warm there. And that's where Greville spreads the food. When they eat, he grabs them and wrings their necks. I was there. He showed me how to do it."

Craig grew uncomfortable at the image of the man in the attic, killing pigeons, and of the boy watching him. He thought how little he knew about Joshua, how little *his* father knew about him, how great were the gaps between people even when they lived under the same roof.

Joshua continued. "The pigeon twitched for a while. Then it stretched out its legs and lay there all stiff."

"A person who dies—that's different."

Joshua shook his head. "Like I told you—the claws pull in. It was the same thing with Grandfather's hand. I watched him. I stood right there. He sat in his wicker chair, and his hand suddenly got all tight and closed up. And the rest of him was stiff."

Craig had seen enough of Joshua's powers of observation not to doubt him any longer. But he said, "I'll bet he dozed off for a minute."

"Is that why his hands were all cold? He told me to put more wood on the fire. When he got up, he had to hold on. And when he shaved, he cut himself. You'll see. But don't tell him I told you! You won't tell him, will you?"

Craig watched his son as the boy ran toward the house,

his hand pressed against the pocket where the gold coins were tucked away. Craig waited until Joshua was out of sight; then he turned into the path to his father's house.

# = 17 =

THE STORM HAD ripped leaves and branches off the trees and littered the lawns and paths around the Matlock cottage. In the morning the garden had still been resplendent. But now one could see everywhere the dark filigree of branches, especially of the espaliers against the house. The bright leaves had been raked into great heaps, waiting to be carted off.

Craig was not surprised to see his mother in the garden. He recognized her from a distance by her light coat and the long yellow scarf she had wound around her head and throat. She loved gardening, no matter what the weather. To see her standing there, up to her ankles in grass and leaves, was a picture from among his earliest memories; a piece of his life, like this house, this garden. It was unthinkable that it would ever change.

He walked across the grass to his mother. The children were loading the piles of leaves onto wheelbarrows.

"Were you still on the water when the storm came up?" Rose asked her son. Almost twenty years had passed since two of her sons had drowned in the Sound, in just such stormy weather. Each time she remembered, her fear of the Sound returned. She stood beside him, leaning on her rake, gloves covering her hands. "Wasn't that reckless of you?"

"Not much more reckless than going to war." He pointed to the small hill of branches and twigs she had raked together. "Why don't you wait until tomorrow? There will be another storm tonight. Then it can all be done at once."

Rose looked over at the children. "Look how they are enjoying themselves. You know I like being outdoors. I like it best when I have something to do." She was right. He, too, had loved to garden in the fall when he was a child. Full of impatience, he had waited for the first storm. To wade through rustling leaves and burrow his arms in mountains of golden foliage. . . . "Are those the same wheelbarrows we used?"

"Of course. They've had a couple of coats of paint over the years, but they're the same ones. Hugh Sewall's father made them out of hackmatack. They will still be here for your grandchildren to use." Rose had spotted Alice, who had stepped out on the porch. She waved at her vigorously. "There you are at last. I had them looking for you everywhere. Come along. A little bit of wind won't blow you down."

Wrapped in a three-quarter-length wool jacket, Alice hesitantly descended the steps into the garden and wandered toward one of the flowerbeds containing larkspur.

"Just take the seeds out of the ripe pods," Rose called. To Craig she said, "It's hard to believe that she is my daughter. I can't bear to watch when she busies herself in the garden. She has two left hands."

"And you have two right ones. You mustn't expect everyone to be as clever as you."

"That sounds like a compliment."

"It was intended to."

"How was New York? We haven't had a chance to talk since you got back. Did you see Langdon and Irene?"

She could not have put her questions more casually, yet Craig preferred to ignore them. The pile of leaves and twigs the children had amassed was now big enough to set fire to. Craig thought he recognized the man who was pushing the burning chips under the foliage. "Did you enlist McCallum for garden work?"

Rose pulled her scarf tighter, a gesture of discipline that was transferred to her face. "McCallum is getting everything ready for our departure," she said. "This is our last day."

"You've decided to return to Albany?"

"Tomorrow morning."

"Isn't that rather sudden? This morning no one said anything about it."

Rose was not a woman to discuss her husband's sudden whims even with her children. "This is the longest we have ever stayed in Willowbeach," she said. "Thank goodness for the storm. It makes it easier to tear myself away."

"Where is Father?"

"In his room." As Craig turned to leave, she added quickly, "It's better if you let him alone. He asked us to. We'll meet at supper. I'm sure he'll be down. I hope you and Margaret will join us."

"Of course."

Rose gave her son a searing look. "I promised myself I wouldn't start anything, but it won't leave me in peace. When I see Margaret going to the beach alone in the morning and coming back in the evening alone. . . . And you go your own way. What's wrong between you two? Is it the trouble between Father and Loftus Poynder?"

"I told you before, their quarrel does not concern me," Craig broke in quickly. "I mean it. Let Father and Poynder do as they like. It's their business, not mine."

Rose was not offended by Craig's vehemence. She understood him. Now she was certain that she would have to have a talk with him. She had waited for an opportunity for days, while the questions had accumulated. "What is going on?" she began. "You have been back two months. In the mornings you leave for Sewall's Harbour; at night you come back. And every week you disappear to New York for a day or two. Why don't you take Margaret with you to Sewall's Harbour? She's not a bad sailor, and she's been looking forward to going out with you all these years. I'll bet she would enjoy going to New York with you too, after four years of Willowbeach."

Craig listened to his mother attentively. Her questions were the same ones he asked himself over and over. How could he make her understand that he did not have the answers, for himself or for her? It would have been so easy to come up with a few reassuring phrases if he were talking to anyone else, but he could not palm platitudes off on his mother. He could lie to everyone, even to his father, but not to his mother. And it was just this that angered him now. "What is it you want to talk to me about?" he asked. "My marriage or the quarrel between Father and Loftus Poynder? As far as the quarrel goes, I've straightened it all out with Margaret. She agrees with me. It's none of our business."

"Perhaps that's what is wrong."

"Are you trying to turn me against Loftus Poynder or against Father?"

"I'm only trying to say that sometimes we cannot remain neutral. You are a Matlock. You can say you don't care if those two old men bash each other's brains in, but you can't keep it up."

"Let me ask you again: which side are you trying to get me to take?"

"I want to turn you against yourself. You wait, you watch, you brood. Someone like you cannot live like that for long. When you were little, you wanted to have a jack-knife. Everyone was aghast, but you insisted. I brought you one, and that was the end of it. One year, when you were supposed to go back to school, you threatened to jump out the window. I opened the window and explained to you how far you would fall. You didn't jump. I was always opposed to rules and regulations, especially in your case, because in the end you always knew exactly what was good for you."

"And what do you want me to do now?"

"I want you to decide. Your situation is difficult. I cannot advise you. But for you to play the bystander—that's simply not possible."

Craig stared at his mother. The scarf wrapped closely about her face emphasized her high cheekbones and narrow gray-blue eyes. It was a simple face that had been marked by many emotions—joy, sorrow, anger, loneliness, curiosity—but not by dissatisfaction. It was this that made her seem so young and so beautiful. He admired her. Suddenly he knew he had always measured all women against her.

"How did you manage," he asked, "to keep your own mind with a man like Father?"

Taken by surprise, Rose Matlock raised her head. "Did I? I think most women have a mistaken view of marriage. They abandon themselves until they are only a shadow of their earlier selves. I never did that. I was a headstrong child, and I never changed. And I was lucky enough to marry a man who respected that trait because he himself was strong enough. I probably would have played fast and loose with a weaker husband."

"Does that mean you would still marry him if you had it to do over again?"

"If he wanted me again, certainly."

"You never tired of him? You were never on the point of packing up and leaving?"

"I didn't say that. There were times when I hated him —or, let us say, I hated myself because my feelings for him no longer seemed suitable. Love and emotion are all well and good, but what determines the quality of a marriage is something quite different: dependability. Dependability is better than faithfulness. A man cannot love a woman the same way for decades on end—nor can a woman. But a marriage . . ." She looked at her son. "That takes more than the feelings between a man and a woman. A house, the children—that is the foundation that gives meaning and order to life. Those ordinary things that make up a woman's life: seeing to it that there's food on the table, that all the clocks in the house are running, that all the lamps are in working order, that the water main does not freeze up in winter, that no birthday is forgotten. People who are happy often complain about the endless routine, but when you are unhappy, the trifles get you through the day and, when you've made yourself tired enough, through the night as well."

"For whom are you speaking now? Just for yourself? Or Margaret? Go ahead. You can tell me."

"It applies to Margaret, that's true. It seems to me, she has shown it enough."

"And now the other side. What comparisons can you draw between Father and myself? You spoke of something like hate."

"He had a few affairs, yes. Perhaps there were more of them than I know about. But he never gave me cause to lose my esteem for him. He kept them from me, from the family. If it had not been for a few overly zealous friends determined to sow dissension at any price, I would never have known a thing. It was very bad for me, but a marriage must withstand such things." An embarrassed silence set in between mother and son.

"Did Langdon say anything to you?" Craig finally asked.

"No. Nor would I have listened. Is there anything you want to tell me?"

"No."

Rose looked squarely at Craig and then abruptly smiled. "Fine. Go now. Unless you want to help with the gardening."

\* \* \*

On his way to the house Craig encountered Alice who seemed to have been waiting for him. "You two certainly had a lively conversation. What was it all about?"

"Alice!" Rose's voice rang through the garden. "Please keep on working. For once, please finish something."

Craig laughed. "She still has us pretty well under her thumb." He followed his sister toward the bed of larkspur.

"Such a lot of foolishness," Alice grumbled. "For years Mother has been taking larkspur and mallow seeds to Mrs. Kavanagh in Albany, who has never gotten them to flower there. All she can raise are some scrubby little plants not half as high as these. The climate in Albany just doesn't suit them, or the soil doesn't; whatever. But every year she takes the seeds to Mrs. Kavanagh. If she didn't presumably the world would come to an end. All because Mrs. Kavanagh has the best voice in the church choir. Here, hold this for a minute." Craig took the bag of seeds.

"Have you heard? We leave tomorrow."

"Yes, Mother just told me."

"If you knew how glad I am. This year went wrong from the start. I've never been so angry with Father in my life. Do you think he has relented about Everett? He doesn't give an inch. If only Father weren't such an awful tyrant! The older he gets, the worse he is. He watched us all get ready to leave, calm as you please. He didn't say we were staying until after the train got here. Now, suddenly, we're told that we're going to Albany tomorrow. I have half a mind to take my chances and not pack at all this time. Then *he* would have to wait, for a change. Do you think he talked to Everett about a partnership while he was here?" The memory of her husband's visit to Willowbeach seemed to release another train of thought. She leaned against her brother and giggled. "Did you ever notice that almost all the Matlock grandchildren are born in June, hmm? Because we poor things return to our husbands early in October, starved." Alice was given to fluctuating between stuffy arrogance and hysterical mirth. "The renovation!" she went on. "Did you look at the plans? The money it's going to take would build each of us a separate house of our own. If he had at least given the job to Vinnie's husband. Do you think he's getting to the age where he starts throwing his money away? That would be like him: so we couldn't get our hands on it."

"We won't, in any case," Craig said. "You have your share. All of us have our share."

"Maybe we could talk to Langdon."

"We could, but I doubt that it would do any good. Did you hear from Everett? Does he agree? You don't have to ask him, you know. The stocks are your property. He has no control over them."

"That's why I wanted to talk to you." She carefully looked all around. "Something funny has happened. Did you really mean it when you said you wanted to buy my shares in the Empire State?"

"Yes. It seems like a good move. They fell so far that you lost a fifth, like all of us. I'll pay you fifty dollars a share. That way you don't incur a loss."

"I know, I know. But guess what? Langdon made me an offer too, quite unexpectedly. He'll pay sixty dollars."

"Langdon—" Craig remembered that his brother had made him the same offer. "Are you sure that Father isn't behind it?"

"For heaven's sake, no. Langdon particularly stressed that no one must know—no one, least of all Father. He didn't make his offer just to me; he asked Vinnie and May, too."

"At sixty per share?"

"Yes. And that's not all." As soon as money was involved, Alice was all Matlock. "When Father dies, Langdon will give each of us an additional hundred thousand out of his inheritance." Again Alice looked around. "I have it in black and white. I can show you Langdon's letter. Vinnie and May also have letters."

"And what do you expect me to do?"

She gave him a cunning look. "I agree, it isn't nice to think about Father's dying; but if you will compare your offer with Langdon's. . . . I'd prefer to sell my ,shares to you, because I can't help remembering that all these years Langdon watched calmly as they dropped and dropped. But you understand—business has nothing to do with personal feelings. I have to consider my children."

He wanted to turn on his heel and leave her standing there. But he controlled himself and said, "I'll pay you sixty dollars. The same as Langdon. Provided you make up your mind soon."

"And the hundred thousand?"

"Do you really believe that part? If anyone promised me something he didn't own yet, I would be more than cautious."

But Alice insisted. "What does a hundred thousand dollars matter to Langdon once he's inherited the whole estate?"

"He hasn't inherited it yet. Wait. For example, I could promise you that Everett will be made a partner in the factory."

"You would do that?" she said, surprised. But she quickly added, "How can you make such a promise?"

"And I would guarantee Vinnie's husband the commissions on all the buildings owned by the railroad. These are promises that can be kept. Langdon might not be able to keep his promises—or he might not want to. In any case, I'd like an answer. Think it over carefully. With me, you can be sure that no one will find out. Another thing—I'd advise you, as well as Vinnie and May, to ask Langdon for the stock certificates now and to deposit them in a safe place."

She smiled. Craig noticed the small folds on the bridge of her nose. She was the only member of the family to have inherited them from John Tyler.

"What do you suppose I did—Vinnie and May, too?"

"You have the certificates?"

"I got them right after you made me your offer. They're in the bank in Troy."

"Clever girl." But his tone left Alice thoughtful as he turned and went toward the house.

There was enough for Craig to think about, too, as he made his way through the silent house to his father's room. Now he saw his brother and sisters for what they really were, Langdon above all. "The good Langdon," Irene liked to call him. Langdon, the loving son whose life was taken up with waiting for his father to die. And Alice, Vinnie, May, who crowded the Willowbeach house each summer with their broods of children. For them, too, John Tyler Matlock was only the person who kept them from what they believed was rightfully theirs. Craig grudgingly admired his brother's latest move. Langdon knew very well that nothing was to be gained by appealing to his sisters' feelings. They could expect nothing more from their father; they had already been given their portion of his estate. And he had treated their husbands badly.

Langdon merely had to throw them the bait and they would snap at it blindly, without thinking.

So that was how it was. Moral indignation was not congenial to Craig. What troubled him went much deeper. It lay in the realization that the family, which had once seemed so solid, was in danger of breaking apart. It was as much his fault as the other children's. He had wanted to gain possession of his sisters' shares, a move which, admittedly, was due less to sober judgment than to a hunch of his. He had been scouting around, and now he suddenly knew all he needed to know. With all his willfulness, Craig had, until now, always felt bound by one overriding principle—the family. No matter that they were an eyrie of vultures; none of them had ever thought to pluck out of the others' eyes. But now this was no longer so. He felt free.

Craig could not remember his father ever calling him to his room for a conference. Such interviews—reproaches, admonitions, confrontations—had always taken place in the smoking parlor.

He entered without waiting for an answer to his knock. Joshua's report had prepared him for a sick man, but everything seemed normal. The door to the balcony was closed, and the curtains were drawn. John Tyler Matlock sat in the wicker chair close to the roaring fire. The sight of the old man for whose death the family was waiting sent a wave of affection through Craig. He was more conscious of it than he had ever been before.

"How are you?" Craig asked. "You wanted to see me?" He was not in the habit of giving explanations, but now he added, "Joshua came looking for me. I was sailing and only just got back."

"You were out in the boat when the storm hit?"

Craig nodded. "I didn't know you cared so much."

"I've never been able to understand what it means to you—sailing. I worked off my excess energies in other areas. Hunting . . ."

He pointed to the gun cabinet from which no rifle had been taken in years. "Today I need only have stood on the balcony, and the ducks would have flown straight into my sights. The storm aroused them, I suppose."

"Mother didn't want any more ducks. I hear you're leaving tomorrow."

There was no reply.

"You won't mind if I take off my coat?" Craig sat down near his father. He noticed the razor cuts on the old man's left cheek and over his lip, but they were faint against the tanned skin. Craig suppressed a remark. For him these minor wounds, which would be healed over tomorrow, were a source of real pity. Meanwhile, Langdon was making deals behind his father's back. Craig could have told his father, but he saw no occasion to. His only advantage lay in keeping his knowledge to himself. Two months ago he had come to Willowbeach solely to speak to his father about Thomas Wilmurt. He had wanted to tell the old man that he had nothing further to fear because Wilmurt's documents were in good hands and out of circulation. But he had not told him. At that time he did not even know why. Now he knew, or was close to knowing. He could have joined the party of the others, Langdon and his sisters. Why did he hesitate? From a sense of justice? Justice for whom? Perhaps it was proper justice when a man like John Tyler Matlock was surrounded at the end of his life by children who had only one feeling left for him: eagerness for his death.

Craig held his hands to the fire. "Hugh Sewall has offered me a partnership in his shipyard."

"You'd have to be a fool! Hand-carpentered yachts, with anchors crafted in a jeweler's shop. His father was a fool before him. I made him a first-rate offer at one time. To head my shipyard in New York. He would have made more money in a couple of months than he could get in a year in his dump."

"Hugh showed me a storage shed full of wood. Pine, oak, hackmatack. His father bought it, and Hugh added to it."

"All the Sewalls have always been fools. Investing capital in wood! If I ran my business like that, I'd . . ."

Craig knew the recitation by heart. He had heard it so often that he had long ago stopped listening. He let his father talk. It seemed impossible that earlier that afternoon there had been such a seizure as Joshua had described. John Tyler's voice, his lively features, his erect posture—his father seemed to be the mighty tree he had always been. Craig noted all this with satisfaction. It seemed only right to him that when his father was on the point of defending his property, he should be in full control of his faculties.

John Tyler Matlock concluded his observations on wealth: "So it is. That's the way of the world. It is not a pleasant world; but for my part, I've tried to make the best of it."

"What was it you wanted to see me about?" Craig was overcome by a sudden burst of impatience.

Matlock leaned forward in his chair, picked up the poker to nudge the burning log. His movements were calm and strong. And again Craig felt satisfaction.

His father pulled the telegram out of his coat pocket and handed it to Craig. "Read that. If you have any questions, ask them."

The wrinkled telegram had been sent from Albany and was signed by Langdon. He informed his father that the state legislature had revoked the Broadway concession granted by the New York Common Council. Craig read the telegram twice. As he handed it back to his father, he said, "Two hundred and fifty thousand dollars for a concession that's worthless. How could you fall into the trap?" After a pause, he added, "Langdon doesn't usually make that kind of mistake."

"I know. But he lost this round." He threw the telegram in the fire.

"You're taking it calmly."

"In war one must be able to accept setbacks."

"I can't remember anyone ever handing you such a setback before. And such an unnecessary one. Don't you have a lawyer to check what statutes apply?" When his father did not answer, Craig continued. "You *do* realize that now Empire State stock will fall even more? And this time there won't be any need for manipulation."

John Tyler Matlock grasped the armrests of the chair. The wicker creaked under his grip. "Damn! Of course I realize it. But it won't happen a second time. Poynder will regret this. When I'm through with him. . . ."

Craig was watching his father closely. A part was sympathetic with the old man; he wanted the Matlocks to win this "war." At the same time he felt alien and hostile to the Matlock aspirations. "Are you so certain?" he asked.

John Tyler's face flared with anger. White splotches appeared on his face. "I am not waging this war for fun. It is a matter of survival, and I intend to be the survivor, as I have always been."

"Couldn't you still reach an agreement?" Craig asked. "Is there no other way?"

"If I had thought along those lines, I wouldn't be where I am. Reaching an agreement means sharing, and sharing means losing. That's how it is in life: if you want only part of something, you get nothing. To get everything, you have to want everything."

"You talk as though you were going to live forever."

Matlock raised his head. Looking straight at his son, he spoke slowly and with urgency. "I am, I really am going to live forever. My father lives on in me, and I will live on in you. I have two sons—" He leaned forward slightly. "I do have two sons?" he asked.

Craig rose. This was the moment toward which they had inexorably been moving. He had waited for it, and yet he had done nothing to bring it about. On the contrary, he had avoided it, postponed it, not out of fear but to gain time, time to be better prepared. "Two sons, yes; but only one heir." He spoke blandly, without expression.

"What does that mean?"

"Just that. I only wanted to remind you of a situation you yourself brought about. You always gave me to understand that you did not need me. I respected that and drew my conclusions accordingly."

Matlock did not take his eyes off his son. He, too, had been prepared for this moment. Of course Craig was his son, but his marriage to Margaret had given him a relationship to Poynder as well—a factor of uncertainty and thus potential danger. Besides, his younger son had returned from the war a changed man. Until his twenty-fifth year, a new gun, a new horse, a new sailboat had been enough to keep Craig in a good humor or, as Matlock put it, "to control him." Then, quite surprisingly, he had married Margaret Poynder and renounced his inheritance. Soon after he had enlisted. Before these events, John Tyler Matlock's assessment of his younger son had been that he was erratic, changeable, and without a conscience. The old man reasoned, therefore, that Craig, like his phlegmatic older brother, did not have what it took to assume his father's mantle.

"I cannot remember that you ever showed an interest in my business. You were a spoiled child, preoccupied with horses, yachts, and girls, flighty and moody. That's all right. You may even have inherited that from me. But the essential ingredient has been left out—the determination to put all your qualities at the service of profit."

"Understand me," Craig said. "I don't want you to have any illusions. You will not in fact live forever. At your age you should be more realistic. What did you do with us? The fact that Langdon adapts himself to the life of a perpetual crown prince is his business, but it could have been different. Did you never think about that? Not every man of nearly fifty has such a thick skin and allows himself to be ordered around."

"Langdon has to be told what to do. Otherwise he won't do anything."

"You see! That's how you talk about your heir. Do you need us or don't you? Of course you do, though you would bite off your tongue before you'd admit it."

John Tyler pushed back his chair and jumped up. "Go to the devil," he said roughly, and a second time, "Go to the devil."

Craig shook his head, smiling. "Oh no. You sent for me. Here I am. You'll just have to listen. You were just saying now you would live on through your sons. Through two sons whom you always sought to put on the shelf because you considered them incompetent and useless, no match for you. And you plan to live on through them? Not even Langdon would be flattered. For that, he would have to love you, and I doubt that he does. Please let's have no sentimental outpourings. Only this: I never once thought about how long your eternal life will last. I have never nourished any hopes that are in any way connected with your death. Please feel sure of that. Nor did I expect that you would remember me, that you would need me. I assume that you never thought that day would come either. You really imagined that you would live forever, and that you would always be lucky. But now, suddenly, you find yourself in a situation you can't deal with alone. Now you're the one who needs me. Go ahead, tell me about it."

John Tyler Matlock stood staring at the floor. "I think we need more wood on the fire."

Craig had never heard his father ask for anything. He had always managed to replace "Please" with "I think we need." Craig, too, had found pleading the most difficult task. He took two logs from the basket and laid them on the fire. When he straightened up again, he said, "What is it you want me to do for you?"

Matlock nodded, as if he had never expected the conversation to take any other turn. "I have Langdon in New York," he said guardedly. "He made a mistake, but it is not his fault. He did only what I asked him to do. I was too sure of myself, and that always leads to trouble. But Langdon will be reproaching himself, and that will stimulate him to greater efforts. He must stay in New York. I need him there. He attends the exchange, and it may be that soon we will have to buy up New York Railroad shares on the quiet. Langdon is the right man for that job. What he cannot take care of, and what I need you for, is practical matters. I mean the nuisance tactics against Poynder's railroads. Derailments, collisions, fires, interrupted telegraph traffic—that's what wore down the Confederacy, and that is what will wear down Poynder. Besides, it will turn public opinion against him. Langdon was too negligent. That sort of thing is not in his line. It isn't his style; he is too soft for it. He thinks you can do such things with kid gloves. He doesn't have any ideas, either; and he does not get along with my line manager, Taylor. Taylor is a rough lout, a slave driver. You'll get on with him much better."

Craig, sitting with lowered head in his chair before the fire, felt his father's eyes on him. "I'm listening," he said without looking up.

"From now on this will be your bailiwick," Matlock continued.

"You will have an office in Albany, and from there—in safe harbor, as it were—you can control the whole operation. I think you should leave right away. Come with us tomorrow. Then we can call all our men together the next day and decide how we will proceed against Poynder. Taylor too, of course. He's the best man to advise you about taking on people. I'll give you a free hand—unlimited funds. It's important that we continue to harass Poynder—more intensely than before and with harsher methods. I believe I can contribute a few ideas. The vulnerable spots on Poynder's railroad are his depots in New York, especially the one on Twenty-sixth Street. If, for example, we could infiltrate enough of our people so that a strike——"

"Stop." Craig interrupted his father. "It is careless of

you to speak so openly before you've ascertained whether
I'm prepared to take on this 'bailiwick.' "

"What is that supposed to mean?"

"Nothing more than that you don't yet have my consent.
I know now what you want me to do for you, but I don't
know what you are going to do for me."

"I don't understand you."

"Oh yes you do. You understand me perfectly. I'm supposed to go to Albany with you. I'm supposed to work
for you. You have just outlined what you want from me.
Now I want to hear what you are offering in return."

"You will profit. An enterprise that unites the railroads
of Loftus Poynder with the Empire State will hold an ab-
solute monopoly. Your shares will climb to twice their
value, perhaps three times."

"But for the present, they will fall considerably," Craig
said. "You're the one who wants something from me.
That's why I'm asking you—what are you offering?"

John Tyler Matlock measured his son with a long look.
He had underestimated Craig, just as his father had once
underestimated him. "Fine, I respect that. At your age, I
also put myself first. Well then, what are you asking?"

Craig had driven the conversation step by step to this
point, but spontaneously, feeling his way as he went. And
the answer he now returned to his father was born of the
moment. "I am asking for half."

Matlock drew a deep breath. "Half of what?"

"Half of everything. Half the shares in the Empire State
for Langdon, the other half for me. The rest does not interest me."

"The rest does not interest you? Is that so? And what
role did you have in mind for me?"

"If it matters to you, you can be president of the company. The ownership, however, should rest with Langdon
and me. In equal parts. You have just turned eighty. It
seems the perfect retirement age."

Matlock sat back in his wicker chair. Whatever might
be going on inside him, his face betrayed nothing but
alertness. "I must say, your language is very direct."

"The only language you understand."

John Tyler's features remained unchanged. "What's the
saying? 'There is more joy in heaven about one lost sheep
that returns to the flock. . . . Can you finish it?"

"Mother could, but I get the meaning."

John Tyler nodded. "It's good to know that inside you there still lives a Matlock."

"I'm expecting more than a Bible quotation." Craig's voice was chilly.

Matlock stood up again. The warmth of the fire, rising to his face, was suddenly unbearable. "We will take care of all that in Albany. I do not want to arrive at such decisions behind Langdon's back; you understand, that would hardly be fair."

Craig saw his father groping for the chair back. He said, "In that case, my answer is no."

John Tyler Matlock was not often put in such a position. He understood that Craig, who seemed determined to force the decision here and now, would not agree to any delaying tactic. "Your proposal is not acceptable to me," he retorted.

"I knew that. That's why I said no."

"Does that mean you will now change sides and join Poynder?"

"No. You don't have to worry about that." Craig picked up his jacket. "I had better leave now," he said. "I assume we'll meet at dinner."

John Tyler Matlock did not answer. He had interfered with the natural order of things when he delayed his return to Albany. He had given in to weariness, and already his enemies were growing up out of the earth and surrounding him, setting traps for him, pressing him with their demands. Even his body threatened to desert him. But he would return to his post. Today he would resume his place at the head of the family table. That should be sufficient to restore order.

# 18

IT WAS COLD in the attic, but the rain had stopped. It no longer beat on the skylight, though there was still a gurgling in the gutters as the water flowed off.

Margaret Matlock knew it was the end of summer when she went to the attic to store the things with which the children had played on the beach and to get out the toys for the winter months. She had carried up a large basket and had already filled the shelves with boats in all shapes and colors, wooden ducks, two cork alligators, and a dozen bright-green rubber frogs. But there was still more: buckets, molds, and spades for making sand castles.

When she heard the voices of the construction workers drifting across from the Matlock house, she briefly interrupted her work and opened the skylight. The air was cold and damp, but the sun seemed about to break through. Raindrops hung on the branches of the leafless trees, and the slate roof of the Matlock house gleamed like dark blue glass. A week after the family had left Willowbeach, the workmen had come to excavate the foundations for the new wings. Standing at the window, Margaret saw Craig and the twins watching the workmen. Even now, when his family had gone, Craig was drawn to the house. The thought hurt her. The pain was caused not by jealousy but by a feeling of failure.

Margaret stepped back from the window, but she could not bring herself to go back to her chore. She had thought everything would be much easier, but she had not reckoned with the magnetism emanating from the Matlock house. She had believed that once she was married and had children, her father's house would automatically lose its chill and cheerlessness. But her plan to refurbish the house according to her own tastes had been dropped when Craig left for the war. There had not even been any pleasure in installing the bedroom furniture she and Craig had bought during his last days in New York. Since 1861 the room had been locked, and she had remained in her old bedroom. Even after Craig's return nothing had changed. She slept in her room, while Craig slept in his study on the same floor.

Margaret had kept silent about the arrangement. She was too proud to force herself on him, and she could understand that a man who had just finished with four years of war needed time, solitude. His letters had often spoken eloquently of all they would do together when he returned and how much he was looking forward to it. But he had gone sailing alone, traveled to New York alone. She had kept silent. Perhaps that was a mistake, but she could not have done otherwise. There had always been the hope that the change would come as soon as his family had left Willowbeach.

Margaret returned to her task. But while earlier she had taken the time to lovingly choose a place for each toy, now she hurriedly put them on the shelves in whatever order she happened to pick them up. She had an idea and wanted to put it into action while she was alone in the house.

It took her less than an hour to arrange the bedroom. Now, content and a little excited, she stood at the center of the room and examined her work. She had drawn the curtains, the better to imagine what it would be like at night, when the fire would be roaring in both fireplaces, its reddish glow flickering over the silvery gray silk of the wall covering. Instead of the children's winter toys she had brought down several things she had not handled for a long time. On the back of the chair, before the vanity, hung the straw hat with the blue ribbons, which she had worn the first time Craig took her dancing in Carbondale. She pulled off her shoes, took the nightgown from the bed, and went to the pierglass where she held it up before her. It was so transparent that at the time, in New York, she had been embarrassed to buy it. Though Craig had once said that what he liked particularly about her was her modesty, perhaps he had only been trying to help her overcome it.

She was still lost in thought when she heard Aunt Edna calling her. The older woman had been in Southport to consult Doctor Shyne. Margaret was glad she had finished her preparations in the bedroom before Edna's return.

"Margaret, where are you? Answer me."

The voice came from the stairwell. Margaret could have gone to meet her aunt and prevented her from finding her here, but she overcame her foolish shame and remained. She merely opened the curtains. "Here I am," she called. "In the bedroom."

Edna Child appeared in the doorway, still wearing her coat. "Where are you? What are you doing here?" She looked around the room with disapproval.

"You were gone a long time," Margaret said. She was already regretting that she had not stopped in the hall. She stepped into her shoes, which were still standing at the side of the bed. "Did the rain delay you?"

Edna had noticed the nightgown flung across the bed. She grimaced. "Must we talk in here?"

It was impossible to avoid Edna, whether she wished to discuss the children, a menu, or some minor matter she had blown up into a disaster. Edna never let her victims escape but followed them through the house and if necessary pursued them outdoors until she had managed to say everything that was on her mind. In the vague hope that this room might block Edna's stream of words, Margaret said, "Why not here?"

"It's indecent." Edna was clearly offended.

"What can be indecent about a married couple's bedroom?" Margaret tried to make light of the matter and not let herself be infected with Edna's mood.

"At one time it was your parents' bedroom."

"Was it? So much the better if nothing remains to remind us of it. The whole house was something or other once. Now I intend to turn it into *my* house, *our* house. . . . Please don't make me angry. And don't stand there as if the devil incarnate were about to rise up in front of you." Margaret left the room, and Edna followed. In the hall she took off her coat. She was wearing a black taffeta dress. In all the years Edna had lived at Willowbeach, Margaret had never seen her in anything but black. "Must you always go around in mourning?"

"Does it bother you?"

"Yes, it bothers me. And it bothers Craig. Your black dresses and your perpetual air of discontent can't help but bother a man."

Edna made no answer but instead stared at the white bandage on her left wrist. Margaret's voice was not much more cordial when she said, "What did Doctor Shyne have to say about your rash?"

"You don't care how I am."

"No, tell me." Whenever Edna could talk about her ailments, she forgot everything else. Her mood improved considerably and became more conciliatory. "I hope it's nothing serious," Margaret continued.

"Doctor Shyne is a most understanding person. I can't see what people have against him. But what else can you expect from untutored fishermen?"

"Did he find out what it was?"

"Just what I expected. He only confirmed my supposition. It is caused by flour. Bleached flour. When I left the doctor, I had the driver take me directly to Hasell, who boldly admitted it. Do you know what he said? 'Nobody uses any other kind of flour anymore. People want their bread white as snow, and the millers give it to them.' But Hasell will bake our bread separately if we can get some unbleached flour for him. He said I wouldn't be able to find any. But that is where he is wrong. I'll write to my brother this very day. He'll take care of it for us."

The two women had gone to the kitchen. "Why write him?" Margaret said quickly. "You've been wanting to pay Hogart a visit for a long time. Why not now? It isn't even four hours from here to New London. The train makes it all so easy. Every time he writes, your brother asks when he'll get a look at Joshua and Sinclair."

"You mean you want me to take the boys along?"

"This time next year they will be in school, and it will be too late. You could take the early train."

"The early train?" Edna was playing with the catch of her purse. "Why don't you come right out and say it? You want to be rid of me."

"We could manage to get along without you for a few days."

"Me and the children both. You want us out of the house. So you can finally be alone with him. Did you think I hadn't noticed how nervous it makes you that the Matlocks stayed longer than usual?" She added immediately, "A French bed!"

"I'll send Greville to the station to get the tickets," Margaret said, as if she hadn't heard Edna. She was deter-

mined not to be provoked. To get Edna out of the house
—for that, she could swallow a thing or two.

"You just don't want to hear what I have to say,"
Edna's voice was sharp. Her hands were still toying with
the clasp of her purse. "I just happened to run into young
Place. You know the one I mean—Daniel Place's son.
He delivers the telegrams in Southport. He was on his way
to Sewall's Harbour." She opened her purse and pulled out
an envelope and held it up triumphantly. "Young Place
was delivering this: a telegram addressed to Craig Matlock." She waited in vain for Margaret to reach for it.
"To Craig Matlock," she repeated, "care of Mr. Hugh
Sewall at Sewall's Harbour. Odd, don't you think?"

Margaret saw Edna's eyes—no longer her whole face,
only the eyes. It was like the time the twins were born,
when the midwife's face consisted only of two eyes that
stared at her while a voice said, "Go on breathing steadily.
The important thing is to breathe deeply and steadily."
Margaret breathed that way now. She said: "If it's for
Craig, please put it in his study so he will find it."

Edna was not impressed by Margaret's calm. Margaret
had always been like that, even as a child. Even when she
was being spanked, she had not flinched. But Edna knew
that under the hard shell, there was a vulnerable spot, and
she was determined to find it. "I suppose you think
that's how it should be. But this isn't the first telegram.
Young Place hardly has time to do anything else. Often he
has to go to Sewall's Harbour twice a day, in every kind
of weather, and not just since yesterday, either. It's been
going on for weeks. Special-delivery letters and telegrams,
sometimes both in one day. Where does Craig live anyhow? There or here?" But again she waited in vain for
some reaction. "You can't fool me. You're afraid. You
shut your eyes. You don't want to see the truth. I suppose
it would be too terrible if he were deceiving you. Do you
think Daniel Place doesn't know what's going on? After
all, he receives the telegrams. He knows what they say. Do
you want to become the laughingstock of the whole town,
thanks to a Matlock? I always knew nothing good would
come of your marriage. People don't try to hide things they
don't have to be ashamed of."

Margaret could no longer endure Edna's voice. She took
the telegram. "I really would like it very much if you left
in the morning," she said as calmly as she could.

Edna lowered her eyes. She was sorry now that she had not given in to her original impulse to unseal the telegram and read it. It had been within her power to open Margaret's eyes. Finally, after long, stubborn waiting, she had tangible proof of the sinfulness of this particular Matlock. And she had squandered her chance. Now, instead of showing Craig Matlock the door, it was being shown to her. "You will regret this," she said, hysteria flickering in her voice. "You will regret it. Open the telegram, do. I beg of you: open it, and you will see that I'm right."

But Margaret had already left the room. She went up the stairs and laid the yellow envelope on the desk in Craig's study. When she stepped back out into the hall, she noticed that earlier she had left the door to the bedroom open. She hurriedly closed it.

Craig did not find the telegram until after supper. The envelope lay on the desk on top of some old newspapers. At first he thought it was an old one he had neglected to burn. The maid had straightened up while they were eating and must have found it in the suit he had laid out to be brushed. He was annoyed at his carelessness but was not concerned. Neither Margaret nor Edna looked after his clothes.

It was only when he picked up the telegram to burn it that he noticed that the envelope was still sealed. It was stamped with that day's date and had been received in Southport that afternoon. He uttered an oath. So stupid! But it had to happen one day. He was drowning in this foolish flood of telegrams and letters from Kitty. Why hadn't he put a stop to it long ago? Then he remembered that Aunt Edna had been in Southport during the afternoon. He knew Edna; it wasn't difficult to figure out how she had presented Margaret with the evidence.

His anger, which until then had always been directed at himself and Kitty, now turned on Margaret. Who else but she had put the telegram on his desk? She had not blatantly displayed it, so he would notice it at once, but had slipped it in with some old papers, as if it were of no special importance. The noble gesture enraged him. All this time she had known about the wire. But she had gone to the Matlock house as usual to fetch him and the children to supper. No, she had given no sign all through the meal. She had asked about the progress of the construction. She had anticipated his wishes, as always, explaining

Edna's absence by saying that she had a lot to do before taking the children to New London. Then she had asked him if he would drive Edna and the boys to the Southport station in the morning. So much self-discipline. So much duplicity. Such coldness—even though it was a kind of blackmail.

He knew he was doing Margaret an injustice. Her ability to let reason rule, even in situations where any other woman would have lost her head, was not due to coldness. Many people thought that his mother, too, was cold and unfeeling because she avoided sentimentality. Margaret was too proud to give any clue to her feelings. Since his return, he had had many occasions to be glad enough of it. It made life easier for him. No searching questions, not even those silent ones other women knew so well how to employ. Because she had not demanded any explanations, he had not been forced to lie. She acted as if everything were going along perfectly. As he examined himself now, he had to admit that, in this way, something new had grown up between them. He did not know what to call it, perhaps an unwritten pact that guaranteed him his freedom. Only in that way had he been able to lead his double life. He had never appreciated her consideration, the trust she had always placed in him, more than he did now, at the sight of the telegram.

He sat down at the desk but did not open the telegram. Kitty's letters—well, they were all right; but how could she bring herself to dictate her telegrams to a clerk? He could see her now at the counter, the clerk facing her, smiling at him, making some ironic remark. He was angry, too, at the thought of Daniel Place, who took down these words, not intended for any stranger's eyes, from a machine on a white strip of paper. Then Place cut it and pasted the strips on. . . . Kitty had no sense of shame. Hadn't she invited him to go with her the very first time they met? What could he have been thinking of! An adventure, fine. But to take her to his apartment! He should have done anything but that. Trouble, nothing but trouble and complications had she brought him, and if he did not watch out, there would be more trouble.

He opened the envelope. At the sight of the figures that met his eyes, he thought for a moment that he had been mistaken and that the telegram was not from Kitty after all. But there was her name: "With love—Kitty."

He laughed aloud, bitterly and furiously. The wire consisted entirely of some outstanding bills that had to be settled: $15 for photograph albums, $80 for spirits, $45 for flowers, $22.50 for visiting cards, $120 for repairs to the fountain in the entryway of the house. There was more. The total came to nearly a thousand dollars. The wire ended with a repeated "urgent" and a triple "With love Kitty." On his last visit he had paid all the bills she had run up before then and had left her some cash.

Craig had lived through many sobering moments with Kitty. But she had always been with him, near him. She had always managed to make him forget his chagrin. as if she were both the poison and its antidote. But today he was alone. This time she could not console him. During the past weeks Kitty had always been present in his mind, no matter what he was doing—sailing in the Sound, hunting ducks, or reading in his room in the evening. Any occupation was only an expedient for passing the time until he could be with her again. But now, as he reread the list of expenditures, with its double "urgent," he felt she almost deserved to be punished.

He took a clean envelope and wrote her name and the Laight Street address on it. Then he tore up the telegram, put the scraps into the envelope, and sealed it. She would understand.

Within an hour he had driven to Southport and mailed the letter. That way, he worked off his anger, at the same time making sure that he would not change his mind before morning.

When Craig got back, the lights were still burning downstairs, but Margaret was neither in the parlor nor in the library. Edna's and the children's valises, packed and ready for the morning, stood in the hall. He turned down the lights and went upstairs. He knocked at the door of Margaret's old room, but there was no answer. He pushed it open. Raising his lamp, he saw that the spread covered the bed. When he returned to the hall, he thought he heard a noise, and when he passed the bedroom, he saw that the door, which had been closed earlier, now stood ajar. He looked into the room which was dark except for the glow from the two fireplaces. The fires gave a reddish sheen to the silvery-gray wall. For a moment he hesitated. Then he entered the room and closed the door behind him.

# ≡ 19 ≡

THE FOUR-YEAR-old sorrel had been in his stall a long time. Though Greville took him out every day, he trotted awkwardly in harness. As long as the children and Edna were sitting in the two-wheeled chaise, Craig had spared the horse, but now, on the return trip from the Southport station, he drove the sorrel at a fast trot.

Margaret had not gone to the station. They had agreed on an excursion to Carbondale, but she wanted to go to St. Andrew's first. Craig was going to call for her on his way back. He urged the horse on as the small whitewashed church came into sight amid the bare trees.

St. Andrew's had once been the center of the fishing community, but since the village had spread to the northeast, along the railroad tracks, and many fishermen had been forced out of their trade, the little church had been shunned. Nowadays there were some wintry Sundays when the Reverend Yarring read his service to empty pews. Even the cemetery was seldom in demand since the new one had been opened on Mill Hill. The Reverend Yarring stayed in the good graces of the rich, however, and the rich kept him occupied with marriages, baptisms, and deaths. The walls of St. Andrew's always shone with snowy white paint, the church was always heated, the pews were always polished, and the cemetery was always well cared for. Three generations of Matlocks lay in the cemetery, and there was room for many more.

Craig stopped by the low wall that enclosed the cemetery. It had been cold in the morning in spite of the sun, but this only meant that, at this time of year, the day would be clear and beautiful. He threw open the canopy and laid the wool blanket on the black leather upholstery.

A woman stepped out of the church and looked around searchingly. The long, dark cape and black lace veil around her head and shoulders made her look as if she

203

were in mourning. Craig did not recognize Margaret until she began to walk toward him.

He had expected her to wear something bright and soft for the excursion, something to express relaxation, to let him know that the night they had passed together had set everything to rights. But the dark garment seemed to reproach him. "Did the Reverend Yarring console you? What words of comfort did he use? Is that how you're planning to go?"

Margaret stood very still, close to the carriage, and put her hands in the folds of the cape. The black lace veil made her face pale and her eyes darker. For a moment it seemed that she would turn away and walk on without speaking. But then she said, "I couldn't very well go to church any other way. I went to my mother's grave. Yesterday was the anniversary of her death." Margaret took off the veil, revealing her thick, chestnut hair. She unbuttoned the cape. Under it she wore a light-blue dress.

"I'm sorry," he said. "Shall we go?"

She got in the chaise. The picnic basket stood on the rear seat, topped with the straw hat with the blue ribbons. She put it on and tied a bow under her chin. Craig took up the reins, but Margaret leaned over to ask, "Will you let me drive?"

"All right. Urge him on. It's good for him to work up a sweat once in a while. And watch out—he always heads for the left side of the road."

She nodded. "The plan is the same? We're going to Carbondale?"

"Yes."

"Was the train on time?"

"To the minute. Do you know how long Edna will be gone?"

"We didn't discuss it. But I suspect she will not hurry back." She flapped the reins, and the sorrel perked up.

"It's been a long time since we were alone," he said.

"In the summer," she replied hesitantly, "in the summer no one is ever alone."

Silently, looking straight ahead, Margaret drove the horse on. The road became a narrow lane, and soon they were driving on a wooded track. The chaise bumped over the broken branches and roots that grew across the bare ground. The sorrel slowed down to a walk, his muscles taut and his hide steaming. When they reached the plateau, with Carbondale visible in the distance, Margaret urged him to a faster trot again.

They had not spoken again. Craig was made as insecure by this silence as he had earlier been by the dark cloak. He did not know what it concealed. The unsureness built up in him and tortured him, so that he feared he would again be carried away into becoming abusive, as he had at the chapel. It had turned out not to be so simple after all: a night spent together could not put everything right. There was still Kitty. His decision to break with her, which he had come so near making yesterday, had not grown firmer. He had merely made up his mind to control his relationship with her more rigorously. He had no intention of risking a scandal, no matter what; but to give Kitty up altogether—he did not want that either. And yet, Margaret and Kitty were only a minor problem compared to the one that had absorbed him since the conversation with his father.

The day after the family's departure, Craig had also left, to clarify the situation concerning the Empire State stock. He had to act quickly, for if his father were to find out, Craig would not have a chance at his sisters' shares. He therefore undertook the tedious journey to Troy, Utica, and Rochester. The Empire State shares had, in fact, fallen further as soon as the revocation of the concession became known. The loss had worked out to Craig's advantage in his negotiations with his sisters. They had sold him their shares after much persuasion and the promise of additional payments if the stock doubled in value during the next six months. Now the certificates were in the safe of his New York bank, but the matter was still not settled. Craig had been able to give his sisters only ten percent of the total sum he owed them. He had hoped that his bank would grant him the necessary credit, accepting the shares themselves as collateral. But the bank had refused, as had four others, and had made it clear why. For the first time he had been made to feel his father's power—and the limits of his own.

It was an important experience, more important than anything else that had happened. If the "No" he had given his father was not to remain an empty threat, he needed money. That meant he needed Margaret. As things now stood, the money could come only from her.

* * *

The place was called Carbondale because of the charcoal-and potash-burners who used to live there. When Craig's grandfather built the house at Willowbeach, one could see the reflection of the flaming charcoal pile floating over the forests day and night. But the forests had been cut down. Only the cabins—five of them remained—served as a reminder of the period. Lovers had rediscovered the place, giving an innkeeper from Greenfield Hill the idea of consolidating and improving two of the cabins and building a large outdoor dance floor. During the summer Carbondale was one of the most popular excursion spots, but in September the restaurant closed down. Craig and Margaret had the place all to themselves. Craig took the harness off the sorrel, rubbed him down, and let him run free. He carried the blanket and picnic basket to one of the wooden tables, wiped it clean, and cleared the bench of leaves.

It had grown warmer. Margaret left her cape in the carriage and ran to the dance floor. The surface was buried in yellowed chestnut leaves. She ran through the leaves, watching them whirl up around her, only to sink back with a hushed rustle.

"Shall I unpack the basket?" Craig called.

"No, no," she called back. "Come here."

Craig went to the edge of the platform and watched her walking through the yellow leaves in her blue dress. Her face was transfigured, not only as if she were recapturing the hours they had spent here in the past, but as if they were happening for the first time. "Have you been here since?" he asked.

Without looking up and without pausing, she shook her head. "But I often wished that one day you'd bring me back here."

He climbed the steps to the platform. "That time, you wore a blue dress, too—and the same hat with the blue ribbons." He wanted to put his arm around her, but she bent down to pick something out of the leaves. It was a narrow, plain bracelet, the silver stained brown. She threw it in the air. It fell back into the foliage.

"Shall we eat?"

"Don't you remember? I was never hungry. I wanted only to dance with you." She leaned against the rail. "And there were always so many other girls who wanted the same thing. Even then it was that way."

The remark, coming at this moment, took him by surprise. He said, "You put the telegram in my room, didn't you?"

Margaret nodded.

"Did Edna bring it back from Southport?"

Margaret was relieved to hear Craig speak so easily about it, so coolly. It was refreshing. The night they had spent together had not been enough to allay her doubts either. And yet she did not consider the telegram important. She would never have opened it, not even if she had discovered it by herself. Perhaps she would have burned it. But open it—never. No, she was plagued by different doubts. Was she really the right wife for Craig? Could she give him everything a man required? She was a prisoner of her inhibitions. She did not have the courage to trust him. Even last night it had been that way. She was haunted by the fear that she would never be able to give herself completely.

"Oh, that stupid telegram," she said. "Edna gave me enough grief over it. You know what she can be like."

"I could try to explain." Craig stopped and asked himself how to begin.

"Explanations can be painful," Margaret said. "The truth might mean that you have to hurt me, and I assume you want to avoid that. I would rather believe that you love me, and that would mean you have no choice but to lie to me." Suddenly she smiled. "I don't want an explanation. Out of pure selfishness. I know myself well enough to know that I don't have what it takes to spy on someone. Scenes: no, I don't think they can make anything better."

Craig was on the verge of saying that there would be no more telegrams, but he stopped himself. When she spoke, everything seemed simple; but then he was perplexed. How much did Margaret really know?

"I think I'm hungry now," Margaret said. She spread a cloth over the wooden table and began to unpack the hamper. From where they were, they could see the Sound. The coast was over seven miles away, but on a clear day like this, one could see the shore of Long Island.

While they ate, they decided not to go back to Willowbeach for dinner.

"If you knew what a pleasure it is for me to be out of the house for a change," she said.

Craig recalled the earlier conversation. The more he could distance himself from it, the more he admired her attitude. Margaret had avoided undue emotion. Nor had she tried to wrest any promise from him. She had not exploited any of the advantages that were hers in the situation. "Edna really is a problem," he said. "She's your relative, but it begins with the food we are served and ends with her influence on the children."

Margaret was thoughtful.

"The biggest problem is the house."

"The house?"

"Yes, the house. I know you've never felt at ease there. You've never been able to consider it your home. We need a place that belongs only to us, like here."

"We talked about it once before, about doing the house over. You had so many plans."

"I didn't want to make any changes while the war was going on." She lowered her head. "You were away four years. You had far different experiences. But at home we saw only the dead being returned for burial. You couldn't open a newspaper without being reminded. I'm superstitious about such things. If you remember, I didn't buy anything for the babies until after they were born." She swept the crumbs from the cloth. "Certainly there are many things we could do to the house, but I don't believe they'd do much good. It's the house itself. It was built for an unhappy, sick woman. That's in the walls and I can't get rid of it. It will never be my house, our house. I can run after Edna and take the antimacassars off the chairs, but it's no use. I don't notice it so much in the summertime, when the children and I can be outdoors all day, but the long winters. . . ."

"And I always thought you were attached to the house."

She shrugged her shoulders. "I grew up there."

"Would you be willing to leave Willowbeach and move to New York?"

"Why not? My father asked me the same thing. But he was talking about Warren Street. What I mean is a house of my own. The boys will be going to school next year. I wouldn't mind if in the meantime we moved into the apartment on Laight Street."

"The neighborhood is no longer livable," Craig said. He was thinking of his resolution to move Kitty out of there during his next visit to New York. "You wouldn't know it anymore. They're tearing down the park, and there are tenements all around. Besides, the house itself will be demolished soon. If we do make the move, we should look for something suitable from the outset. What it really comes down to is money, and that depends on what I will be doing."

He had deliberately introduced the subject of money, but when she did not reply, he said, although he had long since abandoned the idea, "I wondered if I should go into partnership with Hugh Sewall."

"Sewall? Not with your father?"

"That's out of the question. I thought we agreed on that."

"Yes. But I know your father. I thought he would try to win you over to his side."

Craig leaned back. Because the plans whirling in his head since the conversation with his father were still too nebulous to be discussed, he said, "I'm serious. With my capital, Sewall could enlarge. There's a future in boats. It would be a good investment."

Margaret loosened the ribbon around her chin and let the hat slide down her back. "Surely there's also a future in baling wire, lightning conductors, and cough remedies. But for a Matlock to concern himself with such things? Shipping, railroads—those are concerns for a Matlock, and you are a Matlock. You'd soon be bored with boat-building. You are like your father."

"Like my father?"

"Perhaps people don't know that kind of thing themselves, but you are like him."

"Are you saying I'm selfish, moody, tyrannical, egotistical, thoughtless of others? That's what comes to mind when I think of my father. Maybe that's the way you have to be if you want to get ahead as far as he did. Is that what you want?"

"Whether I want it or not won't change anything. You are like him."

"He has hurt a lot of people, and not just friends. His wife, too."

"Yet she loves him."

"Let's just say she's loyal to him."

Margaret shook her head. "She is loyal to him because she loves him."

They were straying from the subject that had to be settled. "The matter is simply this," Craig insisted. "I have enough money for the boats. The other things you mentioned. . . ."

"We could sell Willowbeach," Margaret said.

"Are you serious?"

"The property is in my name. I can do with it as I please."

"I didn't know you felt that way."

"Edna would take it as a personal insult, but I'm sure Father wouldn't mind. Edna could live with her brother in New London. She seldom passes up the opportunity to threaten to return there. I would pay her an annuity, and I'm sure she could go back to giving piano lessons. If we could get a reasonable price for the house. Also, there's still my mother's estate."

"First we need a house in New York," he said. "By the way, I've purchased my sisters' stocks, railroad stocks. But I could only make a down payment. I don't have much time, and it may be that I will find myself temporarily strapped."

Margaret, who had begun to repack the lunch basket, interrupted what she was doing. Her face was beaming. "You see, you married the right woman after all. Nobody understood how a Matlock could bring himself to marry that Poynder girl. But you were on the right track. I *told* you you're like your father!"

He reached for her hand and pulled her close. Shy and embarrassed, she let it happen. Again, as in the night just past, it was precisely this that excited him: when, behind her reserve, he detected something like alarm at herself. "When are Edna and the boys coming back?" he asked. "Not tomorrow, I hope."

"No, not tomorrow."

He cupped her head in his hands and kissed her. He thought: she still kisses like a young girl who has never known a man.

# ═ 20 ═

Since the excursion to Carbondale, Craig had not been back to Sewall's Harbour. The weather was fair during the final days of October, and he had gone on other excursions with Margaret. At night, both fireplaces in their bedroom were lit.

There had been no response from Kitty. If letters were waiting for him at Sewall's Harbour, he did not know about them and, he told himself, he did not want to know. But then Kitty showed up.

The message was delivered by Sewall through Miln Parker. Craig knew Parker only by sight. He was one of Sewall's carpenters. During the summers he was a member of the band hired by the Carbondale innkeeper to play on weekends. That day, for the first time in a week or so, Craig had walked over to his parents' house, where the workmen had finished the foundations of both wings. From there he had caught sight of Parker standing in front of the Poynder mansion, talking to Margaret. She pointed to the Matlock house. The carpenter bowed, and as Margaret went back in the house, he came across the lawns, his blue cap still in his hand.

Miln Parker was a strong young man. His hair was strewn with sawdust. His errand seemed to make him uneasy. "Hugh sent me," he said. "He wants to talk to you. I already asked at the other house."

"Don't I know you?"

"I'm Miln Parker, I work for Hugh."

"In the summertime I've sometimes seen you in Carbondale. You play the horn, right?"

"When there's a chance to earn a little on the side, you grab it; that's all." He put on his cap, as if to go.

"What is it that's so important?"

"Hugh only said it's urgent, something about a yacht."

But Parker acted as though he did not believe his own words. Craig looked at the Poynder house. No one was in sight, yet he had the feeling that Margaret was standing behind one of the windows, watching him. He was sure that Sewall would not have sent Parker if there had been another way. It had to be something to do with Kitty. Some news of her, or maybe she herself had come—a possibility that had crossed his mind more than once recently, against his will. But he did not want to ask any more questions. If Sewall had not taken Parker into his confidence, he must have his reasons, and in that case Parker could not have told Margaret anything.

Craig took the shore path, letting Parker walk ahead. The grass was damp, and there were a few sailboats out on the water. To Craig, it seemed as if months had passed since he last walked here. Sailing, shooting ducks—right now, he could not believe that he had spent weeks that way. It seemed as though time lay far, far behind him.

Sewall must have been watching from his window. As the two men approached the cabin, he came to meet them. "Thanks, Miln," he said to Parker. "Everything is in order. We should start cutting the wood. We need three-inch boards. Get Jim to help you." He waited until Parker was out of earshot. "I had to send him. I hope he found you right away. Something pretty unpleasant has happened."

"Kitty?" Only then did Craig notice that Sewall was not wearing his cap. His face, with the scarred, sunken eye, seemed oddly empty and vulnerable. Craig was about to climb the steps to the porch, but Sewall stopped him.

"Wait," he said. "The doctor is with her."

"The doctor? Let me go."

"Control yourself, Craig. The men are watching us. I haven't told anyone who she is. But I can't keep them from thinking what they want to think. Come on, let's walk on the beach."

"I want to see her."

"The doctor is with her. He's the only one she needs right now." Sewall walked ahead to a spot where a few fishing boats lay keelside up for repair and tarring.

"What happened?" At heart Craig was glad Sewall had kept him from going into the house. It gave him time.

"She just showed up here," Sewall said, "without notice, just like that. About two hours ago. Since those last letters I gave you, nothing more came. I must say, I liked it that way. I thought you had finally settled it. But suddenly she turned up. Higham drove her from the station. I was in the woodshed, selecting logs, when I saw her standing on the porch. She asked me where she could find you."

"Did she tell you her name?"

"She didn't need to. When I saw her, I knew who she was."

"I never described her to you."

"I knew just the same." He looked out at the water.

"I sent back a telegram last week," Craig said. "That's also the reason why I haven't been back here. I didn't expect any more letters. Was she angry?"

"Angry? You're taking the matter damned lightly. Angry! She must have been desperate."

"She's capable of it."

"What are you talking about?"

"Ensnaring someone. Someone like you. Now tell me, what mischief did she make? So she was desperate? I can assure you, she has often driven me to desperation."

"She didn't say much, she was very calm. She asked about the house, about your wife, but mainly about the house. She wanted to see it. Said she wanted to see how you live here. 'I don't want to make trouble for him,' she said. 'I just want to see the house.' I talked her out of that. It wasn't all that hard. I even had her where she was promising to take the first train back to New York. She seemed very reasonable. She wore a light summer outfit. I suggested that she come in and get warm. There was lots of time before the next train. She sat down next to the stove, and then she asked me if she could have something to drink."

"And she tied one on."

Sewall was still looking out over the water. "You do have a heart," he said, "but sometimes it gives you trouble, and then you feel like tearing it out. No, she did not touch a drop of liquor; she asked for a glass of water. Only a glass of water. Not even coffee. She sat next to the stove and shivered. She really wasn't dressed for this weather. I gave her the water. Then I had to leave her for a few minutes, because one of the men needed to see me about the saw blades. She must have taken it then."

Craig leaned against one of the boats, tracing the cracks in the paint with his fingernail.

"When I came back she was sitting there just as before," Sewall continued. "But suddenly she was in a great hurry to leave. I asked her if she didn't want to leave a message, but she said no. She intended to walk back to the railroad station in Southport. She was dressed for the dog days, so I said I'd send for a carriage, but she laughed—she really laughed—and said the walk would warm her up. 'You have no idea how cold you can get in New York.' Those were her last words. She was already out the door on the porch, and she waved again and turned back and laughed and waved. I thought, well, that went off all right, after all."

The saw started up in the yard. Its shriek ripped the silence. As the blades gradually ate their way into the wood, the noise diminished, settling into a dull, even, rhythmic buzz. Clouds of yellow sawdust welled out under the open door of the workshop. Sewall was so used to this noise that he barely noticed it.

"It wasn't until Parker came that I knew something was wrong. He has a little house up the shore. Lately he hasn't come to work until after noon because he's rebuilding his second floor. There's a shortcut, straight along the beach. That's how he came across her things. He thought nothing of it, just that it was odd—a woman's clothes on the sand—the shoes, the purse. In Owenoke there's a sect. They make holes in the ice in winter and bathe—you know, Allanson Sweet, the water worshiper—and Miln just thought she was one of them. My workmen got a big kick out of it when Miln told them about it. It was their laughing that attracted my attention. When Miln gave me a description of the clothes, I knew what had happened."

She's dead, Craig thought. She's dead. But the thought brought no emotion—no horror, no guilt. Then, quite suddenly and without any connection, he thought of the storm he had lived through on Captain Beelt's clipper and of Beelt's words: "In a hurricane the only safe place is at the center, at the eye of the storm."

"That's just like her," he finally said. "Just like her."

"We went out in the boat. When she saw us, she swam even farther out. She didn't have much strength left, but she fought like a wild cat. She didn't want to be pulled in the boat. Like I told you, when she was in my house, she took something. The doctor says it was a sleeping draught, but I guess she didn't trust it and wanted to make absolutely sure. She must already have been dazed. She didn't come to properly until we were about to pull her in the boat, and she fought like crazy. She must have swallowed a lot of water, and maybe that was lucky, because when we got her in the boat, she vomited." He brushed his face with the back of his hand. "That's it. I took her back to my house and sent for Doctor Shyne and for you."

Craig had left his place at the boat. His eyes traveled past Hugh Sewall. The two men silently walked back to the house. They went up the steps to the wooden porch, Craig in the lead. The shadow of a man was visible behind the window next to the door. Craig's hand was already on the latch, but he dropped it again. "I can't," he said. "I can't go in. Please, you go to her. And if she lives, I'll marry her. You can tell her that. Go to her. I can't. Not now."

To Sewall's ears Craig's words sounded like a threat. "Pull yourself together," Sewall said. "I'll talk to the doctor."

"Does she have a chance?"

"You'll know soon enough."

"You can tell her," Craig repeated, "that I'll marry her."

"I certainly won't tell her any such thing. If she dies, it won't do her any good; and if she lives, you won't keep your promise. You two seem very much alike. If you want something, you don't seem to care how you get it. Don't you understand—that's exactly what she was trying to do? So don't lose your head now. Watch out, the doctor is coming."

Dr. Philip Shyne was a man of sixty-five, corpulent but with a remarkable constitution, considering the amount of food he consumed at a meal. He allowed himself to be paid in kind by many of his patients—chickens, eggs, meat—and if ever a lobster strayed into one of the fishermen's nets, it was sure to end up on Dr. Shyne's table. He was from the South. No one knew for sure whether he was legally entitled to be called Doctor. There were people who claimed that he had never managed to get beyond an apprenticeship as a hospital orderly. But that did not make much difference in a time when even an academic medical degree could be earned in a six-month course. He had come to Southport forty years ago, married the widow of his predecessor, and taken over the dead man's house and practice. His wife died soon after, nor was long life granted to either of her successors. Shyne was now married for the fourth time. The fact merely enhanced his reputation.

The door opened, and Dr. Shyne stood in the doorway in his vest, his shirtsleeves rolled up to the elbow, drying his hands and arms. Expecting only Sewall, he looked at Craig with curiosity. "You must be Craig Matlock," he said. "Unmistakable. A doctor doesn't often get a chance to lay eyes on a Matlock, except during confinements."

Hugh Sewall broke in. "How is she?"

"Not so fast," Dr. Shyne said.

"How is she?" Sewall insisted, as though Craig were not involved.

"She will recover. I turned her on her head and managed to empty her stomach pretty well. We'll see. Right now there's nothing more I can do." They had entered the cabin. Dr. Shyne pointed to the door in the rear. "Keep her warm. If necessary, put a couple of hot stones in the bed. No food, but she won't feel like eating, anyway. Coffee, yes. The stronger, the better. You mustn't let her go to sleep. Don't be afraid to use force. Keep her awake by any means necessary. If you have to, walk up and down the room with her." His eyes shifted from Craig to Sewall and back again. "Who is she, anyway?"

"If you mean, who will pay your bill," Sewall said quickly, "I will. She's my cousin."

Dr. Shyne took his Prince Albert from the back of the chair. "I have to tell you, you're very lucky. Normally I don't see such cases except in the morgue. If you want to pay me now, that will be six bits. If you want me to send you a bill, I'll have to charge a dollar." Sewall reached for his brown leather bag. "Do you know, this is the first fee I've ever collected from you?" he said. "Even though you practice a high-risk trade. No, a doctor can't get rich here. The climate is too good, the rich people are too healthy, and the sick people are too poor." He turned to Craig. "That, by the way, is a saying of your father's."

"I'm familiar with his sayings," Craig replied. "As far as he's concerned, illness is nothing but a flaw in a man's character."

Dr. Shyne laughed heartily. "And how would your father describe a young woman who wants to take her own life?"

"He would have no sympathy whatever."

Hugh Sewall opened the door for the physician. "I want to thank you for coming so promptly."

"Lots of hot coffee," the doctor repeated. "Don't let her sleep. I'll look in again later. Included in my fee."

Craig and Sewall were silent for a while after Dr. Shyne had left. Sewall put another log on the fire and set the kettle to boil. He rinsed out the green bellied pot and dropped in ground coffee. As he turned down the draught of the stove, Sewall said, "I'd better go out to the yard. All you have to do is pour in the water when it boils and let the coffee steep."

"Thanks, Hugh. Can she stay here?"

"Did I tell you different?"

"All I meant was, there's never been a woman here before."

Sewall pulled his cap down low over his face. At the door he turned and said, "Don't make any promises."

The tiny back room was little more than a cubbyhole. So much heat was being generated by the stove that the window panes were steamed up. There were a bed, chair, clothes cabinet, and narrow shelf. Kitty's eyes were closed, and her breath was barely audible.

Craig knew that Sewall understood the situation. There was no sense in making further mistakes. She had surely made enough trouble for him already. But all these thoughts vanished as he stood at her bedside.

Kitty's head was turned to one side, her hair dark with moisture, her skin very pale.

"Kitty," he said. "Kitty." He thought of the doctor's brusque cheerfulness. He could not believe that those eyes would ever open again, those lips ever speak. Suddenly he could no longer look at her. Her things lay across the chair. He picked up the dress—crêpe de chine in October!—the silk gloves, and the little handbag and locked them in the cabinet.

Craig left the door open as he went back into the big room, where he filled a mug with coffee, sipping it gingerly. It burned his lips. He put the mug down and got the whiskey bottle in the kitchen cabinet. He took a long drink and replaced the bottle.

Kitty did not stir as Craig bent over her. He put one arm under her head and propped her up, holding the mug to her lips. "Come, please drink this." But she still seemed to be unconscious.

He put the mug down on the windowsill and, using both hands, shook Kitty until she finally opened her eyes. But they did not seem to see. She was looking past him at the ceiling. Her eyes fell closed again. Then her lips moved. Her voice was very low. He could hardly understand what she was saying. "Has he gone?"

"It's me—Craig. Who are you talking about?"

"Send him away, please."

Craig let her fall back on the pillows and went to get the coffee. Again he propped her head up and held the cup to her lips. "You must drink this. Please try. The doctor says you're over the hump. Drink it down like a good girl. You'll see; it will make you feel better." He kept urging her, trying to keep her awake, anything to keep the silence from returning.

Finally she sipped the hot coffee. Then she closed her eyes again; but he forced her to empty the mug. She did not look at him, but once she suddenly spoke. "I didn't want it. I didn't want to make trouble for you." Then she did not seem to know he was there. There was no clock in the room nor in the big room. He had no idea how much time had passed. It was growing dark. From the window where he was standing, Craig could see the Sound. Sometimes a ship passed Sewall's Harbour. At one time Craig had been able to tell time by the ships that passed. It had been a favorite game, and he had won many a bet. But now he had lost all sense of time. Occasionally he put another log on the fire or took a sip of whiskey. He gave Kitty some more coffee and then returned to the window.

Craig was standing there when Sewall cautiously looked into the room. He looked toward the bed and signaled to Craig.

"How is she?" he asked when Craig joined him in the other room. Sewall had carefully closed the door behind him.

"I don't know. I can barely keep her awake. I wonder if Doctor Shyne isn't being overly optimistic. But she's calm now."

"I hope you are, too. Margaret is here. She's waiting outside. Luckily, she didn't want to come in; but I think it's better if you don't keep her waiting." He motioned toward the other room with his head. "Don't worry, I'll look after her." Then he noticed the whiskey bottle. "Did you drink all that?" he said, holding it up to the light. But Craig had already left.

## = 21 =

HE DID NOT see her at once. It was almost dark, and fog was rising from the water. He felt the cold air all the more, coming from the warm house. He had slammed the door behind him and rushed down the porch steps. Now he tried to walk more slowly, but his legs would not obey. Finally he stopped, with the curious feeling that his legs were continuing to move. Margaret was on the dock, where the outlines of a new boat were recognizable. The ribs had already been installed. The ship's body floated in the dusk like a sea monster.

Margaret spoke first. "I thought I would come and get you. Who is this boat being built for? Hugh Sewall wouldn't tell me. What's wrong?"

"Come to get me?" he said.

For an instant she was irritated, but then she replied, "Yes, it's been such a long time since I was here. Just about all summer. I thought you might be pleased."

"You thought. You're always thinking something, aren't you? Are you sure you didn't want to spy on me?"

Margaret grabbed for her scarf as if the wind had loosened it, but the air was still. Even the surface of the water was as smooth and dark as enamel.

"Are you struck dumb? What were you looking for here?"

"You've been drinking."

"Then think about that. Try hard. Think about why a man drinks."

"I think I'd better leave."

"It would have been better if you hadn't come at all." He knew he was making a mistake, one that might never be set right; but he could not help himself. "Wait," he said. "I'll take you home."

"That isn't necessary. It's not dark yet."

"I know what is proper. It is important to preserve the amenities between married people, you know. One has a certain style. One does not spy on the other but one merely comes along. Of course I'll take you home. One does not let a lady walk alone in the dark."

Margaret had turned away. She walked ahead slowly, mechanically, like a sleepwalker. Then the house loomed up, large and dour, its windows dark. Margaret stopped. "You needn't come any farther," she said.

"Once in my life I beat a woman," he said. "Really beat her, without mercy, right in the face."

"Really, I can go the rest of the way alone."

He grabbed her hand so hard that she had to suppress a cry of pain. "It was in Atlanta during the last days of the war. We had occupied the railroad station, and that morning two carloads of horses blew up. Concealed mines on the tracks. We cordoned off the area and posted guards. We had discovered still other mines on a side track, where the cars with provisions were. In spite of the guards, though, suddenly there were two women. How they got there, I don't know. But there they were—two women, one down at the tracks with a wheelbarrow, and the other one up above, inside the car. She threw the food out to her friend through the open door, while the other one put it in the barrow. I didn't care that they were looting, but the car stood directly over the mines. I could still see those horses. We had just finished carting off the carcasses. I ran over and shouted at them to get out. But it wasn't good enough. I had to pull them away by force. They swore at me and fought me hand and foot. I couldn't think of any other way, so I grabbed one of them and hit her in the face."

"I understand," Margaret said.

"I did it because I did not want a catastrophe."

"I understand. Really I do. Please let me go. You're hurting my hand."

Craig let her go and watched as she went to the house.

He waited until the windows became bright, first down-stairs and then on the second floor.

He knelt in the damp sand and scooped up water with his hands, dipping his face in it again and again, until his face and hands were burning with cold and his head began to clear. Then he returned to Sewall's Harbour. He had behaved like a fool. And at the very moment when they had found their way back to each other. He had never seriously entertained the thought of leaving her, but it seemed almost as farfetched to give up Kitty. He wanted both of them. And now it seemed that he had lost both.

Craig could not believe his ears when he entered Sewall's cabin. He heard laughter, not loud or boisterous, but un-mistakably Kitty's. Jerking open the door, he saw that she was sitting up in bed. Sewall was sitting on the edge of the bed, holding a hand mirror so that she could examine her face. She was holding a comb. "You are one moment too early," she said in a voice that, though weak, reminded him of the voice she sometimes used when, lying next to him, she spoke in her sleep. "I didn't want you to see me like this. Hugh said you were here all the time, and I never noticed. I must have looked awful. I'm sure it can't have been an edifying sight."

"Hugh?" he said. "Are you already calling him Hugh?"

"He's your friend, isn't he? What do you want me to call your friends?"

Sewall had gotten up. He laid the mirror on the coverlet. "I'll make some fresh coffee," he said. "She drank it all."

Kitty ran the comb through her hair, but it was a point-less gesture. "I didn't want to make trouble for you," she said. "Really I didn't. Come, sit here. You see, I'm quite all right again." Her hand fell and a shudder ran through her. She pulled the blanket closer. "It was certainly the stupidest thing I could have done."

"It certainly was." Craig was still standing at the foot of the bed.

"That doctor is a rough old man. I think I'll never be able to eat again. That ought to save you some hefty bills." Craig said nothing. "You'll hate me because I'm making such a lot of trouble for you," she said. "But when the telegram came back in scraps, I thought I had lost you. I always do everything wrong. I promised you so often to be sensible, and now you won't believe me when I promise again. It was just the telegram. I thought, he's not brave enough to tell me to my face or to write that it's all over. Is it? Is it all over?"

"Are you really feeling better?"

"If you only knew how much I missed you. I was so angry at you. Do you know what it's like to be alone in that apartment? Just sitting and waiting for you to come? Nothing to do, nobody to talk to, just sitting, waiting, thinking, what is he doing now? Where is he now? How are things going with him? When will he write? When will he come?"

Craig smiled.

"Sure, you think I enjoyed it. You're remembering the time I said I'd have my revenge if you left me alone. I'd turn the whole house upside down. But I never saw anyone. And Joe Cristadoro isn't all that amusing, you know." Suddenly she was tired. Chills shook her body. She sank back and closed her eyes.

He took the mirror, comb, and handbag and sat down on the edge of the bed. Sewall came in and silently put down two mugs, then left again. Kitty resisted when he wanted to make her drink some coffee. "Come on," he said. "Be sensible."

She looked at him. "I promise you it will never happen again. If I were dead now, *she's* the only one who would benefit by it. Does she know you're with me?"

"Please, let's not start."

For a while they were silent. They Kitty said, "I could go back to work. I think that would be best. That's what drove me crazy—so much time on my hands all of a sudden. One has to get used to being idle all day long. I bet Ben Pocock would take me back."

"It doesn't have to be Pocock." Craig was glad to explore the idea further. "You could open your own shop and sell gloves."

"My own shop? Do you really mean it?" She sat up. "Give me the cup. I'll drink the coffee." After she had handed back the mug, she again burrowed under the covers. "My own shop? I could do more than just sell gloves; I could make them. Gloves are very fashionable now, and in a good neighborhood with rich customers, I bet I'd make enough to pay you back quite soon."

"We will buy you a shop," he said. "In a good neighborhood. And you don't have to pay me back."

"Not pay you back?" She stared at him. Kitty loved every line in his face, but she never knew what really went on behind it. "You're going to buy me a shop, and then you'll leave me. Is that what you mean?"

"Please, Kitty. Don't twist my words."

"A shop isn't a bad idea. 'Kate Schoffield, Gloves. Latest French Styles'—how does that sound?"

"Wonderful. Do you think you could get out of bed and walk a little?"

"You'll take me back to New York?"

"As soon as the doctor says it's all right. First get well. You can stay here. Tomorrow I'll buy you a few warm things, and perhaps we could go outside for an hour."

"I mean, will *you* take me back?"

"Of course. Come, try to get up now."

"And you won't leave me alone again?"

"Come on, try." He put his jacket across her shoulders and led her back and forth in the narrow passage between the bed and the stove, four steps one way, four steps back.

It was late when Craig prepared to walk back to Willowbeach. Kitty was asleep. Doctor Shyne, who had come by once more, appeared pleased with his patient, which was to say that from his point of view, he was displeased. "There's no way for me to make any more money here," he said to Sewall, "much as I'd have liked to pocket another fee from you. Your cousin has a remarkable constitution. If her temperature doesn't rise, she can get up for a few hours tomorrow."

The time had passed quickly. Craig looked after Kitty while Sewall brooded over boat plans in the front room. Now, as the two men stepped outside, Craig wearing a coat of Sewall's, it was almost midnight.

"How did it go with Margaret? Was it bad?"

"I behaved like an idiot."

"Did she notice anything?"

"She came for me. I don't know what was the matter with me. I don't even remember what I said exactly. I only know that I did it all wrong. Now she'll be thinking God knows what."

"It'll all come right," Sewall said. "Margaret is a sensible woman, and—" He hesitated. "And she knows you'll never leave her."

"What makes *you* so sure?"

Sewall did not answer. They stood in the dark on the porch. "Will you look in on her tomorrow?" he asked after several moments.

"Yes. Perhaps a little later. I want to buy her a few things."

"Will you be taking her back to New York?"

"Of course. You heard what Shyne said. She won't be bothering you much longer. She's never made trouble for anyone but me."

"You?"

"I know. You and she hit it off right away. She's good at that. She can wrap anyone around her little finger."

"We didn't talk much. You can't say that she's had a charmed life—and you're no good for her, that's for sure. Even though she thinks you are." Sewall stared into the night. "She's . . . like a boat without a rudder. No balance. But you know her better."

"I fell into it like an amateur."

"You talk only about yourself. And she talks only about herself. That's where you're alike. Except that she lacks your toughness."

"I'll take her back as soon as possible." Craig wanted to make it clear to Sewall that he did not wish to discuss Kitty any further. "I imagine in two or three days. I only ask one more favor of you. When the time comes, will you take her to the station in Southport? I'll get the tickets ahead of time and join her at the last minute. I'll explain to her why you're taking her to the train. I think it's better that way. Every soul in Southport knows me."

"You're a hard man," Sewall said.

"I've had enough trouble. That's finished now."

"And to think you almost became my partner."

"What do you mean?"

"The boatyard would have flourished, that's for sure. But I don't know how long our friendship would have lasted."

"The Sewalls have always been dreamers, my father says."

"He may be right."

"Then it's better this way. I'm going to lose a lot of friends in the months ahead. But I'd like to keep your friendship."

Walking through the night, Craig had time to reflect on

his own parting words. He had not planned them, but they did express what was going on inside him, what preoccupied him. Kitty's suicide attempt, the confrontation with Margaret—they were just externals; the crucial problem he faced was himself. It was a matter of direction. He would have to make many sacrifices. He would indeed lose friends. Some of them might even become enemies. His father had often paid this price, and he had not hesitated when it was necessary.

# ═ 22 ═

THE NEW YORK & New Haven was a line which, in spite of poor balance sheets, liked to build costly stations. But Southport was not one of them. It was little more than a freight yard, but it did have two platforms because here the trains from New York and New Haven crossed. There had not been sufficient money to roof the station over.

From a distance Craig could see Kitty and Sewall waiting. Kitty was wearing the navy-blue coat he had bought her, while Sewall sported his cap and an otter jacket, his winter uniform. The temperature had fallen to the freezing point overnight. Kitty and Sewall were not alone on the platform; there was an unusual number of travelers, more than Craig had ever seen here on a weekday.

Craig turned to Greville, who was holding the reins. "Let me out here. You can go home."

The new wooden pavement muffled the horses' hooves on the platform in front of the station. It was the only feature Southport shared with the ocean spas that were its model. Craig refused Greville's offer to carry his luggage, a small carpet bag, to the platform. "I'll see you tomorrow, Greville. At the same time. I'll be arriving on the eleven o'clock."

Craig waited until the gardener turned the rig around. He had bought the tickets the day before. Just as he was about to cross the tracks—there was no overpass—the station master came rushing toward him. McIdden was a tall man, and his black custom-made uniform with the gold braid deserved a grander station, as McIdden steadfastly suggested to his superiors. He raised his cap.

"Have you heard? What a terrible thing. It's hurting all of us. You're on your way to New York to find out more? I hope the train's on time. It's the first one today. All the earlier ones were canceled." He pointed to the other platform. "Just about all those people came to take the early train."

Craig was in no mood for a long conversation. He did not answer.

"You hadn't heard? Of course, it's not official yet, and the New York papers haven't come in today, either. It's more or less a telegraph rumor, as we call it. Place found out about it from other telegraphers unofficially. Must have been quite an accident—well, maybe *accident* isn't the right word. We just don't know the details. Only that there was a fire, and they say there are fatalities."

"Fatalities? Where?" Craig looked over at Kitty and Sewall, who had spotted him.

"All of us have been hurt. Not just the New York Railroad. These things give a bad name to the whole railroad system, and God knows we've had enough of them lately. I only hope the train comes in on time."

"Where were the fatalities?"

"In New York, in the depot on Twenty-sixth Street. Just recently the bridge accident—and now this. The newspapers will latch on to it and blow it up. They say there was a strike. . . ." As he spoke, McIdden watched the signalman at the southeast end of the station. When the man began to wave his red flag, McIdden said, "The train from New York, believe it or not." He looked for the train through slitted eyes as it came into view. "Then the train from New Haven can't be far off either," he said.

Craig crossed the tracks and mingled with the other passengers, all of whom looked alike in their dark, fur-lined coats, their heads swathed in caps and scarves. It was as he had feared: almost everyone knew him. But he avoided conversation.

The train from New Haven still was not in sight. The signalman at the northeast end of the station sat on a tripod between the tracks, his flag rolled up under his arm.

The train from New York pulled slowly into the station, a black locomotive pulling the cars of the New York & New Haven line. At the rear, looking alien and conspicuous, was a single scarlet parlor car.

The scarlet color struck Craig rather like the word *strike* when McIdden said it. Deep inside, something like an alarm went off. Only the New York Railroad used shiny red cars, but he searched for the identification to make sure. He saw *New York Railroad* lettered in black on the red background.

Brakes screeching, the train had come to a stop. Craig could see only the feet of the descending passengers. No one left the scarlet car, nor could any passengers be seen behind the windows, since the curtains were drawn tight. A workman now appeared to uncouple the red car from the rest of the train.

Craig glanced at the signalman who was watching for the train from New Haven. His flag was still furled, so there was time yet. Craig crossed the tracks behind the red car. On the other side, too, the windows were draped and the doors were closed. He looked down the length of the platform. The station master stood near the locomotive, talking with the engineer and the stoker. Baggage was being unloaded; bundles of newspapers came flying through the air. A string broke, and the papers fluttered apart. The dining-car stewards hurried to refill the carafes of ice water. In the midst of this activity, the scarlet car stood silent and abandoned.

But now the rear door opened. Three men stepped out, one behind the other, aloof, their heads ducking down between their hunched shoulders. All were wearing dark clothes. Silently they came down the steps. Two of them were unknown to Craig, the third man was Justin Kramer.

Again the alarm sounded inside his head, this time so loudly that he could not ignore it. He went over to Kramer. "What happened? Where's Poynder?"

Kramer had come to a stop as if colliding with someone in the dark. His eyes widened and blinked. "Excuse me," he said and went past Craig down the platform.

Craig felt as if he were dreaming. The distant whistle of a locomotive seemed unreal. He stopped one of the other two men by grabbing his arm. "Listen," he said, "my name is Craig Matlock. I'm Loftus Poynder's son-in-law. What happened?"

It seemed he would still get no answer. But then the younger of the two men spoke. "I am Dr. Nicholls of Bellevue Hospital." His remarkably small hand pointed to the scarlet car. "We are bringing Mr. Poynder home."

Craig stared at the open door of the car. He saw walls paneled in dark, polished wood and the back rest of a settee covered in red leather. The vibrations of the train from New Haven, just pulling into the other track, caused the door to swing closed.

"What does that mean, you're bringing him home? Speak up, I don't have much time. My train is coming in over there. What happened?" When Dr. Nicholls did not reply, Craig asked, "Is he dead?"

"If you ask me, he should be, considering the injuries he sustained." Dr. Nicholls spoke plainly, making no attempt to soften the impact. "He's a dying man, and he knows it. That's why we're bringing him here. It was what he wanted—over my objections, by the way. I never thought he'd survive the trip."

The trains were standing alongside one another. Craig ran around the engine to the second platform. The passengers had already gotten on the train. Sewall waved him over and held open the gate. "Hurry up. She's in the third car." But Craig ran past Sewall, along the windows, until he found Kitty. She stood behind the closed window, pale, still wearing her coat. He rapped on the glass until she raised the window.

"I can't come with you," he said. "I'm sorry. Did you see the scarlet car? They brought Loftus Poynder." He stopped. What did that name mean to her? Of what interest could it be for her that a man was dying in the scarlet carriage? But how else could he explain to her that she must make the trip to New York alone?

She stood at the window, her hands clutching the frame. She did not speak.

"I can't come with you. Please understand. Maybe tomorrow. I'll try, anyway."

A faint smile appeared on Kitty's face. "I was looking forward to it so much. Every time I look forward to something too much, it turns sour."

"Please don't. Please don't say that. I'll follow, just as soon as I can. You'd better look for a shop. Broadway would be a good location. Perhaps you'll have found some-

thing by the time I get there. We can make the final arrangements just as soon as I get to New York."

She continued to smile. Then the bell on the station
building began to ring. Kitty sat down. The bell rang a
second time. The smokestack of the locomotive emitted a
puff of yellow vapor, and white jets of steam shot out from
the wheel pistons. A third time the bell sounded. Then the
couplings between the cars clanked and became taut.

Craig walked alongside the train. Kitty sat upright and
rigid, looking straight ahead. He knocked on the pane.
"Shut the window. All the smoke and soot will get into the
compartment." But she did not look at him. "Tomorrow,"
he yelled, but then he gave up. He ran with the moving
train for a few yards more, until the yellow cars sped past
him too quickly.

Both trains had left. Only the scarlet car was left. The
tracks shone in the sunlight. The signalmen had left their
posts, since the next train was not due for two hours.

The two men were alone on the platform. Hugh Sewall
said, "I should have known. You had to think of a reason
to let her go alone."

A switching engine rolled up to the scarlet car to pull it
to the siding in front of the freight shed.

"Will you take me home?" Craig said. "I sent Greville
back with the carriage."

"You sent him back? You mean you really intended to
go with her?"

"I can hire a cab." Craig was still looking at the scarlet
coach. "I have to get home before they do. I don't know
how to break it to Margaret."

"You don't mean old Poynder . . . ?"

"They say he's dying."

"I'll drive you."

Craig handed Sewall his valise. "If you wouldn't mind
going ahead, I'm going to try to have a word with
Kramer."

The crowd that had gathered around the scarlet car was
so large that McIdden had difficulty getting the carriage
to the car. Craig had to use his elbows to force his
way through. The people hemmed him in, but he pushed
them aside. As he reached the cars, two men were raising a stretcher from the train. Poynder lay on it, a
bandage around his head, and his body was covered with

a scarlet blanket, the kind used only in parlor cars, with the initials NYR embroidered on it. The crowd murmured. Then the stretcher bearers brought him down, passing close to Craig. He saw Poynder's face, or what was still recognizable of it under the thick bandage and dried blood. The only part of the face that seemed undamaged were his eyes. They were wide open, staring without showing a sign of life. Craig had forgotten that he wanted to speak to Kramer. The crowd, recovered from its shock, pressed closer again. Craig had only one urge: to escape the crush, the shoving and pushing of other people.

"You, you! Are you one of those from New York?" A Southport station employee was standing on the carriage step. "Oh, it's you, Mr. Matlock," he said as Craig turned around. "I found something. It was on the floor. He must have dropped it when they carried him out."

For a moment Craig took in only the bright reflection. Then he recognized the object: Poynder's chrome-plated watch. "Thanks," he said. "Thanks very much."

He put the watch in his pocket and left.

# ═ 23 ═

CRAIG HAD LAST seen Poynder's watch on his desk, in its accustomed place. He was reminded of their conversation when, inside his coat pocket, the watch struck the half-hour. He reached for it and snapped open the lid. Then he opened the back cover. The inscription contained Poynder's name and birth date—January 1, 1800, the first day of the new century. A strange gift to a newborn child.

The road from the station to Willowbeach was rutted and full of potholes. Hugh Sewall was taciturn. He drove with all the speed the bad road allowed.

Craig put the watch in his pocket again and picked up the newspapers he had bought at the station. But he did not find what he was looking for until he came to the back pages, where only a few lines appeared under the heading

Late Bulletins: Strike on New York Railroad. Heavy Property Damage. Some Personal Injuries. What surprised him were two almost identical editorials on the subject of the monopolistic position of certain railroad entrepreneurs. Both appeared in papers with which, as he well knew, his father was on excellent terms. The editor in chief of one of them was the man Craig had met in Langdon's office.

He scanned the editorials. Both were an open attack on Loftus Poynder and the New York Railroad. Both expressed the "increasing concern of the public in the face of the growing monopoly of a single entrepreneur." And both closed with the threat that it would not be surprising "if the mob, which is in the habit of expressing its interests only by rioting," might one day proceed with force against the owner of such a railroad.

There was no doubt that he was looking at editorials that had been planted. The authors appeared to have known in advance what was going to happen. A strike at the New York Railroad. The word *strike* would not let go of him, as if it were the key to everything. They had passed the gate to the Poynder estate. Craig was glad no one was in sight. Sewall had driven much faster than the heavy carriage bearing Loftus Poynder. Still Craig did not have much time. Sewall stopped the rig in front of the house, and Craig picked up his valise and hopped out.

"Your newspaper," Sewall said.

Craig shook his head. "I don't want Margaret to see it." He looked at the house. Apparently no one had heard them drive up. "Many thanks." The men exchanged a look, but neither had anything to say. Sewall started the rig up so abruptly that the gravel spewed under the wheels. The house was quiet. No one was in the garden.

Craig spun around as Margaret called his name. She had come from the greenhouse, a gardening smock tied around her waist, her arms full of roses. On this cold day, with its pale sun, she was a picture of summer. Her hair, skin, and lips glowed. She stopped close to him, bringing with her a sweet earthy odor. "Weren't the trains running?" She had not mentioned the incident of the night when she came for him at Sewall's Harbour. "I've been putting off straightening up the greenhouse. This morning I gave myself a push. . . . Was something wrong with the train?"

The heavy carriage came up the drive, rolling toward

the house. A second, lighter, turnout followed. Margaret gave Craig a questioning look. He put his arm around her. He had come to spare her the sight, to prepare her for the horrors ahead. But why didn't he take her in the house? Why didn't he shut her in until her father had been taken to his room? After all, that was why he had come.

The noise of the carriages had stopped. The coachmen fastened the reins and climbed down from their boxes. The doors were opened. Almost immediately the courtyard was filled with people.

"Who are these men?"

It was too late. He could spare her nothing now. All he could do was remain at her side. "They're bringing your father."

He could not prevent her from moving away. Margaret took a step, then looked down. She untied her apron, letting it fall to the ground. Greville hurried over and picked it up. Two men stood ready with the stretcher, while two others lifted Poynder out of the carriage. They put him on the stretcher and spread the scarlet blanket over him.

Margaret stepped closer but did not cry out. She was still holding the roses. She did not notice Justin Kramer approaching her, hat in hand. Then abruptly she came to life, opened the front door herself, crossed the hallway, and climbed slowly up the broad staircase ahead of the men with the stretcher.

Poynder's bedroom was on the east side of the house. Margaret opened the door and pointed to the marble floor. She was warning the stretcher bearers that it was slippery, or possibly merely that they had reached their destination. She put the roses on a table, took the blue coverlet off the bed, and closed the shutters and the French door to the balcony. The room was suddenly quite dark.

She remained standing at the door to the balcony while the men placed her father on the bed. Dr. Nicholls was giving orders. Craig remained at the door, to wait for Kramer and the other man who had come with them from New York. But they did not appear. He closed the door.

Not until now did Margaret go to the bed. She stood at the foot and put her hands on the wide, wooden rim. Craig went over to her. Poynder was no longer covered up to his neck. His chest was exposed, and the stiff collar and stock had been removed. The two top buttons had been broken off. The broad chest rose and fell regularly.

The stretcher bearers left the room. "Would you like me to leave also?" Craig asked.

"Please," she said without looking up.

Craig remembered that he was still carrying the chrome watch. It had always been important to Poynder; perhaps he would miss it. Craig took it out of his pocket and snapped open the lid. He laid it on the bedside table. The watch ticked loudly. Then Craig left the room.

The carriages had left. The men's baggage stood in the entrance hall next to Craig's valise. Greville seemed to have been waiting for Craig. "Are they staying?" Greville asked. "All three of them? Here are their bags. They asked me to carry them in. What's wrong with Mr. Poynder? Was he in an accident? He looked awful."

"Where are the other gentlemen?" Craig said.

"I asked them to go in the library. There's no fire in there yet, 'cause you were going to New York. I bet it was an accident. It sure looked like it."

"Start the fire in the library. And if the gentlemen are staying, I'll let you know about the valises and their rooms. I'm certain they'll stay for dinner. Tell the girl to lay the table in the small parlor for four. Mrs. Matlock will not be joining us." He went to the library.

They still wore their coats. They stood before the cold grate, interrupting their conversation as Craig entered the room. He felt their hostility.

"You asked that your bags be brought in," Craig said to Kramer. "Are you staying?"

Kramer made no effort to be polite. "I assume that decision is up to Mrs. Matlock," he said. He appeared not to have slept all night.

Greville came in with a basket of wood and lit the fire. After he left, Craig turned to Dr. Nicholls. "You said you are on the staff of Bellevue Hospital. Did you treat Mr. Poynder before?"

"No. It was pure chance. Bellevue was the nearest hospital." Without the dark hat he looked younger, but he too seemed not to have slept; and he was unshaven, though his blond stubble was barely visible.

"You told me at the station that there is no expectation of recovery. Why not? I don't want you to raise false hopes, but . . ."

"I wouldn't if I could. It is as I told you. Given his injuries, he should have been dead hours ago." Dr. Nicholls placed one foot on the fender. "I was told that Mr. Poynder is a very strong-willed person. Perhaps that accounts for it." Dr. Nicholls looked briefly at Kramer, who had retired to the corner near the grand piano. "Perhaps he will regain consciousness, as Mr. Kramer hopes. That won't change the facts, however. The only thing I can do for Mr. Poynder—the only reason I'm here—is to spare him pain."

Craig gazed into the crackling flames. "What's the matter with his eyes?"

It was the first time Nicholls had hesitated. "He is blind. He is blind, and he has lost the power of speech."

"Blind?"

"Now do you understand?"

"How did it happen?"

"The injuries?" Nicholls took off his overcoat and laid it across a chair. "I wasn't called until it was too late. The horses trampled him, he must have fallen directly under them. They dashed in his head. The horses were startled by the fire. It started in their barn, and they broke out. I'm told there are close to a hundred horses at the depot. When I arrived, a lot of them had still not been caught. They were running through the streets. It's odd: when you see them harnessed to the cars, with their blinders, they seem like machines. But when the fire broke out in the depot, they were just wild creatures intent on saving their lives. But you had better ask Mr. Kramer. He was there." Dr. Nicholls pulled out a flat case and took a cigar from it. He did not light it.

"What is the nature of the injuries?"

"We took him to Bellevue. A group of four physicians were consulted. You can believe me: everything possible was done. I have seldom seen such severe head injuries." His glance strayed back to Kramer. "As I told you, he may come to once more. I don't know if I would wish it for him. In any case, Mr. Kramer still has hopes."

Greville entered the library to tell Craig that Margaret wished to see him. She was waiting in the hall, dressed to go out. He wanted to go with her, but she refused. "I must get some fresh air. I have to walk. I'm just going to the beach. I'll be back in a little while." He told her that Kramer had asked to see her.

"Later," she answered. "I've given instructions in the kitchen about dinner; the guest rooms will be ready soon." She left the house quickly.

When Craig returned to the library, Dr. Nicholls had gone upstairs to Poynder's room. Justin Kramer had made himself comfortable in front of the fire. "My wife has gone for a walk," Craig said. "She will see you when she returns —if it is necessary." He became aware that Kramer's companion had taken a book from the shelves, a volume of the collected works of James Fenimore Cooper. "I'm glad to see you feel at home," Craig noted.

The man rose stiffly. "James Garbutt."

Even Kramer seemed to feel that the time had come for an explanation. "Mr. Garbutt is Mr. Poynder's attorney," he said. "You should remember him. It was in his office that you signed your marriage contract."

"Why is he here?"

"I would prefer to discuss that with Mrs. Matlock," Kramer replied.

"I care very little about your preferences," Craig said with sudden sharpness. "It would be better if you became used to the idea that my wife leaves such matters to me."

"It was always clear that the danger existed. Even Mr. Poynder was aware of the possibility," Kramer said. "It was for this reason that Mr. Poynder was about to change his will."

"Surely he never made one in my favor?" Craig said. He was determined to be reserved, to rein in his temper and his tendency to sarcasm.

"By no means. The will now in Mr. Garbutt's safekeeping provides that his entire estate, aside from a few minor bequests, goes to his daughter."

"Well then, everything is in order."

Kramer held back for a moment. Then he said, "If you wish, we'll gladly put all our cards on the table. According to the marriage contract, you are not entitled to any part of your wife's estate. Nor would that change in any way after Mr. Poynder's death. But Mr. Poynder did not consider this provision alone sufficient. Mrs. Matlock still had the option of transferring the management of her property, and of the company, to you. To forestall such a decision, Mr. Poynder intended to change his will."

"But he hasn't done so yet?"

"He charged me with writing a new codicil," Garbutt

intruded. "He came to my office last week. I was to draw up a legal document which would determine exactly in whose hands the management of the estate and the business were to fall. That was his wish. I can swear to it at any time, even if Mr. Poynder should no longer be in a position to testify to his wishes."

Craig stared at Kramer. "Was this your idea?"

"I can only say that I approved and supported Mr. Poynder's decision."

Again Craig had to restrain himself. Until now, Justin Kramer had been little more than a name to him. At best, he had thought of him as a man who had risen from being a minor tax official to the position of chief clerk in Poynder's enterprises. Craig wondered whether Kramer was now to become Poynder's successor. He did not doubt the attorney's words for a moment. Poynder was the kind of man who continued to refine the legal disposition of his affairs. What was it Nicholls had said? He did not understand what kept this man alive. Could it be that he wanted to make sure that this last provision was duly recorded? But how could he?

Whatever happened, anyone who took Poynder's place would need Kramer. Kramer knew about everything. He had been in a position to observe every detail. Whether or not Loftus Poynder would still change his will, Kramer was the key figure.

Craig looked at Kramer, appraising him. He was the kind of man that only New York could produce. They came out of nowhere, bringing with them nothing but their hunger and determination. Kramer was such a man, a man one had to take into account.

"I am grateful to you for your honesty," Craig said. "I think it makes it easier for both of us."

# ═ 24 ═

THEY HAD DINED in the small parlor. Margaret still had not returned from her walk. As they ate, there had been no conversation. At the thought of the man lying in his bed upstairs, none of them felt hungry, and so the maid had found herself taking most of the bowls and platters away much as they had been brought in.

After dinner the guests went to their rooms, and after they had made themselves comfortable and rested a little, Dr. Nicholls returned to Poynder's bedside, while Kramer and Garbutt went back to the library. There was a reason for Craig's joining them: he wanted to find out what had really happened at the Twenty-sixth Street depot.

Craig was more composed now. He was beginning to take a calmer view of the matter. He had searched his memory. There had been the conversation with his father the day before the family returned to Albany. His father had mentioned the word *strike* in outlining the tasks he foresaw for Craig. Matlock had said, "The vulnerable spots on Poynder's lines are his depots in New York, especially the one on Twenty-sixth Street. If, for example, we could infiltrate enough of our people so that a *strike*—" That was the word. He wished now that he had not interrupted his father. But Craig felt he already knew enough.

He waited until the girl had served coffee in the library. Garbutt was immersed in Cooper again. Kramer stood at a window, looking out at the garden. He had shaved a second time and changed his shirt.

"A large house," he said as Craig joined him. "A house that does not suit him. And now he will die in it. To think. . . ."

Craig suddenly realized that Kramer was genuinely fond of Poynder. He said, "Why didn't you send for Margaret to come to New York? It would have been easier. How did he make you understand that he wished to come here?"

"You don't trust me?"

"No, no, I just wondered."

"He wrote. A few words, that's all."

Craig asked Kramer the question that had troubled him all day, "How did the strike come about?"

Kramer continued to look out the window. He shrugged.

"Listen to me," Craig said. "Whatever you think of me, I have nothing to do with anything that was or is between Loftus Poynder and John Tyler Matlock. Their quarrel began before I returned from the war; and after my return, I kept out of it. How could there be a strike? Poynder was on good terms with his employees. If they thought they had a legitimate grievance, surely they would have gone to him and discussed it. Wouldn't they?"

Kramer turned to face Craig. He left his hands crossed behind his back. "Why do you want to know? It won't change anything."

"A strike doesn't just break out. It is preceded by protests, resolutions, demands. Was it a strike?"

"What do you mean?"

"Tell me what you know."

"There were rumors of an impending strike. They began about ten days ago. None of us took them seriously. Mr. Poynder least of all. He even forbade me to speak of it in his presence. Until the leaflets turned up—quite primitive ones. They showed a coffin, and under it, Poynder's name and a call to strike the depot, not to dispatch any more trains. Then the usual rhetoric: the big boss who rakes in the money, who does not care about the safety of the workers and the passengers, allusions to the accidents that have occurred recently, and so on. Quite primitive, as I said, and not very effective. Yesterday morning the depot was flooded with the leaflets, but our people voluntarily gathered them up and burned them."

"Were you able to find out who—"

"Who printed them? Who distributed them? Not so far."

Craig continued to probe. "That was yesterday morning. What happened then?"

"You'll find it all in tomorrow's papers."

"I'd rather hear your version."

"It is not my version. I'm only reporting what occurred."

"I'm listening."

"It was quiet all day. We really thought the matter was finished when we got rid of the leaflets. Then in the evening we were alerted by Philo Jones, the superintendent. The evening shift had begun a work stoppage. The train to Greenbush did not leave, and four freight trains remained to be unloaded. Mr. Poynder decided to go to the depot at once. I should have stopped him, but talking to the people—he was good at that. He had a way with them. We got to the depot shortly after nine. The depot was lit up as bright as day. We had had new arc lamps installed only recently, and all of them were burning. It was true: the men had downed tools. They were standing around in small groups, arguing. The train to Greenbush was still standing there, and the freight cars still had to be unloaded. All the same, I had the feeling that the men didn't know what was supposed to happen next. Mr. Poynder climbed up on a flatcar to talk to them. I was sure it would be easy for him to settle the whole business."

"Doctor Nicholls mentioned a fire in the horse barns."

"Everything was under control until the militia arrived. Mr. Poynder was speaking, and the men were listening. Then in came the militia. That's what set it off. Suddenly there they were. The militia attached hoses to the hot-water faucets, intending to disperse the workers. Up to then, everything had been peaceful. But when the shooting started, there was panic. The men began to tear up the place. They pulled the hot boxes out of the locomotives. It was an inferno. Then all of a sudden, the horse barn was in flames. Mr. Poynder . . ." He turned away from the window and paced along the walls of books. "That's all I know," he said finally.

Craig knew that any more questions would only betray his thoughts, and that was more than he wanted to reveal. Nevertheless, he said, "Militia? Where did they come from? You know Poynder better than I do. Was he really a man who would call for the militia? You said yourself that he thought he could deal with the strikers peacefully."

"He did not call in the militia."

"He didn't? Then who did? You? Jones?"

"None of us did. That much is certain."

"Someone must have alerted them."

Kramer avoided Craig's eyes. "Believe me, I've been asking myself the same question. If I knew the answer . . ."

"But you have some suspicions?"

"You asked me what I know, and I told you. I leave conjecture to you."

Craig knew he had gone too far. He had betrayed too much of his own thinking. But why not? Let Kramer believe that both of them had reached the same conclusion. "Fine," he said. "Let's leave it for the moment. But you and I—am I right in thinking that we won't be content with guesses? Maybe we will arrive at the same conclusions. Then we should talk again. Perhaps our interests are not so far apart after all."

Craig noted with satisfaction that he had succeeded in confusing Kramer. Though the man was biased against him, in one way or another he could be won over. First, however, Craig had to clarify the plan that had been taking shape in his mind during the past few hours.

Through the window he saw Margaret returning from her walk. "You will excuse me," he said and left the library. He was just in time to help Margaret off with her cape. Her face was pink with cold. "You were gone a long time," he said. "Weren't you cold?"

"You don't notice the cold when you're walking." She was grateful for his ordinary, everyday question. "Did you eat?"

"Yes, everything was all right."

She looked at the door to the library. "Are they staying?"

"Justin Kramer has something he wants to discuss with you. About your father's will."

"He wants to do that *now?*"

"That's what he says. But he can wait. Just the same, you shouldn't be afraid to talk to him. Your father trusts him."

"Please do me a favor. Send Edna a telegram. I want her to bring the children back."

He was reminded of his mother and her self-control, her ability to think of those close to her, and especially of her determination to maintain order, no matter what. "You want the boys here now?"

Margaret was already at the foot of the stairs. She said. "Perhaps father will want to see them."

"I'll send the telegram." Craig thought of his plan. If he let too much time pass, he might be too late to accomplish anything in New York. If John Tyler was behind the strike and if there was proof of his involvement, it could only be discovered right then.

"Margaret," he said, "I don't like to leave you alone now, but I should go to New York—for your father's sake. It will only take me a few hours. I'll be back the same day. It's something that has to be taken care of immediately. Otherwise I would, of course, postpone the trip. But we can wait and see how he is in the morning."

"Is the doctor still with him?"

"Yes."

"I'll spell him."


Loftus Poynder tried to interpret the noises. There were many different ones, confusing him. But he knew that he was not in the Warren Street house. Of all the familiar Warren Street noises, there was only the ticking of his watch. And even that was louder than usual. No, it wasn't resting on his leather-topped desk. In the Warren Street house he could have figured out the room and the time with his eyes closed. The time. Between the moments when he was alert, there were stretches that were blank. How long did they last? Minutes or hours? The rattling of the shutters by the wind, the crackling of the fire. Was it day or night? Had they really brought him to Willowbeach? Justin Kramer might have respected his wishes, but you could never trust doctors. Poynder listened. Sometimes late at night, when he was working in his office. . . . He lost track of the thought. Gravel. Gravel paths. A wheelbarrow on a gravel path. That meant Greville and the garden at Willowbeach. But what was Greville doing out there in the middle of the night . . . night . . . the bright arc lamps over the depot. The horses! Watch out, the horses. . . . When he was working in his office, when he was absorbed in work . . . Kramer might come in without his noticing. Wasn't he alone, then? He could not see anything; he could not speak. But why didn't he hear anyone? Surely they wouldn't leave him alone here when there was important work to be done. . . . "I'll bleed you. I'll bleed you until there's not a drop left in your veins." John Tyler Matlock's voice in the library. . . . There was so much to think about, to put in order, to do. He felt the energy in his body. Why had they taken away the pad and pencil? . . . It was three miles to the schoolhouse in Lebanon Springs, and in winter. . . . No,

not those old stories; of course they had had only the
one slate and stylus, and there had been quarrels over
them. Lebanon Springs. The meeting in the schoolhouse.
The militia. . . . The militia! Where was Kramer? His
hand groped over the coverlet, feeling for the pad and
pencil. The wind, the fire—but there was something else.
The rustle of a woman's dress. He felt someone bending
over him. Why couldn't he hear her?

"Father? It's me, Margaret. Can you hear me? Father."

Of course. He could hear her. He tried to speak. The
taste of blood. But he could use his hands to make
her understand that he wanted to write. Why didn't she
say that she understood?

# ═ 25 ═

SINCE CRAIG DID not know how long he would need for
his investigation in New York, he had not told Greville
to meet him at Southport station. Loftus Poynder's condition had been unchanged in the morning, and Dr.
Nicholls had refused to make a prognosis. Craig therefore took the first train and now, in the early afternoon,
he was back.

The carriage left him at the main gate. McIdden had
told him that Edna Child and the boys had arrived two
hours earlier, but as he approached it, the mansion
seemed empty.

Across the way, at the Matlock house, everything was
lively. Construction was proceeding rapidly. The workmen were taking advantage of the good weather. And
next to it, the Poynder mansion. He remembered Kramer's
remark that the house did not suit Poynder. Quite the
contrary, Craig thought; they did resemble one another;
the somber house and the somber man. Both had been
denied love.

The thought that Kramer might be standing at the

library window, watching him, made Craig get off the drive and take the path that branched off behind the gate and circled to the back entrance within the cover of trees and bushes. He did not want to discuss with Kramer what he had learned in New York. He did not feel like talking at all, nor did he feel a need for other people.

The back door faced east. As Craig approached it, he looked up at the second-story windows of the room where Loftus Poynder lay. The shutters were still closed, as was the door to the balcony. Greville came across the yard with a wheelbarrow full of leaves.

Craig pointed up at the windows. "How is he?"

Greville set the barrow down and wiped his hands on his apron. "I don't know, but they're with him all the time." He shook his head. "A man like that, a man with so much energy, and then to see him like that, like a cripple!"

"Did Joshua and Sinclair get back?"

"I picked them up at the station a couple of hours ago. Them and Miss Child."

There was a noise in the house. The two men looked up. Someone was busying himself with the shutters of Poynder's bedroom.

"They haven't been oiled in a long time," Greville said. The shutters banged loudly against the masonry, and Margaret stepped out on the balcony. She went to the parapet and rested her hands on the stone. She stood, a slim figure in a bright dress, looking out at the Sound.

Craig went to the back door, up the stairs, along the hall. At the door of the bedroom he encountered Kramer, who stepped aside to let Craig pass. He rushed through the room without a glance at the bed, out onto the balcony to Margaret.

She was still standing there with her hands on the railing. She did not turn around at once. It seemed to him that she was more relaxed than when he had last seen her.

"Father is dead." Her voice held the same distant calm that radiated from her face.

From the yard she had seemed to him in need of protection. Now he did not know what he could do for her. It was cool, she was wearing a light dress. Come inside, he wanted to say; but then he remembered that they would have to walk through the room where the dead man lay. "I should not have left you," he said.

She shook her head. "It wouldn't have changed anything. He did not want to see you. He didn't even ask for the children." She crossed her arms. "Kramer and the attorney—they were more important to him. His railroads, his money—nothing else." Her voice expressed no sorrow or shock, only deep bitterness.

He took her arm. "Come inside. It's getting cold." He walked ahead. She avoided looking at the bed as she closed the windows she had earlier thrown open. The chrome watch was still ticking on the night table. Next to it someone had placed writing materials; the lid of the ink well stood open. Craig thought of Kramer's expressionless face in the hallway. What had it meant? What had happened while Craig was in New York?

He led Matgaret through the door. In his secluded study they would be less likely to be disturbed. Strewn over the oval table in front of the fireplace lay the red-white-and-blue rods of a game of jackstraws.

"I brought the children in here," Margaret said. She began to gather up the brightly colored sticks. "I told Father that Joshua and Sinclair were here, that I had sent for them. But all he wanted was Kramer. I was there, and I gave him a pad and pencil. But he wrote just one word: Kramer."

"He did regain consciousness, then?"

A furrow formed on Margaret's forehead. She slipped the ivory rods into their leather pouch, but Craig was aware that she was moving mechanically, her thoughts elsewhere. Nor did she seem to have heard his question. "My mother died in the same room, the same bed. Father waited for her to ask for him, but whenever he was with her, she turned her back. She wanted to see no one but me, to have no one else around her. It was terrible. As soon as I came, she either wept soundlessly or tried to set me against Father. Every day I had to promise her something else. That I would never, never move into the house on Warren Street. That I would never marry a man Father had picked out for me. That I would never name a son of mine Loftus. That I would never . . ."

Margaret had never told Craig any of this. Her mother's death was something she had locked away inside herself since she was fourteen years old. It was a story that clung to her like a secret flaw. Over the years she had made an effort to change the image of her mother, to reshape it into something she could like better. Now she knew that she had only been deceiving herself.

"Her final days were the worst. It was always about Father. She reminded him of everything he had ever done to her. She forgot nothing. A gift she had disliked, a forgotten anniversary, careless remarks that had hurt her. . . . I had to listen to it all. I was afraid whenever she sent for me. Finally I hid in the attic. But it was no use. Her shouts filled the whole house. You could hear her through closed doors: insults, curses, oaths, weeping fits. After she died, Edna discovered that she was no longer wearing her wedding ring, and in her will—she made me sit there while she dictated it—she decreed that her headstone be marked only with her maiden name. Up to the last second, she was all hate."

It was as if Margaret were only just now recalling Craig's presence. "And how did *he* die?" she asked rhetorically. "He thought of nothing but his property and his money—nothing else. As if he had only lived for that, as if nothing or no one had ever meant as much to him. As if only one thing made dying difficult: the thought of having to leave his property to others. I can't mourn him. I couldn't mourn when my mother died, and I can't now. And they are my parents, the two people who should have loved me the most. . . ." She spoke quietly, as though speaking to herself. "All that's left of them are questions, questions for which I will never have the answers."

He could not help her. He could only listen—that and try to bring her back to firmer ground. "You said your father called in Kramer?"

"Father wrote. Kramer talked to him for a long time. It was about money, about your father, about you, about the will. It was awful. I couldn't bear to listen, so I left. They didn't call me until the end."

"I don't know whether Kramer told you, but the will is made out in your favor. But your father wanted to add a codicil setting up an executor. Presumably the person he had in mind was Kramer. Did your father sign anything?"

"I think so, yes."

There was a long silence. Margaret's indifference should

have disturbed him, but it served a purpose. Emotion was out of place here; it only muddied the view. "Do you think your father knew what he was doing?"

For the first time she reacted spontaneously. "Did he know what he was doing? He knew only too well. Just as my mother knew."

"Did you see the will?"

She looked up. "What do you mean? Did I do something wrong? They simply wouldn't budge from his bedside. I don't want them in the house any longer. Tell Greville to get the carriage ready and take them to the station. Now." The brightly colored rods slipped out of her hands and fell on the table, scattering apart.

Their luggage stood in the hall. They were waiting in the library, as they had the day before. Dr. Nicholls' and James Garbutt's hats and coats lay on a chair. Only Justin Kramer was dressed for the outdoors. They themselves had asked Greville to get the rig ready and take them to Southport. This time Craig's appearance in the library did not interrupt a conversation, nor did he feel like talking. He went up to Kramer, who was standing to one side by the grand piano, busying himself with buttoning his gloves. Craig said. "Your persistence paid off, then. Are you satisfied?"

Kramer slowly raised his eyes; his fingers continued closing the buttons. "It would be best if you would agree to a meeting with Mr. Garbutt right now," he said. "Only a formality. You must make a deposition that you acknowledge the will."

"You seem to be in a hurry."

"Me? I assume you are the one who will want to get things settled. I didn't get a chance to speak with Mrs. Matlock; it would be most convenient if she could join the meeting with Mr. Garbutt." His voice, which he did not have under control as well as his face, betrayed nervousness and exhaustion.

Garbutt, who had heard this exchange, broke in. "We can take care of it anytime, whenever it suits you. I only ask that you give me some advance notice." He seemed to have been infected with Kramer's nervousness.

There was an embarrassed silence. Then Kramer resumed. "I have only one request. Let a few days pass before you come to New York to take over. Also, under the circumstances, you will surely not want me to continue to exercise my function in the company."

"Just a moment, Kramer—"

But Kramer would not be interrupted. He wanted to get it over with. He had carefully planned every word, and now he made his speech as if he had committed it to memory. "Of course, I am at your disposal until you have decided on someone to replace me. In any case, I shall begin at once to prepare everything for a smooth transition. You can be certain that everything will be done correctly. An inventory of all the movable and immovable assets was made at the same time as the original will. You can examine it in Mr. Garbutt's office. There have been no changes since the inventory was compiled."

Greville opened the door. He had not knocked, and even now, in the presence of the visitors, he made no effort to be polite. "The carriage is ready. The luggage has already been put in it. The gentlemen should hurry."

Garbutt and Nicholls got their coats and then shook hands with Craig. Justin Kramer bowed stiffly. "It was his last wish, and I respect it," he said. "I await your instructions."

Craig stood in the doorway until the carriage was out of sight. Then he went back in. Somewhere far away he heard the children's voices. What had happened? Who could explain it to him? Margaret? Obviously she did not realize what had taken place in her presence. He went up the stairs to the room where the dead man lay, as if that were the only place where he could find the answer to his question.

There was no doubting the facts. Loftus Poynder had named him—but why? What had been his motive? He looked at the dead man. The powerful body, the sturdy hands. . . . He felt uneasy, something he could not define was troubling him. Finally he realized that he missed the ticking of the watch. He went to the bedside table. The watch had stopped. He picked it up, reset the hands, wound the spring, and put it back.

Margaret was still in his study. The jackstraws lay scattered. "Have they gone?" she asked.

"Do you know what happened? Your father . . . he changed his will, but not the way Kramer wanted him to. He put in my name."

"*Your* name?"

"He wanted to appoint someone to carry on his business after his death, and he chose me. Do you understand that? Can you explain it?"

Margaret pressed her fists against her temples and held them there for several seconds. To Craig, it was like watching something secret, and yet he could not take his eyes off her.

"Why did he always do things in such a way that one couldn't help but misunderstand?" she said. "Why? When he was here the last time, in July, the boys asked him if he'd brought them a toy that he'd been promising them for a long time. He didn't answer, and I assumed that he had forgotten. The boys were terribly disappointed. The next morning, after he had gone back to New York, I found the package on the hall table."

Her bitterness toward her father had made her insensitive to pain. Now suddenly she was robbed of this protection. "I knew what he was like! Afterward I always reproached myself. I always promised myself to be more reasonable the next time. But then, when he came again, when he stood there so stiffly, barely daring to hug me, barely looking at Joshua and Sinclair—then I always wished he hadn't come."

"I don't know what made him do it," Craig said after a silence. "But he must have expected something. He must have expected something of me. And that's why I want to tell you something. Please listen. I told you I had to go to New York. It had to do with your father, with the strike. I very much suspect—"

"Must we talk about that now?"

"Yes, Margaret. You must listen to me. I suspect that my father engineered the strike. I learned several things. On the morning of the strike, leaflets were passed out. I found out that they were printed in Albany. That's one thing. Kramer remarked that the workers were standing around as though they didn't know what was supposed to happen next. I found out that on the day of the strike, there were workmen at the depot whom nobody had seen before. Everybody thought they'd just been hired and didn't pay any more attention to them. But the day after the strike, not one of them came back to the depot. In hindsight, the workmen were puzzled. That's another thing. But the important one is the militia. The militia was the crucial spark. That's what Kramer called it. No one will admit that he called the militia. I asked at all the station houses. The militia was not mobilized. No one called for the militia. That can mean only one thing: they weren't real militia; they were hired. The newspapers, too, never mentioned the militia. They carried detailed reports of the fire in the horse barn, dramatic descriptions of the mob—but not a word about the militia. Of course, none of this is conclusive. Maybe I can't get real proof. But I have no more doubts about who was behind the incident."

"The militia . . ." The word released a memory in Margaret. "Did you know that my grandfather was shot by the militia? It was the state militia. Lyman Matlock, your grandfather, called them out against the farmers in Lebanon Springs." She repeated to Craig what her father had told her.

"That makes his decision even more puzzling," Craig said.

She shook her head. "Oh no. Not to me. To me, it only makes it more logical. Don't think that he suddenly discovered his love for you. He hoped——" She looked at Craig. "Surely you won't continue this senseless battle?"

Craig did not answer. He was wondering whether that was the real explanation.

Margaret pulled a slip of paper from the pocket of her dress. She glanced at it and handed it to Craig. "Now even this makes sense. Here, read it for yourself. He gave it to me when he was near the end."

Craig took the scrap of paper. Large, shapeless letters, not all of them legible. "Craig," it said, and then something he could not decipher, and finally, "He is a Matlock."

"Do you understand?" she said. " 'He is a Matlock.' That means, only a Matlock can beat a Matlock. That's how he died—still hating your father. That's his heritage to you: his hatred. But surely you won't go on. Two vengeful old men! They had achieved everything they wanted. Why couldn't they say, that's enough?"

"That was their strength," Craig said.

She wanted to object, try to persuade him. Instead, she quickly gathered up the jackstraws and said, "I must see to the children."

Three days later they buried Loftus Poynder, a man who was born on the first day of the new century and who had died on October 31, 1865. No announcement had been run in the New York papers. Besides the family, only Hugh Sewall and Daniel Place from Willowbeach attended the rites. Justin Kramer, Philo Jones, and Captain Catull came up from New York. Langdon Matlock had sent a formal letter of condolence. Rose had written to Margaret. John Tyler Matlock abstained from any sign of sympathy.

After the funeral service at St. Andrew's and interment in the old fishermen's cemetery, Craig arranged it so that Kramer shared a carriage with him on the drive back to the house. He had come to know Kramer as a man who did not stand on ceremony. Now he, too, steered toward his purpose without a lengthy introduction.

"I've had time these last few days, to think matters through carefully," he began. "I would like you to keep your position."

Kramer—sitting stiffly, his coat collar turned up, his top hat resting on his closed knees, both hands spanning it—did not answer at once. "You may have thought it over carefully," he said at last, "but it does not strike me as a very good idea."

"Why not?"

"Very simple. You cannot trust me."

"Is that a euphemism for: *You* cannot trust *me?*"

"That may be. But one way or the other, the end result is the same. Perhaps it has nothing to do with you personally. I worked for Loftus Poynder. To work for his son-in-law is quite a different matter. I can't imagine it."

"What did Poynder pay you?"

"Enough. More than enough."

"No one ever earns enough."

"Believe me, it would be better to drop the subject. Besides, I have had quite enough of the reporters who come to my office all day long asking who will succeed Poynder. Do you have any idea what will happen when it becomes known that Loftus Poynder named you, a Matlock?"

"The stock of the New York Railroad will go up," Craig answered drily.

Kramer gave Craig a suspicious look.

Craig continued. "They will go up if for no other reason than that everyone will believe that a merger between the New York Railroad and the Empire State is imminent."

Kramer smiled tightly. "Isn't it imminent?"

"It certainly is not what Poynder had in mind. I believe his last provision had quite a different purpose. Also, I am certain that he counted on your continued loyalty to his cause."

"You are speaking in his name." Kramer made no effort to hide his feelings. "A year from now the name of Loftus Poynder will be forgotten. By then you will no longer be the son-in-law; rather, Poynder will be the man who was lucky enough to marry his daughter to Craig Lyman Matlock."

"If you have such apprehensions, wouldn't they be an additional reason for remaining at your post?"

"I see it, rather, as a reason for leaving," Kramer said harshly. "You can save your pretty speeches. You won't convince me."

"Listen to me, Kramer. I can't put it any plainer: *I need you*. I am a stranger in this business. I need someone who knows his way around. I need you because you know the exchange. I need you to tell me what to do in the jungle of laws and taxes." He raised his voice. "I need you, quite simply, to carry on."

"Carry on? What do you mean by that?"

"Whatever Loftus Poynder meant by it."

For a moment Craig Matlock had succeeded in luring Kramer out of his retrenchment, but he quickly withdrew again. "You're overlooking only one thing," Kramer said. "I was against this fight with your father from the outset. I never made a secret of my opinion. I told Poynder that he would lose. Unfortunately, I was right. He couldn't win, not against a man like your father, who—"

"So you did have your suspicions," Craig said with emphasis.

Kramer sounded resigned. "You were in New York. Did you learn anything? I mean, do you have *proof?* Proof capable of standing up? I feel certain that you don't. Whatever John Tyler Matlock does is done thoroughly."

"This point, at least, seems cleared up between us. We need no longer pretend to one another."

"Whether you are pretending or not, whether you are trying to deceive me or telling me the truth—don't make the same mistake Mr. Poynder made. Do not think that you can win. You cannot succeed any more than Mr. Poynder could."

"He must have believed that I could succeed."

For several seconds there was silence, broken only by the sound of the horses' hooves and the turning of the wheels. Soon the Poynder mansion would come into view. "I think I have a clear idea of how this battle can be won," Craig said. "Would that be reason enough for you to stay?"

Kramer gave Craig a searching look. "How do I know that you're being honest? No, I would never be able to forget what has happened."

"I need you, Kramer."

"There would be only one reason for my staying—one reason alone: to see you lose." Kramer could not tell whether it was a smile or simply a reflection of light that scurried across Craig's features.

"As long as you stay, I am not interested in your reasons," Craig said. "Think about it. You needn't give me your answer until I come to New York." The house loomed up ahead, and Craig flicked the sorrel's reins.

BOOK FOUR

# NEW YORK CITY

January 1866

# ═ 26 ═

ON TUESDAYS LARS Wixell always parked his cab in front of the slaughterhouse. If he was lucky, he could earn more in one day than all the rest of the week. The dealers, their trading completed, had themselves driven to the banks to deposit their gains, and they were in a spending mood. But on this Tuesday, January 9, it was snowing. Thick, fluffy flakes fell on the city from a pale-violet sky. Wixell had pulled his new cloth coat with the velvet collar out of the chest and driven at a leisurely pace to the St. Nicholas Hotel.

Patiently Wixell waited in the line of horsecabs in front of the hotel. If he crinkled up his eyes a little, Broadway became the Kungsgatan in Stockholm. The Swedish landowners who stayed there often engaged a cab for the whole day, and their compensation was princely. After twelve years in New York he could hardly believe that in Stockholm he could predict almost exactly the tip a fare would bring him. In New York he stopped guessing. You never could tell in this city.

Wixell had sworn to himself time and again to take things as they come, to spare himself any disappointments, but when he saw the white-haired gentleman in the expensive fur coat, escorted by a page holding an umbrella, coming through the front door of the hotel into the snow flurry, he did hope for a nice long drive outside the city, somewhere no wheel, no hoof had yet disturbed the snow, where it was so still you thought you could hear the falling of the snow flakes.

He jumped down from the box, an unusual gesture in front of hotels, and opened the carriage door. He noticed that the old gentleman's coat was of sable, and the knob of his cane was highly polished silver.

Wixell's passenger gave his destination in a low voice:

"Corner of Broome and Crosby Streets." And for a moment Wixell went so far as to think that he might refuse the old man. He had waited in line for more than half an hour, and now he was getting a fare who wanted to go one measly block, a ten-cent ride and no tip. That was typical: staying at the St. Nicholas, probably in one of the luxury suites, and then expect to be driven one lousy block. But before Wixell could lose his cheery mood, he decided to amend his bad luck by taking a carefully concocted detour, so that he would increase the fare. If the old gent were only the least bit generous and not demand his change, he might end up with a quarter.

At the corner of Broome and Crosby there was a four-story brick building. The façade was painted red, with the window frames and masonry outlined in white. This time Wixell stayed on his box while his passenger dismounted.

Leaning on his cane, John Tyler Matlock stepped up to the box. Softly and cordially he said, "You're a good driver." He cast a look over the carriage and horse. "A good horse. And the cab has excellent springs. In New York, that's almost a miracle."

Wixell considered it proper to get off his box after all. "Thank you," he said. "It's my own horse and my own carriage. The trip comes to twenty cents."

Matlock smiled. "You included a small detour. If you had simply driven down Broadway and then turned into Broome. . . ."

"At this time of day Broadway is clogged with traffic. Of course, if you had walked. . . ." It was always the rich ones who complained about the fare.

Matlock was doodling in the snow with his cane. "How much do you make a day?" he asked.

"It depends on the day and the weather."

"January should be a good month."

"Some years, sure, but not this year. December was slack, too. No snow, no rain, much too dry. Today's the first real snow we've had all winter; but you can't tell if it will stick."

"All right, then, how much do you take in?"

Wixell shrugged. "On a day like today . . ." He decided to play it safe and double the figure. "Maybe five, seven dollars."

"That's not bad."

"You saw for yourself that the cab and the horse are

in good shape. That eats up a lot of profit." He was enjoying the conversation.

Matlock scrutinized the pattern he had drawn in the snow. "I'll engage you," he said in measured tones, "for the next three weeks. I will pay you two gold dollars a day."

Wixell thought it over. The offer was all right. An assured income for three weeks, but still somewhat shabby for such a rich gentleman. "In the city?" Wixell asked.

"Only from the St. Nicholas to here and back again. Three times a day—morning, noon, and evening. Now and again, my wife will need you for shopping excursions in the city. After you have taken me back to the hotel in the evenings, at seven, you're through for the day."

"That means I have to stand around all day," Wixell said cunningly. "That's not good for the horse, not in this weather." He thought he'd bargain the old gent up to four dollars, but he swallowed his words unsaid when he felt himself reproached by a severe look.

"Two dollars in gold each day," Matlock said. "I will pay you every evening after the last ride. If that suits you, fine. If not, I can find someone else."

"Done." Wixell's voice was husky.

"Return here at one o'clock to take me back to the hotel—by the direct route. And no other passengers in the meantime. Agreed?" He turned to go.

The house with the red front glowed in the snowy winter light. Matlock came to a stop at the front door. He waved to Wixell and handed him the cane on which he had been leaning. "Put that in the carriage." Seeing Wixell's wondering look, he added, "A cane makes one look so old, don't you think?"

It had been a long time since John Tyler Matlock had been in his New York office; of the ten clerks on the tall stools, he recognized only two. And while he went toward the frosted-glass door of Sydenham's cubicle, he became aware of the new gas lamps, the new stove, and the new shelves.

Matlock had carefully planned his entrance into the New York office. He had always been a man who left as little as possible to chance. And since his apoplectic attack he planned each step with even greater care, especially if he was going to meet someone who had not seen him for a long time. What came easily to him, and what was always impressive, was his upright posture. It expressed his attitude, his awareness that man is the only animal that strides across the world with head raised high.

He could rely on his bearing; the mirror in the St. Nicholas had confirmed that fact. The same pier glass, unfortunately, also revealed to him that his walk could easily betray him. Unless he was moving quickly, he tended to place his feet farther apart, and his steps seemed rather unsteady, like those of a baby learning to walk. It was a matter of balance. At home, in familiar surroundings, it was not so noticeable because he bridged the moment of unsteadiness by stopping to support himself on something. But in the hotel dining room, when he suddenly needed to clutch the back of a chair, it was obvious to him that it might be advisable, after all, to listen to Rose and consult some physicians in New York.

But now, as he caught sight of the man with the bent back and the thin arms in gray sleeve protectors bent over the desk, his self-assurance increased. He held out his hand to Sydenham. This gesture was his greatest sign of affability, and it disconcerted the chief clerk.

"Mr. Matlock!" Fear and pleasure were mingled in Sydenham's voice. "You—in New York! After all this time." He threw a glance at the big wall calendar. "Seven years, three months, and eleven days," he said. A shy smile filled his eyes. "But you haven't changed at all."

"You, on the other hand, ought to get out more, Sydenham. More fresh air. More exercise. How is your mother?"

"She's very well, thank you. She doesn't grow any older; I'm the only one who ages. Sometimes I can't believe I'm her son."

Matlock was standing at Sydenham's desk. He took the topmost piece of paper out of the filing basket and held it up to the green shade of the gas lamp. "Watermarked paper for simple postings?"

"An auction lot," Sydenham said.

"I'm sure there have been many changes here. A lot of new young people. Probably they are being paid more and working less."

"Your son did not mention that he was expecting you."

"He doesn't know about the happy event."

"You are staying at the St. Nicholas?"

"Yes. There have been some changes there, too."

"I'll see to it that the bills are sent straight to us."

"Fine. And please have five gold dollars ready for me each evening."

"New York has become very expensive," Sydenham said. "Formerly that might have been enough, but . . ."

"I want it to remain the same. The more you have with you, the more you spend."

"Won't you take off your hat and coat?"

Matlock made a gesture of refusal. "Is Langdon in?"

"Yes, sir. In his—in the big office."

"What do you mean? Are you telling me that he uses *my* office?"

Sydenham loosened his shirt collar. There was no safe answer.

Matlock put his hand on Sydenham's shoulder. "I'll see you later. And don't forget—five gold dollars."

As he walked toward the big office, his office, he could still hear Sydenham's remark. That was how time passed. He had not yet spent a full day in New York, and already, at every turn, he noticed signs that made it clear to him what a long time seven years can be and what changes they can bring. It had begun in the hotel. The old hall porter was no longer there, nor was the bar man who had always waited on him. New faces everywhere, and it was not easy for him to become accustomed to them. But the worst was Sydenham. Wizened like a dried pear. That people had to die was a fact you had to accept, but to have to watch this kind of dying . . . . How could someone let himself go, he thought, as if the signs of age he had noted in Sydenham were nothing more than a breach of etiquette. Watermarked paper. What could Langdon be thinking of?

When Langdon Matlock had taken over the management of the New York office, he had counted on the probability of his father's occasional unannounced forays, and although the event had not happened thus far, he remained prepared. But now, when the door to his office opened without a knock and he suddenly found himself facing his father, it was a shock all the same, especially since his father had surprised him and Irene in the midst of a marital tiff. Because he must control himself in front of his father, he directed his anger at Sydenham for not warning him. John Tyler Matlock, he was sure, had first looked in on the chief clerk.

For Irene, on the other hand, John Tyler came as the answer to a prayer. His appearance put an end to the quarrel, at least for the time being; and, as she immediately judged from the old man's expression, Langdon would have to eat crow, which would serve him right. She greeted John Tyler with her most radiant smile. It had never cost her any effort to embrace a Matlock, but this time her hug was particularly warm.

"You're looking marvelous," she said. "How do you do it? You should tell Langdon your secret. Look at him. He gets fatter every day. How long have you been in New York? Is Rose with you? Why didn't you let us know you were coming? Where are you staying?"

"At the St. Nicholas."

Langdon, still visibly taken aback, also embraced his father. He helped him out of his coat. "Yes, why didn't you send a telegram? Last Friday you didn't mention that you were coming."

John Tyler took a few steps back and looked around the room. "I wanted to surprise you, and I see that I succeeded. When did you start using this office?"

Though Irene was in favor of Langdon's being put in his place, she did not intend his prestige in the firm to suffer seriously. She had a better topic. "You could have stayed with us," she said.

"In your new house? I heard you have enough room. But you know, Irene, I hold fast to some traditions. I have always been the first to be told when there is a new family member and when new houses are acquired. I would have liked to see the plans ahead of time. It's even possible that I could have given you some good advice. But so many who have been there have described it to me, I feel I already know all about it. According to report, it's not exactly a Matlock house. That's why I prefer the St. Nicholas. Besides, it's closer to the office. It used to be the custom to live as close as possible to one's place of work." A gesture made it clear that he was not interested in further explanations. "Be glad that I'm not staying with you. I'm not a good guest. At the hotel I can order the people around all I want, because there I pay. I assume you were intent on dragging Langdon off to the tailor," he said to Irene. "You're right, you know. If Langdon goes on this way, it will affect his heart. Do you eat too much? How much excess weight are you dragging around?"

Irene had put on her coat. "I'm sure you won't object if I leave you now. Not that I want you to think that I come to the office all the time to keep Langdon from working. This was pure accident."

John Tyler Matlock scrutinized his daughter-in-law with the same critical look he had given the paper in Sydenham's office. Irene was without a doubt the handsomest of the Matlock women, but she was also the most expensive one. "You're going to catch cold in those slippers," he said.

She smiled. "You don't miss a thing."

When she had gone, John Tyler said, "Old Man Schermerhorn kept his money together just so his daughters could throw it out the window. I do hope Irene pays for her clothes out of her own pocket. Is the pearl necklace a gift from you?"

"Our twentieth anniversary, yes. As for the rest, she doesn't even use up her income. And as far as the house goes, it's built on a plot from her father's estate. Old Schermerhorn left his daughters not only money but also the talent for managing it." He checked to see whether the door to the anteroom was closed.

"One builds that kind of house after he has assumed his inheritance, not before," John Tyler Matlock said. He pointed at the leather chair behind the heavy desk. "Where is my chair?"

"Your chair? Oh, that one. In the board room."

Matlock walked around the chair and examined the seat. "Too soft. It will give you curvature of the spine. What are you waiting for? Send for my chair."

He made a ceremony out of exchanging chairs. One of the secretaries was told to dust the chair and brush off the velour upholstery. During all the activity, John Tyler discovered that the desk was not quite in its old place and himself pushed it back.

Finally he seemed satisfied and sat down behind his desk. His heart was calm, his hands and feet were warm. He experienced no constriction, no nausea. Everything was shipshape. But he found one more source of complaint. "It's hot in here," he said. "Open the window."

When Langdon gingerly opened it a crack, he snapped at him, "Wider. It's stifling in here. Now sit down so we can talk."

Langdon sat facing his father like a visitor. He would have liked a drink, but did not want to call attention to the contents of the desk. He ran his hands through his hair, which he had been letting grow a little longer lately in order to conceal the first gray strands at the temples. "How long will you be staying?" he asked.

John Tyler Matlock occupied his hard chair with the straight back. "If you are asking because of the office, you'd better plan on settling back into your old quarters. I intend to stay until the stockholders' meeting on the twenty-ninth. If necessary, I'll stay longer."

"Do you mean to come to the office every day?"

Matlock began to pull open the desk drawers. "I want you to move your things out during lunch." He shook his head. "Is all this drink for you? Now I know what makes you so fat. Liquor in a place of business!"

"We have visitors——"

"Visitors!" He did not let his son finish. "Don't talk to me about visitors! Since when are those people visitors? Do you do business or do you give parties? Pure waste of time. I dealt only with people whose time was as valuable as my own."

Langdon was sitting in a draft and was gradually beginning to feel the cold. But he did not get up to close the window. This too shall pass, he told himself—this hour and the next three weeks. The calmer I keep, the better.

"Have you heard from Craig?" Matlock had finished his inspection of the desk. "Where is he? Why doesn't he make a move? Didn't you let him know that he should report in?"

"As far as I know, he's been back in the city since the first of the year. He sits in the Warren Street building and won't let anyone near him. He made Justin Kramer negotiate the new freight contract."

"I want to see him."

"You want to see Craig?"

"Didn't I just say so?"

"Here in . . . your office?"

"Where else? I do not discuss business in barrooms

or at evening receptions. And surely he does not expect me to make the pilgrimage to Warren Street."

"What do you want with him?" Langdon stood up. "Aren't you getting cold?"

"It's finally becoming comfortable in here. When it's too warm, one falls asleep."

"Will you have a glass of sherry?"

"At nine in the morning? But don't stint yourself."

Langdon went to the drawer that held the bottles. He poured himself a glass of white rum and left the bottle out on the desk.

"You must have a cast-iron stomach," Matlock commented. "All right, you heard me. I want to see Craig. That's all I need from you for the present. And have them clean out this desk. Would you like to have dinner with Mother and me?"

"I have an appointment with Irene at six."

"At six. Very well. I don't tell you how to arrange your workday. Anything else?"

Langdon poured a second glass, then said, "If you must see Craig, fine. But you should know that he's following in Poynder's footsteps. He won't let up about the strike. He's still trying to find out who ordered the flyers. And of course he's interested in learning what kind of people we got to infiltrate Poynder's depot. But most of all he wants to know where the militia uniforms came from. He won't let go. And do you think he's doing all that just to pass the time? He's hired two detectives who do nothing but sniff around."

Matlock scribbled a note. He did not wear glasses. It was not necessary, given his large, well formed script. "All of that will stop," he said. His voice became harsh. "I wanted to see Poynder on his knees, not in his grave. It would be better if you didn't remind me."

The reproach was not new to Langdon. Until now, he had kept silent; but this time he could not hold back. "You talk as if it were my fault. But who had the brilliant idea in the first place?"

"I loathe incompetence. One can do anything just so long as he does it well. That is the one thing I reproach you with: bungling. It never bothered my conscience how I achieved my purpose. Heaven is a stock exchange where I do not speculate. First Wilmurt and then Poynder. Two deaths are too much for me. Especially the business with

Poynder. People can be put out of commission, just as they can be checkmated. That's fair. Everybody has the same number of men at the beginning, and the same number of moves. But not this way. Slaughtering him in cold blood! I've fought my way through much worse situations in the past without recourse to such methods. It was sheer bungling. Don't ever again tell me that was what I wanted."

"Not what you wanted!" Langdon forgot that he had promised himself to stay calm. "What did you think would happen? The hell with it. A strike is like a fire. You can control everything except the way the wind blows. That business with the horse barns—that was your idea. I was against it because I could tell—"

Matlock's fist came down hard on the desk top. "You failed. I let you get away with the Wilmurt matter, though I don't know why. Wilmurt should have been a lesson to me. But now my eyes have finally been opened. That is why I am here. That is why I must speak with Craig. I am an old man. I must put my affairs in order."

Langdon had sat back down. He had himself under control again. He spoke matter-of-factly. "To be honest, I consider it inadvisable for you to make the first move with Craig. It is the worst possible moment, in that you still intend to devour the New York Railroad. The limb they're sitting on is shaky. All we need to do is wait for the next storm." Leaning forward, he said urgently, "Craig is sniffing around in our business, but I have information too. The tax office is pressing him hard. They say there's a lot of money at stake. Do you think he would have signed the new freight contract with us on the same old unfavorable conditions if he weren't forced to? Now, in winter, when the Hudson is frozen over and we're the ones who can't get along without the New York Railroad! We were the ones in a bind! You should have seen Kramer sitting right there, tame as a pussycat. No more big noises. We are practically there, Father. We need only wait. And Kramer—who knows how Craig managed to keep him. They say he's paying him twice what Poynder paid him. In any case, Kramer isn't the man to snub money. He also has political ambitions. It's possible that a generous well-timed offer would turn him against Craig. He would be a good replacement for Sydenham. Anyway, the question must be settled, sooner or later."

Matlock examined his hands. "Are you finished? If so, listen to me. You haven't understood anything. I want to make an end of it. Do you understand? An end."

"Do you want to be more accommodating to Craig than you were to Poynder?"

"I will make him a proposition that he will accept."

Langdon looked out the open window. A thin mantle of snow already covered the sill. "Don't you think I'm entitled to know what kind of proposition you have in mind?"

Matlock said, "I won't exclude you from the negotiations." He smiled. Langdon was familiar with the smile; it was not a good omen. "I will offer him half," Matlock said, and in the same breath, "I think we should shut the window now."

Langdon was glad to be able to escape his father's eyes for a moment.

"To anticipate your question," Matlock continued. "By half, I mean fifty percent of our shares in the railroad. You will hold the other fifty percent. I wish to have this clearly settled by the time of the general meeting. I shall resign, and the two of you can split the management of the Empire State between you."

"Split? Do you expect me to relinquish half?" Langdon regretted the question even as he put it.

"The whole still belongs to me," his father reminded him. "We are here in my building, in my office, and the firm we are talking about is mine." He hesitated before continuing. Again he smiled. "I merely want us to understand each other. If I take you into my confidence, that is a gesture of family loyalty, an act of politeness, whatever you wish to call it; but it is by no means an attempt to obtain your consent. If necessary, I can do without that."

Langdon cupped his empty glass carefully, as if he were worried about its fragility. He felt only one emotion now, and that was hatred. Was this what he had waited for all his life? He had an urge to shout out his hatred, but even now, his reason prevailed. What had it gained him to be reasonable, though? Right now, there was no help for it. If he was going to salvage anything now, it would have to be through prudence. He must think. He needed time. The last word had not yet been spoken.

"You must know what you're doing," he said evenly.

"I do know. Harsh as it may sound to you, you haven't got the stuff to be my successor. It's not easy for a father, either, to have to admit that to himself. That may account for the fact that I have closed my eyes to it for so long. Don't forget that. I don't wish to discuss it ever again. There is no chance that I will change my mind."

Langdon set the glass down on the table. "I will see to it that the desk is cleaned out at lunch time," he said.

Matlock looked at the note he had written and then asked, "How are the preparations for the stockholders' meeting coming along? I'd like to see Sydenham with the books."

"I'll tell him."

"What about the ballots? Have the proxies been printed?"

"I'll find out. They should be going out to the stockholders for their signatures any day now."

"I want to see the printer. Yes, personally."

"Excuse me."

After the door had closed, Matlock leaned back in his chair and closed his eyes. He was tired. He had prayed for seven sons. Now he found it difficult to deal with two. And it had taken a stranger to open his eyes about Craig. That was the shock he had suffered at Poynder's death. A stranger had recognized his son's qualities.

A few minutes ago, he had been too warm; now he was shivering. I'll have a steam bath in the hotel, he thought. When Sydenham entered the o..ce with the books, he found Matlock sitting in his overcoat.

# ═ 27 ═

AFTER A QUARREL with Langdon, Irene usually got rid of her anger by a tried-and-true method: she went shopping and spent a lot of money on luxuries. Then she had them delivered to the house, making sure they would arrive when Langdon was at home. She paid for such sprees with her own money, but since Langdon would one day be her heir (as, of course, she was his), he would see himself deprived of part of his inheritance by her extravagance. In a marriage like hers and with a fortune like hers, money was the ideal weapon for domestic warfare.

True, since Craig had returned to New York, Irene had a better reason for her trips downtown. She was looking for an apartment where she could meet Craig discreetly. She had come to this decision without having spoken to him. It was enough to know that he was holed up on Warren Street. She had also found out that he was building a house on Gramercy Park so that his whole family could move to New York. Soon, therefore, he would always be nearby. Everything else she could safely leave to time and chance.

Thus for weeks it had become her favorite occupation to drive around and look for an apartment. She had become familiar with neighborhoods she would not earlier have set foot in. But that was part of the adventure. Her face hidden behind a veil and speaking in a French accent, because she intended to rent the apartment in the name of her onetime French governess, she had inspected numerous apartments. But until now, she had not taken the crucial step. Her reluctance was not rooted in a guilty conscience. If qualms assailed her, she reminded herself that she was eleven years younger than Langdon and by temperament really only half his age. What held her back was the consideration that it would make little sense to pay rent on a vacant apartment.

Since the middle of November she had waited to see Craig. She did not want to write to him and she could not very well go to Warren Street. She had therefore kept on hoping that Langdon would finally feel ready to resume relations with his brother. Irene had often begged her husband to make the first move. Only this morning, that had been the cause of their quarrel. This time she had appealed, not to Langdon's brotherly love, but to his cunning. She pointed out that Craig now occupied a different social position and that, whatever happened, it was to Langdon's advantage to be on good terms with him. But that was just how she had put her foot in it. For Langdon read the same meaning into Poynder's will as the rest of New York did: that he had practically made

Craig his heir, something that touched Langdon like a personal injustice. This time he reacted with particular irritation in spite of Irene's attempt to be diplomatic. Fortunately, John Tyler Matlock's entrance had ended the scene.

At that moment Irene had made up her mind not to wait any longer. She had the driver take her directly to Twenty-ninth Street east of Fifth Avenue, where she knew of a small, secluded house that had not been occupied for some time. It was a little run down, but it was hidden from the street and had a separate entrance. It was also halfway between her house on Thirty-ninth Street and Gramercy Park, where Craig would soon be living. The custodian with whom she negotiated the rent came down by a third when Irene said she would pay a year's rent in advance.

That same morning she had withdrawn the sum from her account, and by noon she had the keys to the house. She immediately had a duplicate made, then spent the rest of the day buying things for the house. The time passed so quickly that it was almost six o'clock before she remembered her appointment with Langdon. She took one last walk through her new domain—the wood-paneled salon, the small turquoise bedroom—planning to return the next day. She must not forget Craig's brand of cigars, nor the champagne, for instance. Driving to Kane's, she made notes of everything she could think of, ending up with a long list.

Kane's was on Broadway, near Prince Street. Actually it was a men's restaurant, where business was discussed over a glass of whiskey and a light meal. On the few occasions when someone was accompanied by a woman, you could be fairly certain that it was not his wife. This was one reason why Irene enjoyed meeting Langdon there. If Langdon was late and they had no other plans, they stayed for supper.

Langdon had been waiting for some time. He was sitting at a corner table, a glass of whiskey in his hand. Irene noticed that it was not his first. Langdon did not drink to excess. After the last drink he conducted himself as he did after the first, but his mood changed from one of defeat to one of impotent rage directed at himself. In neither mood was he approachable. In between, however, there was a phase of sentimental self-pity, and if one recognized it in time, one could do anything with Langdon.

Irene took a seat next to him, her reticule containing the key to the garden apartment in her lap. This secret knowledge gave her a feeling of superiority. The waiter appeared, and Langdon silently pointed to his empty glass.

"And Madame? Nothing to eat? Perhaps just a little bite? We have fresh strawberries." Irene always ordered strawberries even when she ate nothing else.

"Why don't you have the strawberries?" Langdon nodded at the waiter. "I'll stick with this." Impatiently he pointed to his empty glass once more.

Irene asked for a glass of champagne. The waiters in Kane's were apt to get a little frosty if you ordered less than a bottle, but she was in a mood to irritate those around her.

"You're late," Langdon said.

"You weren't bored, though, were you? That's not your first drink."

"God knows it isn't. Nor my last. Today was the last straw. And to think that tonight we have to have the house full of people."

"Was it so very disagreeable?" she asked. "You had no idea he was coming today?"

"None. On Friday, in Albany, he didn't say a word."

The waiter brought the drinks. Irene picked up a straw, a habit that always annoyed Langdon. He found it absurd to order champagne only to stir it "until it's nothing more than sugar water."

"Did you invite him for tonight?" Irene asked.

Langdon took a swallow. "Of course. He refused."

His drinking had begun when Langdon took over the New York office. Earlier, on Staten Island, he sometimes went for weeks without touching a drop. But here in New York, when the first telegram from Albany arrived in the morning with long, detailed instructions of what he was to do, with whom he was to dine, and so forth, he found that he needed a drink.

"Did he say how long he was going to stay?"

Langdon turned his head like someone who is addressed unexpectedly. "Imagine," he said, "the old man is giving up. He wants to make an arrangement with Craig. Now——just like that." He did not dare tell Irene the worst part at once. He would lead up to it gradually. "It's supposed to be my fault again. He's hanging everything on me. Tells me that I failed. That hypocrite. He didn't want anything to happen to poor old Poynder. But Father was always like that. The people who pull his chestnuts out of the fire—he kicks them when it's all over. And this time I'm the scapegoat. He wants to make an arrangement with Craig!" Langdon took another swallow of whiskey. "He threw me out of the office. After seven years he walks in and wants his chair. Can you imagine what he would have done if we hadn't kept it?"

Irene put her hand on the table. The only thing that interested her was the part about Craig. "I don't understand you altogether," she said cautiously. "It was always you who urged your father to make arrangements. You didn't approve of those drastic measures against Poynder. You were in favor of putting an end to them. You constantly preached peace. I should think you'd be glad that your father is finally listening to reason." Suddenly she saw a chance to get her way. "I'm certain Craig will be reasonable. You'll all benefit by it."

Langdon laughed out loud. "Then I must tell you what's going on in the old man's head. He wants to offer Craig fifty percent of his shares in the railroad. Half! Do you realize what that means, Irene? I do. I waited thirty years —for nothing. I took it all. I did whatever he wanted. For the last seven years I've spent every day looking at the crooked backs of clerks and that penny-pincher Sydenham. I do the dirty work, and Craig walks in and pockets half. Can you tell me by what right? He always did as he pleased. He didn't give a damn for his father's wishes. I'm paid a ridiculous three thousand dollars a year, and if I try to get back the costs of my business entertainment, I get a lecture from Sydenham. Has Craig ever had to be responsible for anything? When he married Margaret, everyone laughed at him. Now he has the last laugh. And I'm supposed to relinquish half my inheritance, just for him. Can you think of one reason why I should agree to that?"

Every week when Langdon returned from Albany he unloaded his dammed-up anger on Irene; but she had not expected an outburst like this one. Only a moment ago she had been reveling in his anger, but the idea that this day might possibly have cost Langdon half his inheritance quickly sobered her.

"He says he's going to step down," Langdon said. "Step down—him! Craig and I, we're supposed to share the management of the company. Do you believe he will relinquish the reins?"

"That will depend on you and Craig. What could he do if the two of you work together? Your father is eighty. He might live another ten years. That means you wait another ten years for your inheritance. True, he's taking away half; but in return, you'll have your share *now*. And even if the Empire State pays only seven percent in dividends, you can double your capital in ten years. That way, you won't lose a cent. You have it now, *and* you're your own boss."

Irene could not have argued more cleverly. Langdon was a man of compromise. He got along best with people of similar temperament. Irene had always approved his tactic of watching and waiting. She had never stirred him up, never made the waiting harder.

"The question is, will I be my own boss with Craig next door?"

"In any case, it will be an improvement. The important thing is that your father actually retires. You'll manage Craig. You're the older brother. You've been in the business longer. You know all the directors, the influential people. Craig will see that." She felt sure enough of herself to add, "Don't you think we should ask Craig for tonight, after all? If we were to send him a telegram. . . ."

Langdon did not reply at once. He had leaned back and was looking out the window at the snow-covered street. "I think you're right," he said. "But just the same, it's as if there were a magic spell that let him come out on top again. He signs a marriage contract that no sane person would put his name to, and now he controls the entire Poynder fortune. Margaret doesn't know the first thing about it. He's just soft-soaping her, he was always good at that. She'd go on defending him even if she knew that he's cheating on her."

Irene pushed her chair back so that her face was no longer immediately under the lamp light. After a moment she asked carefully, "Does he?"

"You bet. He doesn't even try to hide it. He's installed a girl in the Laight Street apartment." Langdon was too absorbed in his grievances to notice the effect of this news on Irene. "The people in the house aren't exactly blind. They notice when she has flowers brought in by the carload and champagne by the case."

Irene pushed her glass, still half full, to the center of the table. She had at first thought Langdon had found out something about her and Craig. She should have been relieved that he was not talking about her; instead, it was the reverse. "Another woman?" she asked. "In Laight Street? That can't be true."

"I thought you knew about it. Didn't I tell you before?"

"No. Who is she?"

"Who can she be! What sort of girl lets herself get that involved with a married man? They say she was a seamstress in a glove shop. A factory worker. She's said to give wild parties."

"How do you know?"

"He bought her a shop on Broadway and paid for it with a check written on his own account. I know his bank. That little girl knows how to part him from his money, I'll say that for her."

Irene told herself that Craig had always been this way. She had never been upset by those short-lived affairs. She was the one he always returned to. That was how Craig was. She had even considered it one of his greater attractions. Then why was she so upset by this tale? "How long has this been going on? When did it start? Just recently?"

"How do I know? Ever since he came back from the war."

"All this time?"

"I think so. They say she even went out to Willowbeach and stayed with Hugh Sewall, of all people. Imagine that. He cheats on Margaret right on his own doorstep."

"You seem to know all about it. Do you know her name? How old is she?"

"A young thing. I don't know her name, but her shop is on Broadway. One of the best locations, right next to Appleton's Bookstore. You know the place. They sometimes do printing for us—stock certificates, things like that."

"Did you hire detectives?"

Langdon said, "What's the matter with you? Are you cold?" He held his hand to the window to check for drafts and then reached for her hand. "Your fingers are like ice."

Irene had difficulty meeting his eyes. She was reminded of how it had started between them, after they had gone skating on the Harlem River. On the drive home she felt cold, and Langdon had put his greatcoat around her and, holding her hands, had warmed them, as if it were the most important task in the world.

"I'd like to go now," she said. "It's going to be a strenuous evening for both of us. No, everything is fine. I'll have a hot bath when we get home. That always makes me feel better."

"It's too late to call off the reception."

"Don't worry," she said. "There's nothing for you to be concerned about. Let's go."

After he had paid there was another wait while the doorman found a cab for them. It was still snowing, and carriages were hard to find. They did not speak during the drive home, nor was inviting Craig mentioned again. Langdon had probably forgotten all about it; Irene did not remind him. The farther up Fourth Avenue they went, the thicker the snow was. Irene sat quietly next to Langdon, her reticule on her lap—the bag with the duplicate key that had become so useless. And she had paid the rent for a whole year!

At home she bathed and changed into evening clothes. Every time she passed the pier glass, she thought of what Langdon had told her. By the time he entered her room, she had come to a decision.

Langdon was relieved to find her fully dressed and bright and beautiful, as always.

"Will you please tie my cravat?" he said. "I can't seem to manage it."

"Of course. Sit down." While she deftly knotted the soft material, she asked casually, "Did you tell your father about it?"

"About what?"

"About Craig and the girl."

"No. That kind of thing only impresses the old man. I'll bet you he's sown some wild oats himself."

"Did you tell him Craig is looking for evidence against

him in the business of the strike? Who really was behind it?"

"I tried. But Father was deaf to all arguments. It's a mystery to me what made him change so completely. He says Poynder's death, that was going too far. But Poynder has been dead for two months. Whatever the reason, he's backing Craig, and there's no way to dissuade him."

"He still hasn't talked to Craig. We must see if we can drag the matter out. Don't be deceived about Craig. He's no longer the nice boy who lives only for today. The war changed him, and not for the better. Once he owns half . . ."

"Hold on. An hour ago you were talking quite differently. You said just the opposite. You even wanted me to invite him this very evening. Have you forgotten?"

"Certainly not. But I've had time to think. Now I think my first advice was wrong."

Langdon frowned, trying to understand. The cravat had been a pretext. He had not been able to stand it any longer, alone in his room with his thoughts. He had to be near someone. Of his own volition, he would not have broached the subject again. He was all the gladder, therefore, that Irene was worried, too. He was only too happy to agree with her now. His father's insult had hurt.

"But what can I do? Sure, I can hold Craig off for a few days, but Father will find a way to see him. The matter is settled, as far as he is concerned. He was very explicit about that. And don't forget Mother. She's sure to have had a hand in Father's decision. Her life consists of holding the family together. I can't see any way of preventing Father from asserting himself. Should I have him declared incompetent?"

He laughed. The idea was absurd. Irene sensed that she should join his laughter. She had always believed that she had protected herself against the day the affair with Craig would end. It was inevitable and natural. Even if she meant more to him than any other woman, that day would still come. She had said it herself over and over again. Perhaps that was how she had been able to hold him for so long. But why did her good sense desert her now? She had told herself so often that she did not love him, that he merely represented the adventure that kept her young. How could she hate him now? How could she want to pay him back for what he had done to her? Was it his fault that she had become obsessed with the idea of an apartment? The little house, the linens she had bought today, the key in her purse—the thoughts were almost beyond endurance. She could not live with them; she did not intend to suffer a minute longer than was necessary. But to satisfy her humbled pride, she must have revenge.

"I shouldn't have started," Langdon said. "We should go downstairs. Our guests will be arriving."

"How can you take it so calmly? There are times when compromise isn't possible. We're talking about your *rights*. Surely you don't want to stand by and watch Craig triumph."

"I see no way of preventing it. If I knew of one. . . . I've even thought of involving Margaret."

"I would advise against that." She was grateful to him for playing into her hand. "You said yourself that she trusts Craig blindly. Margaret is like your mother in a lot of ways. No, Margaret is out. She would only stick closer to him. I'm thinking of that girl, that . . . glove-maker."

"What good is she if you can't play her off against Margaret?"

"Maybe we can play her off against Craig. Maybe he would not welcome a scandal at this time."

Langdon shook his head. "I doubt that Craig would let something like that influence him. If I know him, he'd simply drop the girl."

"Just leave it to me."

"You?"

"Why not? Women do these things much better."

They left Irene's room. From downstairs, the butler's voice could be heard. The early arrivals were there.

"What do you intend to do?" Langdon asked. When Irene did not answer, he searched her face. But he saw only the golden hair, the pearls decorating her earlobes, the smooth shoulders. Her slight pallor only heightened her beauty. "What are you planning?" he asked again when they reached the top of the stairs.

Irene took his arm and with her right hand gathered up the folds of the gold-colored evening gown. "First I'll drive downtown tomorrow to buy some gloves."

# = 28 =

"IN THE FUTURE you should let me wait on the customers if there's both a man and a woman, whether they're married or not." Mary Schoffield looked after the couple that had just left the glove shop. "They won't be back. Believe me, she was mad."

"But I didn't do anything," Kitty replied. She began to replace the stack of elbow-high white gloves in the flat boxes. "What is it about me that made him make such eyes!" She laughed. "I prefer men customers anyway. They know what they want, and they don't inquire about the price first off."

"Mother could tell you exactly what it is about you. As far as she's concerned, you're a creature of the devil, if for no other reason than that you married her precious John. But I mean what I said: leave the couples to me. The men who come in alone want you to wait on them. It's pure magnetism. As far as they're concerned, I'm invisible."

Mary Schoffield—or Win, as she was called—was the sister of Kitty's dead husband. At seventeen, she had pale, thin hair, freckles that did not fade even in winter, and slightly protruding teeth. Before Kitty had taken her into the glove shop, Win worked in a haberdashery. She was a master of the trade Kitty had yet to learn.

"You're the boss here," Kitty said. "Without you, I'd have been lost after the first month."

Win took care of the accounts. She never forgot an order or the due date of the rent or taxes. She checked the inventory and saw to it that the window washer came regularly. Now she said, "If you don't stand over the caretaker every minute, he does nothing. The whole sidewalk is already buried in snow again. I'll have to see to it that it gets swept."

275

"Leave it. As long as the storm lasts, it's going to drift anyway. If you happen to run into the telegraph boy, send him in here."

For an instant it seemed as if Win were going to say something, but then she threw the woolen triangle over her head and shoulders and hurried outside. The many telegrams that were delivered to Kitty were the only topic that was never mentioned between them. The telegrams came at any time of the day, and usually Kitty left the shop soon afterward. Sometimes she was gone only a little while; sometimes she did not return for hours. Whatever Win thought of it, she refrained from comment. Her discretion, oddly enough, cost her an effort only when the telegrams stopped coming.

Kitty had put the gloves away. Behind the shop was a small sewing room where a pile of work was waiting for her. But she could not bring herself to tackle it. She was annoyed at herself for having let slip the remark about the telegraph boy. In this way she had admitted to herself how anxiously she was waiting. For ten days Craig had not been by. It was enough to drive her crazy. They lived in the same city, separated by less than a mile—and she waited for a telegram from Craig that would call her to a café, to an auction house, to Laight Street. True, she was partly to blame for the situation. After all, in Sewall's Harbour she had acquiesced in everything—in the shop, in the new apartment she had moved into. She knew that Craig was busy, and she understood that he must be careful. But she was coming to loathe these last-minute appointments. "Meet at ten at Mercer." "Phoenix Bank half-past two 45 Wall Street." "Tonight Laight Street." Usually the telegrams contained nothing more. Often they were not even signed. To her they were beginning to sound like commands.

A customer had come in. Kitty waited on her, wrote out the sales slip, wrapped the three pairs of gloves, and walked the old lady to the door. Win came in from outside, bringing the scent of snow. It was warm in the shop, and the ornamental gas jets burned brightly. Every item of the furnishings was expensive: the oval tables where the gloves were shown, the dainty side chairs, the desk where the customers could write out addresses and checks, the engravings on the walls. Six months ago she had been in Ben Pocock's workshop, cutting out gloves for six dollars a week. Kitty had not forgotten. Nor had she forgotten the attic rooms she had shared with other factory girls. Win's excited voice interrupted her reverie. "Look, will you. She's coming here. Most of them only act rich, but this one really is. Oh, I hope a lot of people see her coming in here."

A carriage stood in front of the shop. Not one of the battered rigs for hire, but an elegant private carriage. The horse blankets were fringed, the coachman was in livery, with white gloves and top hat. He had stepped down from the box and was opening the door.

Kitty threw a hurried look at the mirror and patted her hair. The doorbell jingled loudly. The coachman had opened the door wide and stepped to one side. The scent of lily-of-the-valley spread through the shop as the lady entered. Win was inspired to make a deep curtsey. The lady's costume of moss-green velvet was enhanced by a stole, a cap, and a muff of sable. Her hair was a golden blond. Her beautiful, smooth face reminded Kitty of the rich girls she had known at the Convent of the Sacred Heart; they seemed to look through you as if you were air.

"May I help you?" Kitty asked.

"Show me what you have in stock."

"May I see your hand?"

"My hand? Oh, yes, of course." She put her muff on the table and took off her gloves. She wore a wedding ring on her left hand and a large diamond on her right.

Kitty brought several boxes. "Did you have a particular occasion in mind?"

The customer's eyes slid over the gloves Kitty was spreading out before her. "The fawn-colored ones, the gray, and two pairs of the black. No, there's no need to try them on; I know my size. Your shop is new, isn't it? It's in very good taste."

"Are you sure you wouldn't like to try them on?" Kitty said. "At least one pair?"

The lady turned to Kitty. Brazenly her eyes probed every detail—Kitty's face, dress, figure. "This is your shop? You are Mrs. Schoffield?"

The scrutiny was making Kitty uncomfortable. She nodded.

The woman's eyes were still riveted on her. Their irises were golden brown. "May I speak with you alone? No, no, of course I'll take the gloves, but I would like to have a word with you in private." She pointed to the door at the rear, which was covered by a curtain.

"I'm sorry," Kitty said. "That is only the workshop. If you want to talk, we can talk here."

"I'm on my way to the Customs House," Win broke in, all eyes and ears. "I have to inquire about the shipment from Paris." They were not expecting a shipment from Paris, and Kitty wanted to stop her from leaving. Something told her that it was not a good idea to be alone with this stranger. But Win had already flung on her shawl.

The strange woman pulled a visiting card from her muff. She held it out to Kitty, and when Kitty made no move to take it, she placed the card on the counter. "I do not intend to play hide and seek. I simply thought you would prefer to keep this conversation between the two of us."

Kitty picked up the card. It was exactly like her own—the same paper, the same bluish-gray color, the same typeface. *Irene Matlock.* For an instant she thought the unknown woman was married to Craig, but then she remembered the daguerreotype she had found in the Laight Street apartment. She was relieved when another customer entered the shop. But this woman, this Irene Matlock, did not let the newcomer distract her. She used the time while Kitty was waiting on the customer to give the room another inspection—the writing desk, the chair in front of it, the engravings. When they were alone again, she said, seemingly without embarrassment, "Really, a very pretty shop. Did you pick out the pictures yourself? The desk seems a genuine Adams, if I'm not mistaken. You have stinted on nothing. But I see you know what you have to demand, too. Don't you think that's somewhat high, fifteen dollars for the two pairs of gloves you just sold? Of course, the location has to be paid for. You're quite right to include that in your price."

Irene Matlock's gaze returned to Kitty, and her scrutiny began again. Irene forced herself to a self-tormenting precision. She did not know exactly what she was looking for, but what she found—what leaped at her from every detail of the woman standing before her—was youth. Irene estimated the girl's age at nineteen or twenty. Her daughter's age. Irene felt her palms grow moist and cold. Hastily she pulled on her gloves. She had never made a secret of her age. She had used it as a flirtatious device. But now she understood what it meant to be no longer young, never to be allowed to be young again. She was more beautiful than this Kate Schoffield, but she was no longer young. That's what it was. That was why she had sat in her cab for an hour in front of the St. Denis, waiting for Craig.

"Did he pay for all of this?" Irene asked without transition.

Kitty put the calling card aside. She felt the blood rising in her cheeks, all the way up to her forehead; a hot pain pulsed between her eyes.

"But my dear! I had no intention of offending you. I respect you very much. You are a clever little thing. You could have made him give you jewelry, furs. But you thought of the future. You made provisions. That shows good judgment. How long can feelings last? Surely we can learn to understand each other. I am Craig's sister-in-law. You don't mind if I call him Craig, do you? I'm married to his older brother, so I'm really impartial in this matter. Nor am I here at his wife's request. You know that he's married and the father of two adorable little boys?"

"I realize just how impartial you are," Kitty said.

"You really should make an effort to understand me. What brings me here are not motives of morality. You can be sure of that. I want to make you a proposition."

"Please." Kitty's voice was icy.

"You should listen to me, in your own best interest. Craig is a Matlock. Do you know what that means? The Matlock men have a distinct weakness for the female sex, and no wife has ever kept them from giving in to that weakness." She raised her voice. "But there isn't a single Matlock who has ever even remotely considered a separation or a divorce. Divorce involves money, settlements, and Matlocks marry to increase their fortunes, not to share them or give them away. Craig Matlock is no exception. If you thought so, you were making a big mistake. Just a moment—I'm almost finished. His passion—his only true passion, the one that will outlast all others—is possession. Of course he was never a poor man. But his father-in-law's death made him the executor of a considerable fortune. It doesn't belong to him—not yet—but he has his hands on it. You should know that he would *never* do anything to jeopardize any of it. Never. No emotion in the world is worth it to him."

Again a customer interrupted them, and Kitty took a long time waiting on her. She could have shown this Matlock woman the door. It could be done without causing a stir. But what would be gained? She did not know yet what Irene Matlock wanted from her. If only there had not been ten days of waiting to hear from Craig. Much of what Irene Matlock had just said, she had thought all week. She gave Irene a questioning look when the customer left.

"Surely he paid for all of this," Irene said. "How much did it come to? A thousand dollars? Yes, I think that's about right."

"It will take me less than a year to pay back every penny."

"You can pay him back this very day. The whole sum, a thousand dollars. I'll give you a check if you'll do as I tell you; and later you'll receive the same sum again for yourself. Think about it—two thousand dollars. Or if you prefer, I can drive to the bank at once and get you the cash."

"What do I have to do?" A couple had come to a stop before the shop window, looking at the display.

"Do you close during the noon hour?" Irene asked. "Perhaps we could meet somewhere in the neighborhood where we can talk undisturbed."

"We stay open," Kitty said.

"But surely you can get away for an hour. Shall we say eleven o'clock?"

"Where?"

"I knew you would see it my way. You know André's Hairdressing Salon on Park Row? There's a little coffee-house next door. I'll be waiting for you there."

The couple entered the store, and Irene left.

The coachman was not quick enough off the box to open the door for her. "Just drive for a while," she ordered. "Then I'll tell you where to go."

She sank back into the cushions and closed her eyes until the horse started. Never had she felt such a stranger to herself. Irene Matlock, a woman who always knew what she wanted and who had always gotten what she wanted. She had managed both her everyday life and her adventures with the same circumspection. And now, out of the blue, this. She must have been out of her mind. But the half-hour in the glove shop had cured her. Her view of the situation and herself was as level-headed as ever. An aging woman fighting for her lover. Worse, a woman who was seeking revenge for his betrayal. Truly, she must have been insane. The visit to the glove shop was not her only foolishness. There was also the rental of the little house. Between the two, there wasn't a scintilla of difference. Crazy! In retrospect, she could understand why the caretaker had looked at her so strangely during the negotiations over the rental. How could she have let herself go so far? An aging woman running after a young man. Until now that had, at best, been a subject for gossip among friends.

The brougham rolled on. Sometimes, when it braked abruptly, Irene was thrown back against the upholstery. Age. Finally she had discovered her real enemy. She was still beautiful; she was still able to arouse pleasure; she was still desirable. She could find a replacement for Craig any time she wanted. But that would change nothing, because it would not give her back the years. Nothing would bring them back. Never again would she be young, no matter what she did.

She leaned forward and rapped on the window. When the coachman pushed the glass aside, she said, "To the Metropolitan Bank. And then to André's."

Later, at the beauty parlor, as she reclined in the chair while Monsieur André himself combed back her freshly washed hair, she observed herself in the mirror: the pink throat with the high, tight collar, surmounted by a stranger's face which made her ask: is that me? When did it happen? When did I stop being young?

André held two strands of the freshly washed hair, now ash gray, up to the light. "The same tint again?" he asked.

For a moment she hesitated. Then she answered, "Yes, the same blonde."

# 29

THE CHROME-PLATED watch lay in front of him on the desk, its lid open. It was well known that Matlocks could become more easily attached to the souls of things than to the souls of people. Craig Matlock was no exception.

The watch had lain on the bedside table after Loftus Poynder's death. Craig asked Margaret's permission to take it. She had nodded wordlessly. She showed no interest in any of her father's personal effects. Although in the meantime she had twice come to New York for the day, always staying at the Prescott House on Broadway, she had not come to Warren Street to look for any objects that might interest her. Edna Child had said repeatedly that there must be quite a few things that Loftus Poynder's only daughter should take: the silver spade with which ground was broken at the beginning of Poynder's construction of his first railroad, engraved with the names of the participants; and the silhouette of the locomotive that made the maiden trip on that railroad. But Margaret wanted none of it. She had made up her mind to forget the past.

When Craig had gone to Warren Street, he had placed the watch on Poynder's desk in its customary place. Everyone, especially Justin Kramer, had expected Craig to make changes; the rumors even included a move from the old house. But he left everything as it was.

He sat at Poynder's desk, using his writing instruments, as if he were still seeking the answers to the questions he had asked himself at Willowbeach, at the dead man's bedside.

At first Craig had spent only a few hours a day in the Warren Street building. But day by day he began to stay longer. Then he spent a night there, and that became his custom. It had been a long time since he had returned to

282

Laight Street in the evenings. He used his father-in-law's private rooms, and in the morning he could be seen crossing the street to have breakfast at Captain Catull's.

There was only one innovation on Warren Street. Poynder's old safe was now located downstairs in Kramer's office, while Craig had acquired a new one, the combination of which only he knew.

The watch showed eleven thirty. Kramer would soon be coming in for the daily morning conference, bringing with him the first news from the stock exchange. Even now, two months after Poynder's death, Kramer still comported himself with reserve. Craig had increased his yearly salary and given him to expect further increases; in addition, should a merger between the New York and Empire State railroads come about, Kramer had been promised the position of treasurer. Kramer had accepted the news without comment. He gave Craig all the information he asked for, but he never took the initiative, and he never attempted to influence Craig's decisions. Their relationship was marked by mutual respect and mutual caution.

When Craig heard Kramer coming up the stairs, he put down his pencil and waited. As always, Kramer had paused only briefly to take off his hat and coat, in the secretaries' anteroom. His face was still flushed from the cold, and snow still clung to his boots. "It took me half an hour to get here," he said. "I'd make better time walking. The streets are jammed. No one can deal with such masses of snow." His forehead and fine, light-brown hair still showed the outline of his hat. From his extensive wardrobe of blue suits he had today selected a smoke-blue one, and with it he was wearing a sand-colored vest.

Neither bothered with a formal greeting, in exchange for which they granted themselves each morning a moment of mutual silent scrutiny. Since the death of his father-in-law, Craig wore only dark clothing; that, too, was a matter of annoyance to Kramer. Craig—as far as he was concerned—belonged in light suits, raw silk, white linen. But the image of the rich scion of a wealthy family had long since vanished.

"How is the market?" Craig asked.

Justin Kramer sat down, placing a green file on the desk. He was reminded that Loftus Poynder had always wanted to know about the exchange first. "We're still climbing. Not by leaps and bounds, but climbing."

This was a miracle—and Craig had predicted it. Since Poynder's death the shares of the New York Railroad had inched upward—slowly, with remissions, but undeniably upward. They had not yet reached their old high. Losses still predominated. But in part they had already recovered.

"Any sign that my father is buying?"

"No. I would have heard. It is just as you supposed. People simply will not believe that the rivalry between the New York Railroad and the Empire State can last much longer. Everybody assumes that they're witnessing a phony struggle between father and son. By the way, Mr. Matlock Senior is in New York. He arrived two days ago. He wants to see you."

The snow on Kramer's boots had melted and formed transparent pearls on the brown kid. "The news doesn't seem to take you by surprise." He studied Craig's face, but it was like an open door leading into a void. Once again, as so often before, he asked himself what Craig could have done to earn Poynder's trust. And once again he found no answer. He merely felt rising within him a vague rancor toward the dead man.

But Craig had succeeded to the extent that Kramer stayed at his post. What was it that granted Craig Matlock such power over others? Kramer saw its effect every day. The clerks in the building, the workmen at the station: after biding their time briefly, all now swore by him. What was it that this man, who never gave an inch, used to win the hearts of others?

Justin Kramer suddenly suspected that Craig knew about everything, that he was only playacting to deceive him and the public. "I met your brother at the exchange," Kramer said. "Your father's unexpected appearance apparently surprised him more than it did you. I have the feeling that he sees this development as somehow sinister, as if he were afraid that his father and you might come to an arrangement at his expense."

"You've still got that on your mind," Craig replied. "You still won't believe that I will see this battle through. All right. What did my brother actually have to say?"

"That your father wants you to come and see him in his Broome Street office."

"You didn't—"

"No, I told him I wasn't sure that I would be seeing you today."

"Excellent. I'll think it over. I'll give you an answer for my brother before you go to the exchange this afternoon." He pointed to the green file. "Is that the final list of the embezzled mail fees?"

"*Embezzled* is a harsh word. Yes, it's the list. It took a little longer, but I did not want to ask any of the clerks to compile it." Kramer pushed the folder across the desk. "You'll find everything in there. Altogether, it comes to about a hundred thousand dollars that we overcharged the government during the last few years."

"Poynder knew about it?"

"Every invoice crossed his desk."

"What does the total consist of?"

"Two-thirds of the amount arises from false declarations about the weight of the mail we carried, especially letters. The rest is made up of excessive rents charged for the cars used to transport the mail. Of course, such manipulation is illegal. But you can rest assured that Poynder wasn't the only one. I know of no railroad company that does not improve its profits by machinations of that sort. I'm certain that the books of the Empire State would reveal much more sizable peculations."

"I'm not worried about that. But I do not want a scandal. I don't want the matter brought to light at the wrong time. We're dealing with John Tyler Matlock, don't forget. He would be delighted to call the courts' attention to our problem. I'm not about to run a risk, not the slightest. We can't afford to leave ourselves uncovered."

"I compiled the list because you asked for it, but I don't think we have anything to worry about. The Empire State is too deeply enmeshed itself."

"Thank you. I'll look it over. That's all for the moment."

After Kramer had left, Craig studied the list. Then he opened the safe to put the file away. His eyes fell on the tall stack of stock certificates: those from Poynder's estate, his own, and the ones he had bought from his sisters. Another shelf held the envelope with Wilmurt's papers.

Craig had sworn to himself that he would proceed slowly, that he wouldn't act on emotion or impulse. Being alert, more alert than all the others, avoiding all risks, not leaving himself wide open, accumulating ammunition, being armed. And waiting for the right moment. Was it approaching? What did his father's coming to New York mean? Was the old pirate growing weary? Would he make him an offer now, two months after Poynder's death? Was he willing to grant what Craig had demanded that day at Willowbeach? There had been a few changes since that memorable conversation. At the time, Craig's demand had been something of a shot in the dark. But in the meantime there was a new situation. He had taken Poynder's place. But could he really refuse to see his father? Would he not at least have to hear him out? To underestimate one's opponent was dangerous, but it was equally dangerous to misjudge one's own strength.

Craig paced through the two adjoining offices. They had become his world during the past two months. He knew his way around, and not just superficially. He had seen below the surface. Now he understood why Justin Kramer had advised against combat and in favor of a settlement. It was true: Poynder's position had not been secure.

On the desk was a sheet of paper that contained the bare figures. In the last six months, since the struggle between John Tyler Matlock and Loftus Poynder had begun, the total losses of the New York Railroad came to about five million dollars: losses on the stock exchange and decreased income through the loss in passengers and freight revenues. Some were purely paper losses, already compensated for to some extent by buying back the shares at lowered rates. And they would be minimized even more now that the shares were climbing.

But other factors were cause for concern. In looking through the account books, he had run across items pointing to the fact that Poynder had not been a selfless builder of railroads. There were entries such as "judicial honoraria," nothing more than a euphemism for bribes. There were doctored balances, entries for construction and repair work which, in reality, had never been carried out—all of this merely to furnish proof that the company was unable to pay its shareholders dividends of more than ten percent.

Two situations were particularly touchy. Poynder's will showed that he had left a total estate of twenty-seven million dollars. But year after year he had declared under oath to the tax office that his personal fortune did not exceed seven hundred and fifty thousand dollars. The tax commission of New York City was now retroactively attempting to collect some of his tax lien. No official notification had yet been served, but the word had filtered down that the true state of affairs was known. Kramer had negotiated with the tax commission, pointing out that it would be child's play to convert Poynder's estate into tax-free debentures should criminal prosecution be instituted. The matter was still open. The chance that it would come to nothing was considerable, but at the moment it represented a threat that had not been averted for good. The other sore point was the mail subsidies he had just discussed with Kramer.

All of this was sufficient reason to seriously consider an offer from his father. Should he go to Broome Street and see what the old man had to say? But what if his attempt at reconciliation was merely a sign of exhaustion? What if John Tyler Matlock felt that his time had run out? What if his visit to New York was connected with the general meeting of the Empire State at the end of January? Was his father afraid of losing his power? If that was so, then every accommodation, every compromise, would be a mistake that would rob Craig of the chance to get his hands on all of it.

His restless pacing had brought him back to the desk. The chrome watch showed twelve fifteen. Had he been so lost in thought that he had not heard the noon train come in?

He threw open the window. The snow was falling so heavily that he could barely make out the outlines of the station. Quite unconsciously the rhythm of the timetable influenced the course of his day, and the fact that the train had not come in on time irritated him more than anything else.

# ═ 30 ═

THE STATION WAS smothered in snow. It had piled over the tracks, which were being shoveled free. The accesses to the ticket windows and depot sheds were hidden between yard-high banks of snow. Two men stood on the roofs over the two platforms and swept off the snow so the weight would not cause the roof to collapse. There was no sign of the noon train.

Every workman was outside shoveling snow. All of them seemed to be enjoying themselves. As Craig passed, they smiled at him. But they could not tell him why the train was delayed. No one had seen Bryan, the station master, in the last quarter of an hour. This was unusual, for Henry Bryan was one of those men who always seemed to be in three places at once.

Finally Craig spied Bryan's scarlet cap. He was coming from the line's telegraph office, and he was beaming. This was not necessarily a sign of good humor; his round, bright eyes always beamed in his chubby, red-cheeked face. "I was on my way to see you," he said. "I only stopped to make sure about the delay. You're here to ask why the train is late, aren't you? There was nothing that made Mr. Poynder as angry as a delayed train, especially toward the last."

"What did happen? The train is twenty minutes overdue."

"No cause for worry. It's only the snow. Eight inches in the last two hours. It doesn't look as if it's going to stop any time soon, either. Of course, we were prepared for it, in theory. But it always takes a day to get all the machinery going. You're seeing it for the first time, but I've been with the line for fifteen winters, the last five here and the ten years before that in Albany."

"When do you think it will get in?"

Bryan looked at the station clock. "It was blocked outside Poughkeepsie. They're shoveling it out now. Why don't you come to the telegraph office with me? You'll be able to see for yourself."

The telegraph clerk's table was littered with strips of white paper, but the instrument was still clattering away. The clerk, too, seemed infected with Bryan's high spirits. With a broad grin he indicated the table. "It's the worst mess I've ever seen. It's been like this for half an hour." He snipped off the paper ribbon. "Up in the northern part of the state, it's been storming and snowing without letup since yesterday." He rummaged among the strips and pulled one out. "Fifteen trains of the Empire State are stuck outside West Albany. Most of the passengers have given up and are hoofing it to town through the snow-storm."

Craig grew impatient. "I care about what is happening to *our* trains."

"We've had a message that three of them were stopped a mile south of Greenbush. One passenger train and two freight trains. Four others are snowed in on the way to Poughkeepsie."

"Get in touch with Jones. I want all available workmen on the line. I want to be kept in constant touch. Let me know if there's any change." He glared at the tangle of white strips. "Save all messages. Send everything to my office. I want to look at them—everything that comes in."

As they left the telegraph office, Bryan said, "If I may be allowed to say so, don't take it too hard. Once we get our crews on the line, we'll have the tracks cleared by early afternoon. Philo Jones has been through it before. Neither of our lines presents a problem—smooth tracks, straight as an arrow, very little elevation. Take it from me, you can relax. We can handle it. But the Empire State—it's stranded in weather like this."

"You're familiar with Albany?"

"You bet. I spent ten years there with our company, five before that as station master of West Albany, for the Empire State. I can tell you what Albany looks like right now. It's worse than any strike. I lived through it often enough. But fifteen snowbound trains—even I never saw that happen. It's a record. Do you know what it means? Those are the trains from Syracuse, from Rochester, from Buffalo. Some of them have been on the road for fourteen hours. Their supplies are used up. They can't keep the trains heated. They can't even give their passengers hot coffee. They're stuck, and there's not much they can do about it. Either they freeze in the trains, or they leave their baggage behind and walk to Albany. That's a long hike, especially in the dark."

They had reached Porter's office. "Am I talking too much about the Empire State?" Bryan said with a grin. "May I offer you some whiskey? I'm on duty, but if you'll have one with me? It warms your insides."

They entered the little office, and Bryan took off his cap. After they had had their drink, Craig said, "Tell me some more."

"The rights of way are level, but near West Albany, there's a damned steep incline. I've seen six locomotives fail to get a train up it. Three locomotives pulling and three pushing, but the train wouldn't budge." Caught up in the memory, Bryan stared into space. "But passengers who get off at Albany are better off than those who have to go on to New York. In my day they didn't have the railroad bridge over the Hudson. The ferries were stuck fast in the ice. If you wanted to catch the train to New York, you had no choice but to walk across the frozen river with bag and baggage." The memory amused him. "Those were the days. Hysterical women, carrying children, furious men storming our ticket windows, trying to reclaim lost baggage, asking for their money back. I'm telling you: a strike isn't half as bad. Winter is a miserable time for the Empire State. And it isn't just the Albany line that gives them trouble. Their network of lines runs through a lot of snow traps up there. It always hits West Albany the hardest, though; it's like a bottleneck on the way to New York. I can remember one year when the connection at Albany was out of service for a week. All of us had had it up to here. And the gentlemen of the management weren't any better off. For them it was a matter of money. You wouldn't believe what a day like today costs the Empire State. I remember somebody telling me: 'Bryan, pray to heaven that it stops snowing. If it keeps up like this for two more weeks, we can shut up shop.' Another drink?"

Suddenly Craig was in a hurry. "No, thanks. See that I get all incoming messages."

\*     \*     \*

Craig found some of the white strips, pasted on sheets, already on his desk. After studying them carefully, he spent a long time standing before the large wall maps showing the rail lines of the New York and Empire State. Back at his desk, he picked up the sheet of paper with a column of figures and added them up. After he had done this, he took down from the shelf behind him several volumes containing the legal statutes and decrees that had to do with railroads. He leafed through several volumes before he found what he was looking for. He marked the place and turned back to his calculations.

That was how Justin Kramer found him. Without looking up, Craig pointed to the chair by the desk. Even when, as now, Craig was concentrating, his features remained relaxed; only his eyes were veiled. Kramer took in the situation with the attention he gave to everything connected with Craig Matlock.

When Kramer had decided to keep his position, he also made up his mind to eliminate as far as possible his bias against Craig Matlock. But without that bias, Craig had become an unknown quantity to him. Thus Kramer had to reassess Craig every day. At the beginning of November, after Craig's first days in the Warren Street office, Kramer marked his standing as zero on his private stock exchange. If his extrapolation had been correct, it would have been downhill from there. Instead, Craig's quotation, no matter how critically Kramer evaluated it, had risen and had since reached a price which, expressed in words, would go something like this: a man who can find his way around any situation. Almost daily, Kramer received evidence of this capability. Yet he was still waiting for the moment when its limits would be revealed.

"It looks bad out there on the line, doesn't it?" Kramer said. To his surprise, Craig nodded in agreement and asked him to study the railway map.

Craig pointed to a spot west of Albany. "The Empire State must be in a state of chaos," he said. "Fifteen trains are snowbound. Bryan thinks that if the weather continues this way for a week . . ." He trailed off. "Bryan gave me an idea," he resumed. It was as if he were talking to himself. "I think that's it. This is what I've been waiting for."

"Henry Bryan is our snow expert," Kramer said, not

understanding what Craig was getting at. "Snow—that's his element."

Craig Matlock returned to the desk. "Come, let's sit down." Holding the piece of paper with the columns of figures, and looking at Kramer, he explained. "You know that the Empire State is holding its general meeting on January twenty-ninth. I've copied a few figures from recent annual reports. I'd like to go over them with you."

"You mentioned an idea——"

"Wait." Craig looked at his notes. "The Empire State has a stock capitalization of twelve and a half million dollars, distributed in two hundred and fifty thousand shares with a face value of fifty dollars each."

Kramer nodded.

"I've noticed that only some of the two hundred and fifty thousand shares are ever voted. The actual figures vary, but no more than a hundred and sixty-five thousand ever exercise their voting right. My question is: do you think the situation will be different this year?"

Kramer tried vainly to establish a connection between the snowbound trains and the figures concerning the general meeting. What was Craig aiming at? "You can safely assume that nothing will change," he said. "It is quite common to find a third of the stockholders giving up their right to vote. They neither attend the stockholders' meeting nor send in their proxies."

"That would mean, then, that control of about eighty-five thousand shares would be enough for a voting majority at the stockholders' meeting."

Kramer was still unsure what was in Craig's mind. He remained silent.

Craig had laid aside his pencil and put down the paper. "By the time the meeting rolls around, the general meeting at the St. Nicholas Hotel, we—we will have the majority."

A hint of skepticism and defensiveness appeared in Kramer's face. "Forgive me," he said, "but I cannot see how you expect to achieve that." His glance wandered to the safe. "You know that during the past year, on Mr. Poynder's instructions, I have bought up shares in the Empire State. It was a very favorable time. The price was unusually low, for your father had pushed it down himself in order to be able to buy. But twenty thousand is not eighty-five thousand. It's a long way still, and the meeting is eighteen days from now."

Craig pulled out his cigar case but left it unopened. "There was no need to speak of it before," he said, "but the safe contains far more Empire State shares than that. My father paid off my sisters and me in Empire State stock. Altogether, there are fifty-eight thousand shares. All of them in the safe there."

"You owned the shares even before Poynder's death? Your father would not have handed them over afterward."

"Yes. Before the strike."

"Why didn't you mention them when we talked after the funeral? It would have been an argument I would have been more likely to trust."

"I did not consider it necessary."

"You are a farsighted man," Kramer said. "But even so, we hold barely more than half of what we need. How are we to get the rest?"

"I've been thinking about that." Craig Matlock looked at his notes again. "I have learned that the city of New York holds twenty-five thousand shares in the Empire State. And I've also learned that the city representatives have withheld their votes in the last few years."

"Your father has not paid dividends for some time," Kramer said matter-of-factly. "The city is annoyed. It didn't vote against him, but it didn't want to give him its votes either."

"I need the city's votes."

Kramer nodded. He was slowly catching on, but he was careful to conceal his feelings.

"I need those votes," Craig repeated. "And I want you to get them for me. Speak to the right people on the Common Council. You're much better at that sort of thing than I am. You know how to handle them, how much the votes will cost us. Tell me honestly—do you think it's possible?"

"Honestly?" Kramer pulled his cuffs out of his coat sleeves. "Yes, you can count on the votes of the city. You won't even have to bribe them if I can promise them in your name that in future under your direction, the Empire State will pay ten-percent dividends."

Craig smiled. "Did you say under my direction? You seem to be getting used to the idea that it's possible."

"Adding it all up," Kramer said, eager to bring the

conversation back to a more factual, neutral level, "that gives you eighty-three thousand shares. We need seventeen thousand more to be on the safe side."

"We'll buy them."

"The value of Empire State stock has risen much faster than ours in the past couple of months. At the current rate——"

"I have the figures here," Craig interrupted. "At the current rate, seventeen thousand shares would cost us well over a million."

"Just about all we have in cash reserves. Do you want to take such a risk? Think what would happen if your father finds out that we're buying. No matter how careful we are, in the present situation, it would be noticed, and you know what would happen next. He'll see to it that the shares go up. All he has to do is put out the rumor that the Empire State will pay hefty dividends this year. He's already done that within the exchange; that's why his shares have been rising so rapidly."

Craig opened his cigar case, held it out to Kramer, who refused, and put it back on the desk. "I am not counting on Empire State shares going up again soon. I am counting on their falling. Considerably."

"I see no reason why the quotation of the Empire State should go any lower." The watch on the desk began to whirr and then gave off a single clear note. One-fifteen. "If we buy, the market will go along," Kramer continued. "That means the price will not go down but up."

"I tell you, the price will go down, Kramer, it will plummet. Beginning tomorrow, to be precise. Wall Street will long remember tomorrow. If everyone does not sell all his Empire State shares at a loss tomorrow, I'll eat my hat."

He spoke with so much assurance that Kramer remained silent. Craig had reached for a clean piece of paper and began to write. For a while there was no sound but the scratching of his pen and the impatient thrust with which he dipped it in the inkwell. Finally he finished and looked up.

"I believe this will bring them to their knees." He picked up the sheet of paper and read aloud to Kramer what he had just written. "The New York Railroad herewith renounces all agreements with the Empire State Railroad heretofore in effect. It will no longer convey passengers and freight of the Empire State in transfer trade. Tickets of the Empire State are invalid on the New York Railroad effective immediately. Beginning on January 12 at 12:01 A.M., the New York Railroad will convey passengers and freight to and from its station in Greenbush only. New York City, January 11, 1866."

"I'm beginning to understand." Kramer's voice was husky.

Craig rose and went to the wall map. "Here," he said to Kramer, who had followed him, and pointed to where the line of the New York Railroad ended on the eastern shore of the Hudson, outside Albany. "Greenbush. That's where our trains will stop. That will be our railhead. A few of *our* passengers will be annoyed that we won't take them any farther. We will lose some revenue. But that won't do much damage. Over there, however"—and he pointed to Albany, on the other side of the Hudson— "over there on the other side of the city, at the Empire State station, all hell will break loose. For the Empire State, through traffic is the chief source of revenue. Travelers from Rochester, Buffalo—all of them want to go on to New York. But from now on, they will be stuck in West Albany. First they have to get to town. Then they have to get across the frozen Hudson. The bridge does them no good, because our trains stop in Greenbush. Do you see, Kramer? That's the way to cut off their lifeline. Not a soul will travel by way of Albany if it means that much trouble. They'll take the Erie instead. And the Empire is the loser." He echoed Bryan's words: " 'It's worse than any strike.' They'll be on their knees to us."

He did not wait for an opinion from Kramer, but hurried back to his desk and handed Kramer the paper. "Put that in the proper form. Have the original sent to my father. At the same time, get copies to the newspapers. Tomorrow you'll see the Empire State shares tumbling down."

Kramer stood with lowered head, holding the sheet of paper. He asked himself from what source Loftus Poynder had drawn his knowledge of Craig's talents. Justin Kramer was convinced that this move could not help but lead to Craig's victory. He admired the simplicity of the plan at the same time that he felt a slight shudder at the realization that young Matlock had concocted it to destroy his own father.

"This will cause quite a stir," he said at last. "The newspapers will have a heyday with the story. They won't be very flattering about your methods. And one thing more." He held up the paper. "It violates a law that obligates every railroad company to keep its lines open to connecting traffic. The Empire State will take it to court."

"Let them," Craig replied. "That will take weeks. The Empire State doesn't have that kind of time. No, Kramer, the way I see it, my father will understand at once that he must give in. The Empire State Railroad cannot withstand the loss of all their connecting traffic for even as much as a week. They must and will try to reach an agreement with us. We will be accessible. We will promise them a new contract. They will agree to anything, just so long as we remove the blockade. But we will use the negotiations to buy up as many shares as we need to give us a majority at the stockholders' meeting."

Kramer still felt doubtful. Surely all this had happened once before, when even Loftus Poynder had been certain of being able to put John Tyler Matlock in his place. And Loftus Poynder was dead.

"Why so pensive?" Craig asked.

"I was thinking of Mr. Poynder. There was a time when he too predicted victory."

"Are you determined to see me lose the battle? That day at Willowbeach, you said it would be a good reason for you to remain."

"It doesn't make any difference, does it?" Kramer said.

"What do you mean?"

"Whoever wins the battle, it will be a Matlock." Kramer bowed formally. "I shall dictate an official declaration and see to it that it is distributed properly."

"Wait until this evening. Don't issue it until the office has closed. But get it out in time to make the morning papers. And get everything ready for buying."

"If I should see your brother at the exchange this afternoon, do you have a message for your father?"

"No. I can't be reached. By anyone. Not today or for the next few days. Not until the Empire State is ready to negotiate. What matters most is for them to believe that all we care about is a new, better, more favorable contract. They must not find out what we're really after. Believe me, Kramer, in three weeks you and I will be attending the general meeting of the Empire State in the St. Nicholas Hotel, and they'll be eating out of our hand."

After Kramer had left, Craig returned to the railroad map. The decision had been taken, and he felt wonderful. He got his coat from the wardrobe, but before leaving the office, he took his cigar case from the desk and snapped shut the lid of the watch.

Kramer, watching from the window of his office, saw Craig walk down the street. Hands in his pockets, he strode through the heavy whirls of snow as if the weather were tailor-made for him.

# ≡ 31 ≡

TOWARD EVENING THE snow had stopped falling. The air grew colder, and the snow crunched underfoot. Parts of the sidewalks had been swept clean, but St. John's Park lay deeply buried in snow. Yes, Craig thought, the snow, especially in the dark, together with the light of the gas lanterns, restored to the neighborhood some of its lost splendor. Perhaps, though, it only seemed that way because tonight his whole world was beautiful.

He had not returned to Warren Street that afternoon. Matters were taking their course; there was nothing more he could do. He had gone to see the architect to discuss the house on Gramercy Park. He had been lucky at an auction: for his future library he had purchased a complete linden boiserie from a French chateau. It was damaged in one place because some barbarian had had a hole cut to accommodate a stovepipe; but the elegant piece of furniture could easily be repaired. Afterward he had spent an hour at the Turkish bath, and finally he had dined at Musgrove's, where they served the best smoked salmon and most delicate chablis. In midafternoon he had sent off a telegram to Kitty.

They had never spoken about Sewall's Harbour and

what had happened there. It had been a good idea to buy her the shop on Broadway; now she was independent. She had enough to do so that she was not constantly waiting for him. And she seemed to understand her position. For the first time it occurred to him that he might keep the apartment on Laight Street even after the house on Gramercy Park was ready to move into.

From a distance he saw Joe Cristadoro sweeping the sidewalk in front of the house. Joe wore only a thin jacket over his multi-colored shirt. "That's some weather," Cristadoro said as Craig came up. "Not so much as a flake in December, and now all of it at once. My wife is already sick from all the snow; but I enjoy it. Would you believe she comes from some village up north, where it snows for six months out of the year—and I'm from Naples!"

"Has she arrived?" Craig said.

"She was here," Cristadoro replied. "But she left again right away."

"What do you mean?"

"She came in the afternoon. Just for a minute. She asked the cab to wait."

"What time was that?"

"Around five o'clock."

Craig unbuttoned his coat and shook off the snow. Kitty must have had the telegram by then. He was not worried. He had told her seven thirty. She must have come earlier to light the fires in the apartment. "She'll be back soon," he said. "You needn't tell her that I'm upstairs."

He entered the house and went to the top floor. Kitty's strongest dislike was unheated rooms. The apartment, and especially the bedroom, would be pulsating with heat. In this expectation he unlocked the door, but the vestibule was chilly. He walked through the rooms. There were no fires in any of them. The bedroom was tidy; the neatly spread coverlet reminded him how long it had been since he and Kitty had met there. But why had she come by?

He spied the handbag lying on the mantel. The jet beads with which it was embroidered shone dully. The bag matched the evening gown he had given Kitty for Christmas. He picked it up. His fingers could not detect the oval vanity case, the little bottle of perfume, the mirror, and the countless objects with which Kitty usually stuffed her reticules. It felt soft and full. He opened it and looked in amazement at the contents: bank notes, new bills, carefully banded. He counted the money. It came to one thousand dollars in ten-dollar bills.

He laid the bag down in consternation, only to pick it up again. This time he found one of Kitty's business cards tucked in among the notes. On the back she had written in purple ink: "If you have any further demands, let me know. Kitty."

What the devil was the meaning of this? In a rush of anger he picked up the empty purse and flung it to the floor. He put the money and card in his inside pocket and left the apartment.

Joe Cristadoro looked up in surprise when Craig left the house after such a short stay. The caretaker set down the bucket of salt. He considered it prudent not to ask any questions. It seemed that Craig would pass him in silence, but then he stopped.

"You told me Mrs. Schoffield was here. Did you speak to her?"

Joe Cristadoro was always ready to defend Kitty. "She'll be here, don't worry. No, we didn't speak. She was in a big hurry. Out of the cab and into the house. Since she has the shop, she hasn't got as much time as she used to. A beautiful shop, by the way, I must say. I was there and looked it over. And does she ever know how to get along with customers!" Suddenly he remembered. "Maybe it has something to do with the lady . . ."

"What lady?"

"Somebody's been spying on the two of you."

"Who would spy on us? You must be seeing things."

"I don't think so. Fancy private carriage, coachman in livery, a great lady, but she spies all the same." Joe hesitated, trying to figure out how far it was safe to go. "It wasn't your wife, but she asked questions like she was. Whether I knew Kate Schoffield. She knew the name. How long she had been living here. How often you meet her here. Whether you stay all night. That was about it. She offered me a ten-dollar bill. Early this morning."

"If I know you, you didn't turn down the money."

Cristadoro grinned. "One time, many years ago, you could get money by shoveling snow. But that's a long time ago. Sure, I took the money. But she didn't find out anything from me."

"May I see the ten-dollar bill?"

"It's true. I wouldn't dream of telling her anything."

"That's all right, I'm only interested in the bank note." Craig scrutinized the bill. It was as new as those he had found in Kitty's purse. He handed it back to the caretaker. After thinking briefly, he said, "If the lady comes back and asks more questions, tell her that Mrs. Schoffield has left New York. Did you get that—she has left New York, and you don't know when or if she's coming back."

In the walk over to Broadway he had quickly gotten over his anger. He had long since become used to Kitty's tides, as he called her moodiness. Even at his last meeting with her, he had sensed that something new was in the wind. Until now he had always been able to manage her; it should not be difficult for him to do so again.

The row of buildings along Broadway where Kitty's shop was located was built in the style of an Italian Renaissance palace. Each window had its ornamental gable; the five floors were separated by decorative ledges; and a colonnade extended along the shops on the ground floor. One of these was Kitty's.

Broadway was aglow with the light of its new gas lanterns. The cold had become severe, and few people were on the streets. Craig glanced at the window display. It was lined with green velvet on which reposed a single pair of white elbow-length gloves. Nothing else, no price tag, no decoration, merely the silver shop sign in the form of a coat of arms: Kate Schoffield, Designer Gloves. It looked extremely elegant.

The doorway stood between the glove shop and the jeweler's next door. Kitty's apartment was on the fifth floor, a luxurious mansard apartment, all of whose windows looked out on a quiet, inner courtyard. There was also a small roof garden. As Craig entered the front hall, hot air rushed at him. The central heating apparatus provided not only for the apartments, but for the halls and staircases as well. At the fourth floor, the red carpet ended; the last flight of stairs was covered with plain green linen.

Craig had arrived at the foot of the last flight of steps when he heard voices and, for a moment, the sound of an orchestrion. Two men and a woman came down the stairs. They were tipsy. The girl was in the middle, arms linked

with both men. The three took up the width of the staircase. They could only have come from Kitty's rooms.
Craig stepped aside, but they did not notice him. As they
stumbled past, he heard the girl say in an unsteady voice,
"I never saw anything like it . . . a party that's over before
it's even properly dark. She used to drink us all under the
table, every man jack of us."

An odor of cheap perfume and alcohol remained behind, and their racket could be heard until the door below
slammed shut. Craig went up the rest of the stairs. The
door to Kitty's apartment was ajar. The orchestrion started
up again, playing an English waltz that was a current hit.
Pushing open the door, Craig went in. Out of the dusk,
Kitty's voice shrieked at him. "Out! I told you to get lost! I
can't stand your faces any more! Out! Get lost, there isn't
any more. The party's over————" She broke off. The
hand holding the vase, ready for the throw, was lowered
as Craig closed the door behind him.

She was wearing an extremely low-cut gown which he
had not seen before. She looked for a place to set the vase
down. When she could not find one, she simply let go, and
the vase fell on one of the many pillows strewn around the
room. Kitty took a step toward him, caught her foot in the
edge of the rug, which was turned back, clumsily reached
for the sofa, and tumbled onto it. The room was in an ex-
treme state of disorder. Any rooms containing Kitty, if
only briefly, tended to chaos, but the present turmoil sur-
passed anything Craig had seen. Chairs were overturned,
trays holding empty glasses and bottles littered the floor,
newspapers and articles of clothing were strewn about.
For a moment he was on the verge of leaving, simply
walking away, closing the door behind him, getting far
away from the house. Fresh air to breathe—fresh, cold
air. But then he forged his way to the orchestrion and
turned it off. In the silence he heard Kitty's moans.

He went to her. She was sitting up, and her breath
reeked of whiskey. Even now he was not certain that she
knew who he was.

"My God," she said, "I feel so rotten. . . . I think I'm going to die." She was white as a sheet, and her eyes seemed
sunken. She stared at him. Then, as if in sudden recognition, she pushed him away, gathered herself up, and ran
out of the room.

A door slammed shut with a loud crash. She was in the

bathroom. Craig could hear her retching. He stood at the
fireplace and stared into the flames. Finally there was silence in the bathroom. He lit a lamp, tore open the windows, and began to clean up the mess. He put all the
glasses together, straightened up the overturned chairs.
Candy had been spilled on the floor and ground into the
rug, which was also spattered with candle drippings and
cigar ashes. I should have had a restaurant carpet put
down, Craig thought. She had no sense of values. He was
disgusted. A single shoe lay on the floor in front of the orchestrion. He kicked it under the sofa.

The orchestrion had been one of his first presents to
her. It was an expensive piece of equipment, imported
from Switzerland. It played six selections—two marches,
two polkas, and two waltzes. The first day Kitty had kept it
going for twelve straight hours. The orchestrion had stood
for years in the display window of a watchmaker's shop on
Second Avenue. Kitty had often passed by just to see if it
was still there. "But never," she said, "never in my life did
I think that one day I'd own it." Now she owned it, and
what difference did it make? Was she any happier than
she had been when she worked for Pocock?

All was quiet now in the bathroom. He could leave. Another opportunity would not come again soon. An end
without scenes, ugly quarrels, or tears. Tomorrow morning, when Kitty had slept it off and could think clearly
again, she would remember that he had been here. She
would remember the condition she had been in when he
found her, and she would know that she had lost him. As
he was thinking, he recalled the money in his pocket. He
pulled out the roll of bank notes and looked around for a
place to put them. He was about to place the money in a
bowl containing calling cards when he was brought up
short. Diffidently he picked up the top card. It differed in
no way from Kitty's own—the same format, the same
typeface—. "Irene Matlock" was engraved in dark letters
on the bluish-gray card.

Kitty was lying diagonally across the bed, only half un-
dressed, a white cloth over her forehead. It was a small
chamber, with room for little else besides the bed. The
walls were lined with deep purple velvet, and it was even
warmer than in the parlor. She had not pulled the curtains;
the bright planes of the snow-covered roofs and the chim-

neys, their smoke rising in a straight line, were visible. As he walked over to the bed, she raised her hands to her face. "I feel so rotten," she said. "Don't look at me . . . no more light, please. I don't want you to see me. . . . How can anybody feel this rotten?" Her legs dangled over the side of the bed. He raised them up and pulled the covers over them. "Don't get up," he said. "I'll open the window. Fresh air will make you feel better." He changed the cold compress on her forehead and looked around until he found the headache powders in the bathroom. He rinsed out a glass, dropped in the medicine, filled the glass with water, and sat down next to her. He pushed another pillow under her head. "Drink this. Bottoms up."

She shook all over after she had emptied the glass. At the foot of the bed lay a mauve dressing gown which she slipped on before crawling back under the covers. She looked at him. Her eyes were clear; even her voice hardly gave a sign that, only a short while ago, she had had far too much to drink. "We've been here before," she said. "You at my bedside. It probably doesn't mean a thing if I tell you I'm sorry."

He put the glass aside. "Who were those people?" he asked.

"Does it matter?" Her face was enclosed by her pale loosened hair. Snowy light filtered through the window. "I'm cold."

He closed the window and drew the curtain. Beside the bed a small lamp was lit. "Who were they?"

"The girl worked with me at Ben Pocock's. We roomed together. I haven't seen her for a long time. She came to the shop today to bring me a shipment, so I asked her over. I didn't know the men; they came with her."

"Two at a time?"

She did not try to avoid his eyes. "I guess she thought I meant something else when I asked her to come."

They were silent for a time. Then Craig asked, "Are you feeling better now?"

"Much better. They brought the stuff with them. I had forgotten what cheap junk we used to drink. I'm not used to it anymore. That's how it is when you move up in the world."

"Why did you invite them?"

"Can you believe it, Ben Pocock is one of my suppliers. That was a big moment. Mr. Pocock took the trouble to come to see me himself and ask me if I would not like to take gloves from him. He came a couple of times. The first time I pretended to be out. So he left his card. With his best compliments. That cutthroat! Today he came again. I ordered five dozen pairs of fur-lined gloves. And the best part is, no payment until I've sold them. He choked, but he agreed. And that same afternoon June came with the merchandise. With Mr. Pocock's compliments. Five dozen gloves on commission. I never would have dreamed that he'd agree. But that's the way it goes—money changes everything."

She looked at Craig. "Is it always that way? I used to make six dollars a week. Now all I think about is whether I'll take in as much in January as I did in December, when there was Christmas buying."

"Speaking of money," he said, "where did you get a thousand dollars?"

Kitty sat upright in the bed. The compress fell to the coverlet. She grabbed it and threw it against the door. She looked at him furiously. "You rotten bastard! Why do you have to remind me? That bitch. But at least now I know where I stand. No, there's never been a divorce in the Matlock family." She was beside herself, but he preferred her like this to being drunk.

Craig repeated the question. "Where did you get the money?" He held out the calling card he had found in the bowl. "Was it her? Did Irene give you the money?"

Kitty clutched her head. "My head hurts. Do you have to torture me now?"

"She came to see you at the shop?"

"And how she came to the shop! The great lady. You should have seen her entrance. She drove up, the coachman opened the door for her, and—does she always wear lily-of-the-valley scent? How long have you been having an affair with her?"

Craig got up from the bed. "Either you pull yourself together or I'm leaving."

"Why don't you go? Go. There's the door. What are you waiting for? Oh, I remember—you want to know what she wanted from me. A thousand dollars—that's a lot of money. The Matlock family doesn't throw that kind of money around for nothing. That's what you want to know, isn't it, that's the only reason you came? So you found the money."

Craig stood at the foot of the bed. "Yes," he said, "that's what I want to know. It might be important—for both of us."

"All of you Matlocks can talk. She made me quite dizzy with all her talking. She wanted to speak to me alone, in private. I'll never forget the way she looked at me. Usually only men look at me like that. You can deny it all you like, but I'm sure that you've slept with her, maybe not recently, but something definitely went on between the two of you. I'd stake my life on it. And you know something? I'm not even jealous. God knows, neither of us is any better than the other. Women like you, and men like me. Did you give her up for me?"

"I did not have an affair with her," Craig said coldly. "You judge everything according to your own standards."

"Why? It would be a compliment for me, wouldn't it? Little Mrs. Schoffield sharing her lover's bed with a lady in high society. Who knows? Some day I might make it to the same standards if I continue my schooling among the Matlocks."

"Perhaps you'll tell me what she wanted."

"She's your brother's wife, isn't that right? We've known each other for more than six months now, and I don't know a thing about your family."

"If you don't want to talk, then don't."

"I don't mind if you know. Perhaps it's better that way. She can keep herself tightly under control, but this time she let herself get carried away. I bet she's lying awake right now wondering whether her measly thousand dollars will buy her what she wants. At heart she's trying to get at you. You say you didn't have anything going with her; but if that's true, there'd be no sense to the whole business. It's an old story, isn't it? Very sophisticated. Your brother and your wife don't seem to have stopped you. She explained at great length why you would drop me at once if there was any danger of your being involved in a scandal because of me. That you'd sacrifice everything for money. But fortunately, I'm so sensible—*clever,* she called it— that I had safeguarded myself with the shop. She really did confuse me. 'May I speak with you alone?' Heaven only knows why I agreed to meet her at that coffeehouse. I was angry with you. I hadn't heard from you in such a long time. But I was more angry with myself afterward. So elegant, so ladylike—and such a hypocrite."

"What did she give you the thousand dollars for?"

"I'm supposed to get another thousand."

"Why?"

"She gave me the address of a doctor. I'm supposed to go to see him." Kitty pushed her hair back with both hands. "The great lady told me to go to this doctor, and he would give me a certificate stating that I am pregnant."

There was a silence.

"Are you?"

Kitty could tell that he was frightened, although he concealed it well. "What would you do if I were? It is possible, isn't it?" It gave her a strange satisfaction to leave him in doubt, to see a man like him squirming with fear. It gave her a feeling of superiority. "She must know you well, much better than I do. She counted on achieving something with you. It's you she's trying to pressure. No, I'm not pregnant. I'm not expecting your baby. You can rest easy about that. I told her so, too; but she laughed and said it wasn't necessary. All I had to do was go to the address she gave me, and the doctor would certify that I was expecting a child—yours. Did she want to run to your wife with the information?"

When Craig remained silent, Kitty continued. "Just to think that I'd see the day when I'd try to force a man to go on seeing me with that trick."

"And you? What did you tell her?"

"I was getting fed up with her, but when I didn't agree at once, she threatened me."

"You promised her that you would see the doctor?"

"Just so she'd leave me alone."

Craig went to the window. He was sure Kitty was telling the truth. Yet he found it inconceivable that Irene was capable of such a step. Irene, jealous? Jealousy that expressed itself this way? No, that couldn't be. There must be another reason. "Will she be back?"

"Yes, but next time I'll throw her out."

"You took her money."

"Matlock money," Kitty said contemptuously. "You wanted to pay me off with Matlock money, and now I'm paying you back with Matlock money. That's called higher justice, isn't it? Then, when I got your telegram, I knew what I had to do." She seemed about to weep, but instead she sank back into the pillows. Her voice was weary as she said, "What did I do wrong?"

Craig sat down on the edge of the bed. He had come to a decision. She would be hurt, but he had no choice. When he thought of the possible consequences of what Irene had done, there was no other way. He saw through her motive for going to Kitty. "You should get some sleep," he said. "That's the most important thing right now. You have to get a lot of sleep, because tomorrow you have to get up very early."

Kitty gave a tired, timid laugh. "I always made it too easy for you," she said. "That was my mistake. I should have said no, no, over and over again. That's how it is. You rich people only want what you can't have. That's your kind of love. Please go now."

A boat without a rudder—that's what Hugh Sewall had called Kitty. She would never be any different. "Listen to me," he said. "Tomorrow you will take the early boat to the Catskills. I want you out of the city. Just for a little while. Let me finish. I'll explain."

"I can't leave. The shop . . ."

"Win can take care of it. Or you'll simply close down for a while. I'll cover your losses. It's only for about three weeks. It has to be this way, trust me. I'm involved in a fight with my father. A great deal is at stake. That's why Irene came to see you. She's afraid I'll dispute her husband's inheritance. That's why she wanted to use you to get at me."

"Is that true?"

For an instant emotion threatened to overwhelm him. She was so easily managed, so easily put into a different mood, so pliable, agreeable to anything you might want from her; but that was just why she was dangerous. "You told me yourself that you thought she was planning something against me. She'll be back. She won't leave you alone. It's beautiful in the Catskills at this time of year, and you will be staying at the hotel you told me about. Maybe I can join you for a couple of days. It's better for me, too, if they see as little as possible of me in New York. Take the money she gave you and use it for the trip."

Kitty was again on guard. "I won't touch the money," she said vehemently. But Craig knew that he had broken her resistance.

"Be reasonable. Please."

"I'm always being reasonable."

"It's only three weeks, Kitty. You can come back on January thirtieth."

"And then it starts all over again—waiting for you to send me telegrams."

"I'd been looking forward to tonight," he said. "I thought I'd get there and the apartment would be nice and warm. . . . And the snow in St. John's Park. It looked just like it used to."

"Do you love me at all? Do you know what it means to love someone, or is it enough for you to know that somebody loves you, that everyone wants you?"

"Please, Kitty."

She snuggled deeper under the comforter. "Did you lock the door?"

"I think I did, but I can check."

"No, leave it. What are you waiting for?" She took his hand. "Here, feel how cold I am."

"I really understand her," Kitty said later. "I understand her very well. Even when you're not here, all I have to do is close my eyes, and I can feel your body. Yes, I can, its warmth, its smell, its energy. It must be bad for her to know that it's over for her."

"Don't, Kitty."

"I'm not jealous anymore," she said. "Really I'm not, not anymore."

She was still asleep when he left. He had a cab take him to the North River. It was icy cold. He wondered whether ships could get up the Hudson. But the river was navigable as far as Schodack Landing. He bought the ticket and sent a telegram reserving Kitty's room.

He was not convinced that Kitty would not make difficulties at the last minute. But when he returned to the apartment, she had already packed and discussed arrangements for the shop with Win.

She was quiet, but on the drive to the pier, she suddenly cheered up and started talking about what she planned to do on her vacation. Before she went on board, she said, "I brought all my fanciest clothes, and if you don't look after me, I'll play the widow and go on a manhunt in the most decent way possible."

Craig took this with a smile. He had already bought the morning papers. Snowstorms were still raging in northern New York. The trains of the Empire State were either snowbound or experiencing considerable delay. And all the papers had reprinted the New York Railroad's notice in bold type. While he stood on the dock waving at the departing Kitty, he imagined his father reading them in his suite at the St. Nicholas. Not only his father—the bankers at breakfast were reading the newspapers, as were the brokers and the stockholders of the Empire State. The shares would tumble. And Kramer would buy. It suddenly seemed a long time to the general meeting.

# ═ 32 ═

LANGDON MATLOCK DID not know how he would survive this day. In any case, the house on Murray Hill was the least suitable place imaginable for a man in his frame of mind. He remembered his father's comment on the day of his unexpected appearance in the New York office: "That's the kind of house you build after you inherit, not before." What had happened in the three weeks since that day had not let him forget it.

Langdon stood at the foot of the staircase and stared at the polished steps. And on this day of all days, Irene had to act crazy! Dr. Morley had been with her for half an hour. It used to be that when she had a headache, Irene went for a walk; but for the past three weeks, she had called the doctor for every little thing. Yesterday the eye specialist had been to see her. She had not come down for supper; Langdon had found her in bed, a compress over her eyes. Finally, today she had not gotten up at all and had sent for Dr. Morley. The clock in the hallway said one o'clock. Two hours before the general meeting at the St. Nicholas. Time for him to dress. He would have to allow at least a half-hour for the drive, since the streets were clogged with traffic slogging through the snow and slush. Surely the frost they had been enduring since January eleventh could have lasted one more day. In the middle of the night the temperature had changed abruptly, bringing rain and wind. Dr. Morley's report on the condition of the streets and on the storm damage was not encouraging.

To call in a doctor for a headache! What women could think of, and at the oddest moments! But what mattered was that Irene be well enough to attend the dinner for the shareholders. He was more afraid of this dinner than of anything else, but John Tyler Matlock was pitiless.

Langdon breathed a sigh of relief as the doctor came down the stairs.

"Don't worry too much," the physician said while the butler, who had appeared silently, helped him on with his cape and handed him his hat. "Your wife is a summer person. She cannot help but be ill in this weather. Yesterday it was barely twenty degrees, and today it's in the low forties. Even a robust frame can't easily assimilate such drastic changes. For sensitive persons, they come as a serious shock."

You gasbag, Langdon thought. The butler left, and Dr. Morley continued in a low voice. "In addition—excuse me if I put it this way—your wife is approaching forty, a very, ah, complex age, believe me—not an easy time. A readjustment of the body, and the spirit protests. The spirit says, I am young and I want to remain young. I don't want to have anything to do with this aging body. But in ten years, she'll be past it."

"Is that what you told her?"

"For pity's sake, of course not. I'm telling *you*. A physician must be as careful in prescribing the truth as a druggist is with poisons." Langdon's dislike of Dr. Morley usually increased in proportion to the confidentiality of the doctor's tone. "Only once in my career did I make the mistake of advising a patient to take a lover. It was a good diagnosis, but don't ask me to tell you the consequences." Morley glanced at the large mirror and pulled his soft felt hat lower on his forehead. At the front door he stopped. "All right, then, be especially nice to her. Don't pay any attention to her moods. See that she has distractions. Best of all, a change of scenery. The city makes Mrs. Matlock ill. Is there a particular reason, do you know?"

"Not to my knowledge."

"Take a trip with your wife," Morley said. "A different climate, different people."

With an effort Langdon extended his hand. "Excuse me, I'm in something of a hurry."

"Yes, of course," the doctor replied. "The stockholders' meeting. I must tell you, it's a brilliant tactic your father thought up. To let everybody believe that the Matlock family is divided into two warring camps. But I didn't sell my shares, not even when they fell. I wasn't deceived. My compliments. What is medicine compared to the science of money? That's the true science of this world. I should have specialized in that field."

"Well, I'll be seeing your bill soon enough," Langdon said, opening the door. The storm almost tore it out of his hand, and he had difficulty closing it again.

He really should look in on Irene now, but he was afraid that they would quarrel over what Dr. Morley had said. Lately they had had arguments about even more trivial matters. Irene seemed to be looking for fights, and not just with him. She picked on the children, the servants. Yesterday the dressmaker, who had delivered the gown for the dinner, had left the house in tears.

In going to his dressing room, he therefore stepped lightly past Irene's door. While the water ran in the tub, he sorted out his clothes for both the afternoon session and the dinner. He thought about Morley's remark about the lover. Had the doctor been trying to tell him something? What impertinence, if he were. Really a most disagreeable gasbag, that Morley. And then his comments about the stockholders' meeting. How nice if he were right.

A bad dream—yes, that was what the past three weeks had been. The New York's notice about stopping all connecting traffic had been a blow. It had stirred up a lot of dust. The newspapers were on their side, while the public had been outraged. But what good had that been? They had brought suit, but John Tyler Matlock would not let it come to trial. The Empire State had withdrawn its suit and ten days later had accepted the new contract—a complete capitulation. The new contract obligated the Empire State to pass on to the New York Railroad all passengers and freight throughout the year. And for this "privilege," the Empire State must pay an additional hundred and fifty thousand dollars to the New York Railroad for the use of the rolling stock and other equipment—precisely what Loftus Poynder had always aimed at. During the ten days of negotiations, the standing of Empire State stock fell—

no, plummeted. They had lost face before their share-holders. What a jolly general meeting this was going to be.

What had upset him most was that his father had en-dured all of this with stoic calm. He had not interfered in the contract negotiations which Kramer conducted with them. He left it to Langdon, locking himself up in his of-fice, accessible to no one—just like Craig. No one saw Craig during these weeks. He was said to be out of town, though everyone knew he was in his office on Warren Street. Not even Rose Matlock had succeeded in seeing him. And Langdon was not at all sure whether they had yet come to the end of their humiliation. Yes, he feared this afternoon.

Having shaved and bathed, he now stood at the mirror, fiddling with his cravat, when he heard Irene's voice in the bedroom. She was angrily scolding someone. All right, so she was nearing forty. But after all, he was fifty, and his nerves were shot to hell; yet he did not call in a battalion of doctors. Suddenly angry himself, he jerked open the connecting door.

Irene was holding one of the shirts he had laid out and was crumpling it before the eyes of the housemaid. "That's what you call ironed? Look at the collar. And the cuffs. You call that starched? What are you waiting for? Take it away."

To his horror Langdon saw that she was tossing his fa-vorite shirt at the terrified girl. But he thought it best to keep silent. When they were alone, he put his arm around his wife. "Why do you get so upset over a badly ironed shirt? Calm down. You should be taking care of yourself. What did Dr. Morley say?"

"You probably would have worn that shirt! That's what you get for being so good-natured. How often have I told you, you should give her back a shirt every once in a while. Throw it at her feet. It keeps them on their toes. After all, I'm not paying good wages for laziness. Climbing into bed with the butler every night, and too tired during the day to lift an iron. I want you to fire Daniel."

"Please," he said, "remember your nerves. Yes, I'll fire him. How would you like to go away after the general meeting? A change of scenery might do you good."

"I know that, but it's easier said than done. I don't even want to think how things would be around here if I didn't get out of bed for a week. What's the meaning of that?" she said, pointing to the valise Langdon had set out.

"I don't want to have to drive downtown twice in this weather," he explained. "I'm taking my evening things along now and change at the hotel. Father and Mother have a large suite. Maybe I can grab half an hour's rest before dinner."

"Rest! That's all you care about. If I could sleep like you, I wouldn't need Dr. Morley."

"You had better leave for the St. Nicholas as early as possible. In weather like this, the drive takes twice as long."

Irene was playing with the cord on her dressing gown. "I don't care if every carriage in New York breaks down in the mud. I won't need one. I'm not setting foot out of this house."

"Do you think I enjoy it? I agree with you—the dinners should be abolished. All those stupid shareholders, provincials every last one of them. They come to town once a year and want to live it up. Fortunately, this year the meeting is on a Monday, so they're already gone through the weekend instead of adding it on, as they usually do. The worst thing about the dinners is the food. Six main courses and God knows how much else in between. You stuff yourself, and later, you feel sick. Every year I'm determined to do what Father does—go outside midway through and stick my finger down my throat. Forgive me, but that's actually what he does. Then he comes back and goes merrily on eating. I can't manage it."

"You and your stomachs. You can digest anything."

"You can lie down during the afternoon. It's only once a year." He gave a forced laugh. "As long as we don't pay them any dividends, let them at least have a little fun."

"Langdon, I'm sorry, but you must understand. I've endured it so many times. But not this year. Even if I wanted to, I couldn't."

"And if I beg you?" he said. "I need you."

"You have your family. They'll all be there—your father, your mother, your sisters. No one will miss me."

There was something in her voice that made him take notice, a helpless tone he had not heard before, the sound of genuine illness. He looked at her. She was well groomed, as always. True, she was no longer twenty, but the only difference was that in his eyes she was more beautiful.

"No one will believe that you're ill," he said. "You know my family. Illness is not allowed. Yes, all of them will be there. Father himself arranged the seating. Your absence would be noticed. And you know how he is about such matters."

"Go on, dance to his tune. Craig is taking it away from you, and all you can think of is the seating and your father's moods. No, don't try to change my mind. Do you expect me to sit next to Craig, as I used to? Is that how it is? Did your father put me next to Craig? He did, didn't he?" She took a few irresolute steps. "I'd better stay home. I couldn't be responsible for my conduct this evening."

Langdon lowered his head. Right now anything he could say would be a waste of time. But no matter how violent Irene's moods were, they usually passed. In the end, reason always triumphed. "Think about it," he said. "The dinner is at nine. On the second floor, in the banquet hall. And after it's over, we'll take a trip; we'll go wherever you want. You always wanted to see Europe." He began to fold his evening suit and put it in the valise.

Irene watched him struggling with the clothes. "Let me do that," she said. Her smile, the familiar gesture of gently pushing him aside, seemed to promise reconciliation. "Thank you," he said.

When his things were packed and he was ready to leave, she asked, "Will Craig get his way?"

Langdon suddenly remembered their conversation at Kane's and Irene's resolve. Whatever she had done in the matter, she had said no more about it, and he had not asked. "I can't tell," he replied. "We have to be prepared for the worst. I'm quite sure that Craig has been buying up the stock. He's put his name on the ballot against Father. I don't know how the vote will go. But even Father seems to be counting on the possibility that we will lose. I don't know. I only know how hard it is for me to go there."

Irene seemed on the point of speaking, voicing a protest, but instead she remained silent. As if she were in pain, she pressed her fingertips against her temples, a new variant of a familiar gesture.

Barely an hour before the general meeting, Langdon entered the lobby of the St. Nicholas Hotel. Signboards at the entrance and in the lobby indicated the way to the rooms on the second floor, where the stockholders of the Empire State were to meet.

The lobby was crowded, and those who had come late stood in small groups, arguing loudly. Many recognized Langdon and spoke to him. He shook hands, exchanged a few words, and was annoyed that he had not used the side entrance. The reporters were there in full force, and he found himself surrounded. This was what he had dreaded most, but he succeeded in smiling, countering their questions with empty phrases. To his astonishment, he found that it was not difficult to dissemble, in fact, he was enjoying himself.

"Wait. You can see that I'm very optimistic, in any case. I can promise you this: both the outgoing and the incoming president of the Empire State are named Matlock." With this he escaped the reporters. The door of the elevator closed behind him. You have your family, Irene had said. He recalled her words as he entered his father's suite. Even the anteroom hummed with voices; they penetrated through the closed doors. There it was, the family, and Langdon would rather have been anywhere else.

All of them were present, filling the drawing room, which was furnished with copies of baroque furniture, with an elaborate stucco ceiling. The day of the general meeting had gradually grown into a kind of family reunion, attended even by distant relatives whom John Tyler had seen fit to invite. Langdon's eyes traveled over their heads. He was surprised to discover his own son, whom John Tyler had recalled from college for the day without telling Langdon. Vinnie and May had also brought their sons. All were staying at the St. Nicholas, on the same floor. At the center of the group was Rose. She sat near the fireplace, surrounded by her daughters and sons-in-law, all of them holding glasses, chatting cheerfully, and laughing.

Yes, there they were, the Matlocks, the real ones and the ones who had married into the family. All of them were equally noisy and high-handed. It seemed to Langdon that this was their only reason for being: to rob him of his birthright. It had not always been so. There had been a time when there were only the three of them—Father, Mother, and him. He had been the center of attention. Everything had belonged to him then: Father, Mother, and each ship for whose christening they had traveled to New York. No sisters, no brothers-in-law, no cousins—and most of all, no Craig.

"May I take your hat and coat? And the valise, sir." Reluctantly he accepted help. "Take my things to Mrs. Matlock's room, Mrs. Rose Matlock." The steward left.

Langdon forced his way through to his mother, but Alice, glass in hand, blocked his way. "There he is, my big brother." She summoned a waiter. "What would you like?"

Langdon refused a drink. "Are you playing at hostess?"

"Still mad because I sold my shares to Craig? You've always been jealous of him. Not even Father made such a fuss about it."

"Langdon!"

He was glad when his mother called him. He leaned over and kissed her on the cheek.

"Father is waiting for you," she said.

"I asked them to take my bag to your room," he said. "It's all right if I change here tonight, isn't it?"

"Of course. How is Irene? I hoped she would come with you."

"The weather troubles her. She's not feeling very well."

"Would you like me to look in on her? I have no plans for the afternoon."

"No, no, that won't be necessary. You won't be able to have your nap, though."

"I didn't get up until nearly lunchtime. That's what I enjoy when I'm away from Albany—the change. I often think that if I were a rich old lady without a husband and children, I'd travel all over the world and spend my life in hotels. Do you know what Father promised me for my birthday?"

"Probably the same thing he's been promising you for fifty years—that he will take a trip with you. He'll never get beyond making the plans."

She shook her head. "Did Alice tease you?" Rose Matlock rose and took her older son's arm. She picked up a freshly filled glass. As she raised it, the voices grew quieter and all eyes turned toward her. "So you can stop trying to figure out why Alice is looking particularly pretty today, I'll tell you: she is expecting."

Rose Matlock's voice was drowned out in the hubbub that greeted the announcement, and for a time all conversation centered on the future family member. Watching from the sidelines, Langdon felt like a stranger who had no part in any of these goings-on and who did not want any part. "Where is Father?" he asked his mother. "What kind of mood is he in?"

"Never better. Yes he is, believe me. He went for a walk bright and early this morning, in this weather. Then he spent nearly two hours in the steam baths. It's become so easy since they installed them in the hotel. He was annoyed about the prices they charge, but that's just his way. He's really feeling very well. The time in New York has rejuvenated him. I know you're worried about the meeting, but if he can be so calm————"

"Where can I find him?"

"In his bedroom." Rose put her hand on Langdon's arm. She seemed to be searching for the right words. "Trust him just a little. If he can be cheerful, surely you can, too. He must have a reason. He is old, but not so old that he can be discounted."

He had expected to find his father fully clothed, but John Tyler Matlock was stretched out on a couch, naked. Joe Finney was bent over him, massaging his back. John Tyler raised his head and looked at his son. "There you are at last." He sounded as if he had been ready for a long time, dressed and waiting to leave. "Why are you so late?"

Langdon had difficulty controlling himself. He nodded to the dark-skinned masseur. "Hello, Joe. I waited for you this morning."

Joe Finney shrugged, indicating John Tyler Matlock.

"Don't distract him," John Tyler said. "Yes, that's right, Joe; the shoulders and neck."

Langdon glanced at the clock on the mantel behind the couch. "You have twenty minutes," he said to his father. "Don't you think it's time to get dressed?"

"I can't remember a general meeting ever starting on time," John Tyler countered dryly. "Joe Finney is a true master. How can you stay so fat if he works you over twice a week? I wish I could take him back to Albany with me. The best we have there are no better than lumberjacks. In such matters, Albany will always be a backwater."

Eighty years old, Langdon thought as he looked at his father. Not an ounce of fat, no sagging flesh. The glow of the fire lent an additional smoothness to the brown skin.

"All right, Joe," John Tyler said. "Be sure to wipe off the oil. I can't get it out of the shirts."

Langdon watched impatiently while Finney helped the old man into the dressing gown that had been warming before the fire. "I must say, you don't give any signs of being disturbed," Langdon said when they were alone. "Could it be that you're actually looking forward to what's in store for us?"

John Tyler glanced at his son from under lowered lids and began to dress. "Usually I'm bored by these annual clambakes," he said. "Fortunately, now and then there is an exception. Do you remember the year we bought up the separate lines to make the Empire State? Do you remember their faces when we suddenly produced a majority no one had counted on? Those were the days. Stockholders' meetings used to be fun. I'm an old war-horse, that's all. I need to smell gunsmoke."

"And what if this time defeat awaits you?"

John Tyler was standing before the mirror. He had just begun to adjust his stock, which always irritated him. He jerked around. "Pah. What do you know about fighting? Every victory is only defeat that has been averted. There's only one thing that can't be deflected—age. Age, my dear boy, is one uninterrupted defeat. Day after day. Yes, that's how it is, and we must accept it. There's nothing we can do about it, but it is the *only* thing we can do nothing about."

"Do you realize what may happen today?" Langdon was still not soothed. "A son holding a knife to his father's throat—that is more than defeat. Perhaps you're prepared with some edifying phrase for this eventuality? I really can't bear to listen any longer. Maybe you won't mind a defeat, but I will—very much."

John Tyler chuckled. "We'll see."

"We'll see!? What is that supposed to mean?" Langdon was having one of his rages. "Yes, we'll see. You will. It will happen. Craig has a stranglehold on you. Because he wants the lot. He didn't even think it worth the trouble to give you a hearing. He's been quietly buying up shares. He's opposing you in the election. He wants it all, and you say, 'We'll see.' I suppose you're enjoying all this."

John Tyler had hooked his thumbs into his blue silk suspenders. He stared at his son with undisguised contempt. "Control yourself," he said. "Leave it to me."

"Hold still. Say nothing. Leave it to you. Just as I've always done. That was my mistake." The voices from the drawing room grew louder, and a wave of laughter broke against the closed door. It undid Langdon. What was there to celebrate? But that was how they always behaved, as if life were one long feast. "When it comes right down to it, it's all the same to you," he said to his father. His voice was sharp and bitter. "The main thing is that the Matlocks have something to celebrate. What I am losing . . ." He knew he had exhausted his arguments, that he was only fighting a holding action.

"Have you finally figured it out? Pretty late. I'll tell you something. You should be glad it is Craig who, as you put it, has a stranglehold on us. If it were a stranger, the outlook would really be bleak. That's the way it is—the better man wins. Or you can put it this way: in order to win, you have to be either young and hungry and mean as a wolf or an old sly fox like me. Other rights mean nothing. You're the oldest, but a right is worthless if one is not in a position to defend it. I don't like to repeat myself, but you force me to. I would be afraid for the Matlocks if you were my only son and heir. It was not always this way. But since the business with Wilmurt and Poynder, my eyes have been opened."

"You're digging up the past. Surely that has nothing to do with what has happened since."

"No? You're very much mistaken." John Tyler's eyes were cold and hard. "What really happened with Thomas Wilmurt? Who killed him?"

"He was a ruined man, ruined by you————" Langdon broke off as he began to comprehend the scope of the question.

"Was it you?"

"Me? Are you out of your mind? How can you even say such a thing?"

John Tyler cut his son off with a peremptory gesture. "There was an investigation. You can count yourself very fortunate that I knew the man in charge. The dead man had a skull fracture, which clearly contradicts the suicide version. I wanted the documents, not a corpse."

"A skull fracture? I swear to you, I had nothing to do with it. I instructed two men to get the documents from him. It was clear, of course, that if need be, they weren't going to behave like perfect gentlemen. But violence was never included. I swear to you. I was the most shocked of all when I heard how he was found."

"Just once I'd like to see you stand up to something. Damnit, I almost wish you *had* done it. I wish, for once, you had the courage."

Langdon laughed. "Perhaps that's what I should have done. Now that would have made headlines. But I wouldn't have covered for you. I would have implicated you."

"Take a lesson from Craig," John Tyler said. "No alarms, no smell of gunpowder, only silence." He buttoned his coat, went over to the night table, and lit a cigar. Langdon had not seen his father smoke for years. John Tyler drew a few puffs and rubbed out the stogie. He pointed to the walking stick lying across a chair. "Hand me the cane," he said. His voice was as calm as ever.

Leaning on the stick, John Tyler preceded his son to the door. "When it's time for the voting," he said, "you bring in our ballots. Leave everything else to me." And then he added something totally unexpected. Langdon did not know what to make of it. "There must be an end to it," John Tyler said. "There must be an end of it with me."

# ═ 33 ═

LOFTUS POYNDER'S CHROME watch pointed to two fifty. They would be late for the general meeting, in any case, but that was Craig's intention. The election of the board of directors was planned for five o'clock, and he himself did not plan to make his entrance any sooner. There were only two propositions to be voted on. One recommended John Tyler Matlock, the other Craig Lyman Matlock.

Justin Kramer was silent. His pale face indicated that he did not entirely share Craig's confidence. Besides, for several weeks, he had not slept well.

"Nervous?" Craig asked.

"Yes, to be honest, a little. This morning I walked around the block for half an hour, near where I live. I saw your father. He, too, picked Washington Square for his morning walk. The storm didn't seem to bother him in the least. He was in the company of a banker. They headed for the bird pavilion, unpacked a pocket chess set, and played a game. Steady nerves seem to run in your family."

"Are you bothered by the weather?"

"Yes, perhaps the weather, too."

"He is not," Craig said, as if it were understood that at this time he could only be speaking of his father. "This weather suits him perfectly." He looked at Kramer. "I would bet you that he is only now tying his stock. For him, there is no greater pleasure in life than to keep a meeting of two hundred people waiting." Craig looked at the watch again. Time was standing still. The morning had passed quickly. He had made sure to crowd it with appointments. At twelve he had met with his architect in Gramercy Park. If the thaw lasted, excavation would begin soon. After that, he had called for Margaret, who was coming in from Southport, and taken her to the Prescott House.

Kramer's head was lowered. He was plucking at the skin of his fingers.

"There's no reason to be nervous," Craig said. "Even the weather is playing into our hands."

Kramer could not suppress a smile. He, too, had started the day with this thought. The rain and the storm were sure to keep some of the stockholders away, and the fewer of them turned up at the St. Nicholas, the more assured was Craig's majority. Why was he nervous, then? Everything had gone beautifully. The mighty Empire State had had to bow to the will of the New York Railroad. They had the shares they needed for a majority voice, having bought them up at prices they had not dared dream of. One victory after another, right down the line.

"Did you prepare the statement?" Craig asked.

Kramer opened his document case and took out a white piece of parchment. The text declared that the undersigned empowered the treasurer of the Empire State Railroad, Wendell Sydenham, to hand over to the authorized representative of the New York Railroad, Justin Kramer, all business papers and books, as well as all documents, of the Empire State Railroad.

Craig read the statement word for word. "I won't rest easy until my father's signature is on this paper," he said.

"Why are you so hard?" Kramer said. "If you are elected, control of the company automatically goes to you. What difference can it make whether you get to see the books a few days sooner? I see no necessity for such an affront. We'll have to collaborate with them in some way. Whatever happens, you control the largest shareholder group by far, and you can demand the appropriate directorships."

The men's eyes locked. During the last two weeks there had been a change in their relationship. Though they still carefully kept their distance, they had become comrades, fighters in a common cause. But it was not only the shared goal that had forged this intimacy. Loftus Poynder had been a workhorse. Although he was one of the wealthiest men in the city, he had never been accepted by the old New York families. Nor had he striven for such recognition. Of his own free will he had remained an outsider. He had persisted in his social anonymity. But Justin Kramer had suffered from this neglect. Since Craig had taken over, the situation had changed. The Matlocks were something like a public institution. They stood in the limelight, and Kramer stood with them. He was honest enough to admit to himself how much pleasure it gave him to be an important and well-known person.

What Kramer was still not clear about, however, was Craig. What made him take this step?

"I don't understand," Kramer said. "I cannot approve of such harsh measures."

"I know Sydenham—and, most especially, my father. I don't know what will happen to the books in two or three days. My father isn't easily beaten, and even when he is, he remains dangerous. I want to be on the safe side." He handed the document back to Kramer and glanced at the watch once more. He had already put on his coat when he thought of something. He unlocked the safe and took from it the yellow package with Wilmurt's documents. "Let's go," he said.

The rain was coming down heavily, and the wind was undiminished. Though the carriage windows were shut tightly, the gale penetrated the joints and cracks, so that the curtains blew every which way. They had discussed everything. Each knew what he had to do.

The carriage proceeded slowly, the coachman swearing whenever someone did not get out of his way quickly enough. Craig was holding the yellow envelope. He had not reacted to Kramer's questioning look.

They had reached Broadway, and the St. Nicholas was about to come into view, when Kramer broke the silence. "You must be feeling in good spirits," he said. When Craig did not respond, he persisted. "Isn't it a good feeling to have achieved one's whole purpose?"

"I don't know," Craig answered. "Perhaps I'll feel it later."

Through the window he saw the front of the hotel. At the sight, a hot, burning sensation rose in him—no longer the gnawing restlessness of the last few weeks and days, but pride and triumph.

"So I won't see you lose after all," Kramer said.

"Are you sorry?"

"No. And yet, there is one thing I'm sorry about. However one may feel about your father, he is a great man, a giant, a sequoia; and I hate to see such trees toppled. Poynder, too, was a giant, and it was terrible to see him fall. I feel no different about John Tyler Matlock. Are you sure there's no other way?"

The carriage had stopped. They waited for the door to be opened. Then they got out and stood at the main entrance to the hotel. Craig shook his head. "No, there is no other way. Believe me, Kramer."

"You may be right. All the same, I'll be glad when it's over."

"I'll be back promptly at five," Craig said. "I'll see you then."

The Prescott House, the hotel where Margaret was staying, was on Broadway, across the street from the St. Nicholas. It was older than the St. Nicholas and less splendid, but it was comfortable and somehow comforting. The service was good, and the room furnishings were genuine imports from London and Paris, rather than from the furniture shops that specialized in copies.

The few times Margaret had come to New York since her father's death, she had always stayed here. Craig had chosen the hotel for her, but as he entered the lobby now, it seemed to him to have been careless to have registered her here, so close to Kitty's glove shop.

He was still holding onto the yellow envelope. He could not say why he had brought it—as a precaution perhaps, as insurance. He rented a safe in the hotel and locked Wilmurt's precious papers in it. But the thought of Kitty gave him no peace, and he quickly left the building.

The rain had stopped. At the edge of the sidewalk the melting snow was gray with filth. The first week Kitty had written him from the Catskills, but there had been no letter or telegram since.

Fortunately there were no customers in the shop. Win Schoffield almost curtsied to him, his appearance was so unexpected. "Mr. Matlock! Excuse me, I'm just straightening up. You've been away a long time. Kitty isn't here."

"I know," he said. Win Schoffield did not seem to know why Kitty had left New York so suddenly. "How have you been getting on these past three weeks?"

Win had recovered from her surprise. "I'll be glad when Kitty gets back. I thought it would be easier. Kitty will be disappointed when she sees how sales have fallen off. We have the same number of customers, but they all ask for her, and nobody buys anything." She smiled at him as if she were only too glad to expand on her last remark, but Craig did not respond. He was in a hurry to get back to the hotel.

"You remember the lady who was here the day before Kitty left?" he asked.

"Of course. The one with a private carriage."

"Has she been here since?"

"She came once, but Kitty had already gone. I told her I did not know where Kitty was. I haven't seen her since."

"Have you heard from Kitty? When is she coming back?"

"Tomorrow, I think. That was our agreement, and that's what she wrote me. I can show you the letter."

Craig waved his hand. "When did she write you?"

"I got the letter day before yesterday. She said she would be on the afternoon boat tomorrow."

"I'll try to meet the boat," he said. "If something should prevent me from doing that, tell her I was here and that I will see her tomorrow evening for sure."

Relieved, he left the shop. Earlier, in the carriage, Justin Kramer had asked him about his feelings. But certainty was better than feelings. Or did he need both?

Kitty—that was feeling, emotion; that was the unpredictable. Margaret, on the other hand, meant certainty. They were like night and day, the two of them, and Craig considered it only natural that he loved both and wanted to hold onto both.

When he knocked on the door of Margaret's suite, he was not in the least uncertain, nor did his conscience trouble him. He was pleased with himself. It was a fact of life that nothing was more important to a Matlock's peace of mind than the awareness of owning something outright and exclusively.

Margaret welcomed Craig joyfully. When she released him, he saw the sketches spread out on the table.

"I see the architect was here," he said. "Did he show you everything?"

"He even took me to the site. The ground plan only confused me. I could not get a clear picture. I wanted to see the actual place."

Only then did he notice that she must have just returned. She was still wearing boots, and a few raindrops glistened in her chestnut hair.

"Too bad you had to run into such dreadful weather. When you come to town, of all days. Isn't it a wonderful place for a house? Wait until you see it when the sun is shining."

"I can imagine it perfectly now that I've been there. By the way, I did something awful, all on my own. I talked the architect out of the glass conservatory."

Craig stared at her. "Do you know that I've been trying to do that for weeks, with no luck? He staked his professional pride on that conservatory. I thought I'd go along with the idea for the time being."

"I think it's only wasted space. This way, we can enlarge the nurseries." Although she turned away quickly, he saw her sudden blush. She went toward the bedroom. "I just want to take off these wet boots. Do you have a little time?"

"Until almost five." He heard her moving about in the bedroom. How simple it was to be with her. How simple and uncomplicated to talk to her. It was possible to agree about anything. She did not see difficulties where there were none, and when difficulties arose, she figured out ways of overcoming them.

"Can you come in here a minute?" she called.

Margaret was in her dressing gown. She had let down
her hair, which fell over her shoulders. "It's about tonight," she said. "I'm not sure all of a sudden that I can
wear this." She pointed to the gown of black moiré hanging ready. "Are you sure it didn't turn out too flashy?
Look at the neckline. To wear mourning, and then cut
so low. I'm sorry to bother you with it, but I just don't
know . . ."

"Wait until you see my sisters and Irene. They are
asking themselves right now whether their gowns are
provocative enough."

"You're only trying to give me courage. But I'll never
be like them. It's too late for that. That sort of thing has
to be learned very young."

"You will outshine them all. Personally I don't care
for gowns as gaudy as Christmas trees. Even if you
weren't in mourning, I'd advise you to wear black."

"Did you know she was here?"

"Who?"

"Irene. When I got back from the house site, she was
sitting in the lobby."

For a moment he was speechless. He was afraid his
voice would give him away—if his expression had not
already. "What did she want?"

"I couldn't make heads or tails of it, quite frankly. I
asked her to come up, and it seemed that that was what
she'd expected. But she suddenly changed her mind. She
said she had just stopped by to say hello. She never took
the trouble before."

"That's typical of Langdon. He must be behind it. He
turns with the wind. He's adjusting to the new situation,
and he sent Irene on ahead. You know how Langdon is.
He wants to be on good terms with everyone." Craig had
reasserted control over himself as he spoke. His explanation sounded plausible even to himself.

Margaret remained thoughtful. "Do I really have to
take part in the dinner? I know that it's an important
day for you. But when I think about my father———"

"That's exactly what you should be thinking about."

"I looked at the seating chart. I've been placed right
next to your father."

"That was his doing. He made up the seating arrangement himself, and he knows exactly why he wants you to
sit next to him. He must come to terms with you now."

"I'll be sitting there remembering what happened to my father. And everyone will be watching me. I'm no good at dissembling."

"Remember that this is your father's big day. That will make it easier."

"I'll try."

She took a few steps, and he only then noticed that she was barefoot. Soundlessly her feet moved across the carpet, just as she walked on the beach. He had never before been so conscious that this was the first thing that had attracted him to her—her manner of moving, quite unselfconsciously, without coyness. He stood behind her and put his hands on her shoulders. He turned her to face him and opened the collar of her dressing gown. He pulled it aside so that her neck and shoulders gleamed in the light. He smiled. "Believe me, the dress will look marvelous on you. You can carry off the low cut." She stood very still.

He pulled her closer. Her hair, still damp from the rain, had a stronger scent than usual. She closed her eyes. "Do you have time?" she asked softly. She had thought she would never be able to ask such a question, but now, having asked it, she felt free.

# = 34 =

CRAIG MATLOCK LEFT the Prescott House shortly after five. It was already dark, and Broadway was clotted with traffic. Usually a long row of cabs stood in front of the St. Nicholas, but now only one carriage was waiting, and a vehement argument between two men was taking place. As Craig crossed the street, he thought he recognized one of the disputants; he was a reporter for one of the dailies.

The lobby of the hotel was like a swarming editorial office. Newsmen were lined up at the window of the American Telegraph office, eager to hand in their dispatches. Craig was overcome by a feeling of power. All the activity was because of him. Each of these reports dealt with him. He quickened his step.

The massive doors of the grand ballroom had just opened. Men streamed out into the foyer and side corridors. They laid siege to the free buffet and lit cigars, for smoking was not permitted during the session. In the room itself, lit bright as day by the great gas chandeliers, groups of men were in the center aisle, engaged in heated discussions. John Tyler Matlock, seeming huge on the dais against the back wall, was surrounded by numerous men who pushed their way through to shake his hand.

Craig made his way to the front. Suddenly he felt ill at ease. The table that had been reserved for him and Justin Kramer was placed in the front rows. Kramer sat there, leaning over his opened writing case, quite alone, in a circle of silence. He did not look up. Even when Craig put his hand on his shoulder, it took him a second to react and raise his head. He was pale, his forehead appeared more angular, his nose more pointed. Nothing in his face indicated victory.

"What happened?" Craig Matlock asked.

Kramer gestured toward the dais but did not speak. Now, up close, Craig could see that it was the directors of the Empire State who were surrounding John Tyler Matlock, congratulating him.

"He did it," Kramer said in a strange voice. "He tricked us." His hands nervously searched among the papers on his table. "He got us by a very vile trick."

"But what do you mean? Has the vote already been taken?" Craig refused to accept what he was seeing. He resisted the truth.

Since the tabulation of the vote had been announced, Kramer had been sitting at his place like one paralyzed, but Craig's presence sufficed to put things back in perspective. "Yes, the election has been held. And he won it. You can see for yourself: he has won the election."

Craig, his coat hanging loosely over his shoulders, his hair tousled a little by the wind, knew it was nonsense, but he still felt triumphant. The sensation had taken root in him. It had become part of him. It was a fire, and even now it did not die out. It burned on, a petrified fire— lava, hard, dark, impenetrable. He sat down in the chair next to Kramer's. "Did the city back out on us?" he asked.

"No, they voted for us. That wasn't the problem. Altogether we got a hundred and nine thousand votes, six thousand more than we brought in ourselves. The additional ones came from some shareholders in the hall."

Craig avoided looking toward the dais. "Then how did he win?"

Kramer shuffled the papers and pushed a form at Craig. "Look at that. So primitive, so simple, that I would never have thought of it."

It was one of the printed proxies the Empire State sent out annually to all its stockholders. Those who could not personally take part in the meeting were thus able to exercise their franchise.

"Look carefully. It seems to be an ordinary proxy. The shareholders are supposed to write in their candidates here, in the blank space, sign, and return the proxy. Your father did only one thing: he put his own name here in the empty space. He had it printed in, you see. If the stockholder does not write in a name—and that happens in about half the cases—there is no vote. Your father simply had them print in his name when they printed up the proxies. Just his name—John Tyler Matlock—small and inconspicuous. Pretty daring, but your father seems to have relied on the fact that people sign proxies blindly, without reading them carefully. And it worked. He got a huge number of votes—just about all those that would otherwise be lost to any candidate. Together with his own shares, he managed to get a hundred and ten thousand."

Craig laid the form aside. "We lost, then."

Lost. A moment ago the word had held the weight of catastrophe for Kramer. Now, spoken by Craig, it had become merely a statement of fact. His resistance was aroused. "We could contest the election," he said. "That's why I got hold of a proxy at once. They were just about to spirit them away."

Craig shook his head. "That wouldn't get us anywhere. There's nothing in the constitution of the Empire State that would prohibit the company from inserting a candidate's name in the proxies. It may be unusual, but it's not illegal. No, the mistake is ours. I should have thought of that possibility. My father knew what he was doing. That's why he was so calm."

"We could win if we contested the election."

"No. What else is on the agenda?" he asked.

"The election of the new board of directors, right after the intermission. You're not giving up, are you? I implore you. A motion to contest the election would pass. The general mood here is with us. The shareholders have been pressing your father hard. When he gave the president's report, they interrupted him frequently. The lack of dividends, the losses from the January blockade, the market position. The opposition is strong. When the result of the vote was announced, there were more boos than cheers. The stockholders feel terrible about the outcome. They want to see someone at the helm who can guarantee them profits. Our motion to set aside the vote would only express the general mood."

Craig looked at the dais. John Tyler Matlock was just coming down the steps, heading for a door in the back. The secretary of the meeting still sat on the dais. He had taken off his pince nez and was rubbing his eyes.

"We must gain time," Kramer continued. "I can't think of anything else we can do right now." He fell silent, stopped by the look on Craig's face.

"The air in here is terrible," Craig said. "Let's go outside for a moment." He took a small key from his vest pocket. For a moment his fingers toyed with it. Then he handed it to Kramer. "Do me a favor," he said. "Go to the Prescott House. I've rented a safe in the hotel. You'll find a yellow envelope in it. Bring it to me." He pointed to the door through which his father had gone. "I'll be in there, with my father."

Kramer examined the key in his hand. "Go. Don't worry," Craig said. "The meeting isn't over yet."

The Great Hall of the St. Nicholas, where the meeting was being held, was ordinarily used as a ballroom. John Tyler Matlock had retired to the chamber where the musicians sat during intermissions. The furnishings were modest: a filing cabinet for sheet music, old wobbly chairs, a round table with a scorched top, a shabby red-velvet sofa, and behind it a large mirror tarnished over more than half its surface.

As Craig entered he was presented with a scene similar to the one he had earlier seen on the dais: his father surrounded by his board of directors. Glasses in hand, they were toasting the victor. Perhaps he was mistaken, but Craig thought they were exaggerating their joy, as if they had not yet quite grasped that the victory had, in fact, once more gone to John Tyler Matlock and that all their fears had been groundless.

They were so preoccupied that they were not at first aware of Craig. Then the first man fell silent and exchanged a meaningful glance with his neighbor. The laughter stopped and the voices diminished. Slowly the circle around John Tyler Matlock opened. He stood between the sofa and the round table, which held liquor bottles and carafes of ice water. Since their last meeting at Willowbeach, four months had passed. Craig thought his father was thinner.

It had become quiet in the room. The directors stood awkwardly, not quite knowing what to do.

"I must speak with you," Craig said to his father. "Alone." He had given no thought to his father's reaction. He saw John Tyler's left eyebrow rise slightly. He sucked in his lower lip. How well Craig knew this expression.

"All right, gentlemen," John Tyler Matlock said. "Please excuse us. I assume we won't be long. We can resume the meeting in a few minutes."

One by one, they left, until only Langdon remained.

"I would prefer you to leave us alone," Craig said to his brother. "But the decision is up to Father."

"Go ahead, leave us," John Tyler Matlock said. When Langdon did not respond at once, he added impatiently, "If your interests should be involved, you can count on me to represent you."

At last father and son faced each other. The scorn in John Tyler's face was more pronounced. "Now, it seems, I will get my conversation with you after all. You kept me waiting a long time." He pointed to the table. "Have a drink. The new ventilation system in the hall is worth no more than the old one. The air is enough to make one choke. Two hundred people breathing stale air —but tomorrow it will be over for another year. As far as I'm concerned, there need never be any more stockholders' meetings. They're nothing but a lot of hogwash. What will you have?"

"Thank you, I don't want a drink," Craig said, even though his throat was parched.

"Then pour me one. No, please, no champagne. A lot

of air. Give me some whiskey. And not too much water."

John Tyler sat down on the sofa. Craig remained standing. "I must compliment you," Craig said. "You planned that well. I should have known you had something up your sleeve."

John Tyler raised his glass to the light and took a small sip. "I see you are taking it with good grace. I'm glad. Actually I only wanted to show you that I still have all my teeth, that I'm still the same old John Tyler Matlock. Especially when my opponent is you. Had it been another, I might not have thought it worth the trouble to use that simple trick. Take it as a lesson; it may be the last one I'll be able to teach you. Learn from it that one must never be too sure." He smiled. "Even if it was a marked card, it trumped yours."

In contrast to his voice, a shadow of weariness sped across his face. "No one likes to accept defeat," he continued, "especially when it is inflicted by one's own son. I had hoped to the last that we could arrive at some sort of agreement. But you left me no alternative. And as I said, I had to prove even to myself that I'm not too old."

"Now you're the one who's too sure of himself."

"I know that it can't be a long-lasting victory. I wasn't concerned about that. I wanted to feel what it was like once more to be the stronger. I thought, the last time is more important than the first."

"Your victory will not even last the night."

John Tyler took this as if Craig had made a joke. "If you knew how sick I am of the whole business, especially when I see them all in a bunch like that, the directors, the pillars of my enterprise. You can rest assured, this time I am in earnest. At next year's general meeting I will retire. Between now and then, you can take your time and familiarize yourself with the operation. Then I will vacate my chair for you." He sipped his whiskey and shook himself. "Absolutely unpalatable. They ask three dollars a bottle here in the hotel. Will you take my glass?"

Craig put the glass on the table. "I'm sorry," he said. "I have different ideas about your retirement. Not a year from now. You will vacate your chair today."

John Tyler stretched out his long legs. "I don't appreciate your tone. I am making you a fair proposition, and this is how you react. I'm still the one who says when. That is the great difference. Never in my life have I taken orders. And I wish it to remain that way. Look, it need not be a full year. We can agree on six months. I could justify it by saying I've been told by my doctors to take it easy. Then the company can give me a farewell banquet and transfer the office to you. Let's say July thirtieth, or even the beginning of July, before I go to Willowbeach."

"I said tonight."

John Tyler lifted his bulk off the shabby red couch. He undid the buttons of his coat. "I make you a solemn promise that in the interim the company will not pass any resolutions without your approval. Considering the extent of your holdings, you can control four directorships. I'll throw in a fifth, including the position of treasurer. Your man, Justin Kramer, seems very capable indeed, and it's time for Sydenham to pack it in."

"I didn't come here to bargain," Craig said. For a moment he recalled Kramer's words, his image of a toppled giant. But he said, "I am telling you what you will do." He pointed at the door. "You will go back to your seat on the dais, and you will inform the membership that you have decided not to accept the election."

John Tyler stood motionless, his eyes straight ahead. "You can't seriously expect me to do that," he said at last.

"Yes, I can. And you will do it. I'm sure you'll think of some explanation by which you can save face. Refer to your doctors or simply to your age. Say whatever you want. I don't care how you explain it. You needn't worry about me. I'm sure you will manage it so no one gets the wrong idea. You have never had any difficulty making others believe whatever you wanted."

John Tyler's left hand suddenly sought support from the table. He grasped the edge. The empty glasses trembled. In the silver champagne buckets the ice clattered. The attack lasted less than a minute. Then he drew himself up again. He reached for one of the carafes and poured out a tumbler full. Craig made no move to help him; he did not take his eyes off his father. The hand that raised the glass to the old man's lips was steady. John Tyler drank in little sips, an old man who never forgot for a moment that he must husband his strength even when drinking or breathing. In everything he had subordinated his life to the principle of moderation except in one: his claim to be foremost.

"Will you do it?" Craig asked.

"At least, I'd have to discuss it with Langdon and the directors first."

"It would be the first time you consulted them on anything. It was always your way to confront them with accomplished deeds. And it was successful."

John Tyler had withdrawn from the table as if to prevent himself from seeking its support. His eyes, which until now had avoided looking at Craig, struck his son with all their dark power. Oh no, he was still not giving up. "Can you tell me why I should do this? I understand your wanting to take my place—but to give it up voluntarily? I could have saved myself a lot trouble to get that result."

There was a knock at the door, and Sydenham looked in. "The half-hour is up," he said. "When will we resume the session?"

"A few more minutes," John Tyler said. Sydenham closed the door. Father and son looked at each other. Both suspected that Sydenham had stopped on the other side of the door to listen. Though the occasion was trivial, for a moment they felt closer, recognizing each other as two of a kind. Yes, they were like each other. But it was precisely this that challenged both to see this trial of strength through to the end. "What reason would I have to give in to you?" John Tyler's voice was muted.

"There are reasons," Craig replied, and he too lowered his voice. "I had hoped that I wouldn't have to spell them out. They are excellent reasons, you can be sure of that."

John Tyler did not seem impressed. "A marked card?"

"A whole hand of them. This time you were too sure of yourself. I want to be open. I would have preferred to have charged Poynder's death against you. I left no stone unturned, but the matter was handled too smoothly. Fortunately you committed another error."

John Tyler lowered his head, as if he knew what would come next, as if capitulating in advance.

"I've been saving this trump card. And I'm still hoping that you won't force me to play it. It would be better for all of us, better for the family. What is your decision: will you step down?"

"You wouldn't provoke a scandal. The family name is at stake."

"Don't be too sure. If there is no other way, I will not back away even from a scandal."

John Tyler still did not raise his head. "Tell me something. Who besides yourself knows that you are in possession of Wilmurt's documents?"

Craig was glad that he was unobserved. He poured a glass of water and gulped it down. "You know about them? But that's impossible."

"I know, all the same. I've known for some time. I always thought it very decent of you not to have made use of them." The scornful, aggressive trait had disappeared from his features; what remained was simply the expression of a lively, restless intelligence. "I have often told you that one cannot trust a bank. In July of last year you rented a box in which you kept your shares and a yellow envelope. The bank director is a friend of mine, and he had no more pressing duties than to inform me at once. He didn't know what the shares were, and he didn't know the contents of the envelope, but he found both remarkable enough to tell me about them. When he described the envelope to me, I knew what it was. When Wilmurt offered me the documents 'for sale,' they were in the same yellow envelope."

"Why didn't you give him his share?"

"At the time it seemed better to show him that I was not afraid of his disclosures. If I had acted otherwise, I would have burdened myself with an everlasting blackmailer. Looking back on it, I made a mistake. Tell me, is it true that no one else knows about it?"

"Poynder knew. He could have gotten the documents easily. But he sent Wilmurt away. That was the kind of man Poynder was. A delicate conscience is a luxury."

John Tyler stood motionless, his dark eyes staring straight ahead; yet Craig had never been able to read his face more easily. This was a man who had made his own laws for living. According to these laws, only others fell ill, not Matlocks. Other people might have trouble with their wives, but Matlocks did not. Others might lose their property, other people might die. He had really believed that he was in possession of a kind of eternal life. But now he knew time was running out, that the day was coming even for him when he would have to hand over what he had held on to for so long and with such fervor. The tenancy had lapsed.

When John Tyler looked at his son again, there was something mistrustful, almost stricken in his eyes. "You will destroy Thomas Wilmurt's documents?"

"If you do as I say."

John Tyler raised his narrow, brown-flecked hand. "The stockholders won't even make it hard for me. They have been waiting for something of the sort. But do not believe that in future you can count on my advice. When someone like me downs tools, it is for good."

"If you would care for the honorary presidency————"

"No." John Tyler brusquely stopped his son. "We are too much alike to be able to work together. And I am very bad at being a subordinate." He took his cane, which had been hanging from the back of the sofa, and went to the door.

The dinner ran its course, just as it had in previous years. If there were any doubts about the unity of the Matlock family, they vanished. Of course everyone was talking of John Tyler Matlock's resignation, but by the time dinner arrived, the consternation had already turned to admiration for the grand old man who knew how to say good-bye with the same sovereignty with which he ruled for half a century. The really smart fellows hadn't been fooled for a minute. They had long predicted what had now turned out to be the case. The animosity between the Empire State and the New York Railroad was unmasked as a cunning maneuver "to turn the stock exchange into a Matlock roulette," as one of the newspapers put it the next day.

John Tyler as always presided at the head of the table between his wife, Rose, and his daughter-in-law Margaret. Relaxed and affable, he responded to the toasts drunk to him. Even the most observant spectator would have been unable to see behind the glittering front. The family revealed no vulnerable chink. All were present, even Irene and Langdon, the sons and the daughters, the in-laws and the grandsons. No one thought anything of the fact that John Tyler Matlock retired early. He was a man of eighty. He had been up since six o'clock that morning. And the following day he would have to rise early again to catch his train to Albany. The gesture with which he invited

Craig to take his place at the table was so convincingly affectionate that it was met with a spontaneous outburst of applause.

Of course there were also signs that a new captain was at the helm. Langdon and Irene stayed to the bitter end. No sooner had John Tyler left than the directors of the Empire State pushed their way to Craig's side to assure him that the railroad had long been in need of stricter leadership. Politicians offered him their support, and stockbrokers whispered assurances that Wall Street was sure to give proper recognition to the change of leadership. When the party moved on to the ballroom, the same hall where John Tyler Matlock had announced his retirement, it was Margaret whose company the men sought.

Attentive and cordial, Craig listened to all of them. He let others speak while he watched. Simply by his alertness, he gave the appearance of being talkative and affable. Only his father would have known that the expression around his lips was one of contempt.

It was shortly after one in the morning when Craig returned to the Prescott House with his wife. He asked the porter to give him the yellow envelope Kramer had brought to the hotel. Upstairs in Margaret's suite, not bothering to take off his coat, he went to the fireplace and added another log. Then he sat in front of the blazing fire; the oiled yellow paper of the wrapping resisted the flames for several seconds and then suddenly caught.

"What are you burning?" Margaret said.

"The heritage of a man who wasn't lucky."

She had sat down next to him, still in her evening gown, her mother's black pearl collar around her neck. "That's the only thing that matters, isn't it," she said. "To be lucky."

Craig, thinking of his father, was about to contradict her; but he kept quiet. He got up, catching a glimpse of his face in the mirror over the fireplace. It was the same old face. This was a day of victory. Ahead of him lay a long time, a long road. He would celebrate many more victories before he, too, would have to accept the defeat that his father had suffered today.

# BOOK FIVE

---

# WILLOWBEACH, CONNECTICUT

---

## July 1866

# ≡ 35 ≡

Joshua balanced the telescope against the window sill. He kneeled on the chair and focused on the twin tracks running along the willow-lined stream beyond the garden and the meadow. It had always been impossible to see the tracks from the window of their bedroom; the veil of branches and leaves was too thick. But now, after the storm had stripped some of the trees and damaged others so badly that they had to be cut down, the view to the river lay wide open.

"What do you see?" Sinclair stood next to his brother and plucked at his shirt. "Do you see the train? You promised you'd let me look."

"Wait, there's nothing to see yet."

"You keep on looking all the time. Now it's my turn."

The tracks sparkled in the sunlight. They used to be covered with grass, even when it had been freshly mown, but the hail had battered the grass down to the roots. Now it was tentatively growing back. Though it was still too early for the train, Joshua was afraid that it would come just when he had abandoned the telescope to Sinclair. "It's mine, anyway," he said. "It was my Christmas present."

"Everything always belongs to you. Please let me look. I'll give you something for it." This was always Sinclair's last recourse in his running battles with Joshua.

"All right, here, get up on the chair. But don't turn any part on it."

Sinclair knelt on the chair and pressed his eye against the telescope. After a while he said, "I can't see anything."

"Close your left eye tight. Now do you see anything?"

"Nothing."

"What do you mean, nothing? Can't you see the

tracks?" Joshua grabbed the telescope from his twin's hand. "You twisted it," he said accusingly.

"I did not either twist it. Really I didn't. I don't even know where you're supposed to twist."

"Then you must have different eyes."

Sinclair turned red. He stamped his foot. "How can I have different eyes? We were both born the same day. I don't *want* to have different eyes."

"Come here," Joshua said. "Try again." He was all superiority, all patience, as if he were twice Sinclair's age. "Close your left eye and twist this thing here until you see something. Like this, that's right. What do you see now?"

There was silence. Then Sinclair shouted jubilantly. "The tracks! I can see them, next to the willows at the river. They're up real close."

"Now give it back. The train isn't coming yet. It's way too early."

The boys traded places, and Sinclair asked, "Can I go see the tern afterwards?"

Joshua had found the bird in the garden on the day of the storm, its wing broken. The two boys had been watching him earlier as he struggled against the wind. Time and again, it had tried to fly into the gusts, but the big, clumsy bird could not move off the spot. Then a squall had caught it. The bird had fallen, its wings spread out, head foremost.

"You promised I could go see it." Sinclair insisted on an answer.

"Would you want to feed it too?" Joshua said. He had "owned" the tern for three weeks. Dr. Shyne had bandaged the broken wing, and Greville had hammered together a cage. During the first few days Joshua had allowed no one to get near the tern. It was *his* bird. He had found it. He himself had collected the huge number of insects it devoured. But feeding the bird had become a tedious chore.

"You're going to let me feed it?" Sinclair asked, surprised.

"I'll make you a present of it—for one of your gold coins. It will belong to you, just to you, and you can visit him whenever you want, without having to ask first."

Sinclair seemed afraid that Joshua would change his mind. He rushed to his nightstand. When he opened the wooden casket, he saw that there was only one coin left. Suddenly undecided, he said, "It's my last one. You've already got all the others."

"It's up to you. You've got to decide whether you want the tern or not."

Sinclair handed the coin to his brother. "I'm sure I'm doing the right thing," he said.

Joshua hoped Sinclair would go off to see the bird at once. Then Joshua could put the coin with his others. As it was, he waited patiently; under no circumstances would he reveal his hiding place. He returned to the window and the telescope. The view had improved. The sun was high in the sky. The last cloud had moved on. The landscape stretched out without shadows, without depth, every object clear and close enough to touch.

"The train that brought Grandfather had just one car this year," Sinclair said.

"The train doesn't belong to him anymore. Now the train belongs to Papa. All the trains belong to Papa now."

"What does that mean, 'belong to Papa'? You always use the word *belong*. What does it mean?"

"What a stupid question. They belong to him. He owns them."

"What does *own* mean?"

"It's like with the telescope. *It belongs to me.* I can let you look through it. I can lend it to you for a whole day. But I can take it away from you if that's what I want to do. If I want to, I can throw it on the floor and stomp it into little pieces. That means it belongs to me. I can do with it *whatever I want*. The tern, *your* tern, belongs to you."

"But . . . but I can't . . . crush it?" Sinclair quickly changed the topic. "Do you know for sure that Papa's train is coming today?"

"Yes, Mr. Place's son brought the telegram this morning. Why do you suppose Mama cut our hair today?"

"If Papa . . . owns . . . the train now, do you think he'll take us along one of these days?"

"When we move to New York, we'll all ride on the train."

Sinclair was thoughtful. "What about the tern, then? What should I do with it? Do you think I'll be allowed to take it to New York with me?"

Joshua was too preoccupied with his telescope to hear

all of Sinclair's question; he took in only the words *New York*. "New York is a great big city," he said in the superior tone he loved to use on his twin. "They've got trains right in the middle of town. On every street. Trains under the street, soon. And a station where more than forty trains come in every day."

"I don't want to go to New York if I can't take the tern with me," Sinclair said.

"If you take good care of it, it will soon be able to fly again. Birds are made for flying."

Sinclair looked startled. "But I want to keep it. I gave you my last gold coin for it."

Joshua did not answer. Suddenly he slid off the chair. "You can use the telescope now. I'm going over to see Grandfather. I have to ask him something."

Sinclair looked at his brother mistrustfully. "Is the train coming?"

"No, of course not. I saw Grandfather coming out on the porch. I have to ask him something, something important. You stay here and watch for the train. When you see it coming, call me. I'll hear you."

A gold coin for the tern. As he walked across the lawn to visit his grandfather, Joshua was not convinced that he had driven a good bargain. The gardens of the Poynder mansion were nearly always silent and forlorn, but now those at the Matlock house were equally deserted. The other children had not come this summer. From the yard behind the house, where men were busy splitting branches off the cut-down trees, came the sound of axes and saws. If the other children had been here, he could have earned a great deal more with the tern. He would have shown the bird only for a fee. Of course, his aunts would have paid as well. But this was not the only profit he was losing. After the storm he had found many interesting objects along the shore. Most of them were from the big yacht that had recently been dashed to pieces nearby: lengths of heavy gold cord, glass tiles, and the four life preservers which Joshua now considered the chief asset of his capital. They could support you much better than any rubber tube and were superbly designed as weapons in major sea battles. It really was too bad that this year, of all years, the children had not come. Otherwise, by the end of the summer he would probably have fifty gold coins.

John Tyler Matlock sat in a wheelchair on the south porch, in the shade of the green-and-white awning. A glass of lemonade stood ready for Joshua on the little wicker table. Sinclair seldom came along on these porch visits. The sight of the old man in the wheelchair made him uneasy. But Joshua quite naturally took his place in the rattan chair and pulled up close to the wheelchair after having sipped at the lemonade.

"I was watching you," John Tyler said as he pointed at the window where Sinclair's red mop of hair could be seen behind the glittering brass tube of the telescope. "Does he finally understand how to handle that thing?" It was he who had given Joshua the telescope.

"He's watching for the train," Joshua said. "He'll give us a sign right away."

"It's nice that you came," the old man said. Newspapers were piled up on his lap, but he had not read them. "Actually you ought to be taking a nap at this time of day."

"We haven't taken naps for a long time now. We're too old." Joshua reached into the pocket of his blue linen trousers and felt the gold coin there. "I have to talk to you," he said gravely.

"All right. What about?"

Joshua looked out at the lawn. It still carried black scars where the fireworks they had been allowed to set off on the Fourth of July had been stuck in the ground. Greville had gotten sparklers and Catherine wheels; all Joshua's pocket money for the month of July went into buying them. This still annoyed Joshua, for nothing had remained except the brief joy—and the black spots in the grass. "I have to talk to you about money," he said.

"About money?" John Tyler stared across the table at his grandson. "Shoot. What is it you want to know?"

"The gold coins you've given me. You told me to take good care of them. That I shouldn't use them to buy anything because they're worth more than greenbacks. Two and a half times as much. That's what you said."

John Tyler laid the newspapers on the floor. He did not want to annoy the boy by watching him too steadily, but that was what he was tempted to do.

"You know, since Aunt Edna left, we have a new maid.

Aunt Edna used to talk a lot about money, but the new maid talks *only* about money. Every time she comes back from shopping and goes over the accounts with Mama in the kitchen, she complains that the prices have gone up again. This morning it happened again, and she said— I remember it exactly—A dollar is worth only fifty cents now. And all in one year.' That's what she said."

John Tyler smiled. He had been waiting for Joshua to join him. As soon as he heard the boys' voices in the other house, he came out to sit on the porch. He had discovered the place only this year. In earlier summers he would have found it too noisy. Even in his room or the smoking parlor, he groaned about the children's uproar.

Joshua was impatient. "Why don't you say something? One dollar, only fifty cents?" And his hand slid back into the pocket with the coin. "What about my gold coins, then? Are they worth less too?" The idea had haunted him all morning.

"Your maid was talking about paper money," John Tyler replied. "Coins made of gold are another matter altogether. During the last year, greenbacks have lost half their worth. But your gold coins have not diminished in value. Can you understand that?" He made an effort to speak slowly and to express himself as plainly as possible. "A year ago your gold coins had a value of two and a half paper dollars. Now the same coin is worth almost four paper dollars. It is worth almost twice as much, but, of course, you can't buy twice as much with it. You haven't gained anything; but you haven't lost, either. That is gold. Gold is safe, gold is dependable. The day may come when paper money is completely worthless. It's happened twice in my lifetime. But gold keeps its value. Gold is stable. Do you understand that?"

"I understand." Joshua took a long sip of lemonade. He seemed relieved, freed of a burden. But then he had second thoughts. "You say I didn't lose anything and I haven't gained anything. What about the income?"

This time John Tyler could not help but stare straight at his grandson, as if he had made an important discovery. "What do you know about income?"

"Papa talks about it all the time. He says that Mama doesn't have to touch any of her money. I paid close attention. He said she can live on the income. No, wait;

what he said was, 'You can live on the income of your income.' Is that right? Is there such a thing?"

"Yes, there is."

"And what does that mean—income of the income?"

"I don't know if you can understand that yet."

"I want to understand it."

"If your mother takes away some of her money, it doesn't get smaller. Even then, there gets to be more of it all the time."

"But there are never more of my coins. I keep them well hidden. I don't take any away. But there aren't more. If I buy fireworks with them, there are less."

"You don't really buy fireworks with them?"

"No, I just meant if."

"Do you think a lot about money?"

Joshua nodded earnestly. "In the mornings, I check whether my coins are still in their hiding place, and I count them. And at night I think about them in bed."

"That's the right way." The old man, too, was grave. "If you want to get somewhere, you have to think about it all the time, from morning to night."

"But what can I do to get income?"

Through the silence came Sinclair's high, penetrating shout: "The tra-a-in. The train is coming. Josh-shu-ah, the tra-a-in is coming."

Joshua jumped up out of the wicker chair. "I'll be back," he said. "I want to know how that works. You have to explain it to me."

"I'll explain it to you; don't worry."

Joshua turned back once more. "Nobody has to know about it, right? It's just between the two of us."

John Tyler nodded. "Just between the two of us."

Rose Matlock had stepped out on the porch. Standing next to John Tyler, she watched Joshua as he dashed off, diagonally through the garden ruined by the storm. It did not take long for Sinclair to come running as well; like an arrow he shot past the house to catch up with his brother.

"How could they ever have hit on the name Joshua?" John Tyler wondered aloud. "Joshua Matlock. Actually, it sounds pretty good. Joshua Matlock—yes, not bad."

"Is the train coming?" Rose said.

John Tyler reached for his cane to stand up.

"What's the matter?" Rose asked. "I was just going to

sit with you a while. It's a pretty place, and well out of the wind."

John Tyler's face closed. He leaned on the cane and rose.

"It makes it look as if you were running away from Craig."

"Better that than have him think I'm sitting here waiting for him." Leaning on his cane, he disappeared into the house. He left the door open, but Rose did not follow.

≡ 36 ≡

ALTHOUGH THE RIVER and willows were looming in the windows of the compartment, the train did not lessen its speed. Craig pushed the curtain to one side. "McCallum is determined to break the record," he said to Justin Kramer, who was sitting across from him. "When he doesn't make it, he feels lousy. I'd prefer a different engineer on my trips."

Kramer nodded. When Craig went on one of his surprise inspection tours, which were dreaded by the Empire State line superintendents, the trains were never fast enough for him.

The two men were sitting at the desk in the parlor car. The tabletop was covered with papers and building plans. Craig put out his cigar. He was smoking more than he used to. "I've been thinking it over," he said. "We'll cancel this route. Eight miles of track for two trips a year! It will come in handy for our move to New York, but after that, let's give it up."

"Seen from the profit angle, that's the wisest decision, of course." Kramer wiped a strand of hair from his forehead with a quiet new, relaxed motion. In everything —his speech, his bearing, his clothing—he appeared much more casual. A memorandum of several pages lay in front of him. He turned to the last page. "If you'll just sign here, right there; and the copies, too, please."

Craig put his signature on the contracts they had been discussing. "A fancy price for a piece of land," he said, "but I'm sure it was the right decision. Though I'm having trouble getting used to the idea that soon there won't be any more St. John's Park."

'We couldn't have found a better property. The location is ideal. We can count ourselves lucky that the Common Council approved it."

"That was because of our money," Craig said. "Luck had little to do with it."

He began rolling up the building plans. "In the three weeks out here, I'll look them over once more. You have copies in New York. The whole thing is a little too elaborate for my taste. A freight station need not be a temple to the arts. But they are quite a bit better than the first set of plans we had." He looked over the desk. "I think we've covered everything."

"You should try to persuade your father to sell you his shares," Kramer said.

Smiling, Craig pushed back his chair. "You still can't forget that stockholders' meeting, can you?"

"It's not so much the fact that he still holds over thirty percent of the stock. But when I think he might sell them to someone else, I get nightmares, like in the old days. I keep hearing rumors—that's all they are, though, rumors—from Albany. They say your father met with some of the directors of the Pennsylvania. The Pennsylvania has been interested in gaining entry to New York. If your father would at least give you a first option . . ."

The train was slowing down. "I'll talk to him," Craig said.

"Remember that you started with much less."

After a brief silence, Craig spoke again. "Are you really set on going back right away? How about it? Won't you stay at least until tomorrow?"

"Thank you, but tomorrow the people from Chicago are coming. I want to go over the books before I meet with them. Besides, I promised Mrs. Schoffield that I would see her this evening. I've been promising her for two weeks, and something always comes up."

"Is it about her taxes? I've told her not to be ridiculous. It can't amount to much, after all."

"I know," Kramer said. "But though she's fearless in most things, she lives in mortal terror of the tax office. She has visions of herself in debtors' prison."

"She can't have taken in all that much."

Kramer remembered the early months after the shop had been opened—the small beginning. "You'd be surprised at her turnover," he said. "She has opened a private account. At a different bank. She thought I wouldn't find out about it. She will go far. She's already planning to open a second shop."

"That's out of the question. Talk her out of it."

"I'll try my best. There's something else. Lately she's been hinting that the apartment is getting too small for her."

"Wait, Kramer. Has she been hinting, or are you trying to break it to me gently that she has already rented a larger place?"

"Well, she was rather thinking of a house."

"Is that right? With a staff and servants, no doubt."

"Not exactly. She would take on Joe Cristadoro and his wife when the Laight Street houses are torn down for the freight station."

"I can see she's won you over. Am I right? I warned you, Kramer—she's a dangerous woman. She has taken you in. I assume you endorse her plans." But Craig was thinking that the idea had certain advantages. "I would want to be consulted at least."

"You agree on principle, then?"

"Look for something outside New York, easily accessible but quite a ways outside. Perhaps somewhere along the Hudson, a place like Carmansville."

Kramer seemed amused. "Rent or buy?"

"I wouldn't mind buying. Carmansville isn't a bad investment. But please, let's be sure we understand each other. The company buys the house, and it remains registered to the company."

"Of course."

The train stopped and they got up. The boys' voices could be heard outside. Craig had put the papers in the brown documents case and was locking it. "Take some flowers to Mrs. Schoffield from me this evening," he said. "But don't forget, I pay you too well for you to have to act as a tax accountant on the side."

"It's a purely honorary office." Kramer followed Craig out onto the platform.

McCallum shouted as he came up, "One hour and fifty minutes! What about that? If the New Haven would just put in double tracks, we'd make all kinds of time."

Joshua and Sinclair ran up to their father. "I have a tern," Sinclair shouted. "It belongs to me."

Joshua had eyes only for the two rolls of paper in his father's arm. "What did you bring?"

"These are the plans for the new freight station."

"Will you show them to me?"

"Yes, but you'll have to wait a little longer."

"We found the tern in the garden," Sinclair said. "It belongs to me alone, and nobody else is allowed to feed it."

"Watch out!"

McCallum had disappeared back into the locomotive. Slowly, gently, the train started up and made its turn behind the Matlock house: one locomotive pulling only the scarlet parlor car. Kramer stood on the platform.

"Come," Craig said to the boys, and between them he walked up the slight incline.

Margaret had written him in detail about the damage the storm had done at Willowbeach, but to see it with his own eyes was another matter. The Matlock house, now with its two new wings, was usually screened behind the dense stand of trees when it was approached from this side. Now it stood white and exposed on the hill. Some of the trees were still standing, but they, too, were leafless, and their branches were broken. On the northwest, where the hail had battered the bark, the trunks were blanched. Where the roots had been dug out, the dark scars disfigured the grass. Only the locusts hemming the walk from the outer gate to the house were still standing. But their branches were also bare though it was summer.

Craig saw his mother. Rose Matlock came from the porch across the lawn, to meet him. There was no sign of John Tyler.

Rose was unchanged. Her silver-gray hair was loosely upswept, and her gray eyes were full of life; her skin was clear and light. Encumbered as he was by the document case and rolls of parchment, he could not embrace her. He kissed her cheek. "It's terrible," he said. "The old trees! I hadn't imagined it would be so bad."

Joshua and Sinclair stood by impatiently. "Run ahead," Craig told them. "I'll be along in a minute. Go on, tell them I've arrived."

Rose walked on ahead toward the house. "It *was* terrible," she said. "The whole thing only lasted about fifteen minutes. A beautiful day, not a cloud in the sky, until afternoon. Everything happened so fast. First the storm, and then it grew dark as night. The worst damage was done by the hail. I tell you, stones as big as pigeons' eggs. Even the next morning they still lay six inches high at the cellar door."

"Was it this bad everywhere?"

"No. Across the way, at your house, the damage wasn't half as bad. Of course, the greenhouse took the full brunt of it. Only the steel skeleton remains of the glass roof. But the trees had a much easier time of it; they're still young. In Southport there was nothing at all. Hugh Sewall's shipyard flooded, though. One yacht and three boats were torn off the moorings." They had reached the porch. Rose gave a backward look at her devastated garden. "I don't know if I can plant new trees."

"How can you say that, Mother?" Craig was struck by the silence. "Where is everybody? Alice, Vinnie, May? And where are the children?"

Rose did not reply immediately. Her head turned aside, she stood still, as if unable to take her eyes off the ravished garden. "Perhaps they'll come now," she answered at last. "Now that you're here."

"I don't understand. What do you mean?"

"I mean that we are alone, your father and I, alone in the big house with all its new rooms. They didn't come with us. Of course, all of them had excellent excuses. Alice's baby was born four weeks ago; May had to look after her mother-in-law; and Vinnie can't leave her husband just now. He's working on a commission from you."

"We're building a new freight station. That's his specialty—industrial buildings. I have a horror of stations that pretend to be Oriental palaces. It occurred to me to try him. To keep it in the family."

"Yes, they all need you now. Father no longer matters to them. How long will you be staying?"

"Two, three weeks. No longer. And then we'll be moving soon."

"How is your New York house coming along?"

"Just installing some fixtures. And the painters and paperhangers.

"And the house here? Margaret says it is as good as sold."

"The agreement is signed."

"Then this is your last summer here at Willowbeach?"

"But why?" Craig had put down the valise and plans. He went to his mother and laid his arm across her shoulders. "What's the matter with you? Why must that change? I hope there's room for us here, with you. Of course we'll be coming to Willowbeach in the summer."

Rose stepped to one side. "If I had had my way, we would not have spent this summer here. A hotel, strangers—anything would have been better for your father than Willowbeach. It would have distracted him. But he insisted on coming here. I couldn't talk him out of it. But surely it is necessary to allow some kind of interval, for one's own sake. I don't know how to help him anymore, and that's the worst thing one can say after so many years." She was not complaining, not bitter; she was simply being informative. She did not try to hide her feelings, but she was not carried away by them either. She changed the subject. "How is Langdon? Have you seen him since he came back from Europe?"

"I suspect that he was rather bored, but Irene came back in splendid spirits. They took Celia along, and Irene actually achieved her goal. Celia is going to marry some count or duke, I forget which. They brought him back to New York with them. Irene is in her element. You'd think *she* was the bride."

"But what about Celia's previous engagement?"

"The Boston banker? That was called off even before they left for Europe."

"And Langdon?"

"He's spending a lot of time on his Staten Island farm again. Now I don't want you to think I ousted him. He continues to be a director of the Empire State and receives a salary. But he told me himself that none of it interests him very much anymore. He has returned to his horses. Did you know that one of his nags won the trotting races at the Union Track on Long Island? And he has one three-year-old that has earned twenty thousand this year alone."

"I'll be glad to take Sinclair and Joshua while you

move," Rose said. "Have you picked out a school for them in New York? Or you can send them to school in Albany, if you like. The one you went to is still a good school."

"You'd be willing to take Joshua and Sinclair to Albany? What about Father? Wouldn't it make too much commotion in the house?"

"It was his idea."

Craig looked at the front of the house. Then he saw the wheelchair on the porch and the stack of newspapers next to it on the floor. "How is he?" he asked.

"At least you are asking about him," Rose said. "No, listen to me now. I don't want to say much about the whole affair. Only this: you degrade yourself when you degrade your father. Whether it was necessary to make him resign, and whether it had to be done that way, I don't wish to discuss. You are now the head of the family, and I beg you to behave accordingly. It is not necessary for you to send your father a bill for the use of a private train from Albany to Willowbeach."

"He always spoke of abolishing privilege."

"That does not excuse you. There are things . . ." She gave him a penetrating look. "There are things that come back to haunt us, sooner or later. For you this may be a bagatelle, but for him it's not. Don't forget too quickly who made it all happen in the first place. There's no need to show him so openly that you no longer need him. Just to keep up appearances, why don't you at least let him participate in major decisions? Invite him to come to New York. You'll see. He'll come. For a man who has led such an active life, it is hard suddenly to be condemned to idleness."

She turned around and looked at the wheelchair on the porch. "Yes, he sits here in his wheelchair. But I tell you, his wheelchairs are a joke. He brought three of them to Willowbeach. One is on the porch, one is in his bedroom, and one is in the smoking parlor. But they're just for show. Tell him he has to come to New York to look at the new freight station himself, and he'll be his old self again."

"Where is he? In the smoking parlor?"

She nodded. "I assume we'll see you at dinner tonight. You, the children, and Margaret. She told me, by the way. In December, is it?"

"Yes. You see, there's no possibility that your house will be empty in the future."

"Margaret should eat more," Rose said. "Tonight's dinner is————"

"Fish, and walnut pie for dessert," Craig said.

"That's right," she said. "Some things do not change, ever."

When Craig was a child, the house at Willowbeach had seemed a great palace with innumerable rooms, endless corridors, countless side apartments that he would never be able to find again. Later, when he returned during college vacations, the house appeared to him to have shrunk. But when he entered it now, it was again the mansion of his childhood.

In the smoking parlor, John Tyler was sitting in the old armchair. For years he had refused to have it re-upholstered. A blanket was spread across his knees, and an open book lay on it. The wheelchair stood next to the fireplace.

"Close the door," he said by way of greeting. "I don't feel like catching cold. The whole house is drafty. Just because the sun is shining, all the doors and windows are left open. Are you aware that more people die of pneumonia in summer than in winter?" It was his father's familiar voice, the light, young voice; and it made Craig smile. "I'd like to see the day when you catch cold."

John Tyler closed the book and laid it on the table. "If I so much as leave the house without a hat, my nose starts running. You are forgetting my age. Sit down. You're early."

"McCallum drives like the devil." Craig had decided not to mention his decision to tear up the private spur.

"Are you still employing him? I meant to let him go last year. Why don't you sit down?"

Craig's glance rested for a moment on the wheelchair. The smoking jacket of dark brown velvet hung decoratively over the back rest. Even the book in his father's hands, which he had not, certainly, been reading, the blanket over his knees under which he was surely much too warm—all these were the props of a melodrama. "In any case, you're looking good," Craig said.

"Looks! Looks are deceiving. The doctor says I should get more fresh air, but I can't sit in the garden the way it is now. Did you see what the storm did to us? The first days, I made them keep all the shutters closed. I couldn't stand it. All those beautiful trees—the larches, the locusts, the tamarack tree. My father planted them when I was a boy. And now————"

"But, Father! You used to talk about cutting them down. The fruit trees kept the garden too shady, the espaliers were poison to the brickwork and filled the house with vermin. And the tamarack tree hid the view."

"Well, all right. Parents seldom know much about their children, and children know little of their parents. But the two of us"—he stared at his son—"we know each other, don't we? We can't deceive each other."

"We can keep on trying, all the same, if that amuses you. If you're so well, why didn't you come to Sydenham's funeral?"

"I've buried enough dead recently. At my age, someone is always dying. It doesn't do well to dwell on it too much; it only makes one realize that one is a relic. What did he die of actually?"

"A neglected case of influenza. You know what he was like. Staying home and taking care of himself—that wasn't his way. I don't suppose his heart was ever very strong."

"A miracle that he lasted as long as he did. He was always a watermill. All his strength went to his head, his memory. I hear you hired Vinnie's husband." He pointed to the rolls of paper. "Are those the plans?"

"I brought them to show you." The lie passed Craig's lips easily. He pulled the plans out of their heavy rolls.

John Tyler threw down the blanket. "Let's move to the big table."

He forgot the cane leaning against the chair. Upright and with a sure step, he strode across the room, reminding Craig of his mother's words.

The two men spread out the plans and put weights on the corners. "These are the designs for the freight station," Craig said. "We were able to buy the last lots on St. John's Park. We'll build over the entire park. That should be enough for the next twenty years, even at optimistic rates of growth." He took a pencil from his pocket. "This area here we'll leave bare for the time being. One day there will be a direct connection with Jersey City under the North River, and whoever is going to build it—this is the only possible place for a depot. What do you think?"

"What can you want to hear from me! The matter seems quite settled. Is this Vinnie's husband's design?" Like Craig, he did not use the man's name; he was a son-in-law only, the husband of a Matlock. "Not bad." He pointed to the elevation. "At least he isn't one of those spun-sugar architects. I wouldn't have credited him with it. What does he charge for a design like this?"

"He wants two percent of the building costs, but he will get one percent."

"And the other plans?"

"They're merely preliminary sketches for a passenger station. We haven't got much further with it. Sometime soon, we'll have to expand, and that means that we'll have to abandon Twenty-sixth Street. It's chiefly a question of location. With the city's help, we could get some parcels of land on Forty-second Street, but there are many opposition votes. I myself am for it, but most of them think it's too far north, too far from the big hotels."

"Don't let them talk you out of it. Forty-second Street is excellent. The city is growing northward. There is no other direction it can go, and someday that will be a central location. It doesn't matter what a few hotel keepers say. The bankers are more important. What do they think?" He leaned over the sketches. "What huge proportions. How do you intend to finance it? With company money?"

"It's still in the talking stages. But we've been in touch with the city administration. If we put our lines underground and keep clear of crossings, the city is prepared to contribute a million two hundred thousand. The sum is based on a tentative cost estimate for all essential buildings to the amount of three and a half million. I figure that we will need no more than two and a half at most."

"Take care. If the contractors give you false invoices, you're delivering yourself into their hands, for all practical purposes."

"First of all, we can buy up a contracting firm for the purpose, and secondly, the contract with the city would include a clause depriving it of the chance to examine the costs of materials and wages after the contract has been signed."

John Tyler stepped away from the table. It took an effort to hold back a word of approval. "Nevertheless, I find it a little too massive. For a station like that, you need a passenger turnover of thirty million a year."

"Since January, we've gone up by thirty percent." Craig was reluctant to continue. He wondered if he had gone too far already and revealed too much of his plans. But he went on. "We have resumed discussions with the owners of the lines from Buffalo to Chicago. If they are successful, we will have a through line from Chicago, by way of Albany, nine hundred and eighty miles altogether."

"Discussions?"

"We intend to buy, but we would be content with a leasing arrangement. I believe there are convincing arguments to persuade them of the advantages of such a merger."

John Tyler turned to his son. "Buy. Lease. Convincing arguments. That reminds me of a conversation I had with Loftus Poynder a year ago."

He had spoken very matter-of-factly, and his son continued in the same ordinary tone. "Successful methods should not be tampered with."

John Tyler took a few steps. "I could not have taught you more than that in one year," he said when he finally came to a stop.

"I don't know why I'm telling you this, but the shareholders can be satisfied with their decision of last January."

"Wall Street, in any case, responded well to the change."

"I see that from the market quotations."

"As long as we are on the subject," Craig said. "About your shares. Are you interested in holding on to them?" He put the question as though he were speaking about a trivial matter.

"At the current rate, I see no reason to sell, and surely you will not want to buy as long as the price is so high."

"Nevertheless, as I hear it, you have sold everything else—the mines, the salt works, the textile plants. And not at rock-bottom prices, either. And in Albany, they tell me, you've been building."

"At my age one starts to think in terms of liquidation. Administering rental housing and banking the income—that's something Rose can do without my help, if need be. I am simply putting my affairs in order."

"Then why not sell your shares in the Empire State, as well? Or if you don't want to sell, I would be willing to take them over against a guaranteed interest."

John Tyler had returned to his armchair, but he did not sit down. He went to the window leading out on the porch.

"Are you interested?"

"If you are so well informed about what I have sold, then I'm sure you have also been told that the directors of the Pennsylvania have been to see me. Surely that doesn't frighten you. They believe it's possible for the Empire State securities to go up to two hundred. In any case, they are prepared————"

"Of course they are prepared—for anything. I cannot understand how you could see them at all. If word were to get out!"

John Tyler turned sharply. "Well, well. Here it is at last. The Pennsylvania. That would give you quite a scare, wouldn't it, if they suddenly controlled over thirty percent of the Empire State? That's how much it is. No one consults me any longer, nor do I want to be consulted; but there it is, that confounded thirty percent. That's *your* problem now—to defend the majority. From now on, that will be keeping you busy."

"Two hundred dollars. They are insane to offer you so much. You're only trying to push me to the wall. I won't pay any two hundred dollars." He lit one of his little cigars. "A hundred and eighty," he said at last.

John Tyler laughed joyfully. "Calm down. I sent the gentlemen packing. They won't be back. They know that my no is final. I want my shares to remain in the family."

"Well, then." Craig made no attempt to hide his relief. "That means you'll sell to me after all."

"I did not say that."

"What does it mean, then?"

"That my shares remain in the family. I have thought the matter through. I believe that I have hit upon a good solution. You took what you wanted. Langdon has enough, also, and I've given him some part of the profits from my recent sales. My daughters have been taken care of. As for the rest, let their husbands work a little harder. No, all of you have quite enough. I must think in larger terms. I must think of those who come after you. There will be another generation of Matlocks when you're gone.

I have decided to leave my shares to one of my grandsons."

"One grandson?"

"Yes. Joshua. Whatever made you pick that name, by the way? There has never yet been a Matlock named Joshua."

It took Craig a minute to recover from his astonishment. "Why Joshua?"

"I am old-fashioned in such matters. He is the first-born."

"They are the same age."

"No, Joshua was in more of a hurry. He arrived twenty minutes earlier."

"You're splitting hairs."

But John Tyler let nothing dim his joy. "Joshua will receive his shares when he reaches the age of twenty-one. For my part, I will do all I can to live to see that day. Sixteen years—it's not entirely beyond the realm of possibility. Should I die before then, you will administer the shares for your son. During that time, you can vote them; but on Joshua's twenty-first birthday all your authority expires, and believe me, I will hedge this clause in with such proper terms and formulations that it will be uncontestable."

"Sixteen years," Craig said. "And you're convinced that you will live to see it. You are incorrigible."

"Until now, work filled my days. I thought it could not be replaced. But quite automatically one clutches at something else. I have discovered that malice is an equally effective elixir."

"I still have trouble understanding it."

"Think. In sixteen years, when Joshua is twenty-one, you will be forty-seven. You cannot imagine that now. Forty-seven, that's as good as fifty. Until you're forty, you have an impenetrable fortress. After that it begins to crumble almost imperceptibly. But a sharp eye will be able to detect the weak spots. You will be spared nothing. For Joshua has a sharp eye—our sharp eye, and our spirit—and with more than thirty percent of the shares of the Empire State in hand . . ."

"You old tyrant! Old incorrigible tyrant!"

John Tyler laughed roughly. "I could hardly wait for my father to make room for me. You couldn't wait either, and one day it will happen to you: there will be someone younger and stronger." He lowered his eyes. When he continued, it was in a different voice. "You can believe me, I envied every tree that fell in the garden. It is a terrible punishment to grow old." He stood calmly, one hand on the window sill, his shoulders very narrow so that his jacket seemed much too large. Only when the voices of Joshua and Sinclair in the garden grew louder did life return to him.

"I'll leave the plans here," Craig said. "You can look them over at your leisure."

The old man standing at the window did not reply, nor did he move until after his son had left. He picked up the blanket from the floor, apparently undecided what to do next. He went to the table, rolled up the plans, and pushed them back into the cardboard tubes. Then he crossed the room slowly, musingly. He pushed open the door to the dining room. The table in the large room which every year had been extended to its full length, now seemed tiny. It was already set for dinner, with silver service plates, blue china, blue napkins, and blue candles in silver candlesticks. Six place settings.

"Grandfather."

The old man turned around. Joshua stood in the doorway, a little out of breath. His father's voice came from outside: "Joshua! Joshua!" The boy smiled and put his fingers to his lips. Once more his father called. Then there was silence. Joshua said, "Do you have time for me now?"

John Tyler nodded. He closed the door on the dining room. Going to the armchair near the window, he pointed to the second one standing next to it. A very young smile transfigured his eyes.

Joshua pushed the chairs closer together. He sat down, and began. "All right, how does it work—about income?"